THE SAINTED TRILOGY

MEGIDDO

BOOK THREE

by

MICHAEL MEDICO

© 2020 Harbour Point Publishing
Harbour Point Publishing, LLC
Northport, New York 1168
thesaintedtrilogy@gmail.net
www.thesaintedtrilogy.net

Printed in the United States by Harbour Point Publishers, Northport, NY

The Sainted Trilogy, Harbour Point Publishers.

Library of Congress Cataloging-in-Publication Data
Revelations, Book Two of The Sainted Trilogy
(Formerly titled The Sainted)
Medico, Michael p. cm.

Fiction—General 2. Fiction—Thriller 3. Fiction—Horror Fiction, I. Title.

Paperback ISBN: 978-1-0879-9883-1
Ebook ISBN: 978-1-0879-9889-3

DEDICATION

To the men and women in the armed forces, police departments,
fire departments, hospitals and all who have been brave while
fighting the good fight in battles near and far,
you are among our Living Saints and our Heavenly Angels
and forever our heroes

"I remember once in the Holy Land seeing a sign in the shape of an arrow along a road. It said, 'Armageddon, 4 kilometers.' If ever there was a sign that made you wonder whether you wanted to continue down a road, this was it."
—Benedict J. Groeschel,

"No One Knows That Day and Hour...
But concerning that day and hour no one knows,
not even the angels of heaven, nor the Son, but the Father only."
—Matthew 24:36

"It's not over, until the Lord says it's over."
—T.D. Jakes

PROLOGUE

The priest sits in the confessional and waits.

The chapel at the Immaculate Conception Seminary is open every Thursday and is reserved for those lay people who wish to partake in the Sacrament of Reconciliation. It is still early and there is no one in the chapel so Fr. Aiden Langford takes the opportunity to read while he waits for his first penitent.

He picks up the book he chose to read, "Handed Down: The Catholic Faith of the Early Christians by James L. Papandrea." The book speaks to the fact that most Protestants believe there is little similarity between modern Catholic orthodoxy and that of Christians in the first centuries. Fr. Aiden finds the book very interesting as it is written by a former Protestant minister who is able to show that modern Catholics and early Christians are in fact staunch in their adherence the rituals and beliefs of the church. Fr. Aiden is especially interested in the author's claim that pastors, teachers and writers, known as the Church Fathers, use the gospel to develop doctrines and practices that define the Christian religion. These doctrines continue today, faithfully kept alive in the Catholic Church. Father Langford's interest stems from his own belief that this premise is true.

He had been reading a short time when the curtain to the confessional opens and a person sits down. Both he and the penitent's figures are cloaked in the darkness of the booth and there is only a thin screen and wall that separates them. The priest puts the book on the side of his bench, turns on the confessional's occupied light and speaks,

"Good morning, welcome and let us pray, in the name of the Father, the Son and the Holy Spirit."

There is no answer.

"Do you wish to confess your sins?"

Still no answer...

Fr. Aiden is a bit perplexed, but he assumes that the person is gathering his or her thoughts or is too embarrassed to speak so he asks, "What is troubling you? Do you wish to confess your sins? I am here to help you."

But, as before, there is nothing but silence

"If you do not wish to confess, why are you here?"

"That is a good question, why am I here?"

Father Aiden loves a clandestine penitent for he knows that it will be a benediction for that person if he or she can be forgiven their sins. The priest replies, "Ah, you can speak! This is the first step to helping you to reconcile yourself with God the Father through the blessings of his Son, Jesus Christ. Do not be afraid or embarrassed for I've heard from many who thought they could never be redeemed and they have found their peace through penance and forgiveness and salvation through the love of the Lord."

The man behind the screen answers, "That is most interesting and comforting to hear."

"Well then, let us start, how long has it been since your last confession?" The priest hears a chuckle from behind the screen.

"It has been ages."

"Ages, so I take it that you are lapsed in your faith and in the Holy Church's sacraments."

"Yes, I think lapsed is an appropriate word."

"Well even your absence from the Church of Christ and its sacraments are not enough to separate you from the grace to be found in confessing your sins. That is why we have the sacrament of reconciliation."

"So, you say that God will forgive me my sins. Well, why don't I just go to the top and confess to God."

The priest smiles enjoying the repartee, "God, through his Son Jesus Christ, anointed the Apostles with the power of the Holy Spirit and He said 'whose sins you shall forgive, they are forgiven them; and whose sins you shall retain, they are retained.' As a priest, I am God and Christ's representative on earth and He has given priests the power to hear confession and forgive sins. The power to forgive sins is a part of the power of the priesthood, to be passed on in the sacrament of Holy Orders from generation to generation."

"Sounds like a lot of power."

Fr. Aiden nearly laughs out loud, "It is! Not only that, but God's mercy is infinite and knowing the nature of man and the nature of sin, God will provide a second chance or a third or a fourth or a hundred if necessary for those who might fall victim to the evils of sin. It might be difficult to believe that sin, even the most egregious kind, can be forgiven, but it is true."

"Hmmm, a hundred chances, so if God can forgive a hundred times, He technically can forgive sins a billion times; is that correct?"

Fr. Aiden thinks for a moment, "I suppose God would forgive such a sinner given in that He is infinitely merciful."

"So, that being said, it sounds like a sinner can go about his or her business and commit all the sins they want and come back here and they are forgiven."

"Yes, but that sinner would find himself or herself in a bit of a dilemma."

There seems to be a genuine curiosity of the man in the booth as he says, "Interesting, what is this dilemma you speak of?"

"Well, you will need to figure that the more you sin, the further from God's grace you are and the harder it is to work your way back. Next some of the sins you speak of may be illegal and in that instance the rule of law instituted by governments have their own statutes and punishments which can be severe in and of themselves. Third, because we never know when the Lord may call us home, you may die with a plethora of sins staining your very soul and no one to turn to for forgiveness for it is then too late."

The man speaks to the priest, "And that is when you are condemned to suffer eternal damnation."

The priest responds, "If you die with your soul stained with mortal sins, that is what scripture tells us and that is my understanding."

"Most curious"

Fr. Aiden considers what to say next to the man occupying the confessional. The priest wants all who try to reconcile to leave with hope in promise that they will be forgiven. "No one is beyond forgiveness and punishment given for committing sins; it is simply the way for you to satisfy a debt you owe to God and to the authorities as the case may be. This satisfaction can be paid in life with penance, prayer and good works. What the tenets of our faith tell us is that any debt owed to God at the time of our death must be paid in purgatory."

"…or Hell?"

Fr. Aiden is sad when he says, "or Hell."

There is an eerie silence that follows and the priest becomes concerned. "Would you like to take this time to recount your sins, my son?"

"Ah, that would probably take more time than you have."

"Well, let us try anyway. Why not confess your sins for, shall we say the past week?"

"How should I begin?"

"You should begin by saying 'Bless me father for I have sinned" and then recite your sins as best you can remember them."

"Can I reserve using the words 'bless me' until after I tell you my sins?"

Father Aiden seeks to provide a measure of comfort to the penitent so he says, "If it makes this process easier for you, of course."

"It does…father I have sinned."

The priest continues, "What sins have you committed in the past week?"

The man behind the screen asks, "By the way, are you still obliged not to repeat anything I say in the act of confession?"

"Yes, I, as well as all priests, am bound by the Seal of the Sacrament. The Code of Canon Law states: The sacramental seal is inviolable; therefore, it is absolutely forbidden for a confessor to betray in any way a penitent in words or in any manner and for any reason. The punishment for a violation of this trust is excommunication."

"So, I can tell you anything and you can't say a word to anyone. Is that correct?"

"Yes"

"…and if you reveal what I say you get booted out of the church. Is that correct?"

The priest says, "Yes"

"OK, sounds pretty fair to me so let's continue."

The priest asks again, "What sins have you committed in the past week?"

"Well, to tell the truth they are many and varied in their scope, duration and severity."

"Go on."

"For example, during the past week there was one incident where I murdered 47 people including children. I must admit that it was an enlightening experience, but given that it is sinful in nature I thought I would start there."

It doesn't take, but a few words before Fr. Aiden comes to the realization that the man in the confessional is mentally deranged. Although he has had training in dealing with people who are afflicted with delusions, the priest is in a quandary as to what he should do. Nonetheless he asks, "Why did you murder these people my son?"

"By the way, let's not use the words 'father' or 'son' because you technically can't screw a woman and get her pregnant although, with you priests, I've seen it happen many times before. And let's not have you call me 'son' because if you ever became a father, believe me, you wouldn't want me for a son."

He wants to keep the man talking so Fr. Aiden says, "If that is what you want it is acceptable to me."

"Good, now that it's settled, what's next? Oh yes, why I murdered those people. Well, they were atheists so who cares anyway. As a matter of fact, maybe that's not a sin at all! Maybe God is pleased with me for killing those bastards! What do you think!?"

"My son…sorry, I mean the taking of innocent life can never be condoned least of all by God."

"Then I guess that's a sin. Oh well, onwards and upwards. By the way I have to tell you that I love your British accent." The man in the confessional now tries to speak with a British accent, "Very public school don't you think?"

Fr. Aiden is now getting very nervous as he is anxiously contemplating what to do next. What can he do or say to placate the madness that has overcome this penitent? The priest decides that he would attempt to keep the dialog going so he simply says, "Let us continue, what are the other sins you have to confess?"

"Well last week I also was able to assist in the torching of a factory in the city of Dongguan in central Guangdong province. I'm afraid that another 417 people lost their lives. I guess we could have done better, you know taken more lives, but we didn't have the time to plan it properly."

Fr, Aiden asks, "Why did you set fire to the factory?"

"I said I assisted, someone else actually set the fire."

"But you were there, so why was the fire set at the factory?"

The man thinks for a moment, "I guess you can say we did it for the same reason that Sir Edmond Hillary climbed Mt. Everest…because it was there!"

"So, you're saying that the only reason you assisted burning down a factory and killing 400…"

"417"

The priest corrects himself, "417 people are because they were there?"

"Yes, exactly! It is important for you to understand the nature of this beast. I am a being of infinite needs and if God is infinite in His mercy, I'm hoping He will be gracious enough to bestow His infinite mercy on my infinite needs."

"What about the families of the people you've murdered? Do you expect them to forgive you? What about those in the criminal justice system? Do you expect them to forgive you? God can forgive you and show you His mercy, but you must do penance and your penance will be meted out at the hands of law enforcement."

The man laughs, "Fuck them. Law enforcement, dim witted idiots the whole bunch. What the hell do they know anyway? I can tell you about some of the law enforcement people I've met…"

Fr. Aiden stops the man from speaking, "This is your confession, so let us continue. What other sins do you wish to confess?"

"Good idea priest why get sidetracked. In the same week…listen, why don't I just tell you that I did a lot of bad stuff, you know beheadings, bombings, murders, rapes, arson, starvation; you know once we starved a group of men, women and children in Africa. Yep, we just shut them in a large room, well more like a cave. They managed to survive for a while, but the first of them died after only 2 days and then the rest just dropped like flies. I once got this guy to embezzle a fortune; unfortunately, the money belonged to some people *who really couldn't afford to lose it. Anyway, the good news is that the guy killed himself. I would have done it, but he killed himself before I had the chance."*

The man stops speaking, but there is silence from Fr. Aiden.

"Hey, I can see you through this screen, why so quiet?"

"Please continue."

"Like I said, I've committed a lot of sins, got other people to commit them too. It's been a trip I tell you, a real trip. Anyway, I've committed a lot of what I guess you'd call lesser sins like lying, cheating, stealing, but they don't count right?"

The priest's mind is racing, "All sins, mortal as well as venial, must be confessed before they can be forgiven."

"I've committed many more sins in the past week. The list goes on and on, but I think you get the idea. Remember I said you didn't have enough time to hear them all. Do you believe me now?"

A worried Father Langford says, "I guess I do."

There is a short silence when the man in the confessional says, "How about we discuss something else, say the eternal struggle between good and evil, what do you think?"

"It appears to me that you are in great need of help, the kind of help a doctor can provide. You appear to be undergoing some crises and these crises are manifesting themselves in the delusions you are experiencing. Murder, arson, rape, crimes taking place all over the world; if you truly believe that you have committed these heinous crimes you must try to get the help you need."

The man considers what the priest is saying and responds, "You don't believe I have done these things?"

"Quite frankly, no."

"Why not?"

"Well, I believe that you believe that you have committed these crimes. However, it seems impossible for you to be in so many places around the world and commit so many heinous crimes while your identity remains unknown, especially to the police and other authorities in all those countries."

"What makes you think that my identity is unknown?"

Fr. Aiden is beginning to feel a bit more at ease. He considers that the man in his confessional has not exhibited any violent behavior towards him, at least so far. The priest also considers that in order to get the man behind the screen to realize he needs help; he must keep him talking. "I suppose because there would have been reports on the news and you would be the focus of a far-reaching manhunt."

"Ah, I see your point, but you are wrong."

"I am?"

"Yes, ever hear of the Lamb of God murders?"

Chills run down Fr. Aiden's spine. "Yes. Are you saying you have something to do with these murders?"

"Yes, and I get by with a little help from my friends." He sings the line from the famous Beatles song.

"Why in God's holy name would you want to say something like that?" Father Aiden Langford is bewildered and stunned that anyone would confess to such horrid crimes.

The man smiles from behind the veil of the screen, "Well, to tell the truth, this is something that's been building up for a long time now. I see it as a way to help redefine the nature of evil in ways that we haven't seen since, well, we've never seen murders quite like these. Of course, I'm not counting the holocaust or the pogroms or the mass exterminations in Germany, Russia, Southeast Asia, the Middle East and China. Those were done by the governments so they are legal and don't count. But in the end, I assure you that the Lamb of God killings will give a whole new meaning to the word genocide."

The priest feels a pain in his chest as his heart is pounding faster.

"Oh, sorry I'd mean to upset you. You've already had a heart attack; I wouldn't want to be responsible for another one."

"What? How…"

"Oh, I know a lot of things. I know that you are considered a biblical scholar so let's have a little discussion. What do you say?"

Fr. Aiden takes a deep breath and reaches for a bottle of water that he has sitting on the shelf next to the seat and takes a sip, "Yes."

"Ah! Glad you are feeling better now where shall we start. Oh, how about Leviticus, who writes, according to scripture, 'Whoever lies with a beast shall surely be put to death.' Sounds pretty extreme to me, after all a goat can be very attractive at times and it's right there in the Bible."

The priest is silent.

"Well come on, tell me what you are thinking?

"God would never have said that, He wound never condone murder."

"So, say you, but let's move on, this one's from scripture according to Exodus, 'Whoever does ANY work on the Sabbath day, he shall surely be put to death.' Sounds pretty extreme to me after all I might want to keep busy, you know an idle mind is the devil's workshop."

"Is it your premise that God would actually condone such a punishment for working on the Sabbath?"

Yep, it's right there in the Bible."

"This is absurd. How can anyone believe that men and women who need to do honest work to provide for their families are removed from the love and mercy of God?"

"Like I said, it's right there in the Bible, but let's continue. It's back to good old Leviticus, 'The adulterer and adulteress shall surely be put to death' sounds like God wants to keep us from having a good time. I like getting laid, don't you? Oh sorry…"

The priest is incredulous, but he knows that if they stop talking the man in the confessional may get violent. He resolves to keep this going until other penitents arrive. Fr. Aide Langford counters, "From the beginning of man's knowledge of God, he has been confronted by temptation and, in the hearts of mankind, what he knows to be sinful is sinful in the eyes of God. However, to say that God would put all adulterers to death because they have sinned assumes God is merciless and that is not true in any sense of the word."

"Oh, come on priest let's take a look at what Moses said in Numbers 31: 15-18, 'Have you kept all the women alive? Now therefore kill every male among the little ones; and kill every woman who has known man intimately. But keep alive for yourselves all the young girls…sounds like Moses was a greedy perv; all the young girls for themselves, and all with God's approval, can you imagine!?"

Fr. Aiden is dumbfounded, "What are you suggesting, that God commanded Moses to commit genocide and rape?"

"I'm not suggesting it, the Bible spells it out."

Father Langford hears some movement in the chapel and he feels much safer now that other penitents are around. He takes this opportunity to continue their discussion. "Your selective readings have one commonality; they are from scripture, but they are not of God. They were written by the men at the time, perhaps inspired by Satan, but not of the Lord."

The man chuckles, "Inspired by Satan, not a bad conclusion on your part. I've seen much evil, especially the evil of man and in most instances, I agree with you and I did inspire such sinfulness."

The priest cannot believe what he is hearing, "You? Inspire? What are you saying?"

"Listen priest and listen well, neither God nor His Son can stop the horror I will wreak on mankind; do you understand?"

Fr. Aiden Langford jumps up from the bench and opens the door to the confessional; he throws back the curtain to the penitent's booth to find there is no one there. It is dark, but he detects something scratched in the wall of the wooden enclosure.

He sees the words "Lamb of God" and they are written in blood. The priest grabs his chest and falls to the floor.

CHAPTER 1

The priest lies in bed, sedated and unaware of his friend sitting by his bedside.

Chief Barese rushed to the hospital as soon as he received word of Father Langford's heart attack. Earlier in the day, the local EMS had received a call from Immaculate Conception Seminary requesting an ambulance. The caller said that the priest hearing confession collapsed in the chapel and fell to the floor. One of the congregants waiting to see the priest for confession knew CPR and she was able to get his heart beating. When EMS arrived, they administered cardio-therapy and medication and they were prepared to give Father Langford electrical cardioversion, but that was unnecessary.

The police were also called to the scene to take statements from the five people in the chapel at the time. The witnesses all reported that Father Aiden ran out of the center of the confessional to open the penitent's side, but everyone present said that there was no one in confessional and no one saw anyone leave. At that moment the priest was heard to scream "Lamb of God" before he grabbed his chest and fell to the floor. The people in the chapel rushed to Fr. Langford's side and they could see the words Lamb of God scratched on the wall of the confessional, and that's when they called the police.

The chief is very worried. He begins pacing the floor in Aiden's room trying to make sense of this all the while hoping Aiden regains consciousness. The priest is Al's best friend and confidant and Al wants to know all the information available and the doctor's prognosis for his recovery. The chief of detectives continues to pace the floor when the treating physician walks into the room. After a brief introduction, Al immediately asks, "Doc, what do you have to tell me?" At first, the doctor is reluctant to release details of the patient's condition, but Chief Barese doesn't hesitate to show his badge and tell the doctor that Father Langford is witness in an ongoing investigation.

Dr. Paul Simonelli looks at the badge and speaks to Chief Al Barese, "Well chief, it seems that Fr. Langford suffered a heart attack, also known as a myocardial infarction or an MI. He is very lucky that he received CPR as quickly as he did otherwise this could have proved fatal. Luckily ICS is so close to Huntington Hospital."

"Fatal, my God, what is being done doc? What are you doing to help him get better?"

The doctor knows that Chief Barese is very worried, but he wants to manage expectations. "Whoa chief, we need to take this one step at a time. I've looked at the patient's medical history and it seems that he's had a heart attack in the past. Father Langford suffers from Thrombosis, abnormal blood clotting. He's already on an anticoagulant and we are continuing to administer the drug to dissolve the blood clots. Because the necessary treatment is being administered as quickly as it is, the amount of heart muscle damage is less and that improves the prognosis. We expect to keep him in the hospital for several days, at a minimum, to detect heart rhythm disturbance and observe for any shortness of breath and chest pain. Once we have run tests and we are better able to determine his condition we may recommend an angioplasty or intracoronary stenting to open an obstructed artery as well as medications that dilate the blood vessels, but it is still too premature to make that recommendation just yet."

"How long do you think it will be before he will be able to speak to me?"

The doctor wants to make this as clear as possible, "I really can't say, but he will need his rest and I do not want to get him excited or anxious in anyway, that can produce a major setback. Do you understand chief?"

Chief Barese knows that the doctor is right. "You're right doc; I didn't mean to come on so strong. He is my best friend and he is involved in an ongoing investigation, I just want him to get better, but I guess his statement will have to wait."

The doctor is very familiar with the concerns of family and friends who have had to confront similar situations. "Chief, I know you are worried, but rest assured that Father Langford is getting the necessary treatment and care he needs."

Chief Barese and Dr. Simonelli shake hands and the doctor leaves the room. Now Al is alone with his friend and the significance of Aiden's condition hits him hard. Al goes back to his seat next to the bedside of the priest and holds his hand. Aiden's hand is cold and clammy and Al becomes even more worried for his friend.

The chief's phone rings and he sees the call is from Dan Orello, his second in command and Al answers in a low voice, "Hi Dan, I'm with Aiden now. Let me find a place where I can speak." Chief Barese leaves Aiden's room and walks to the lounge areas to speak with his associate,

"Dan, sorry about that, but I was in ICU and didn't want to disturb anyone. What's up?"

"Hi Chief, how's Aiden?"

"I wish I had better news Dan. Aiden is still unconscious and he might be that way for a while. I just spoke with the doctor and it's gonna be touch and go until he's stabilized."

"I know how close you are to him and I'm really sorry."

"I know you are Dan. Do you have any news for me?

Dan starts to tell the chief what they found in their investigation so far, "We examined the confessional and Lamb of God was written in blood. It is being analyzed now and we won't know if it's human or not until we get the results back. We also examined the interior of the confessional for prints, but it is going to be nearly impossible to determine who may have left them. It is, after all, a confessional and many people go in and out on a regular basis. We will note whatever we can, but I'm not sure it will lead to anything."

Chief Barese muses, "It's probably a dead end, but forensics should still try to determine if there is anything that we can go with."

"Chief, we also took statements from everyone who was there and witnessed the incident. All the people pretty much have the same story. They claim Aiden ran out of the booth, tore open the curtain on the penitent's side, screams and then grabbed his chest before he collapsed. No one saw anything else, no person entering or leaving…no nothing."

The chief and Dan commiserate, "With all the shit that's going on here in Suffolk, all over the country and around the world what should sound strange doesn't sound so strange anymore. Keep me posted about anything new, I'm going to sit with Aiden for a while."

"Sure, chief and if, by chance, he becomes conscious, tell him we are thinking of him and to get well soon."

Al smiles and answers, "Thanks Dan, I will" and he hangs up.

Chief Barese walks back to ICU and the room is quiet as he sits by the priest's bedside and puts his hand on Father Langford's arm. He takes advantage of the silence to go over all that has happened in the past few weeks. The murders, arson, mutilations, senseless and horrific violence around Long Island, the US and the world itself and the possibility of the forces of hell being the catalyst is making the chief even more frightened. He looks at his friend lying there unconscious and wants nothing more than to hear the priest call him Spartaco, to hear him tell what happened, to make him believe that God could stop all this. Al gives Aiden a slight nudge to his arm hoping to feel some movement, but there is none and that's what's most depressing.

CHAPTER 2

The limousine pulls into the driveway of Beth's townhouse. The driver gets out of the car and opens the trunk. He offers to carry Beth's belongings into her home, but she declines and thanks him for taking her home and she takes her dress and other items and walks into her home.

Beth opens the door and heaves a sigh of relief as she enters her foyer. She throws her evening gown across the chair and finds her way into the living room. She drops onto the couch, still exhausted from the night before; she removes the jacket and shoes that Lisa bought and she closes her eyes. Normally she would have poured herself a glass of wine, but after the prior evening's drunken stupor, Beth decides that she will never drink again.

Knowing that she needs to relax a bit, Beth turns on the TV and switches to ACN half-heartedly listening to the news anchor, Steven Bennett, reading news items from the teleprompter. Beth perks-up when she hears him summarize the lead story related to the "Lamb of God" murders.

"Reports are coming in from authorities around the world who are telling ACN that they are investigating a large number of killings, mutilations and various heinous crimes that are taking place. Here now is reporter Miles Pritchard from our London Bureau with this update; Miles."

"Thank you, Steven, I have been speaking here with the Chief Inspector of London's Metropolitan Police Force, Detective Chief Inspector Martin

Halstead. DCI Halstead, can you give our viewers any information on what you have learned so far in the investigations of the Lamb of God murders?"

The camera now centers on a somber looking Detective Chief Inspector Halstead who starts to speak in a very cautious manner. "In recent weeks we have seen a number of extremely serious crimes that are of such a violent and horrendous nature that I cannot go into the details. All I can state at this time is that these investigations are ongoing and those responsible for such monstrous crimes will be captured and brought to justice."

Miles Pritchard asks, "Do you have any leads? Are there any suspects and what is being done to try and prevent future crimes?"

DCI Halstead responds, "All information relating to any suspects are being kept strictly confidential. All leads are being followed up in a manner consistent with the policies as outlined in accordance with criminal investigation policies and procedures. We have asked the public to be ever vigilant. Stay away from crime prone areas and do not go out alone, especially at night and immediately notify your local constabulary of any suspicious persons or groups of persons at any time they are spotted." DCI Halstead issues these warnings knowing that, given the horrors he has seen, if anyone has been targeted there is little hope they will survive and even less hope their murderers will be apprehended.

The camera turns back to the studio where Steven Bennett continues, "In a related incident, it seems something very disturbing has happened at Immaculate Conception Seminary on Long Island in Huntington. A priest who was hearing confessions burst out of the confessional in what has been called an extremely agitated state by those who were in the chapel at the time. The priest was said to have ripped open the curtain of the confessional only to find the penitent was gone. At that point the priest grabbed his chest and falls to the floor. No one saw the person and the police and EMS were called to the scene. One person who wishes to remain anonymous told our reporter at the scene that the words "Lamb of God" were carved in blood on the confessional wall. Now back to Steve Bennett in our studio."

Beth thinks to herself, "Could this be Aiden?" and here first instinct was to pick up the phone and call ICS to find out. She stopped herself thinking it would be better to call her co-workers to get the details. Suddenly Beth is very depressed and she sinks deeper into the couch regretting she ever turned on the news. The anchor continues for another minute wrapping up the story and continues with the next news item. Beth stares at the screen and a sinking feeling comes to her stomach.

A photo of Tom Houston appears on screen as the anchor continues, "In our next segment we feature one of the Socialist Liberation Party candidates for their presidential nomination and native Long Islander, Dr. Thomas Houston. He held a well-attended charitable fundraiser at his Garden City mansion yesterday in honor of Dr. Spencer Price of the Price Center for Cancer Research." The camera cuts away from the anchor and, on the screen, appear a photo of Tom Houston's mansion. The scene changes to a video showing limousines driving up to the front entrance of Tom's home with a number of the many luminaries getting out of their cars and walking up the wide staircase.

Steven Bennett continues, "The guest list reads like a who's who of celebrities' in the political, business and entertainment industries." Beth sits up as Spencer's photo comes on the screen and the anchor informs viewers, "The fundraiser was held for Dr. Price, who is a pioneer in the fight to find a cure for the cancer. It is being reported to ACN that a total of $47 million was raised for the Price Center and that should make Dr. Price very happy. The party went on well into the wee hours of the morning and it looked as if a wonderful time was had by all including Dr. Houston."

The visuals change again to feature many of the people who attended the event and Beth is staring, wide eyed, at the flat screen TV. Beth is hoping, no praying, that she doesn't appear on camera. She's not famous, maybe they didn't tape her, and as it appears like the focus is only on the rich and famous, Beth thinks she is in the clear. But then she remembers the event a Madison Square Garden and her new found celebrity. A mere moment goes by and the color drains from Beth's face as she sees herself in a series of photos with Tom walking her to the limousine. In one of the photos, she and Tom are looking into each other's eyes and in another he's holding her close and kissing her. Beth just says to herself, "Oh my God."

Steven Bennett continues, "It seems that ACN was able to obtain these photos of Tom Houston escorting his overnight guest, a beautiful young woman, out of his home and into his limousine. Tom Houston has recently been named one of the top three most eligible bachelors in America, and it seems that he could have finally found his newest love interest. Hey, you never know!"

Beth is now near a state of panic, all she can think of is what she will tell her family…friends…co-workers…Chris!? Just then the phone rings in her home and she jumps up, she looks at the display and sees its Chris calling from Chicago. Beth remembers, he's coming home tomorrow and she panics. Has he seen the story? What will she say to him? How can she ever explain this to him and all the people she knows?

She tries to ready herself in order to answer his call, but she stops, she just can't do it. Beth rationalizes that he will be home tomorrow and she will tell him in person. The phone stops ringing and Beth is relieved that she's off the hook, for now. As soon as Chris hangs up, the phone rings again. This time its Tom and she rushes to answer the phone.

Beth is distraught as she practically screams when she answers, "Have you seen the news?! Have you seen the photos? Oh, my God what have I done?"

Tom in a slow measured voice says, "Now Beth you need to calm down."

Now Beth actually screams, "Calm down! Calm Down! This is terrible, what will I tell my family? What will I tell Chris?" Beth is now getting so upset she starts to cry.

Tom exhales and tells Beth, "Listen, I know that it looks like there is something going on between us, but you know and I know that nothing happened last night or any other night and I think that you need to just tell people the truth. You got drunk, you couldn't drive and I gave you a bedroom where you could sleep it off. Spencer was also my guest that night as well as the Chairman of my campaign committee Benton Gallagher and a number of others. Please Beth, you need to calm down and not panic, please."

Beth sniffles in the phone, "That's easy for you to say. No matter how innocent it is, it still looks terrible for me, not you."

Tom tries to take a different approach with Beth. "What do you say I call the television network and tell them that you and I are just…"

Beth is getting panic-stricken, "WHAT! Are you crazy!? That would make things even worse!"

Tom speaks as steadily as possible given Beth's hysteria "Okay! Okay, just calm down. Tell me what can I do to help Beth; what do you want me to do?"

Beth is emotionally exhausted and she heaves a sigh, "I don't know what you can do, I just don't know."

Tom seems genuinely concerned, "Beth, please try to stay calm and see this as the misunderstanding it is. Staying at my home was, in fact, innocent and it was, in fact, done for your personal safety. If you would have left my home in your condition it could have resulted in a terrible consequence for you and perhaps some other unfortunate driver. Like I said before, you should tell whomever you have to exactly what happened; you have nothing to be ashamed of."

Beth just sits there, phone in hand, wiping the tears from her eyes. "I don't know; I just don't know what to do."

Tom says, "Listen Beth, I have something very important to do now, but I know that you are upset, and that is also important. Let me do what I need to do and I'll call you back to see how you are doing. Okay?"

Beth is silent.

"Beth, please answer me; is that okay?"

Beth heaves another sigh and answers, "Okay, I guess."

"Good, now just try and calm down and come to the true realization that this is merely an innocent occurrence taken totally out of context and proportion. I'll call you later" and Tom hangs up.

Beth continues to be distraught when the phone rings again. The display says it's from her co-worker Diane Breuer, and now Beth becomes even more distraught. Beth decides that she can't speak to anyone else at this time and just lets the call go into her answering machine. Beth's recorded message comes on and then she hears Diane speak, "Hey, hot stuff, I want to hear every sordid detail about the evening with Mr. Hunky. Wow, I just thought, I might be friends with the next First Lady! How lucky am I?!!!" and Diane hangs up.

Beth whispers in a low voice, "Shit."

The next hours Beth gets calls from her mother, her brother, her sister, her father. There is even Vincent and Angelica Grometti calling to offer to cater the Inaugural Ball, but Beth does not pick up a single call because she is so upset.

At this point, Beth is totally depressed about what has happened and what her life is turning into. All she wants to do is crawl into some hole and wait until this all blows over, but she knows it won't blow over. She knows it will only get worse and that makes her start to cry…again.

CHAPTER 3

After speaking with Beth, Dr. Tom Houston puts down the phone and sits in his home office, alone. He leans back in his chair and picks up the first report titled, "The Erosion of Christian Thought and Influence around the World."

He must prepare for the meeting he will have for his lord and master, and all must be perfect. It is critical that the inroads being made against Christianity worldwide continue. He's received reports from his offices around the world and what these reports convey are making him smile. The first article he read is one that reports Christians have become the most persecuted religious believers in the worlds for two years in a row. He is anxious to deliver the good news to his master and he knows Satan will be very pleased. The reports are arranged so that they not only cover the relevant news, but also some other updates that go beyond the reach of ACTELECT'S influence.

After he finishes reading the first report, Tom drops it back on his desk and he picks up the next report. This one is from their office in Iceland and a summary statement reads;

> *"ACTELECT recently took a poll of Icelandic youth. The poll was conducted as a result of efforts on behalf of our non-disclosed affiliation with "No God in Our Lives." The sampling*

represents a cross-section of 18–25-year-old young adults from all different income levels and backgrounds. Among the questions asked was, "Do you believe God created the Earth?" The poll found that among all those surveyed 0% believe that to be true. This result is down from a high of 90% just 20 years ago. It is apparent that the covert operations directed at changing the views of young Icelanders has had a very strong and measurable impact. The poll has a margin of error ±2%. This mirrors other polls that have been taken on the same subject."

Tom laughs to himself and thinks, how can the 0% results have a minus 2%? He finishes reading the rest of the report and picks up the next one.

The next two articles are so important that Tom Houston is sure that it will please his master. As reported in the headline reads:

The Vanishing:
Report Exposes Persecution of Middle East Christians as 'Close to Genocide'

Organized persecution of minority Christians in their traditional Middle East homelands is approaching genocide and has driven an exodus in the past two decades, a report commissioned by the British Foreign Secretary, Jeremy Hunt, warned Thursday.

Millions of Christians in the region have been uprooted from their homes, and many have been killed, kidnapped, imprisoned and discriminated against, the report compiled by the Bishop of Truro, the Right Rev Philip Mounstephen, found.

It also uncovered "shocking" evidence that the persecution is worse today than ever with widespread discrimination across south-east Asia, sub-Saharan Africa and in east Asia – often driven by state authoritarianism and intolerance of religious diversity.

Last week it was revealed that the fall in numbers has picked up after the Islamic State, which waged a genocidal campaign against Christians, lost its "caliphate" in Iraq and Syria, as Breitbart News reported.

"Unfortunately, it can be stated that the Islamic State group's anti-Christian campaign was very successful in Iraq, and to a certain extent, successful in Syria," John Hajjar, the co-chair of the American Mideast Coalition for Democracy (AMCD) and co-director of the Middle East Christian Committee (MECHRIC), told Breitbart News.

"I think we have no more hope," Archbishop Vicken Aykazian, the diocesan legate in America's capital and ecumenical director for the Eastern Diocese of the Armenian Orthodox Church of America, also told Breitbart News, referring to the future of Christianity in its Middle East cradle. "Middle East Christians have no nation that protects them openly."

The new report confirms those claims. It was made public as "the world was seeing religious hatred laid bare in the appalling attacks at Easter on churches across Sri Lanka, and the devastating attack on two mosques in Christchurch".

Mr. Hunt, an Anglican, has made the issue of Christian persecution one of the major themes of his foreign secretaryship. He said:

"I think we have shied away from talking about Christian persecution because we are a Christian country and we have a colonial past, so sometimes there's nervousness there. But we

have to recognize — and that's what the bishop's report points out very starkly — that Christians are the most persecuted religious group."

He added: "What we have forgotten in this atmosphere of political correctness is actually the Christians that are being persecuted are some of the poorest people on the planet. In the Middle East the population of Christians used to be about 20%; now it's 5%."

The report shows 100 years ago Christians comprised 20 percent of the population in the Middle East and North Africa, but since then the proportion has fallen to less than 4 percent, or roughly 15 million people.

In the Middle East and North Africa, the report says, "forms of persecution ranging from routine discrimination in education, employment and social life up to genocidal attacks against Christian communities have led to a significant exodus of Christian believers from this region since the turn of the century."

It highlights countries such as Algeria, Egypt, Iran, Iraq, Syria and Saudi Arabia which have worked to make life close to impossible for devout Christians and other minorities. The report goes on to add:

In Saudi Arabia there are strict limitations on all forms of expression of Christianity including public acts of worship. There have been regular crackdowns on private Christian services. The Arab-Israeli conflict has caused the majority of Palestinian Christians to leave their homeland. The population of Palestinian Christians has dropped from 15% to 2%.

Bishop Mounstephen said the study found Christians are "harassed" in more countries than any other religious group, and especially in predominantly Muslim countries in the Middle East and North Africa. His report found 245 million Christians now suffer "high levels of persecution" in 50 countries, a rise of 30 million year on year.

In particular, they have been attacked by extremist groups in Syria, Iraq, Egypt, north-eastern Nigeria and the Philippines, as well as in India and China. He added that the Middle East is witnessing the "decimation of some of the faith group's oldest and most enduring communities" and called for "urgent government support".

Persecutions and Deaths of Christians Worldwide 2018

There were so many incidents of persecutions and deaths of Christians that it is far too numerous to include in this summary report, a separate section has been included so as to provide information pertaining to the persecutions and deaths of Christians and Jews worldwide. There have been a number of instances in Nepal, China and the Ukraine among a number of other countries. However, the following is a highlight of what has occurred recently in Nigeria:

"... the estimated 30 million Christians in Northern Nigeria, who form the largest minority in a predominantly Muslim environment, have for decades, suffered marginalization and discrimination as well as targeted violence, especially in the hands of organized mob violence and violent groups such as Boko Haram and Fulani Herdsmen.

"Hundreds of churches in Northern Nigeria particularly Northeast and North-central Nigeria as well as Southern part

of Kaduna State which is predominant Christian population have also been burnt or destroyed with estimated 16,000 defenseless citizens composed of mostly Christian population killed across the country since June 2015 when Mr. Muhammadu Buhari became Nigeria's sixth civilian President. The estimated 16,000 defenseless civilian deaths outside the law include 5,800 mostly Christians killed by terror Fulani Herdsmen and Boko Haram since June 2015."

During the first six months of 2018, about 6,000 Christians— mostly children, women, and the elderly—were killed in Nigeria alone. The details of these murders, though seldom reported, were often grisly. Many victims were hacked to death or beheaded with machetes;

Others were burned alive (sometimes inside locked churches or homes); and women were frequently sexually assaulted or raped before being slaughtered.

Tom turns the page and is immensely interested in the next article because it is all about his opponent in the nomination of Democrat Socialist Liberation Party. It seems that Helen De Witt's campaign staff has adopted an anti-Catholic and anti-Evangelical Christian position trying to carve out an anti-religious stance in order to compete in appealing to fringe groups and other constituents of Dr. Houston, who do not ascribe to those belonging to organized religions. Tom is curious as he reads the initial paragraphs of the leaked emails.

Emails show Helen De Witt Surrogates' Anti-Catholic sentiment is alive and well in her campaign

The recent WikiLeaks emails of Helen De Witt's surrogates Jessica Proceda and Jeremy Hellman regarding Catholicism have created a controversy. Ms. De Witt's chief of staff, Luther

Crimmens and campaign higher-ups are maintaining a deafening silence as they view this anti-Catholic position as a shock the 21st-century conscience! This is even more galling with an informal perspicuous historical relationship between Catholic voters and the Democrat Socialist Liberation Party.

Tragically, anti-Catholic sentiment seems to be alive and well in the 21st-century Socialist Liberation Party due to positions they have taken with regard to abortion, gay marriage, transgenderism and other controversial issues.

Tom Houston smiles because he doesn't have to read further to know that Christians, Catholics and Jews are on the descent and his master will enjoy the development. He shakes his head and continues to read another article on the same subject.

[Headline:]
"World's First Lesbian Bishop Calls for Christian Church to Remove Crosses, to Install Muslim Prayer Space,"
Breitbart London, October 5, 2015

The Bishop of Stockholm has proposed a church in her diocese remove all signs of the cross and put down markings showing the direction to Mecca for the benefit of Muslim worshippers.

Eva Brunne, who was made the world's first openly lesbian bishop by the church of Sweden in 2009, and has a young son with her wife and fellow lesbian priest Gunilla Linden, made the suggestion to make those of other faiths more welcome.

The church targeted is the Seamen's mission church in Stockholm's eastern dockyards. The bishop held a meeting there this year and challenged the priest to explain what he'd do if a ship's crew came into port who weren't Christian, but wanted to pray.

Calling Muslim guests to the church "angels", the Bishop later took to her official blog to explain that removing Christian symbols from the church and preparing the building for Muslim prayer doesn't make a priest any less a defender of the faith. Rather, to do any less would make one "stingy towards people of other faiths".

The upper echelons of the Church of Sweden, much like other national churches across Europe, seem to be fully invested in the diversity mission. Back in February, a parish church in multicultural paradise Malmö declared it would be holding a service in solidarity with the local Muslim community as a protest against a march by anti-Islamisation movement PEGIDA in the city.

Tom breezes through the rest of the article, but takes note of the closing paragraph. Next, Tom picks up an article on the "Daily Caller" website written by James Zumwalt. Tom is especially interested in the turmoil caused by the influx of Muslims into countries throughout Great Britain, Europe and the United States. He believes that this will greatly contribute to the tensions between the religions and exacerbate the deterioration of relations between them in hopes the conflicts will rise in their intensity.

Tom Houston's staff, as they often do, highlights certain paragraphs that they would like him to read and he finds this helpful.

"Sweden began opening its doors to Muslim immigrants in the 1970s. Today it pays a high price for having done so. The group suffering the severest consequences of such an open-door policy has been Swedish women.

As Muslim men immigrated to Sweden, they brought with them an Islamic culture sanctioning rape. It is a culture bad enough inherently in the treatment of its own women. Under sharia, Muslim women serve little more purpose beyond catering to their husbands' sexual demands. A non-submissive wife runs the risk of being raped by her husband.

But under sharia, this rape culture also impacts upon Swedish women as they are "infidels" and, as such, are — according to Allah's teachings — sanctioned targets for rape by Muslim men. Such an Islamic belief system has born witness to a drastic increase in rapes in Sweden — more than a thousand-fold — since first opening its doors to Muslim immigration."

"A 1996 Swedish National Council for Crime Prevention report bears this out. It noted that Muslim immigrants from North Africa were 23 times more likely to commit rape than Swedish men."

True or not, Tom believes that contributing to the tension is always good and he next turns his attention to an article written in the "Daily Mail" by Sam Webb. The headline especially interests Tom as are the highlighted paragraphs.

[Headline:]
"Sharia law to be enshrined in British legal system as Lawyers get guidelines on drawing up documents according to Islamic rules"
[Sub-Head]

- The guidelines on wills could mean women are denied an equal inheritance

- Adopted children could also face losing out under Law Society document

- The move has been criticized as a backwards step by equality campaigners

"Top lawyers have written guidelines for British solicitors on drafting 'sharia-compliant' wills which can deny women an equal share of their inheritance and entirely exclude non-believers, it was revealed today."

"But as the Muslim population has grown and the pervasive creed of multiculturalism has become ever more powerful, so Sharia law has rapidly grown in influence within some communities.

"Sharia law, imported from theocracies like Afghanistan and Saudi Arabia, first began to be used here in a strictly limited form, dealing mainly with narrow issues like Islamic financial contracts."

"There are now estimated to be no fewer than 85 Sharia courts across the country — from London and Manchester to Bradford and Nuneaton. They operate mainly from mosques, settling financial and family disputes according to religious principles."

On a side note, Tom sees an item that is circled and highlighted that reads,

Muslim gangs are attempting to enforce Sharia Law in East London.

Tom recognizes that these changes to traditions in Great Britain and other countries dilute the impact of Christianity and eventually will contribute to its demise. Tom Houston is confident that this will lead to his master's ultimate triumph over the forces of Heaven. There are many more articles coming from around the world. He is reading of the persecutions of Christians, Jews and other infidels in the Middle East, China and beyond. Tom is satisfied that all is proceeding according to plan and he also knows that, among other things, these disparate anti-Christian and Jewish groups will get his covert support for their efforts. The Founder and President of ACTELECT is taking great pleasure from reading one news feature and report after another as he picks up his next stack of articles.

There is an abridgement and Tom is able to skim through a few of the many items that he takes time to delight in.

- *Recently there have been 875 incidents of arson and vandalism that have taken place in churches throughout the country. (See full article on page 3)*

- *NY Times reported that the Chinese government removed two more crosses from Churches. (See full article on page 7)*

- *There is a movement to take the motto "In God We Trust" off of US currency (see full article on page 13)*

- *Elementary, high schools as well as colleges and universities across the United States have not only forbidden the use of prayer, but any and all references to Christianity itself while allowing for Muslims to affirm their beliefs. (See full article on page 25 - 31)*

- *Bibles have been removed from VA hospitals (see full article on page 32)*

- *A sitting U.S. President has been quoted as saying that "Whatever we once were, we're no longer just a Christian nation; we are also a Jewish nation, a Muslim nation, a Buddhist nation, a Hindu nation, and a nation of nonbelievers." He has also said, "The future does not belong to those who slander Islam." (See full article on page 41)*

- *A US Military Brief labeled Catholics and evangelical Christians as religious extremists, eight churches and Christian organizations were forced to violate the tenets of their faith, and schoolchildren were ordered to sing government-approved Christmas carols. (See full article on page 48)*

- *Catholic University gives award to an avowed pro-abortionist. (See full article on page 56)*

- *A New York City teacher was also told to remove a quote from former President Ronald Reagan that read, "If we ever forget that we are one nation under God, then we will be a nation gone under." (See full article on Page 63)*

- *The Federal judge in Texas forbade students from using religious words such as "prayer" and "amen" in speeches at graduation. (See full article on page 75)*

- *A lawsuit has been filed by the ACLU demanding that a religious-rights law in Mississippi, which protects the First Amendment constitutional rights regarding faith issues, be struck so that homosexuals cannot be refused any service for any reason. (See full article on page 81)*

- *In Nepal, Christmas is no longer a holiday. (See full article on page 86)*

- *Churches have been set on fire in countries including Norway, Sweden and the United States. (See full article on page 92 - 103)*

- *In Egypt, Muslim extremists have subjected Coptic Christians to beatings and massacres, resulting in the exodus of 200,000 Copts from their homes. (See full article on page 118)*

- *In Iraq, 1,000 Christians were killed in Baghdad between the years 2003 and 2012 and 70 churches in the country were burned. (See full article on page 129)*

- *In Iran, converts to Christianity face the death penalty and in 2012 Pastor Yousef Nadarkhani was sentenced to death. (See full article on page 133)*

- *In Russia, many attacks, arsons and acts of vandalism against churches in Russia are reported each year. The acts of vandalism are often accompanied by satanic symbolism and graffiti. (See full article on page 142 - 143)*

- *In Bolivia, an angry mob of Indigenous peoples destroyed the only evangelical church in the remote village of Chucarasi in the Bolivian Andes after beating a congregational elder unconscious. (See full article on page 147)*

- *In Chile, since 2015, twelve churches have been burned in southern Chile, 10 Catholic and two Protestant. Attacks are supposedly from the Mapuche indigenous people, who are campaigning to reclaim ancestral lands, according to authorities. (See full article on page 151)*

- *In Pakistan, critics of the laws say that Christians like Asia Bibi are sentenced to death with only hearsay for evidence of alleged blasphemy. At least a dozen Christians have been given death sentences and half a dozen murdered after being accused of violating blasphemy laws. In 2005, 80 Christians were behind bars due to these laws. (See full article on page 156)*

- *In India, the acts of violence include arson of churches, re-conversion of Christians to Hinduism by force and threats of physical violence, distribution of threatening literature, burning of Bibles, raping of nuns, murder of Christian priests and the destruction of Christian schools and colleges, and the desecration of cemeteries. Much of the violence has been attributed to Hindu Nationalists. (See full article on page 160)*

- *There is a prime-time television program entitled "Lucifer", based on a comic book storyline, featuring the main character as the hero. (See full article on page 167)*

There was one recent storm of controversy that pleased Tom to no end. It concerned the supposed statement by Pope Francis concerning the existence of hell and its place in theological doctrine. One of the articles that summarized the controversy that is swirling around the Pope's statement reportedly said that there is "no Hell" and condemned souls simply "disappear." This position refutes thousands of years of church teaching. It has also drawn outrage by many Catholics and has added to the problems the Pope is having with many of the faithful.

The firestorm over the words is an outgrowth over a conversation between Pope Francis and Eugenio Scalfari, the 93-year-old atheist and co-founder and former editor of Italian newspaper La Repubblica. It seems that Mr. Scalfari's discussion with the pope centered on the question of "hell" and its existence. Mr. Scafari indicated that the pontiff said there was no hell in direct contradiction to church teaching. In a statement from the Vatican, spokesmen tried to clarify the dispute by walking a thin line between the pope's sentiments and theological implications.

Tom doesn't care about what may have been a poor interpretation of the Pontiff's true beliefs because he knows that Satan will also find it very amusing. Tom has covertly funded many of the efforts to undermine the Catholic and Christian Churches and Mr. Scalfari's beliefs made him a willing, if not, unaware acolyte. Tom had many more items in his stack, but he feels that he has enough information to assure that his lord will be pleased.

Tom Houston makes his way down to the lower level of his home and into the wine cellar. He touches the one special shelf and the cellar becomes the cave of horrors that he is very familiar with. He makes his way through the labyrinth of rocks with razor sharp edges to the chosen location where he is to meet his master. Tom goes to his knees and bows down with his head touching the floor.

A frighteningly powerful voice speaks, "What is it you have to tell me?" and then the voice goes silent.

Still in complete subservience, Tom Houston says, "My lord all continues as planned." He tells Satan all he has committed to memory from the reports he received. When Tom Houston is finished, he asks, "My lord, do you wish to hear more, I can provide…" but he is silenced.

"You have told me enough. I am preparing for the final battle to come and I will give you your instructions soon."

"My lord there is so much more to be done. I am proceeding with all due haste, but there are many unfinished…" but Satan stops the man from speaking further.

"Quiet, do you think I know nothing of these things?"

"I am sorry my lord, I did not mean to…" Tom is becoming terrified for he needs to ask the one question he must, but he fears the answer from Lucifer.

"I know what you are thinking. I have given you much, but it is not enough…it is never enough with you, is it?

Tom starts to shudder, "My lord…"

"Quiet you fool, if the battle is to come soon then I will need to provide you with, how shall I say, succor, yes that's a good word, succor."

There is a loud rumbling and the floor of the cave shakes. Still on his knees Tom Houston looks up for the first time. Satan now stands at least 40 feet tall and he is looking at a distant part of the cave. There is smoke and fire and the smell of Sulphur nearly chokes Tom. There appears a break in the billowing smoke that permeates the cave and a lone figure materializes in the distance. Tom cannot make out who or what it is, but his eyes are transfixed on the image. The figure comes closer and closer, but the smoke obscures much of the mysterious figure's features.

Satan looks down at his underling still kneeling on the floor, "Do you not wonder whom it is I have summoned?"

"No, my lord, I mean yes my lord." Tom fears making Satan angry and the wrong answers always make Satan angry.

This time, however, Satan laughs. "Ah, welcome my friend welcome! Dr. Thomas Houston, please welcome Al-Masih ad-Dajjal."

CHAPTER 4

The plane arrives at Islip MacArthur Airport on time. I'm anxious to get off the plane and take a moment to call Beth, but what will I say? I have tried to call her while I was with Harry, but she doesn't answer and, on some level, I was relieved. I am trying to work out in my mind how I can tell Beth about what had happened between Amanda and me, but I have no clue about what to say. I rationalize that none of it is my fault and I did nothing to encourage Amanda, but would she believe me?

I walk through the terminal to baggage claim and wait for my luggage to come down the conveyor belt. There are television monitors located throughout the baggage claim area and they are all tuned to a news channel. I'm looking at the screen as the anchor is ending a story about forest fires out in California that have been burning for weeks.

The news anchor, Greg Talbot is speaking to the camera, "…so far more than 100 homes have been destroyed, but thankfully no loss of life. Firefighters continue to battle the blaze and are they are warning local residents to leave their homes and belongings and find their way to safety. We will be keeping you informed of the status of this important story as updates come in. Now we take you to Kristen Lawrence with our entertainment news report, Hot! Hot! Hollywood. So, Kristen what have you got to tell us?"

"Good evening, everyone, well Greg, here's some very interesting news. Hot! Hot! Hollywood is reporting that one of the hottest actresses in the world has a new guy! Take a look at this video taken just a few hours ago." The screen cuts from Kristen to a video taken on the sidewalk outside of Chicago's O'Hare Airport terminal. It shows me and Amanda kissing and all the color drains from my face.

Kristen Lawrence continues her story. "Beautiful, talented Amanda Sellers has been photographed giving a passionate, long-lasting kiss to this handsome and mysterious stranger. Amanda Sellers, who is notoriously private when it comes to her love life, seems to be quite comfortable sucking the lips off of handsome Mr. Mysterious. Rumor has it she spent the weekend with him at her fabulously wealthy father's country estate. Last week Amanda Sellers told Hot! Hot! Hollywood that she is working on a new movie and the plot is top secret…maybe he's the top secret. We'll be following this story and let you know how it develops, wink, wink! Now onto our next item featuring…"

I'm still standing by the conveyor belt in stunned silence with my luggage having passed by twice. A woman standing nearby looks at the TV and down at me and looks back at the TV and down at me again. All of a sudden, she realizes that I'm the same guy she sees on TV and now the woman gets very excited,

"Hey! You're that guy kissing Amanda! Wow!" The woman reaches for her handbag and pulls out a pen and an old credit card receipt. "Can I have your autograph?" and she thrusts the pen and paper in my face. I stare at the woman and snap out of my frozen stance, grab my luggage and run out of baggage claim. Outside the terminal I frantically look around, trying to remember where I left my car so I can just get out of the airport. I suddenly remember the area where the car is parked and practically run across the lot to the parking space. I get into my car and put the keys in the ignition, but I don't bother to start the engine. All I can think about is Beth and how she would react when she sees the news story of Amanda kissing me. I think about what I should do next and decide that I better get it over with and try to explain to Beth what happened.

I reach for my phone and autodial Beth's number. The phone rings three times and I hear her prerecorded message, "Hi, this is Beth and I'm not available, but just leave a message after the tone and I will call you back as soon as I can. Have a wonderful day…" I am at once upset and relieved; I finally muster enough courage to talk to Beth about this incident, but now I have a reprieve from actually having to tell her. I hear a beep and leave a message, "Hi Beth, this is Chris and I just landed. I need to talk to you so please call me as soon as you can. I'll try to call your cell at the hospital to see if you are there." I pause for a second and then end the message, "I love you and miss you" and I disconnect. I call her cell and I get her voice mail and leave the same message. I also call the hospital, but someone at the nursing station tells me that Beth had taken off today.

Now I'm getting very anxious about the whole thing. What if Beth saw the news report? What if she is not picking up the phone because she knows it is me and she is angry…very angry? What if she' just out shopping and her phone is dead? What if…? All these questions are going through my mind and I have no answers.

I turn on the ignition and the car starts, but before I put my Mustang into gear, the world stops and I have a vision.

The giant of a man stands on the side of the road. He has joined a band of thieves whose leader calls himself the devil. The giant of a man considers the devil to be the most powerful of kings and promises him all his strength and loyalty. The devil king orders his men to march toward a small town where they would plunder and terrify the locals as they have done many times in the past. It is the first such raid for the giant, and he looks intently at his sovereign lord, the devil king.

As the group nears the town, they spot a cross, planted in the ground near the entrance to the main road. The giant looks up at his devil king and sees terror in his eyes and the giant can sense the fear in the devil's heart. It was from that moment on that the giant Canaanite called Reprobus leaves to follow another, more powerful, king.

I am confused; failing to understand what the meaning of this vision was when the form of St. Christopher appears.

The giant man smiles at me, "I am honored that your mother and father thought to name you after me. I am both grateful and humbled."

I stared at St. Christopher and was never so happy to see a saint as I was at this time. "I am in a terrible shape, St. Christopher. I don't know what to do. I am confused and ashamed and I afraid that I will lose Beth."

St. Christopher holds his hand up as if to stop me from speaking, and as it became quiet, there was another vision.

Ancient Lycia is the scene of violent martyrdom for many Christians who live and travelled that realm. The emperor hears of this giant evangelical and considers that he must pay homage. The emperor commands that the giant, Christopher, sacrifice to him, but the saint refuses. The emperor first tempts Christopher with gold and silver, but the saint again refuses. Lastly, two women are sent to seduce him, but rather than succumb to this temptation, Christopher takes these women into his confidence.

"I know that you were sent to lead me astray from my path to the Lord, but I will not allow myself to worship the emperor as my god. There is only one true God and His Son, Jesus the Christ."

The women look at each other and sit on the floor of the cell that is now Christopher's prison. For hours they sit and talk and both women would question Christopher about this God of his. Christopher explains all that he knows, all he has learned and all that was told to him on his life's journey.

"Jesus, the man from Galilee, was sent by the Father to sacrifice his life so that we all may be free of the wages of sin and live in the glory of heaven." The words spoken by Christopher both overwhelm and inspire the women and by the end of their time together they had both convert to Christianity.

St. Christopher looks at me for a brief moment. He must have known what I was thinking, what is in my heart and he told me, "We all face temptations and we must make those judgements that will determine how we proceed. I chose to follow the path that the Lord set before me."

I stammer, but when I answer, "I don't know what to do. I love Beth, but I also have feelings for Amanda. I am so confused on what to do; how will I know if I am making the right decision?"

The Sainted seems to know my dilemma and is sympathetic as he says, "Christopher, I cannot give you the answer to your questions nor can I make the decision for you as you must make that on your own. What I can tell you is that you must look into your heart to find the answer to your questions and the right decision will become evident. What you must always remember is that the Lord is with you always and His will be done."

The words of St. Christopher ring true, but it still means that I need to face up to the inevitable and try to do the right thing.

"St. Christopher, can you help me…", but as I was about to ask him to help me find the right words the vison began to fade and the familiar heavenly light swallowed the giant from Canaan.

CHAPTER 5

St. John sits alone in a small corner of his cave that he reserves for writing. The candle and fire offer little light as the holy man sits at the table. He is old and he is troubled as he writes what has been revealed to him. The man stops to read the script from the parchment and he reads the words aloud to no one.

> "And there came one of the seven angels which had the seven vials, and talked with me, saying unto me, come hither; I will show unto thee the judgment of the great whore that sitteth upon many waters: With whom the kings of the earth have committed fornication, and the inhabitants of the earth have been made drunk with the wine of her fornication."

The man looks up from the parchment where he has written these words and ponders what they mean. He continues to read,

> "And the woman was arrayed in purple and scarlet color, and decked with gold and precious stones and pearls, having a golden cup in her hand full of abominations and filthiness of her fornication and upon her forehead was a name written, MYSTERY, BABYLON THE GREAT, THE MOTHER OF HARLOTS AND ABOMINATIONS OF THE EARTH."

Much has been revealed to John, but much he has been told by the Lord is still a mystery to him and he is intent on finding answers. He knows the truth behind the Whore of Babylon, the true meaning that God has made manifest. He knows that when God speaks to him of fornication, he speaks of the adultery committed is against Him.

John gets up from the small stool that he has been sitting on and paces back and forth in the small room. He ponders the meaning and the impact it will have on the faithful. Who is this whore that the Lord speaks of they will ask? What havoc will the whore reek on all they will ask? John knows that the whore may not be a woman or a man but, it must be someone or something to fear. John reaches for his quill and begins to write a passage given what has been revealed to him;

> *"And I stood upon the sand of the sea, and saw a beast rise up out of the sea, having seven heads and ten horns, and upon his horns ten crowns, and upon his heads the name of blasphemy.*
>
> *And the beast which I saw was like unto a leopard, and his feet were as the feet of a bear, and his mouth as the mouth of a lion: and the dragon gave him his power, and his seat, and great authority.*
>
> *And I saw one of his heads as it were wounded to death; and his deadly wound was healed: and all the world wondered after the beast.*
>
> *And they worshipped the dragon which gave power unto the beast: and they worshipped the beast, saying, who is like unto the beast? Who is able to make war with him?"*

St. John sits in silence for a long while giving him time to ponder the words presented to him by the angel of God. He tries to consider the possible meanings of what he has been told, but the answers do not come. Is the Whore of Babylon the beast? What form will the whore take? How will the whore seduce the multitude?

The old man's body is weak with age and tired from the task he has been given. He lowers his head onto the table he has been writing on and a restless sleep overcomes the last surviving apostle of the Christ.

CHAPTER 6

Tom, still on his knees, looks at the man standing beside him. He finally gets the courage to rise from the floor to get a better look. Al-Masih ad-Dajjal stands at least five inches shorter than Tom Houston and is dressed in the traditional robes of a devout Muslim. His right eye is punctured and it is nearly falling from the socket. As if to compensate, his left eye is larger; nearly reaching his forehead, but there is a luminescence that seems to come from the center of the eye that mesmerizes Tom. The last thing Tom notices the word *'Kafir'* carved into the man's forehead. Tom does not know what the word means.

Tom is repulsed by his appearance, but asks, "My lord, may I ask who this man is?"

Satan looks down at the man and responds to Tom Houston, "Al-Masih ad-Dajjal, the 'Deceiver'. He is the last of a long line of 30 deceivers and I have summoned him from the pit to instill in you the resolve to complete your assigned tasks." Tom wants to protest Satan's characterization of him, but he knows better and remains quiet.

Satan continues speaking to Tom Houston. "I see you are repulsed by the look of your new found friend." Tom is about to say something, but knows he must continue to remain silent. Satan also knows this, but he continues, "So as not to offend your sensibilities, as well as others, The Deceiver will do what he must to hide his true nature from those who think themselves as believers. He will do this before he will walk among them; will you not, ad-Dajjal?"

The Deceiver smiles and says, "Of course my master."

Satan stares quizzically at the man's forehead, "By the way ad-Dajjal, I must say I love the look, but you will need to do something about *'Kafir'*, after all you wouldn't want to give away your secret. Maybe some make-up, what do you think?" Now Satan laughs at his own joke.

Al-Masih ad-Dajjal continues to smile, "Yes my lord, none of those who will follow me will know I am the Kafir."

Satan laughs aloud and tells ad-Dajjal, "Good, well done! Now, will you promise 72 virgins or 72 raisins?" Satan still laughing at the confusion being fostered in translations from the Hadith, "Ah this is most helpful. Perversion of Islamic teachings, and the terror it has wrought, has brought so many young men and women to martyrdom. Now for my eternal pleasure, those who have visited horror on others will suffer unendingly. There is the special place that I have created in lake of fire and it will be their reward."

Tom Houston prefers to keep silent, but he has many questions to ask of his master. He lowers his head so that he does not have to look Satan in the eye, "My lord what it is that we must assure be done so you may proclaim victory?"

Satan turns to face Dr. Tom Houston as the demon commands him to do what is needed to complete his mission. "There is much left for you to do. You will continue to sow the seeds of discord among the bastard believers of God, Christ and The Sainted. Once you are placed in the most powerful position of leadership, you will go out into the world and you will continue to proclaim the absurdity of religion and the false belief of so many that there is a God. That, in great measure, will cast enough doubt in the weak minded among the faithful. As the devastations of famine, drought, pestilence, war and more are wrought upon mankind, the peoples will come to realize the end is near. With nowhere to retreat, you will deliver absolution to the people as many will turn their backs to God and worship me; it is then their souls will be mine. Is that clear to you?"

Tom bows and says, "Yes my lord."

Next Satan turns to Al-Masih ad-Dajjal and makes it known what is expected of him. "I have made your task much easier ad-Dajjal. I have sown the seeds of death, destruction and violence among the Islamic tribes and those seeds are planted very deep…yes very deep indeed." Satan takes the time to relish this development and grins as he continues, "You will take your place in the role of leadership among these wanton killers and professed believers in Islam and consolidate their blinding ignorance into a force to do final battle with the Christians, Jews and others."

Lucifer takes the time to look into the heart and mind of Al-Masih ad-Dajjal and Satan knows that the Kafir is resolute. "Through the millennia the world has borne witness to the death of many millions of Christians and Jews. The forces of evil, that guide so many in Islam, have also seen to it that many Muslims have died in their wanton, but very effective jihad. This slaughter will be made even more potent as most seek to abandon their courage and to run and hide in cowardice. I command that the war my minions foment, grow in scope and size and that this is to continue and it is you who are to be the force to see it is done."

Al-Masih ad-Dajjal assures Satan, "It will be done my lord."

Tom now has regained some of his courage and asks, "How long will we need to complete the work my lord?"

Satan replies to both men, "According to the prophesy, you will have 429 days and on the last day we will do battle with the forces of God and His Son. I will know that you have done what I command when I see the signs have come true."

Both men look at each other and back to Satan and Tom Houston asks, "What are those signs my lord?"

Satan looks up as if to think of what to say next, but he knows the signs well, and he tells his sycophants, "You will know your work is complete when you see these signs; A multitude of people will stop offering prayer to God, this is most important. Dishonesty will become a way of life for many…falsehoods will become virtue…people will abandon their faith for worldly gain…the elderly will be cast aside…there will be no shame amongst the peoples. It is then that drought, pestilence and famine will become widespread and when they plead for God's intervention there will only be silence in response. After this is done, most will lose their faith in the forces of heaven and they will come to worship me."

Satan now instructs Al-Masih ad-Dajjal, "You will follow my commands exactly. You will emerge in a land in the east, Khorasan and you will be followed by the people with faces that appear as none anyone have ever seen. You will travel the land preaching my gospel and bringing death and destruction and because of this you will be unable to enter Mecca and Medina, but should be of little concern as I will see to their destruction as I will also see to the destruction of Jerusalem." As both ad-Dajjal and Tom Houston listen, the strategy of Satan is becoming clearer to both men.

Satan continues his instructions to Al-Masih ad-Dajjal, "You will gather an army of many from Isfahan; it will be soldiered by those who have been deceived. You will then lead them in the war against Jesus Christ and the forces of heaven. My minions, demon beasts from the pit, will join your forces in the battle and defeat is not an option."

Al-Masih ad-Dajjal knows and understands all he has been told. He tells his master, "The Quran then specifies that, in the latter days, the Christians will dominate the earth, and they shall be the cause of all kinds of mischief running rampant. Waves of calamities will rise on all sides and will race down from every height. These are prophesies that will be used to incite fear and retribution against the infidels. We will be relentless in assuring this comes to pass." Then ad-Dajjal turns to Tom Houston and says, "Is this false pride on my part or will you help to assure it will come to pass?"

Tom Houston does not bother to face Al-Masih ad-Dajjal and he merely answers, "It will come to pass."

There is silence for a few moments before ad-Dajjal speaks, "Where will this final confrontation take place, my lord."

Satan tells the sycophants before him, "It will come to pass on the third ethereal stratum of the Plains of Jerusalem in the shadow of Megiddo." Satan smiles at the men as they now understand what must take place. He knows that the men will do what they are commanded and he knows they will not fail…for if they do, there will be hell to pay.

CHAPTER 7

I arrive at home confused, depressed and in total panic. I don't know what to say to Beth or how I will explain the incident with Amanda at the airport. I immediately think to call Uncle Al, but what should I tell him? I reach the conclusion that it is of little use to continue freaking out over the situation. I know that Uncle Al will be able to distill my problem down a more manageable level as opposed to me jumping off a cliff.

I call him and try to formulate some way to let him know what happened between Amanda and me. I can rationalize that I didn't initiate or encourage Amanda, but I was definitely tempted by her advances. I hope Uncle Al can come up with a great coward's way out of having to tell Beth, but I know I need to face the inevitable.

His phone rings and he answers, "Hey Chris, nice going!"

I am puzzled, "What are you talking about, nice going?"

I hear him laughing at the other end of the phone and he says, "You do have a certain charm about you, and now you have two of the hottest girls falling all over themselves because of you. Personally, I don't think you're all that attractive, but hey there's no accounting for some peoples taste." Now Al is laughing again.

"Shit, how did you find out?"

"Well Romeo, I was watching the television and I saw your smiling face, well actually I couldn't see much of your face because Amanda Sellers was sucking it off your skull."

"Shit, that's what I was calling you about. I can't believe that this happened and I need your advice."

"Well Chrissy, I've got nothing but time, I'm just waiting here at the hospital and I …"

Now I become ever more freaked out "What, you're in the hospital!? What's wrong, are you okay? What happened, what have the doctors said?"

Uncle Al tries to calm me, "No…no Chris, I'm not a patient in the hospital, I'm here with Aiden, he's had a heart attack and I'm just sitting here in the ICU. I'm hoping he'll regain his consciousness soon so I can breathe a sigh of relief."

"I am really sorry Uncle Al, what happened?"

"Well according to witnesses, Aiden was hearing confessions when he burst out of the confessional and tore open the curtain, you know, on the side where the penitent usually sits. Well, it seems that when he did there was no one inside, but was heard screaming 'Lamb of God', he then grabbed his chest and fell to the floor."

"I am confused, Lamb of God? You don't mean the Lamb of God, like in the mass murders?"

"One in the same Chris; the words were written in the confessional, in blood, and now Aiden is unconscious and I don't know what happened. He's on life support, he's being medicated, and the initial exam confirmed it was another heart attack. It's not his first so it's really very serious. The doctor says he will need to rest and I was warned by the doctor that Aiden can't get excited. I'm keeping in close touch with my team, but I just know he has something to tell me about what happened and I want to be here when he wakes up so I'm here just keeping my buddy company."

I am now even more depressed and I tell my uncle, "I am so sorry to hear that. I know he is your best friend and he is one of the truly good guys. I'd like to visit him, but that's probably not a good idea at the moment."

"No, he's in intensive care, but I was able to pull rank and they're letting me stay."

I am at a loss for words and just say, "I understand."

Now Uncle Al gets an opportunity to do the thing he loves most, break my balls. He asks, "So let's get to the hot topic on every stupid entertainment show out there; Amanda Sellers and the Mystery Man! Come on, give it up let me hear the sordid detains and don't leave anything out, I'm a trained professional and I will know when you are bullshitting me."

With a heavy heart I begin to tell Uncle Al about my visit with Harry Lieberman and how I met his daughter, Amanda. I told him about how she seemed to like me and how we wound up having a great rapport. Maybe I should have told him about how Amanda tried to seduce me and even though nothing happened, I just can't find the right words to explain it all.

I end my description of the events by saying, "She drove me to the airport and when I got out of the car and tried to say goodbye, she simply kissed me in a way I could not have ever even imagined."

Uncle Al has been quiet for the entire time and when I finish the story he simply exclaims, "Wow!"

"Wow is right, I don't know how it happened, but 'wow' is a good word to use. All three of us had a great time; Harry was a terrific host and Amanda was wonderful and great to talk to, but I don't think I ever gave her any indication that I was trying to get close to her. After all she is a famous actress, she's the daughter of a phenomenally wealthy man, she has dated the rich and famous and she is among the most beautiful women I have ever seen. The whole kissing thing came out of left field and it was totally unexpected."

"So, Chris, it sounds like you are unsure about your feelings for either Beth or Amanda. Is that correct?"

I immediately answer, "No, I love Beth and well, I guess I am flattered by the idea that Amanda Sellers could possible like me, that way. Know what I mean?"

"Well since you put it like that, yeah I know what you mean."

I am beyond depressed at having to tell Uncle Al about all this, but he always knows what I'm feeling and what I am thinking. "What should I do Uncle Al? What can I do to make this all go away?"

"Listen Chrissy, it's not going away. I think you know what will resolve this one way or another, and I think you already know what you have to do."

I breathe a heavy disheartening sigh, "Yeah, I think I know, but I was hoping that you would have another way out for me; you know the coward's way out."

There's a strange thing that happens to my uncle's voice when he imparts advice. He speaks in a way that conveys wisdom and strength and tells me, "Well, sorry to disappoint you, but I see no alternative other than to tell Beth what happened. Listen, you love her and she loves you and being honest with each other will help strengthen your bond with her. It ain't gonna be easy buddy, but it's the right thing to do and I think you know that already."

I heave another sigh and say, "I guess you're right."

Uncle Al and I continue to talk for a while when he says, "Hey Chrissy, you in front of a TV?"

"No, why?"

"There's a news item I think you'll want to see."

"What? What is it?"

Uncle Al is getting impatient, "Just turn on the damn TV to the Long Island News Channel?"

I go into my living room and turn on the TV to the local news channel. There is a commercial currently running so I ask again, "What? What is it you want me to see?"

"Pazienza!"

The commercial ends and the news anchor begins to speak, "Before the break we promised you that we will be following up with our big feature in our 'People in the News' segment. Now here's Molly Turner on location in front of Dr. Tom's Houston's Garden City mansion with a heartbreaking report for many of the women in America." The anchor breaks into an ear-to-ear grin and says, "Well Molly what's the bad news?"

Molly laughs, "Well based on what we've seen in a series of photos, one of American's most eligible bachelors, Long Island's own Dr. Thomas Houston, may be off the market. The Long Island News Channel has gotten a hold of a series of close ups showing Dr. Tom Houston and a beautiful young woman, whose identity is unknown, sneaking out of his mansion. They are standing in front of a stretch limousine, face-to-face and they seem to be staring into each other's eyes. The next photo shows them kissing each other. These were taken the morning after a gala fundraiser was held for Dr. Spencer Price, of the Price Center for Cancer Research. I for one am deeply saddened by this turn of events because I was hoping to be the lucky girl to win the affections of Tom Houston, but alas, if I didn't have bad luck, I'd have no luck at all. This is Molly Turner reporting and now back to you Steve." Molly can be seen laughing on camera with Steve Bennett smiling behind his desk in the studio.

"Well Molly there's always Prince Constantine-Alexios of Greece. I understand he may still be available and you could become a Princess!"

Molly thinks a bit and breaks out into a broad grin saying, "Princess huh? That works for me!"

Chris sits frozen on his chair, staring at the TV, throughout the entire segment. He doesn't speak or react in any way.

Al figures that Chris is silent because he has seen Beth and Tom Houston together, kissing, and he is at a loss for words. Al tries to get Chris to say something, "Chris, you, okay? You still there?"

No answer.

"Chris, speak to me, let's talk about this. I know you feel like you've been punched in the gut, but there may be a simple explanation."

I mumble, "Simple?"

"Yeah Chris, simple."

I take a deep breath before I speak, "When you say simple, what do you mean? She simply spent the night with Tom Houston…she simply left the day after…she simply had the foresight to bring a change of clothes…she simply kissed him? If that's what you mean, then I agree, it seems simple."

Uncle Al knows how I am feeling because he doesn't react to my sarcasm. "Listen Chris, I get that you are shocked and angry at what may appear to be a serious breach of trust, and that's why you need to call Beth and tell her about what happened between you and Amanda and ask her about the photos that you just saw."

I am still angry and I know it will not change until I have a chance to calm down, "I need to take time to think this all over."

"Okay, maybe you should take the time to calm down, but don't wait too long, these things have a way of festering and it will eat away at you. Talk to Beth, find out what happened and one way or another you'll know the right thing to do."

"I have to go."

"Okay, but call me if you want to talk and let me know what happens. I'm always here for you."

"I know and I will" and I hang up.

CHAPTER 8

The mountainous tribal region is situated in a remote part of Afghanistan and is very difficult to reach. It has long been a preferred clandestine area that terror groups use to conceal themselves from their enemies, train for jihad and to regroup and resupply to continue to strike terror in the hearts of the infidels and Muslims alike.

The cave in the tribal region is comfortable enough. The ornate rugs that are scattered across the floor and the oil lamps that rest on small tables seem to soften the hard rock walls that surrounded the cave's interior. A group of the top echelon commanders belonging to al-Qaeda, Boko Haram, ISIS and Taliban have assembled for a secret gathering. The men in attendance do not trust each other, but they have put hatreds aside for the moment and are in deep discussions among one another. There are wide spread speculations about the man they are to meet. No one among them has seen this man; they do not know where he is from and they do not know why they have been summoned. All they do know is that they feel compelled to be here. Is it fear or curiosity that compels them? If they have an opinion, they do not share it with the group.

The members of the terrorist groups are talking among themselves when a cold wind blows through the cave and, all at once, the light from the lamps is snuffed out. The only visible light is coming from the mouth of the cave and one of the mullahs rises from the floor and commands a low-level guard to relight the lamps. The guard moves toward the lamp, but before he has a chance light it, a dark form stands at the cave's entrance and his voice fills the hollow,

"Leave the space dark."

The terrorist leaders strain to see who the stranger is, but they cannot see his face nor discern his stature.

The stranger now says, "Order all, but the select leaders I have summoned, to leave now, we have much to discuss."

Again, the terrorist leaders look at one another in silence until Sheik Alqatil mmin Alkuffar speaks up. "Who is it that dares to command the council?"

The Deceiver remains silent.

"I will ask you only once more, who is it that dares to command the council?"

Al-Masih ad-Dajjal removes the kufiyah that is covering his face and distorted, misshapen eye. The man stares across the darkness of the cave at the sheik until the silence is shattered by screams. Another member of the terrorist council immediately calls out for a torch to light the interior. When all present are able to see the sheik, they gasp in revulsion. They see Sheik Alqatil mmin Alkuffar lies dead on the stone floor of the cave. Blood has erupted from his eyes and ears and a there appears a giant opening in his chest as if it were ripped apart by some unseen force.

The entire council immediately turns around to face the stranger. Al-Masih ad-Dajjal has since covered his features with the kufiyah and calmly tells the gathering, "Are there any more questions?"

The group gazes at the man and then at each other. It becomes increasingly evident that the stranger is one not to be challenged, and all among them shake their heads indicating their answer is "no."

The Deceiver slowly walks among the men present in the cave and looks each of them in the eye. Once he has taken measure of the terrorist leaders, he is satisfied that they will do what he commands. He holds out his hand and orders that there be light in the cave and in an instance all the oil lamps are lit. Initially the brightness makes it difficult for the men to see, but as their sight returns, they have many questions.

An old sheik, who has been quietly sitting in the corner of the cave, asks the strange visitor "Why is it that you've come to us at this time?"

Al-Masih ad-Dajjal tells the assembled, "I come to you from the east, Khorasan, so that you will know that of which is required of you. I am here to make true the prophesy; and you will begin to see the signs of the coming upheaval."

The old sheik is puzzled. "What are these signs you speak of?"

The Deceiver takes his time in revealing what signs are to be observed, "It has already started in the west and you will know these things. The peoples will stop offering their prayers; dishonesty has become the way of life for the infidels and even for some of the believers. You have seen for yourself that there is no shame among these peoples, these infidels. Many are even worshipping Satan; even the telling of falsehoods has become a virtue."

As he says these words, Al-Masih ad-Dajjal looks around at the faces of the men in the cave and he sees them nodding in agreement. He continues, "These things have been told in the Hadith by the Prophet Muhammad, peace be upon him, and it is commanded we must heed and obey the will of Allah. To fulfill this prophesy, you must gather your forces and begin the journey west."

The terrorist leaders look at one another and begin to speak as one of the men say, "To where must we go? When will this journey begin?"

Al-Masih ad-Dajjal considers how to answer and says, "Come outside and I will answer your questions." Again, the terrorists look at one another, but they begin to exit the cave behind the stranger. As they all come to stand outside, there is a collective gasp and they stand frozen in fear.

In every nook and crevice along the mountains surrounding their fortress cave stands tens of thousands of warriors. They are men, but none like any has ever been seen before. These men are dressed in ancient robes wearing Persian blue-black traditional shawls. They have faces that appear as hammered shields and the stranger's army stands in complete silence.

Al-Masih ad-Dajjal extends his arms as if to embrace this force that surrounds hm. He smiles and shouts at his men, "Where have you come from?"

The warrior collective shouts, "ISFAHAN!"

Again, the Deceiver exhorts, "To where do we go?"

"WEST!"

"Where in the west do we go?"

"MEGIDDO!"

The terrorist leaders now are cowering in fright. Al-Masih ad-Dajjal knows that he must perform one more act. He has been given powers by Satan to perform miracles and now he will use these powers to command absolute allegiance of these men.

"Of the unfortunate incident in the cave, I was forced to execute Sheik Alqatil mmin Alkuffar because I cannot tolerate insolence. I know there is still some doubt as to my powers among the council so I ask, if I killed this person and then bring him back life, will those among you still doubt me?"

The men in the council look at one another and answer, "No."

At that moment to the shock and amazement of all present, a dazed Sheik Alqatil mmin Alkuffar walks through the entrance of the cave, alive. The once dead sheik sees Al-Masih ad-Dajjal and immediately falls to the ground and says, "Please forgive me, oh Masih, for doubting you. You are here to lead us in our struggle; you are our path to victory over the non-believers. I pledge my loyalty, my honor and my life to you."

Seeing this miracle all the leaders of the council, and their followers, drop to the ground and pledge undying loyalty to the man they believe has been sent by Allah. They do not know he is The Deceiver.

Satisfied that he has accomplished what needs to be done, he commands the group. "Assemble your men and get them ready for the long journey. You will need sustenance" and as Al-Masih ad-Dajjal spoke, the ground trembles and from it arose all manner of food. Among the food there could also be seen weapons of war, both new and ancient weapons, and among the weapons, can also be seen nuggets of gold and silver.

All those present do not make any attempt to explain the unexplainable. The terrorists shout for their men to collect the gifts that came from the earth.

"I wish to be alone now." Al-Masih ad-Dajjal walks back into the cave to wait as his commands are carried out.

CHAPTER 9

The next morning Beth sits alone on the couch in her great room. Tom had promised to call her back yesterday, but he left word that he had been called into a meeting and that he would in the morning.

Beth made herself a cup of coffee, but it has become cold. She continues to obsess over the predicament that she finds herself in. Chris has called a number of times, but she is too upset to speak to him. She knows that she needs to come clean about her night at Tom's home, but just not now. Beth is consumed by 'magical thinking' as psychologists call it, and she is hoping for a miracle that somehow her predicament will just go away. Beth knows this is fantasy, so she just sighs as she lies on the couch and becomes lost in her thoughts.

The phone rings and startles Beth out from her thoughts. She looks at the digital display hoping it's not Chris; she just can't bring herself to deal with this now. She sees that it is Tom and reluctantly she picks up the phone, but doesn't say anything.

"Beth, are you there? Beth?"

"I'm here."

"Sorry I couldn't call you back yesterday, but there was an important meeting that came up at the last minute. How are you feeling this morning?"

"Lousy." Beth is very depressed and it is evident in her voice.

"Beth, please try to relax and look at this for what it is."

Beth becomes angry and says, "For what it is! For what it is! What is it, Tom? Better yet, what do you assume Chris will think it is?"

Tom tries to add some context to the discussion in hopes that Beth will calm down, "Listen Beth, much as I hate to admit this, Chris seems like a reasonable guy. I am sure that he will understand. I can't believe I'm telling you this, but you need to give him a chance to hear your side of the story."

Beth sighs, "I know that I have to face him and tell him about what happened, but I know that it will make him angry. He may not come out and say it, but there will always be some unspoken suspicion and a lack of trust, and that is what I'm so upset about."

"Listen Beth, I can understand how you feel but…" Tom goes silent and Beth looks at the phone to see if she still has a connection and says, "Tom? Tom, are you there?"

Tom answers, "Beth, turn on the TV to LI News Network."

Beth is puzzled, "What?"

"Beth, just turn on the TV now."

Beth reaches for the remote and turns to the news network and the entertainment segment commentator seems excited as she reports, "Beautiful, talented Amanda Sellers has been photographed giving a passionate, long-lasting kiss to this handsome and mysterious stranger."

Beth literally bolts upright off the couch and stares wide-eyed at the TV. She can't believe what she is seeing; Chris, there on the screen, in a passionate embrace; lip-locked with one of the most popular and beautiful movie stars in the world.

"Amanda Sellers, who is notoriously guarded about her private life, spent the weekend with him at her fabulously wealthy father's country estate. We'll be following this story and let you know how it develops, wink, wink! Now onto our next item featuring…" Beth is in the state of shock and continues staring at the screen long after the image of Chris and Amanda Sellers disappears.

Tom understands the silence and allows this moment to pass. When the moment has passed, Tom asks, "Beth, do you want to talk about this?"

Still more silence.

"Beth, let's talk about this rationally."

Beth is seething, but tries to seem calm and collected, "What a wonderful idea! Let's talk about this, how did you say, rationally."

"Beth…"

"There must be a rational explanation. Let me see; maybe she stopped breathing and Chris came to the rescue and gave her mouth-to-mouth resuscitation. Oh wait, maybe I'm wrong! Amanda Sellers might be giving Chris mouth-to-mouth resuscitation. No, I've got it! Amanda decided to change careers, she's becoming a dentist and she's using her tongue to probe Chris for cavities!"

Tom is trying to remain calm in hopes that Beth will calm down. "Beth, I know you're upset…"

Beth screams into the phone, "Upset! Upset! I'm not upset! This is so far beyond upset that I am about to explode."

"Beth, please try to calm down, there may be a perfectly logical explanation for that incident. I know Amanda and she's a very nice person."

This seems to make Beth even more irate. "Oh, I'm sure that Amanda is a wonderful person, a veritable Mother Teresa. I am a bit suspect about Chris, though. Let me ask you, you're a billionaire, do you think that Chris is formulating some Machiavellian plot to lure Amanda into some amorous liaison so that he can be around when Harry Lieberman retires and turns over the management of his companies to him. By George, I think I've got it!"

"Beth…"

"Don't Beth me! I'm pissed and I want to stay pissed."

"Okay, I'm not going to try and make you calm down. Believe me; I understand why you are pissed. It does appear that Chris betrayed you…"

Beth screams into the phone at Tom, "Appears he betrayed me? Appears he betrayed me? Am I supposed to turn a blind eye to what he did? How can I ever trust him again?"

Tom is about to tell Beth that she is pretty much in the same position as Chris. He could point out that she spent the night at his mansion, but he thinks better of this idea. Tom sees an opportunity to get Beth on the rebound so he says, "Beth, Chris was dishonest and he betrayed your trust and for that I know you are angry and upset. Please try to calm down; you are too fine a person to be treated like this."

Beth is still seething, but Tom's words have a soothing effect on her and she says, "Thanks, Tom, I'm sorry I took this out on you. You're probably saying why the hell did I get involved with all this?"

Tom is solicitous and says, "Beth, that's nonsense, a friend should always be there for a friend and I will always be there for you."

Beth smiles and says, "Thanks Tom I appreciate that."

Tom thinks that there couldn't be a better time to encourage Beth to speak with Chris. He knows the there is so much animosity, "Listen Beth, take time to relax and when you feel you are ready, call Chris and try to work it out."

Beth fumes thinking about all that she has learned, "Oh, I'll work it out alright."

"Now Beth, please don't be upset. You need to try to calm yourself."

"Upset, I'm not upset Tom, not at all. Listen Tom, I've got to go. Thanks for allowing me to vent and thanks for being there."

"You're welcome but please…"

"I've got to go." Beth hangs up the phone and leans back on the couch and she starts to cry. On the other end of the line, Tom hangs up and smiles.

CHAPTER 10

The Deceiver prepares to begin the long journey toward Megiddo. The mullahs and sheik leaders have assembled in the camp and the fires burn bright in the night providing warmth for these terrorists. The only one that does not seem to be bothered by the cold is Al-Masih ad-Dajjal. The men are all anxious to hear the Masih, for now they believe he is the Messiah who will lead his followers to victory over all infidels.

The sheiks are talking among themselves when Al-Masih ad-Dajjal asks for silence. "I am the fulfillment of the prophecies. You are to be my sword to strike down the non-believers. There are prophesies that will be fulfilled and you must be mindful so that you can maintain your place with the true believers of Islam."

One of the sheiks, a battle-hardened warrior asks, "Oh prophet, oh Masih, what is it that we look for? What are these prophecies you foretell?"

Al-Masih ad-Dajjal thinks it important that the sheik in calling him Masih. He will use it as power to control the men before him. He tells them, "You will know by these signs. I am the prophet of Allah and He allows me to perform miracles in his holy name. You have seen that I can make hidden treasures spill forth from the earth at my command and this reward awaits all of you and all of the faithful."

The group is in rapt attention as they answer, "Praise be to Allah!"

"It has been less than three years since I have arisen and now, we are coming to the last of these years. I have sown the seeds of famine, but a greater famine is yet to come. In the third year, Allah will command the sky to withhold all of its rain, and it will not rain a single drop. This will come to pass and He will command the earth to withhold all of its fruits, and no plant will grow. All hoofed animals will perish, except that which Allah causes to live. During these demanding times, those true to Islam, the Mu'mineen will satisfy their hunger through the recitation of Subhanallah and La'ilaha Ilallahu."

The group answers, "Praise be to Allah!"

Al-Masih ad-Dajjal continues as his followers gaze upon him in rapt devotion. "Once, famine and pestilence abound, there will be earthquakes and events of such terror as to drive all infidels to madness. Allah will cause drought to those who disbelieve in him, causing starvation and hardship for them all."

There is a cry from the leaders assembled, "Death to the infidels."

The Deceiver then tells of the rewards to the faithful. "There should be no fear for Allah will protect you, praise be his name. He will send down rains upon those who believe in him, which in turn will cause good crops to grow, trees to bear fruit, and cattle to grow fat."

The group raises their weapons in answer and cheer, "Praise be to Allah!"

"Now we must plan in all due haste to follow the prophecy and make the journey to Megiddo."

The sheiks are questioning Al-Masih ad-Dajjal with one asking, "Lord, this is a long journey. It will take many days and we will need to cross many lands before we find ourselves near Megiddo. How long do we have, oh Masih?"

Al-Masih ad-Dajjal seems annoyed at the question. "We have as long as the prophecy commands. I will stay on this Earth for a period of forty days; the length of the first day will be one year, the second day will be equal to one month, the third day will be equal to a week and the remaining days will be as counted. We will need to proceed immediately so you will gather the men, weapons, the gold and provisions I have provided and be ready to leave by sunrise."

The group, somewhat confused, but answers, "Praise be to Allah!" A quiet comes over the men and there seems to be a detectable reticence among them. The men are looking for answers to questions that they are unable to ask for fear of their lives.

The campfire continues to burn brightly as a sudden noise breaks the silence. Appearing from behind one of a large outcropping of rocks is a giant beast. The beast is a mule, but unlike any mule that these men have ever seen. It is gigantic in size and many of those around the fire move away in fear.

Al-Masih ad-Dajjal smiles at the fear he perceives and tells the men, "Do you fear a harmless mule? If you fear such a beast what will become of you when the holy war against the infidels begins? I seem to observe an abating of your faith in Allah! Are you such cowards?"

The entire group of men feels shamed by the words of the man they see as the prophet of Allah. "No lord, we were merely stunned at the size of the beast. It is like none any of us has ever seen."

Al-Masih ad-Dajjal tells them, "And like none you will ever see again. I will ride this beast all the way to Megiddo and together we will confront the infidels. Our victory is assured except if those who are among us lose their faith. Am I to be concerned that many among you will lose their faith and deny victory to Allah?"

The sheik leaders seem to have new found courage as they shout in unison, "No oh Masih! We will be there, even unto our death, oh Masih! Praise be to Allah and to his prophet Mohammad!"

"Now go do as I command. I am going to pray in the cave and I do not want to be disturbed by anyone, is that understood?"

The groups of terrorists all answer in the affirmative and pick themselves off the ground. They begin to command their men to do the bidding of their new leader, the Messiah…their Masih.

Al-Masih ad-Dajjal, retires to the darkness of the cave. He appears to be alone, but he is not alone and he knows it. From all around the interior can be heard a voice, "Is all going according to the plan and prophesy?"

"Yes, oh lord."

Satan knows the answer, but asks the question anyway, "Are the forces ready?"

"Yes, oh lord. I have done as you command. The warriors will be assembled for the march to Megiddo beginning at sunrise."

"Good. Remember, there is no mercy for failure. I will be victorious or you will suffer beyond the boundaries of comprehension. Is that clear to you?"

"Yes, oh lord, you will be victorious and you will claim the souls of all mankind. It is my sworn oath. It is your will be done."

A blast of hot wind blows through the cave and Al-Masih ad-Dajjal finds himself alone and, for the first time ever, he becomes frightened.

CHAPTER 11

I'm still seething. Even after I spoke with Uncle Al, I'm still seething.

I'm distressed, and worse, I feel betrayed. I need to confront Beth, but I just want to fume, remain angry; I don't want this feeling to go away. How could she do this to me? How could she tell me she loves me and then spend the night with Tom Houston? These thoughts consume each and every waking moment until the world stands still and I am transported into a vision.

> *The holy man sets out to fulfill the goals of his order. He has travelled to Valencia and he has travelled to Algiers where he has ransomed nearly 400 Christians from their fate as slaves. He then travels to Tunis where he surrenders himself as a hostage for another 28 captive Christians, and it is there he runs out of funds to free the captives. The man is now in a prison cell placed there by the Mohammedans as hostage until ransom could be paid for all the slaves that have been freed.*

The vison changes and the man is kneeling before someone important, the governor of Tunis, who is imposing sentence on the holy man.

"You have been charged with blasphemy for your sacrilege against the laws of Islam. For this profanity against Allah, you are hereby sentence to be impaled." The governor's demeanor changes as he seems to have second thoughts on the captive and continues to speak, "But I decree you will be spared as I believe that you may be worth more alive than dead. You will remain captive until your ransom is paid."

The vision changes, yet again. Time has passed and the holy man appears frail and emaciated. He is placed in the center of a large open expanse where he now stares down at a gauntlet of Muslim soldiers.

The governor has decreed that the man will face torture for his continuing blasphemy of converting the Moorish to Christians even while prisoner. Soldiers line the path as the man tries to make his way through the gauntlet. He is beaten mercilessly until he is no longer conscious. Once revived, the Moors bore a hole through his lips with a hot iron rod and padlock his mouth shut as punishment.

The holy man steps out of the vision and I am in the presence of St. Raymond Nonnatus. He does not speak, but just stares at me. I am too upset and irate and I don't want to allow the Sainted to talk me out of my anger.

"Christopher."

"Yes."

"We need to speak."

"I don't want to speak."

"Why?"

"Because I have been betrayed and I am angry and I want to hold onto these feelings, and because it's the only way I can have some comfort."

"Comfort? Christopher, look up at me."

I don't want to look up at him.

"Christopher, look up at me."

Reluctantly I look up at St. Raymond and he points to his lips. There are the two holes made by the iron rods that had been used in his torture. It was where the Moors took a lock and used it to close the mouth of St. Raymond so that he could not preach and convert the Muslims. The saint says, "These are old wounds, but they are still painful reminders of what I had to endure for being accused of doing what my Christian faith commands. For me, the truth and love of God will always prevail and as I was in pain, you are in pain, are you not?"

"Yes."

"Then why do you not want to be free of such agony, free of such pain?"

"I don't know, maybe it's because it's the only way I can feel in control. I let my feelings of love for Beth take over, and now that she has betrayed me, I am left with nothing but regret, but at least when I'm angry I feel in control."

"Christopher, please listen to what I have to say."

I look up at St. Raymond and say, "Okay."

"Anger, while providing temporary dominion against feelings of loss, only drives you further away from God and Christ. Take heed you must always fight the temptation of pride and the feeling that wrests control away from God only to be used for your own purpose, and that purpose cannot be honest."

There is the familiar glow and a light that shines from the heavens and St. Raymond turns to face the light and he is gone. I'm alone again, but even after being admonished I still cannot rid myself of the feelings of anger even after the vison of St. Raymond. I walk to the refrigerator and grab a beer and take it back to the couch and begin to drink it. When I'm about halfway through the beer I realize I need to get the phone and call Beth. I want to get this over with because if I don't, I'll just make myself crazier. I hit speed dial and I immediately hear her phone ring.

A voice on the other end says, "What do you want?"

I am taken back by her nasty tone and I become infuriated. "What do I want? What do I want? What the hell do you think I want?"

"I don't care what you want. By the way how is your new girlfriend, what's her name"? Oh yeah, I think her name is Amanda Sellers, how is she Chris? I hope the mouth-to-mouth resuscitation you administered to her worked or was it the up close and personal dental exam she gave you with her tongue; it was difficult to know given how close you two were."

I am silently fuming as I am trying to think of something just as nasty to say to Beth, but the words don't come.

"Oh, cat got your tongue Chris? Wow, Amanda Sellers! Well, normally I would be impressed, but in this case, I am questioning Amanda's taste in men. What the hell does she see in you? Wait; don't tell me I might lose what little respect I have left for her."

I finally have had enough of Beth's nasty comments and I answer her back. "Well, aren't you a clever little girl. Trying to put me on defense while it was you who was seen leaving, no actually; how did the news reports say, 'sneaking out of Tom Houston's mansion.' That's it sneaking out of Tom's mansion the morning after the gala. Oh my, wasn't that sweet of him to invite you to stay at his home."

I can almost see Beth fuming at my equally angry and nasty reply "What nerve you have lecturing me. Who the hell do you think you are?!"

I am now in the zone trying to muster up every horrible thing I can think of. "Oh, and didn't you look lovely all cleaned and scrubbed the next morning. Good thing you thought of bringing a clean change of clothes, by the way, I never saw those clothes before. Looks like I was right, he wanted to get into your pants and it looks like he did. He probably even bought them for you."

Beth is on the border of rage and she screams, "You are such a piece of shit!"

"Oh, I'm a piece of shit. That's good coming from you. I'm gone two days and I can't even trust you keep your pants on."

"Well, looks like the feeling is mutual. Trust is a two-way street shithead, and you obviously can't keep you pants zippered. I never want to see you again."

"Don't worry, you won't..." but before I can finish telling her off the phone call is cut off and there is only silence.

I just sit on the couch with my half-finished, now warm, beer staring at a blank television screen. Eventually my anger abates, but I am now trying to figure out how I feel and I come to the conclusion that I feel miserable. I am at a total loss and all I can think of is what my life would be like without Beth, and I don't like what I am thinking. I could call her back and try to explain about Amanda, but then I think about her spending the night with Tom and my pride won't even let me hear the explanation, even if she has one.

I am still staring at the blank television screen when a call comes in. I look down at the display hoping that it is Beth, hoping she is calling to apologize. I'm hoping she will give me a chance to apologize to her, and hoping I would be man enough to accept it. But it's Uncle Al and I just can't face him at this time. I send his call to voice mail and I lean back on the couch depressed beyond any point I have ever been before.

CHAPTER 12

After unsuccessfully trying to reach Chris, Chief Barese hits the off button on his phone and returns to sit by the bedside of his friend Aiden. He is very worried and he knows that his nephew is angry, and he knows that Chris could blow up at Beth. He also believes that this could create a wall between the two that might never be breached.

Al's attention turns back to Fr. Langford who is still unconscious, and who is still in grave danger from the impact of his heart attack. Chief Barese feels a vibration coming from his phone and he sees that he's gotten a text from Det. Dan Orello, his second in command, at Suffolk Country Police Headquarters. The text simply says, "Call as soon as you get the chance."

The chief doesn't want to use his phone in the ICU, so he leaves and walks to the hospital's waiting room to call Dan at HQ.

"Hi Dan, this is Al, what's up?"

"Hi chief, sorry to disturb you, but we need to talk."

"OK, I'm listening."

"Chief, I'm here in the conference room with the team." Dan is heading a team of investigators that are looking into horrific crimes that have been committed all over Suffolk County, Long Island. Aside from Dan, the chief's team includes veteran detectives Christian Oliver, Avery Michaels and Christina Shannon and they have gathered all surround the speaker phone to update Chief Al Barese on the details of some of the latest crimes that have been committed recently.

"Well chief, I'm going to let each of the team tell you what they are working on at the moment, but in light of the increasingly large numbers of offenses, we need to limit the call to the most heinous crimes otherwise we could be here all night."

Chief Barese realizes that this will take some time and he wants to be able to concentrate on what he will be told. The chief tells Dan and his team, "Listen, I'm in the hospital waiting room and this isn't the best place to talk. I'm going to get into my car and drive to HQ so let me call you back."

Dan says, "I think that's best, by the way how's Aiden?"

"Still the same; I'll update you when I get in, meanwhile I'll call back in just a few minutes from the car."

Dan signs off, "Thanks chief, we'll be in the conference room."

Chief Barese hangs up and walks back to the ICU. He is hoping there would be some change in Aiden's condition, no matter how small, but he knows that is magical thinking. Back in Aiden's room, Al looks down at the man, his best friend, lying there. The priest has IV tubes going into his body. He has a face mask covering his mouth so he can breathe easier and his vital signs are being displayed on the monitor next to his bed. Al sighs and reaches over to brush hair away from Fr. Aiden's forehead. He whispers to the priest, actually to himself, "I've got to go buddy, but I'll be back." Al turns around and is about to leave, but stops and steps back from the door to the side of the bed to say one last thing to his friend before he goes, "Don't even think about getting up or talking to anyone until I can get back here, understand? There's some really bad shit going on buddy and I think you may have some answers." Aiden is quiet, but somehow Al believes that the priest understands, and he leaves the ICU and heads for the parking lot and his car. Once inside the car, the chief immediately calls back to headquarters and is put through to the conference room.

The team is in the conference room waiting for the call when Dan hears the phone ring. He looks at the display sees it's the chief's mobile number on the screen, "Hi chief, sorry for taking you away from Aiden, but thanks for calling in. I think that you need to hear this and I've asked Christina to begin."

Detective Christina Shannon is the first to give her report. "Chief, I have been involved in a number of recent cases that I think you already know about, but in the last few days it seems like the world has turned upside down. I have been following up on the murder of a boy who was shot by his friend. It seems that they were collecting metal that they would sell to a scrap metal dealer. The killer, a six-year-old, said his friend was stealing from him so he shot him. He told us that he was given the gun by his older brother who's a member of a street gang. It was one of those crimes that you just can't believe and I was discussing this with a friend that I have who works out of the 47th. My friend was telling me of a murder committed by kid in his precinct too. It seems that this kid, also six years old, killed the pregnant girlfriend of his father and the body was discovered by the victim's daughter. He also told me of two other murders committed by kids around the same age in other Long Island communities that are now being investigated by the local precincts."

Detective Shannon continues, "Now, here's one murder that was just discovered last night. There's a young girl who wanted to go out with her boyfriend, but her parents refused to give their permission. So later on that night the young girl, her boyfriend and the boyfriend's buddy broke into the girl's house and killed the mother, nearly killed the father and also murdered the girl's two brothers in the most horrific ways you could imagine. These kids then went about setting fire to the house, you should see the photos. Now, here's the weird thing; one of the detectives out of the 23rd is sort of a police historian. He's been researching crimes committed around the country going back decades right up to present day; he's writing a book about it. Anyway, this officer has been following the series of murders committed by kids and he's discovered something very interesting, but really creepy. The murder that has just been committed by the girl and her boyfriend is exactly like the one committed by Erin Caffey from Texas back in 2008."

Chief Al can be heard over the phone saying, "Holy shit."

"Holy shit is right." Det. Shannon takes a short sip of water before she continues, "Sorry Chief, I needed to have a sip of water. Next, I want to tell you of one of the most tragic cases you could ever imagine. On Tuesday the police took a three-year-old girl into custody for killing her 22-month-old sister. Her parents were drunk and passed out when the crime was committed. The three-year-old is so young that her identity remains unnamed even in the arrest records. You're not gonna believe this, but the incident exactly matches a crime committed a few years ago when another three-year-old girl commits the murder of her 22-month-old sister; same method, same result. By the way, the past murder was committed while the parents were passed-out drunk. In each and every case of the seven murders that occurred during the last two weeks, the crimes were committed by children under the age of 16. In each case they are exact imitations of murders committed in the past. In one case the copycat murder took place more than 100 years ago. I really mean exactly the same as those committed in the past. I can go on, but I think you get the idea."

Chief Barese is quietly listening in his car and the rest of the people in the conference room are also quiet until the chief breaks the silence, "This seems impossible, maybe in the age of the internet these kids could have researched murders and tried to replicate them, but I can't imagine a three-year-old would be influenced in that way."

Dan Orello interrupts, "Chief, we've interviewed most of the alleged murderers and in each case, they readily owned up to their crimes, but during the interrogations these kids never mentioned once that they were inspired in any way by the past crimes. In each instance, though, there was one thing they had in common; each kid we have in custody said that they take their orders from 'The Serpent' or 'The Great Fiery Red Dragon.' I looked it up and this is how Satan or Lucifer is referred to in the Bible, Revelations 12:3. I'm no bible scholar, but this is beyond weird, it's downright insane."

More silence and eventually Dan says, "Chief, are you still there."
"Yes."

Dan continues, "Chief, there's one thing that is different from past crimes and you're not gonna like it."

Chief Barese braces himself for bad news as Det. Orello continues, "Each of the victims had "Lamb of God" written in blood on a wall or carved into their bodies."

Chief Barese is at a loss for what to say next so he just tells the group, "Let's continue with the update. Who's next?"

Detective Christian Oliver speaks up. "Chief, I'll take the next round as this could be one for the record books. There has been an ongoing investigation of a homeless shelter for young women who are prostitutes, addicts, homeless, abused or all of the above, and they have fallen on really hard times. The 'Helping the Homeless Shelter' is located out on the East End and there is a woman who has run this place for the last 27 years, her name is Arlene Lemoyne.

It began when Dispatch received a call from someone who found a woman lying in the street. This woman was incoherent and in very bad shape when she was found. She managed to tell the officers that she escaped some shelter and that while she was there, she was tortured and nearly died. The homeless woman kept babbling something about her friends that kept disappearing and she thinks that the devil is killing these people. At first the responding officers, their names are Timothy Kahn and Mike Vasquez, assumed that the woman was mentally unstable so they took her to the hospital where she is now under observation. Well, no one gave her story any credence until another woman was found near what turned out to be the Helping the Homeless Shelter. She had serious multiple wounds to her body and she was practically bleeding to death when a patrol car saw her lying in the street. The officers called an ambulance, but because she was so badly wounded, they needed to perform emergency triage while waiting. The woman attempted to speak, but all she could say is "Helping…Helping…" The officers, whose names are Carl Paulson and Reginald Jenkins, tried to assure her they would help her, but she kept saying "Helping…" right up to the time that the ambulance arrived. The woman then grabs Officer Jenkins by his shirt collar and screams "HELPING!", but before EMS could try and save her, she collapses and dies."

Detective Oliver needs to take a deep breath before he continues to speak, "Now Officer Jenkins is filling out his report when he overhears Officers Kahn and Vasquez speaking about the other woman who they picked up. They are talking about the whole Satan thing and one officer mentions to another that they are able to identify she came from Helping the Homeless Shelter. That seems to have piqued the interest of the Jenkins so he goes over and talks to Vasquez and Kahn. They tell him about the crazy woman who thinks Satan killed homeless women from the Helping the Homeless Shelter. Well, Jenkins considers that the woman who just died was trying to say 'helping' as in 'Helping the Homeless Shelter.' So, Officer Jenkins goes to the captain and tells him about all he knows and he gets the go ahead to visit the shelter to see if there is anything out of the ordinary. You're not going to believe what he and his partner found."

Chief Barese feels his head starting to pound when he says, "Just tell us."

"Well chief, the door to the shelter is locked and you need to ring an intercom and have someone come to the front entrance to let you in. As soon as the door opens, the officers nearly pass out from the smell. Arlene Lemoyne, who runs the shelter, is covered in blood, literally covered in blood. She has a butcher knife, more like a cleaver, in her hands and a smile on her face. Both officers reach for their guns and they take the cleaver away from Ms. Lemoyne. While they are cuffing her, she invites the officers in and what they found was something like a scene from a horror movie, but not like any horror movie they had ever seen before. In the lobby alone there are at least eight dead women, each having had parts of their bodies cut off. The officers call in for assistance from crime scene back up, the medical examiner, and forensics and officers told them they need to come to the shelter fast. While they wait for the back-up to arrive, Officer Jenkins takes a walk around the main floor and what he discovers is so shocking that he told us he nearly passed out. The last time I checked the team had discovered a total of 76 women; 68 are dead and four are so badly wounded that they are not expected to live. They also found another four women locked up in the basement with wounds that indicate they had been beaten over an extended period of time. Chief, the medical examiner's on-site preliminary report records that most of the women appeared to be suffering from starvation, sexual abuse and major injuries from being tortured. Many of the victims' bodies were covered with needle marks and their hands were burned and mutilated, as well as their faces and genitalia. Arlene also told the officers that she enjoyed biting the flesh off the faces, arms and other body parts of her victims."

Chief Barese exclaims, "God in heaven."

"That's not all, Helping the Homeless Shelter is located on a 26-acre parcel of land, and it is set back far from the road. The team sent a group to explore the area and they found what appears to be a number of freshly dug graves. Not just a few, but what appears to be dozens and dozens of graves. There could be as many as two hundred dead."

Chief Barese's considers the impossibility of what he is being told, but asks the only question he can think of, "Is that it?"

Detective Oliver says, "Afraid not Chief. It seems this crime is exactly like one committed in the 16th century by a one Countess Elizabeth Bathory. This royal sweetheart killed hundreds of young peasant girls over a period of 25 years in exactly the same way the women were tortured by Arlene Lemoyne. If you don't believe me all you need to do is to search similar serial killer crimes and Lizzy's name just pops up."

Chief is afraid to ask the next question, but he has no choice. "Is that it?"

"Uh, sorry, there's more, chief. When we asked Arlene Lemoyne why she murdered all these women she just smiled at us and said 'Haborym.' She said she was in love with Haborym. So, I checked the data base and there's no Haborym convicted of any crime I can find. So, I did a search and it seems Haborym is a Hebrew name for Satan or the Devil or whatever you want to call him."

The chief is incredulous, "Satan? She said Satan?"

"Yep, and she said that Satan commanded her to do these murders and he promised her that they would get married."

"Married? My God, is there anything else you have to tell me Christian?"

"Yes. Here's the final piece of this puzzle, but you're not going to like this. Lamb of God was written all over the walls of the shelter, in blood. Testing is being done, but we are almost sure it is blood from the women who were murdered."

Chief Al Barese is silent for a brief moment when he asks, what he hopes is the last time, "Is there anything else that I need to know about all this?"

"No Chief, that's all I have now. I will be getting an update from the ME and forensics and I will be getting a final report on the dead once the graves have been dug up and bodies recovered. I'll update you then."

"Okay, who's next?"

Dan says, "Next is Avery Michaels. Avery has been working with… well; I'll let her tell you."

Det. Avery Michaels has a notebook in front of her as she wants to be sure she has all her facts in order, "Thanks Dan, hello chief."

The chief is all business, "What have you got?"

"Well like we've been telling you, there has been a tremendous increase in the number of murders, tortures, fires, rapes, kidnapping recently all over the Island and there seems to be no relationship among them, except for one thing; each criminal killed in the name of Satan or subjected their victims to a satanic ritual and Lamb of God is written in blood at each of the crime scenes."

The chief seems incredulous, "Satanic ritual? What the hell does that mean?"

"Each victim was subjected to some of the most violent and cruel torture I have ever had to investigate. Among these crimes was a senseless murder committed by two teenagers who tortured and killed a 15-year-old girl. She was kidnapped and raped before they killed her."

Chief Barese asks, "Did these teenagers ever tell you why they did this?"

Det. Michael checks her notes and tells the chief, "Yeah, they did. At the crime scene there was a satanic shrine set up complete with a pentagram, a sword and other paraphernalia. When the teens were interrogated, they happily confessed that they were able to summon a demon from hell with black magic or 'magick', with a 'k', along with fire made from burning papers and incantations. The teens involved both admitted that the demon commanded a sacrifice and this poor girl was the victim."

There was silence all around, but the chief spoke up, "I'm almost afraid to ask, was there anything else?"

"Yes. Given the fact that all the recent crimes seemed to be copycat ones based on past incidents, we did some research. All the crimes I've been investigating had been literally executed in the same manner some just a few years ago with a number having occurred some decades ago. This one seems to be just like one that was committed by a couple of teens in Texas in 2014. It seems the victim was hung and she had an upside-down cross carved onto her chest. When you read the 2014 police reports you'll see the patterns are exactly the same, well except one thing."

The chief asks, "What thing?"

"At the recent crime scene, the words Lamb of God were written in blood on the wall. The medical examiner will let us know if it was written with the girl's blood, but we have no doubt it was."

The chief is pulling into the parking lot at HQ and he tells the team to continue with their investigations as he wants to make a few calls. He tells them that when his calls are over, they will meet again to discuss what steps need to be taken.

Dan says, "Okay, chief, just let us know when you want to meet again" and with that the team leaves the conference room and they go back to their desks.

When the chief gets back to his office, he immediately picks up the phone and calls Chris, but the phone goes straight into his voice mail. Chief Barese becomes exasperated and leaves a message, "Chris, this is Uncle Al as if you didn't know. Call me back as soon as possible, I've got something really important to discuss with you."

His next call is to Huntington Hospital to ask about Fr. Aiden Langford's condition and he is told that there is no change.

Next the chief then picks up the phone and calls the Los Angeles police headquarters and asks for Captain Roger Thompson. The phone rings and Captain Thompson picks up. "Captain Thompson here."

"Roger, this is Al Barese how are you?"

"Al, great to hear from you, but you won't want to hear how I am."

"What do you mean?"

"Al, I am pulling what little hair I have left out of my skull. You wouldn't believe what we are going through out here in LA."

Chief Barese says, "Let me guess. A sharp uptick in the murder rate and sharp uptick in arson, a sharp uptick in rape, a sharp uptick in torture, a sharp uptick in…"

Captain Thompson responds, "Ordinarily I would be amazed that you know all that, but I suspect that you are dealing with the same insanity that we are dealing with."

The chief sighs, "We are Roger, and I am at a total loss as to what to do. I've got a team working 24/7 on this and I could use another dozen or so detectives just to keep up with the current crime rate. Something very weird is happening and I am afraid to consider the possibilities."

Captain Thompson says, "What do you mean?"

"Roger, this is between us because the information we are about to discuss has not been released to the media just yet."

"Okay, just between you and me."

Chief Barese takes a deep breath and says, "First, we have had more and more crimes, and I mean horrific crimes, being committed by teens and young kids, one kid is only three years old…"

Roger says, "My lord! Go on."

Now Chief Barese confides to his friend, "Roger, there are three other factors that make this about the strangest thing I've ever confronted."

Roger Thompson interrupts, "Now, let me guess; the crimes are exactly the same as other committed in the near or distant past, the murders are connected with some satanic ritual and the words Lamb of God, written in blood, are found at the scene of each crime."

"Shit, I was hoping you wouldn't say that."

"Well, unless you were calling to buy me dinner, I figured that you might be having the same problem. What do you know?"

Chief Al is getting more and more depressed, "Nothing more than a bunch of nuts saying the devil made them do it, but there are no connections between the different victims or the different perpetrators other than that."

"Well, I haven't been to church in a while, but I think we may need to try and find an exorcist, you know one of those guys that gets rid of demons."

Half-joking, half-serious the chief says, "Hey, that's not a bad idea."

"Come on Al, I was just kidding. I can just image the news guys getting hold of that information and crucifying us, no pun intended."

Al begins to think about the conversations he's had with Aiden and the connection with Satan and Lamb of God. He says to Captain Thompson, "Listen Roger, I've got to go, but please keep me posted if anything comes up you think I can use in my investigation, and I'll do the same. By the way I'm buying dinner the next time I'm on the left coast."

"Good speaking with you, I can use all the help I can get. So long and I hope the next time we meet it's over a thick, juicy steak."

Chief Barese hangs up and immediately calls Chris again. "Chris this is Uncle Al, I really need to speak with you. It's not about Beth, but I hope you two were able to work things out. Anyway, call me as soon as you can."

Al leans back in his chair and thinks about what he knows, but more important, what he doesn't know and he truly believes it will get a lot worse.

CHAPTER 13

The monsignor sits behind an antique desk in the office Vatican officials have given him. The small office contains shelves and cases filled with books that he has read and reread over the years and he continually refers to these tomes as an important part of his formal duties. His desk is illuminated by a small lamp as the priest prefers lower light due to his weakening eyesight. His days are long, but he cannot rest as there is much to do. He stares at the pile of documents that are neatly stacked and he begins the ponderous task of selection. The monsignor's facial expression appears grave as he sorts through the pile. Each day the pile is getting much larger than the day before, and this does not surprise him.

Monsignor Amedeo De Marinis had been a local parish priest until the Holy See had taken notice of his special talent. At the age of 50 he became a resident of the Vatican where he continues his long service to the Lord and the Church. His name, Amedeo, means 'God's love' and he was named such by his mother and father who had tried to conceive for many years before they were blessed with a baby boy. Now, just past 80 years old, he finds it more and more difficult to fully execute his sacred duties. The nature of his responsibilities however leaves little room for rest for Monsignor De Marinis is an exorcist; in fact, the Chief Exorcist of the Holy Catholic Church

The priest looks through the stack of papers and his mood turns very dark. He realizes there is far more to the growing number of cases than he has ever encountered in all his years as a priest. One document after the other speaks to the diabolical possession of the victims that he has become all too familiar with. The monsignor suffers from the early stages of Parkinson's so his hand trembles a bit as he picks up the first report. It reads of a young woman, Maria, who lives on a farm outside Caracas, Venezuela. She is 15 years old and the document goes on to say that she speaks and understands many languages which she has never learned or even heard of before.

Monsignor De Marinis knows that this is not a sign of ecstasy brought on by religious fervor such as the gift of the Holy Spirit to speak in tongues. This, he knows from experience, is one of the signs of possession. Maria has been under the care of her family and the local priest has attempted to pray over the girl, but to no avail. The priest has petitioned the Vatican for help and as usual these requests find their way to Monsignor De Marinis' desk. In his customary fashion, the monsignor then places the petition on one of the six piles he has started and picks up the next report.

The next document reports the possession of a 32-year-old man who has long been lost to the ravages of addiction for the past 15 years. Msgr. De Marinis recognizes that demons look to gain access to humans through what is known as a 'doorway'; a vulnerable area in the life of a person. The person then becomes open to vile and malevolent spirits whether through voluntary or involuntary means.

The young man named Henrijs is Latvian. According to the doctors and the local parish priest, who have ministered to the man, now report he can discern many things that he could not have known. The priest confirms distressing events in his communications with the Vatican that include Henrijs being able to repeat, word for word, many literary works including the entire text of 'The Oresteia' trilogy, in the original Greek. The Latvian priest also notes that he had never read or even heard of the book, but he obtained a copy and tested the drug addict on numerous occasions. The priest confirmed that Henrijs was also able to recite the text in his native Latvian as well as German. Given Henrijs' background and his addiction to drugs, the monsignor realizes that this is not mere trickery, but an actual instance of possession. Msgr. De Marinis makes a note to himself to contact Father Jaseps Lielgaidiņš, an old friend, who has performed many exorcisms throughout Russia and Eastern Europe.

The monsignor continues to read the remaining official documents for the next two hours until he stops to consider one occurrence, he finds especially disconcerting. It involves a woman in her early 40's named is Valentia Trullo. She is currently under the care of physicians in a mental health facility located just outside Rome. The report states that she is being kept in a padded cell under restraint as the woman has shown physical strength well beyond the person's natural physical makeup. She has been placed in this facility as a result of a heinous crime she committed; Valentia murdered her entire family in a violent fit of rage more than seven years ago. The local priest originally reported to the police and the doctor that Valentia was a very pious woman. Both she and her family were long time members of their local church and as a young woman she was devoutly religious, living her life at peace with God. Valentia received sacraments on a regular basis. She spent time in daily prayer, attended mass and received Holy Communion at mass every Sunday.

In a recent statement written by the doctors on staff, they have observed disturbing changes in Valentia Trullo's behavior. Some unusual experiences manifested themselves to one doctor, a psychiatrist, who noted that he would have normally assumed that Valentia's behavior was the result of her mental illness, but he now believes that it is much more.

During a recent session with the patient, Dr. Luigi Mastriano recounts a series of very strange occurrences. When he entered Valentia's cell, she was laying on the floor in her restraints, seemingly in a trance, she began to levitate four feet above the floor. The doctor, in disbelief, called for the ward attendants to come into the cell. When he did, she opened her eyes and screamed at the physician, "Shut the fuck up you piece of shit!"

The doctor then ordered the attendants to place her on the cot so he could examine her. As the attendants did, Valentia exhibited enormous strength and broke free of her restraints. Once freed, she flailed at the attendants and sent them flying over a small table in her cell. Valentia then lunged at the doctor and threw him against the wall and said, "She is mine now!" The doctor writes that she reached for his throat ready to choke the life out of him when the attendants, four in all, managed to subdue the patient.

Msgr. De Marinis finishes reading the report and decides that he will personally handle this case. He no longer travels far from the Vatican due to his age and declining health, but he knows that this is among the most violent and least common of the possessions he has experienced and recognizes that he must help this woman.

* * *

The following day Msgr. De Marinis goes to the offices of his immediate superior, Cardinal Agostino Castelli, to seek his permission to perform the rite of exorcism on the poor woman. The monsignor enters the office of the cardinal, an old friend, "Good morning your eminence" and he kisses the cardinal's ring.

The cardinal has a big smile for his dear friend as they embrace, "Ah Amodeo, it is good to see you, it has been a while and I miss our evening discussions very much and our games of chess! How are you?"

"I am well and keeping busy."

"That is not what I hear my friend. It seems that the Parkinson's is becoming more aggressive, is it not?"

"By the blessings of the Lord I am still able to function and I still love my work and that is why I am here."

Cardinal Castelli is curious, "Why is it that you need to see me?"

Monsignor De Marinis' mood turns somber, "The numbers of reports that I must review everyday are getting far larger and it seems to me that there is something far more disturbing than I can ever remember."

The cardinal becomes gravely concerned, "Do you wish to retire? Who would blame you having seen more cursed demons than most? If anyone deserves to enjoy life, it is you."

"No, no I do not wish to stop my work, your eminence, I wish to take on a case that I find to be singularly evil in nature and may provide the Church with some answers to what may be happening." For the next 30 minutes the monsignor tells Cardinal Castelli of Valentia Trullo and the latest incident at the mental hospital.

Msgr. De Marinis is somber as he concludes, "Her doctor says that she is beyond any help he can give her and, although in the past he dismissed possession as a possible answer, he now believes it is the only stone that is left unturned."

Cardinal Castelli is very worried for his friend of advancing years, "Why not send a younger man, perhaps your apprentice Father Fielding?"

"Your eminence, for some reason I believe that this is like no other possession that I have confronted and given my experiences with the forces of hell, I have an uneasy feeling and I do not want to trust this to anyone with little experience in these matters."

The cardinal leans back in his chair and considers what he is being asked to do. "Amodeo, I know that you still believe yourself to be a young man, but in truth, you are not."

"Your eminence, I know I am not young, but youth is not called for in this instance. I believe that if the danger is as great as I fear, experience is what will be needed."

The cardinal stares at the priest and says, "I have never refused you in the past for your work is the work of the Lord, but I am loathe letting you do this exorcism alone, especially in light of your fears."

The monsignor is about to protest when the cardinal holds up his hand to stop him from speaking. "Let me finish. I will allow you to continue your work, but there is a condition."

Monsignor de Marinis asks, "What is the condition?"

"You are to bring Father Fielding as your assistant."

"But..."

The cardinal is firm, "There are no 'buts' Amodeo, you will need assistance and you have reported that Fr. Fielding is very capable, and according to your evaluation he has performed his duties of exorcism very well. He will be an asset to you."

"I know but I have..."

"Then good, it's settled; now how about a cup of coffee and a game of chess old friend?"

The monsignor resigns himself to the decision of Cardinal Caselli and sits back as the cardinal pours him a cup of coffee. After a cup of coffee and spirited game of chess the monsignor returns to his office.

* * *

Once back in his office the monsignor calls the hospital and asks for Dr. Mastriano. A few moments later the doctor picks up the phone and says, "Dr. Mastriano speaking."

"Good morning doctor, this is Monsignor De Marinis from the Vatican."

"Yes, monsignor, what can I do for you?"

"Thank you for your time, I am the director of exorcism for the Vatican. I have read the report you submitted regarding Valentia Trullo, and I am calling to discuss the matter with you."

Dr. Mastriano seems disconcerted as he begins to speak with the priest. "Monsignor, thank you so much for getting back to us here. We have all run out of answers, suggestions, processes, therapies related to the condition that Valentia is suffering from and we have nowhere to turn."

"I sensed that when I read your report. I know that it is not easy for you to acknowledge the possibility of possession, but let me assure you that if what you have written can be confirmed, I believe that Ms. Trullo is truly possessed by a demon, perhaps even Satan himself. She also represents a danger to herself and those around her."

The doctor is worried, "After more than seven years of treating Valentia, this latest manifestation is beyond any medical treatment, and quite frankly monsignor, you are our only hope."

The monsignor reaches for his calendar. "When can I come by to interview Valentia Trullo?"

Doctor Mastriano simply says, "The sooner the better."

"Then I will see you Tuesday at 10AM."

"Thank you, monsignor, I look forward to meeting you."

The monsignor writes the time on his calendar and says, "Then Tuesday it is, good bye doctor", and with that, the priest hangs up the phone.

Monsignor De Marinis calls and sets up a meeting with Father Fielding to discuss the details of the possessed woman and how the rites of exorcism will be conducted. He tells his assistant what they will need to bring and to be ready on Tuesday to meet with the doctor.

* * *

Tuesday is a warm sunny day, but the moods of both priests in the car are muted and somber. Fr. Fielding has been briefed on possible possession of Valentia Trullo from Msgr. De Marinis and he asks, "Monsignor, what is it that we will need to do first. I have read the report and, in all honesty, it appears that the doctors and staff have given up all hope."

"That is true father, but we will first need to interview Dr. Mastriano so that we can have a better understanding of what may have happened prior to his contacting the Vatican."

"Of course, monsignor, I have all holy articles that are required and prepared a list of questions to be answered in accordance to our tradition. Would you like to see them?"

The monsignor thinks he may have a little fun with his assistant. He feigns insult and says, "Father, over more than 50 years I would be negligent in my duties if I could not recite the questions, rules and prayers pertaining to the rite of exorcism by heart."

Fr. Fielding is embarrassed, "Monsignor, please forgive me I did not mean to imply…"

Msgr. De Marinis now laughingly says, "I was having a little fun at your expense James and I know that you did not mean anything by your comment." Father Fielding is relieved and smiles.

The monsignor looks out the car window and says, "Ah, here we are at the hospital; let us go meet with Dr. Mastriano."

The priests exit the car and walk into the hospital. They are guided to the office of Dr. Mastriano as the doctor's aide announces their arrival. Dr. Luigi Mastriano greets his visitors and invites them to sit down so they may talk. "May I offer you a cup of coffee?" asks the doctor and both priests respond no.

The doctor sighs and he begins to detail what he has experienced. "I cannot thank you enough for coming to see Valentia. As you may guess, I am not a believer in such things as possession, but I must relate to you some things that I did not include in the report that are most disturbing."

Both the monsignor and the priest are intrigued as the doctor continues. "I will tell you of things that I have no explanation for. As I wrote in my report to the Vatican, Valentia was a very devote woman. She attended church and received the sacraments often. When she committed the murder of her family, she found her way to her church; the church of Our Lady of Sorrows. We do not know what state she was in, but when she was found by the police she was screaming and cursing. The officers present testified that she seemed to be suffering some form of physical pain, torture if you will. She would speak, but in an unnatural manner and with a voice not her own. Valentia appeared to be helpless and on the verge of complete collapse. Earlier, she had attempted to break down the door and destroy the statues surrounding the altar, but she was denied entry by a force that no one saw or heard. The local parish priest came running towards her to try and calm the situation, but she was able to grab him by his vestment and throw him, single handedly, more than eight feet in the air up against the side of the church entrance. When the police arrived and tried to restrain her, she swore that she would destroy the church and all mankind. Once the police learned of her family being murder victims, she was brought to this facility where she has been committed by the court."

Dr. Mastriano continues, "It would be easy to explain away this behavior as manifestations of hallucination, hysteria and panic. She has been with us for seven years and over the years a number of doctors, among the best in their fields, have had cause to examine and test Valentia. Although numerous examinations were performed no signs of aberrant conduct or behavior could be detected, and each doctor determined she was normal in the fullest sense of the word. No physical illness was evident, and there was no explanation for the sudden rage that caused Valentia to murder her entire family or assault the priest. She says she has no memory of these events."

Monsignor De Marinis asks the doctor, is there anything else that we should know. It is important that we have a full accounting before we meet Valentia?"

The doctor seems hesitant to tell the priest what he himself has experienced, but he knows that to keep it secret is wrong. "There is one more thing that you should know. It is something that I've experienced on my last interview with Valentia. After the latest violent episode, she is now is now being held in a padded cell, completely restrained and unable to move. I wanted to speak with her in hopes of getting her to open up and help me understand her violent actions better. I thought that if I could engage her in conversation that she might provide me with insight into what may help in her treatment. Here, let me play a recording I made of our last interview."

The doctor reaches for a recorder and presses the play button. "This is Doctor Luigi Mastriano and I am interviewing Valentia Trullo, female, age 48, Case No. 1438. It is May 15th 2018 at 10:30AM.

Doctor: *"Good morning, Valentia, how are you this morning?'*

Ms. Trullo: *"I am fine. I hope you had a pleasant night's sleep after you screwed that bitch you've been lusting after."*

Doctor: *"How did…? Never mind. I'm glad you are well. Would you mind if we chatted for a while, I'd like to ask you some questions? Is that good with you?"*

Ms. Trullo: *"Sure, if you let me ask you a few questions of my own?*

Doctor: *"Of course. We have talked of many things in the past, but we haven't fully discussed the deaths of your family members."*

Ms. Trullo: *(There is a notable change in her voice it becomes deeper and masculine in tone. She becomes very agitated and screams at the doctor) "FUCK THEM…FUCK THEM… they are pieces of shit and they deserved to die!"*

Doctor: *"Why do you say that? Everyone we have spoken to says that you loved your family and they loved you. Why would you want to kill them?"*

Ms. Trullo: *(Continuing in a masculine voice) "Because they deserve to die and to rot in the depths of hell."*

Doctor: *"Valentia, you seemed to have changed your voice. Why have you done that?"*

Ms. Trullo: "The bitch is no longer here."

Doctor: "By bitch, I assume you mean Valentia."

Ms. Trullo: "Yes."

Doctor: "Where is she?"

Ms. Trullo: "She is with us."

Doctor: "and who is us?"

Ms. Trullo: "That's for me to know and for you to find out!" (Valentia emits a guttural laugh)

Doctor: "So you wish to keep your identity secret. Well then let us move on."

Ms. Trullo: "Not before I get to ask you a question."

Doctor: "Alright, what do you wish to know?"

Ms. Trullo: "Do you believe in God?"

Doctor: "I don't know if I do? I have questions about the existence of God."

Ms. Trullo: "Ah, a potential convert! Do you believe in Satan?"

Doctor: "I never thought of it, but I suppose if I don't believe in God, I can't believe in Satan. One cannot exist without the other."

Ms. Trullo: *"Very perceptive of you, doctor, but I think that you are wrong."*

Doctor: *"Wrong? Wrong about what?*

Ms. Trullo: *"Wrong about God and wrong about Satan. Want proof?"*

Doctor: *(I check to see if the restraints are strong and sturdy before I answer) "Alright, show me proof?" (At this point I am providing commentary on what Valentia is about to show me as proof there is both a God and Satan, but he goes silent.)*

Dr. Mastriano *(Sounding very frightened as he speaks into the tape recorder of what he witnessing) "Valentia closes her eyes and the room goes very dark although it is mid-morning. She is now unrestrained, totally unfettered, and she rises from the bed she is resting on and the room bursts into flame. Valentia appears before me, not as a woman, but as a demon, a fiery demon. The demon is holding a fiery sword and a crown of fire adorns his head."*

Demon speaks: *"I am here for her soul and you will not do anything to change that. She is cursed to spend eternity in hell and I will see to it that you will suffer the same fate if you get in my way."*

Dr. Mastriano *(speaking into the recorder) "In an instant the flames disappear and the room returns to the way it was before. Valentia in lying on her bed with the restraints fully intact and she is staring at me and smiling. I am questioning my sanity and I rush to the door so I may leave the room. Before I exit, I hear Valentia speak."*

Ms. Trullo: *"Have a nice day doctor."*

* * *

The three men sit in quiet contemplation until Monsignor De Marinis breaks the silence. He asks Dr. Mastriano if they may meet Valentia and the doctor agrees and the men walk to the ward located in the lower level of the hospital. The ward is a long, narrow space flanked by cement walls. The walls are painted an institutional grey color and there are a number of cell doors lining the hallways. A mere glance through the small openings on the doors reveal rooms with padding covering the walls, ceiling and even the floors. There is a small window in each cell that lets in some natural light.

The doctor feels a need to explain to the priests the austere design of the area. "This is the level that we house the most violent and dangerous patients we treat. The cells are designed so that the patients cannot harm themselves as well as offering some protection to the attendants who must feed, bathe and care for the people being treated."

Fr. Fielding asks, "Are all the patients restrained like Valentia?"

"No, some are not, but we still take precautions as some of the men and women can turn vicious with no warning at all. We require that all attendants must work in pairs to prevent them from being overwhelmed in case of a violent episode."

The men stop in front of a door to the cell that has become home to Valentia Trullo for the past seven years. The doctor tells both priests that there is always a danger and, given his experience, warns them not to agitate her.

The monsignor says that he understands and asks the doctor if they may interview Valentia alone, without him being present, "I think that it might be better for all as you might be an unwanted distraction." The doctor seems relieved and he tells the attendant accompanying them to unlock the door, but before the door is opened the doctor warns, "She will appear thin and frail and she refuses to eat anything. She has become emaciated and for this reason she has to be fed through an IV. It is the only way to get nourishment in her, but she grows weaker by the day."

The attendant opens the door and steps aside to allow the priests walk into Valentia's cell. The next sound is that of the cell door being locked behind them and it sends a chill down the spine of Fr. Fielding. The monsignor walks toward the bed where Valentia is lying down. She is even more wasted and withered than he had imagined. There are two uncomfortable looking chairs that have been placed on either side of Valentia's bed and both priests sit down.

Msgr. De Marinis has asked Fr. Fielding to take a recorder, and he motions to his assistant to place it next to Valentia's bed. The interview begins:

Msgr. De Marinis: *"Good morning Ms. Trullo. May I call you Valentia?"*

Valentia: *"You may."*

Msgr. De Marinis: *"I am Monsignor Amodeo De Marinis and this is my associate, Father James Fielding."*

Valentia: *"I know who you are, and he's not really your associate he's your assistant, is that not right?"*

Msgr. De Marinis: *"How are you feeling? I must admit you do not look well at all. Why do you not eat?"*

Valentia: *(Her voice changes to that of someone or something else) "I eat enough to keep the slut alive."*

Msgr. De Marinis: *"Why?"*

Valentia: *"To see that this worthless bitch suffers"*

Msgr. De Marinis: *"Why?"*

Valentia: *"So she may join me in hell."*

Msgr. De Marinis: *"In hell? Are you Lucifer, the fallen angel?"*

Valentia: *"No."*

Msgr. De Marinis: *"Then who are you."*

Valentia: *"Leviathan, prince of the Seraphim"*

Msgr. De Marinis: *"So you are not Lucifer?"*

Valentia: *"Are you an idiot? Can't you hear? I am Leviathan."*

Msgr. De Marinis: *"So you are the demon, the fallen angel who can tempt even the strongest souls into heresy."*

Valentia: *(smiling) "Ah I see you have heard of me."*

Msgr. De Marinis: *"How long have you been tormenting Valentia? Was it you that caused the poor woman to commit the murder of her family?"*

Valentia: *"That was but a small prelude, an insignificant diversion as we prepared for what will be the final confrontation. Do you believe in God, monsignor?"*

Msgr. De Marinis: *(to Fr. Fielding) "Father, let us begin the rite of exorcism with the prayer to Saint Michael." (Together the priests pray) "Let us pray, In the Name of the Father, and of the Son, and of the Holy Ghost, Amen. Saint Michael the Archangel, defend us in battle, be our protection against the malice and snares of the devil. May God rebuke him we humbly pray; and do thou, O Prince of the Heavenly host, by*

*the power of God, thrust into hell Satan and all evil spirits
who wander through the world for the ruin of souls. Amen."*

*As the initial entreaty to St. Michael is being prayed Valentia thrashes on
the bed in a violent rage and fury. The evil spirit possessing Valentia screams
and howls as if in unbearable pain.*

Msgr. De Marinis: *(continuing the prayer) "In the Name
of Jesus Christ, our God and Lord, strengthened by the intercession of the Immaculate Virgin Mary, Mother of God, of
Blessed Michael the Archangel, of the Blessed Apostles Peter
and Paul and all the Saints"*

*There is more screaming and writhing coming from the demon, now in
full force, attempting to break free of the restraints.*

Msgr. De Marinis: *(continues) "…and powerful in the holy
authority of our ministry, we confidently undertake to repulse
the attacks and deceits of the devil."*

*The entire bed shakes and the priests are thrown from their chairs. The
monsignor goes to his knees and Father Fielding follows. Next follows a terrifying mournful shriek from the depths of what reverberates like the cries of
a thousand demons.*

Msgr. De Marinis: *(continuing the prayer of exorcism) "God
arises; His enemies are scattered and those who hate Him, flee
before Him. As smoke is driven away, so are they driven; as
wax melts before the fire, so the wicked perish at the presence
of God!"*

Msgr. De Marinis: *"Behold the Cross of the Lord, flee bands
of enemies."*

Fr. Fielding: *(response). "The Lion of the tribe of Judah, the offspring of David, hath conquered.*

Msgr. De Marinis: *"May Thy mercy, Lord, descend upon us."*

Fr. Fielding: *(response) "As great as our hope in Thee."*

The rite of exorcism continues as the priests kneel in solemn prayer. Msgr. De Marinis reaches over and opens the small case that they have brought with them. Inside the case is a Pyx containing a consecrated host. The Pyx is adorned with a cross and when the demon sees it, he explodes in a violent fit of anger that shakes the room.

Msgr. De Marinis: *(continuing in prayer of exorcism) "We drive you from us, whoever you may be; unclean spirits, all satanic powers, all infernal invaders, all wicked legions, assemblies and sects. In the Name and by the power of Our Lord Jesus Christ, may you be snatched away and driven from the Church of God, and from the souls made to the image and likeness of God, and redeemed by the Precious Blood of the Divine Lamb."*

The screams and howls can be heard all throughout the ward. The doctor and attendants fearing for the safety of the priest rush to the cell door and try to open it, but the key will not work. They pound the door and yell in hope of a response from the men, but all they hear are more screams. It is then that the ground shakes beneath them and they are all thrown to the floor. In spite of the turmoil, the monsignor continues to pray with Fr. Fielding, but it becomes increasingly difficult.

Msgr. De Marinis: *(holding the Pyx and shouting) "O Lord, hear my prayer."*

Fr. Fielding: (shouting his response to be heard above the noise) "And let my cry come unto Thee."

Msgr. De Marinis: "May the Lord be with thee."

Fr. Fielding: (response) "And with thy spirit."

Msgr. De Marinis: "Let us pray."

The demon that possesses Valentia wails a mournful cry and he thrashes about the bed in agony. The presence of the Blessed Sacrament causes Leviathan to spit vomit and spume at the Pyx in an attempt to desecrate the host. The bed, which had been bolted to the wall, breaks from the bolts and smashes against the walls of the cell.

Msgr. De Marinis/Fr. Fielding: (having stopped momentarily, continues to pray the rites of exorcism, shouting) "God of heaven, God of earth, God of Angels, God of Archangels, God of Patriarchs, God of Prophets, God of Apostles, God of Martyrs, God of Confessors, God of Virgins, God who has power to give life after death and rest after work: because there is no other God than Thee and there can be no other, for Thou art the Creator of all things, visible and invisible, of whose reign there shall be no end, we humbly prostrate ourselves before Thy glorious Majesty and we beseech Thee to deliver us by Thy power from all the tyranny of the infernal spirits, from their snares, their lies and their furious wickedness."

The room goes very still and quiet reigns. Monsignor De Marinis and Father Fielding look around and at each other and continue,

Msgr. De Marinis: "Deign, O Lord, to grant us Thy powerful protection and to keep us safe and sound. We beseech Thee through Jesus Christ Our Lord. Amen.

The monsignor reaches into the case again and brings out a vial of holy water. The priests bow their heads and finish the prayer.

Msgr. De Marinis: *"From the snares of the devil"*

Fr. Fielding: *"Deliver us, O Lord."*

Msgr. De Marinis: *"That Thy Church may serve Thee in peace and liberty"*

Fr. Fielding: *"We beseech Thee to hear us."*

Msgr. De Marinis: *"That Thou may crush down all enemies of Thy Church"*

Msgr. De Marinis/Fr. Fielding: *"We beseech Thee to hear us."*

When the priests look up Leviathan is standing before them. Monsignor De Marinis is momentarily stunned, but soon regains composure and lifts the vial of holy water. Leviathan lets out a horrible scream and swipes the hand of the priest and the vials flies from his hand and rolls into a corner of the room. Father Fielding is still kneeling in fear, unable to move, as he watches in horror. The monsignor reaches into his cassock and pulls out the Pyx and holds it up. The demon is more than 12 feet tall and he cries in such pain and suffering that it shakes the room.

Leviathan: *(screaming) "Oh, I cannot bear the pain, the suffering. Stop this torment!"*

Msgr. De Marinis: *"I command you in the name of our Lord God the Father and His Son, Jesus Christ to leave this woman and to go back to the depths from which you came.*

You are condemned to burn in the fires of hell for what you and the fallen angels have done!"

Leviathan: *(screaming)* "You cannot send me back to hell; I am here to prepare for the coming."

Msgr. De Marinis: The coming of whom?"

Leviathan: "Of the Antichrist."

Msgr. De Marinis: "The Antichrist?!"

At that moment Leviathan causes the room to quake and tremble so violently that the monsignor crashes to the floor and the Pyx comes loose and falls through a crack in the floor. Leviathan smiles and grabs the priest by his throat and lifts him more than six feet off the floor when they look at each other, eye to eye.

Leviathan: "There is no joy, only fear! There is no hope, only despair. There is no life, only death! There is no heaven only hell! Mankind will know this to be true when the prophesies are made real. On the Jerusalem Plain in the shadow of Megiddo the truth will come to pass."

The demon tosses the monsignor aside as if he were mere sack cloth and the priest lands in a heap clutching his throat, barely able to move. Leviathan turns toward Father Fielding who is staring at the hellish vision of the demon in horror. The priest, realizing that the demon is looking at him, tries to rise and flee, but the demon grabs Fr. Fielding and holds his face next to his. The priest can smell the vile breath and nearly passes out.

Leviathan: "No, do not pass out, there is one more thing you must see before I free your soul from its earthly fetters."

The demon thrusts one of his razor-sharp claws into the priest's chest and grabs the priest's beating heart. The fiend then reaches into thin air with the other claw as a glowing dagger appears. Fr. Fielding struggles violently to be release from the vice-like grip that Leviathan has on him, but it is futile.

Leviathan: *"It is now time to free your soul."*

Leviathan swings the dagger across the throat of the priest and severs the head from the body. The demon throws the body aside and holds the head in his claw, lovingly stroking the skull of the now dead priest. Leviathan turns to the monsignor who is staring at the head of his dead assistant in horror. The room now quakes more violently than before and the monsignor rolls from one side to the other. Leviathan tosses the severed head at Msgr. De. Marinis and suddenly the devilish fiend morphs back into Valentia who is now bloated to four times her size.

She is getting larger and larger and as she does her skin tears apart and great, gapping wounds appear all over her body. The woman screams in agony staring at the priest, pleading for release from the torment. Powerless to do anything Msgr. De Marinis is unable to help. All of a sudden, the room stops its violent quaking, and Valentia is levitating four feet off the floor. She looks down at the priest and says,

Valentia: *"It is done."*

Her body explodes and covers the room with blood, torn skin and bone. The monsignor stares in horror of the death that floods Valentia's cell. He makes the sign of the cross and says to himself, "It is not done."

CHAPTER 14

I drive through the gate into St. Patrick Cemetery in Huntington to be at the gravesite of my mom and dad. There are beautiful cherry blossom trees that are planted throughout the cemetery and when I am there in May they are in full bloom. This time of year, however it is still a little too early to see the beautiful pink blossoms.

It has been a while since I had visited their gravesite, but I find comfort every time I go. Since my call with Beth, and the horrible way it ended, I have grown despondent and I am hoping to find some peace and a perspective on the situation and what I can do, if anything, to feel better.

I walk down the small pathway through the rows of tombstones until I reach the monument that marks the place where the remains of my mom and dad are buried. As I always do, I stand before the tombstone and I say a prayer that they are together, at peace, and happy in the Lord's care. I heave a sigh and just stare at their names engraved on the monument and think about how much I miss them. I've been coming for years to their gravesite looking for solace and comfort and often finding a place where peace can always be found, except for this time.

My attention turns away from the tombstone that marks my parents resting place to the situation I find myself in. I feel guilty that I cannot let go of the hurt and anger. I should be able to put that aside, if not for myself then for my parents who do not deserve this kind of behavior from their son. This is what I should be doing, but I am not. I am still angry and I let that emotion fester instead of honoring the memories of my mother and father.

I am depressed, mired in self-pity when all around me in present day stops, and I am transported to the time of Christ and the Apostles. I am now observing a vision of St. Jude Thaddeus and the Apostles of Christ.

> *A silent reverence takes over the men; the apostles of Christ. They have banned together as they wait for 40 days after the death and resurrection of the Lord. Each Apostle present anticipates the sign; what they all hope is an omen and St. Jude Thaddeus stands among them. It is then that a flame appears above the heads of each of the Apostles. This is the sign they have been looking for, this is the sign that will guide their future and this is the sign that will affirm their resolve. It is the gift of faith brought down to them by the Holy Spirit.*

St. Jude Thaddeus steps out of the vision and stands before me. He is very somber as he stares at me. I can't face him because I know that he is disappointed in me, and that I haven't shown any desire to take control of my anger at Beth. I try to think about what to say, but I have no words and the scene of the vision changes again.

> *The holy man stands among the pagans. The multitude is screaming and cursing at the man they fear. He has been among them for only a few days. He has shown the pagan worshippers the corrupt and vile nature of their gods and already there are so many questions that the people have no answers to.*

> *St. Jude Thaddeus looks about the Temple and is saddened by what he sees. The statues of gods and goddesses, blindly worshipped by the people all the while ignoring the true nature of that of evil carved into stone. The saint circles the center*

of the large edifice and looks at each stone image as he commands, "You will in the name of the Father and the Son and the Holy Spirit leave this place. You are vile and abhorrent and you will no longer hold sway over these who now worship your unholy existence!"

At that moment, the earth beneath the temple begins to shake and the statues of the pagan gods and goddesses crumble into fragments. As the statues crumble, hordes of demons emerge from their stone prisons and cry hideous shrieks that can be heard throughout the Mesopotamian settlement. The people cower in fear and run from the temple for their lives, but some still remain. They are in awe of what they have seen and St. Jude Thaddeus preaches the true word of God and blesses them all.

I have seen these types of visions from other saints I have known, and I am fully aware of the seriousness of the lessons to be learned. I have forgotten my anger, at least for the moment, and I stare at St. Jude Thaddeus.

He looks at me and says, "Have you nothing to say Christopher?"

"Why have you shown me these visions?"

The entire space surrounding St Jude becomes unnervingly dark and I silently wait. A halo of light appears to glow about the face of the saint. The Pentecostal Flame appears above the head of St. Jude and I see he is holding an axe in one hand and quill pen in the other.

"Christopher, my time here is coming to a close, but I must warn you that your pride, anger and unwillingness to forgive are leading you further from our Lord Jesus Christ. You must find your own way, but there is something else that I must warn you of."

I being admonished and I know it. I am ashamed, but I am frightened of the warning that St. Jude just spoke of. "What warning? What are you trying to tell me, I don't know what to do?"

St. Jude Thaddeus says, "You have seen how the Lord has used me to exorcise the demons from the statues. There is so much evil in the world, but there is so much more to come. You must take heed for the time is coming."

"More to come? What is coming? Please tell me what I need to know."

The vision of St. Jude now begins to disappear and I know that it would be useless to try and keep him here. His last words to me are, "Faith is your strongest weapon, vigilance is your greatest defense and love is your greatest reward."

St. Jude Thaddeus fades into the heavenly light and I am alone at my parents' gravesite.

CHAPTER 15

Tom Houston is shaken by his last encounter with Satan and his new associate, Al-Masih ad-Dajjal. He sits alone at his desk, staring at nothing, lost in his thoughts. Tom knows that to fail Satan in his quest for the souls of the living is not an option. Tom also envisages that the punishment the demon will unleash and he imagines something so heinous that he cannot or will not consider the possibility.

Tom has vowed to Lucifer that he will redouble his efforts to be elected President of the United Sates knowing that in this position he can hold sway over hundreds of millions of people in America and around the world. His election will set into motion the means to give Satan his deepest desires, and to give Tom an eternity of pleasures heretofore never imagined.

As Tom contemplates all that is ahead of him, he takes great pleasure in the latest presidential polls. It seems that his overall approval has risen 5 points and he is favored by more than 50% of registered voters. He grabs a pen and sheet of paper and begins to list the tasks he will assign to his team. This list contains all he must do in the next few weeks to keep the momentum going, but as he does the phone rings and he answers, "Yes?"

It is Tom's assistant, Erin, "Good Morning Dr Houston, I am calling to remind you that you asked to schedule a presentation of the fundraising contributions made on behalf of the Price Clinic for Cancer Research. I have called Dr. Price's office and confirmed that he is available any time next week. I have also checked your schedule and you are available Tuesday through Thursday."

"Erin, give me a moment to think about this considering the campaign and some of the things that need to get done."

Erin interrupts, "Dr. Houston, I thought that you might have an issue so I checked with campaign staff. They suggested that we use the trip to schedule several campaign stops and fundraisers throughout the Miami/Ft. Lauderdale area as well as Central and Northern Florida before you return home. It will be a rushed timetable, but your staff feels that can be done and will provide some very positive exposure for your campaign. I will need to reschedule a number of meetings with your approval."

Tom smiles, "Erin, what would I do without you?"

Erin responds, without missing a beat, "It's hard to imagine Dr. Houston."

Tom continues to smile, "Great, tell my team to get to work and provide me with an itinerary as soon as possible and be sure to notify our public relations group. Tell them I would also like some of our Hollywood friends to be at the rallies and fundraisers" and he hangs up the phone. Everything seems to be falling into place and he knows that with the friendly mainstream media on his side, the trip will be a phenomenal success.

Part of Tom's plan is to be sure that he stays close to Beth. She is going through an emotionally traumatic time and he wants to be there to pick up the pieces. Tom resolves that he will call Beth at least once a day with a sympathetic ear and a shoulder to cry on. On all levels, both personal and political, Tom becomes more relaxed and self-assured. He is becoming more confident that he will be successful in his efforts and his encounter with Satan and The Deceiver seems to take on less significance than it had just a few minutes ago.

Moments later the phone rings. Tom looks at the caller ID and sees that it's Beth. He picks up the phone, "Hi Beth, how are you? I hope you have taken the time to calm yourself and see this all as a terribly unfortunate string of events."

Beth sighs, "Thanks Tom for being there and for your kind words. I wanted to call you and tell you that I will be taking off on a short leave of absence beginning today. I need time to think things over and I thought that I would go to my parent's condo out east."

Beth is heartbroken and she begins to cry over the phone.

Tom says, "Beth, why are you crying what happened? I am here for you; please tell me what happened."

Beth sobs deeply, "I just hung up with Chris. We had a terrible fight and we said some horrible things to each other. I don't know how to feel; angry, jealous, hurt, ashamed, the most awful emotions one can feel and I am feeling them all."

Tom has the urge to say something to soothe her heartbreak, but he thinks better of it and decides to stay quiet.

"I thought he loved me and I loved him, but after what he said, after what he did, I don't want to ever see him again."

Now Tom thinks to himself, "Should I play it safe or should I go for broke with this?" Dr. Tom Houston, candidate for the Socialist Liberation Party nomination for president, never plays it safe so he goes for broke.

Tom, in as gentle a voice as he can muster, says, "Beth, believe me when I say that I am so sorry for what Chris put you though. Chris was not honest with you and that means you will never be able to fully trust him. You've told me that you love him, but that love was taken for granted and now he has shown his true colors. I know how hard it is to accept this, but perhaps, you are better off knowing this now rather than later."

Beth remains silent, listening to Tom and trying to understand the impact of what he is saying. After a few moments she tells Tom, "I guess you are right. It is very hard to accept that someone you loved can betray you so deeply. I feel…I don't know how I feel?"

Tom tries to be even more solicitous to Beth and tells her, "Listen Beth, the most important thing you can do is to try and remain calm and think about yourself for a change. You have spent most of your life looking after others and giving your heart and soul to all those in need. I know you have done this because you are a kind and selfless person."

"Thank you for saying that Tom, I am hoping that taking some time off will help me to put this all into its proper context and perspective."

Tom seeing an opportunity takes another calculated risk. "Beth, I have to leave for a few days next week."

Beth asks, "Oh, where are you going?"

"I'm going to Florida to visit Spencer. I'll be presenting him with a check for $47,000,000; isn't that wonderful! I am sure all that money will be well spent. Spencer will be thrilled and the funds will allow him to continue his research. While I'm there I'll be making a few campaign stops and attending a few fundraisers. Hey, a candidate's work is never done."

Beth is saddened as she tells Tom, "Spencer invited Chris and me to visit the cancer institute. We were planning to spend a week there, sort of vacation, but now that's over."

Tom tries to make it seem like a spur of the moment suggestion when he says, "Beth, I have an idea. Why don't you come with me to the event in Florida! We can fly down on my private jet, you can spend time at the institute and I am sure Spencer will treat you like royalty. When you're there you can stay at my villa in South Beach where you can relax and work on your tan. In the evening you can accompany me to the fundraising dinners and we can have a great..."

Beth now gets a bit nervous and she stammers a bit as she says, "Uh, Tom, that's very kind, but I don't think it's such a good idea."

"Beth, why not? I promise that I will be a complete gentleman and this would be a great personal sacrifice given my status as America's most eligible bachelor..."

Beth now smiles for the first time since her fight with Chris and corrects Tom, "One of three of America's most eligible bachelors."

"Ah, I stand corrected, one of America's three most eligible bachelors and I am sure that once the tabloids find out it will ruin my reputation. I am also willing to take a chance and play the part of a eunuch who has been neutered at far too young an age!"

Beth now laughs out loud. "Tom, I really don't..."

Tom is detecting that Beth's resolve in getting weaker, "Come on Beth you need to get away and this is a great opportunity to spend time with Spencer and have as much time as you need to rest and relax. Come on, it will do you good even if I may be featured in the tabloids as having lost my touch."

Tom can feel that Beth's is close to saying yes so, he continues, "Plus, as an extra added bonus, I will invite Hamilton Cargill, who I have it on good authority, may ask you to be his fourth wife…for real this time!"

Beth laughs out loud again, but she still seems a bit hesitant so Tom pleads with her, "Beth, come on. Come with me to Florida, I promise you will love it and I promise you will have a wonderful time. What do you say?"

Beth relents and simply says, "Okay"

CHAPTER 16

Iam shaken by the events of today, of the vision revealed to me by St. Jude Thaddeus at mom and dad's gravesite and the ominous warning of events he foretold. This vision, on top of the awful and hurtful things that Beth and I said to each other, now has me in a total and complete funk.

I slowly walk back to my car when I hear my mobile phone ring. I am hoping its Beth, but I see its Uncle Al. I figure that given he has left me a number of messages; I decide that I should just get this over with and speak to him.

"Hi Uncle Al, I'm at mom and dad's gravesite and..."

Uncle Al interrupts me and says, "Listen Chris, I need to speak with you. I know how bummed out you are about Beth and we can talk about this after, but I just got out of a meeting with my group investigating an unbelievable surge in the most horrific crimes you can ever even imagine."

I walk to my car and connect to the Bluetooth so I can listen through my car's speakers. Now I am all ears, "What's happened Uncle Al?"

"Chris, I won't go into all the gory details, but there have been murders, rapes; violence of such vile and horrendous proportions that it would baffle the mind of any sane person. Crimes committed by kids as young as three years old, senseless violence and murders in such numbers that this will upend any crime statistics ever recorded in Suffolk County's history and it is being replicated all over America and the world."

I don't know how to react to this shocking revelation by my uncle and all I can say is "Dear God."

Uncle Al now speaks in a tone so serious that I am frightened at the prospect of what he might say next. "Chris, there is something else you need to know."

All I can say is, "What is it?"

"In each and every instance that a crime is committed there are three things that these crimes have in common; number one, each perpetrator has confessed they were inspired by Haborym, Lucifer, the Demon and every other name that you can call the devil, but they all mean the same thing, Satan. Number two, many of these crimes are exact copies of crimes committed by others over the last two hundred plus years."

I am incredulous, "You've got to be kidding."

"I wouldn't joke about something like this. I even called my good friend, the chief of detectives for Los Angeles County and he tells me that the same things are happening in his jurisdiction. I bet if I checked in towns and cities, big and small, anywhere in the US I would get reports listing the same types of crimes, exactly the same; committed under the same circumstances with the same MO."

I take a deep breath and ask the question, but I already know the answer, "What's number three?"

Uncle Al just says, "Lamb of God…"

I know what Uncle Al is going to say next, "…and in each and every case, Lamb of God was written in blood at the crime scene?"

"Now listen to me Chris, you have to ask you friends, you know who, to shed some light on all this horror. Why now? Why is this all happening now? I was hoping that Aiden would give me some insight, but he is still in a coma. Chris, we need help, it seems the whole country, and maybe even the world, needs help."

I didn't think that I could get any more depressed, but I am. "Uncle Al, I just had another vision at mom and dad's gravesite. The vision was of St. Jude Thaddeus, one of the twelve Apostles of Christ. He spoke to me in the vision and told me somethings that I don't understand, but it shook me to the core."

Uncle Al speaks in a low voice that betrays a fear that I have never heard in my uncle's voice. "What did he say?"

"His exact words were; 'there is so much evil in the world, but there is so much more to come. Take heed, it's coming.' Uncle Al, I'm scared like I have never been scared before."

"What do you think he meant?"

Things seem to be falling into place and I say, "Well now that you told me what is happening here, and possibly around the country or even the world, I think this is it. But what I think is most frightening is that St. Jude said there's more to come." Uncle Al is quiet as he is thinking over what I've told him. I realize that there was one other part of the vision that I want to share with Uncle Al because it could be important.

"Unc, there's one other thing that you should know. In the vision, St Jude is preaching among the pagans in ancient Mesopotamia. He is in a temple where he performs a miracle of sorts; he exorcises demons from the statues of pagan idols that were placed all around the temple. It seems that the demons there were controlling the locals and, while some of the villagers fled, St. Jude was able to bring some of them around to his side."

Uncle Al confides, "Chris, there's something that certain of the crimes had in common. In a number of the cases that we are investigating, satanic rituals were performed. Maybe there is a connection to your vision, but I can't see it and that is why I'm hoping we can get answers from The Sainted."

That is the first time that Uncle Al actually acknowledged the saints directly.

He continues to speak, "I only wish that Aiden was conscious; I know he would have something to say, some insight into all this."

I ask, "How is Father Langford?"

"Last thing I heard was that he is still unconscious and in intensive care. I am going back to see him as soon as I can get away, but I don't know when that will be. All hell is breaking loose here with every pun intended. Chris you've got to do something; talk to your saints, hopefully you've can find out what is making all this happen. I know I've said it before, but I am at a total loss as to what to do other than investigate the crimes, imprison the guilty when I can find them and bury the dead. Somehow I think we'll run out of cemeteries and jail cells if we can't stop this from continuing to happen." I can only imagine the sorrow and frustration my uncle is experiencing. I can hear the powerlessness in his voice as he tries to make sense of it all.

"Uncle Al, I know how you feel, what you must be going through and if I had a way to contact the saints and ask them, you know I would. Like I've told you, I don't know when the visions might come and I have no power to contact them. They are in control and all I can promise is to ask them when I see them."

Uncle Al sighs over the phone, "I know Chris, I know. I am just so damned overwhelmed by this evil and I feel powerless to stop the slaughter."

Both Uncle and I stay silent for a while until he asks me a question. "Chris, I hate to bring up the subject, but have you spoke to Beth yet?"

The memory of my call with Beth comes flooding back in my mind and I say, "Yeah I did and it didn't go too well. We had a terrible fight, yelling and cursing at each other. We said some very hurtful things, and it was horrible and I regretted it from the moment I said it, but by then it was too late. The call ended with Beth saying she never wants to hear from me again."

"Listen Chris, I know that it ended badly and I know that you are both in a bad place at the moment, but I can't believe that you don't love each other. My God, I've seen you together and if there ever was a more perfect couple it is you and Beth."

"Well, you wouldn't have thought that if you could have listened to us on the phone."

"I get it; so many awful things are said in the heat of the moment, but that doesn't make them true. I'll bet if you call her, with your tail between your legs, and told here you were sorry and beg her to listen to your explanation she would agree."

When I hear Uncle Al say this to me, I get very defensive and blurt out, "Why should I beg here for forgiveness when she was the one…"

"Listen to me Chris, do you love her?"

I know where this conversation is going so, I answer, "Yes."

"Do you want her back?"

"Yes."

"Well then buddy, you're gonna have to swallow your pride and ask Beth to take you back. Yeah, I know what she did wasn't right, but like you she may have a totally innocent explanation and you need to listen and like she needs to listen to you."

My anger and pride are still festering and I don't want to admit Uncle Al is right, but I know in my heart he is. I reluctantly tell him, "You're right."

"Okay Chris, now what are you going to do?"

I relent and tell my uncle, "I'll call her after we hang up."

"Atta boy, now Chris you need to let me know when you get another, umm, visit from you friends, okay."

Uncle Al has always had a problem saying the word 'saints' out loud, so he calls them 'friends' or some other name most of the time. I ask him again for the 40th time, "Why do you have such a tough time saying the word 'saints?"

"The phones may be tapped and some covert 'black ops' government agency may be listening in. We will be sent to the nuthouse and we may not get padded cells next to each other. If that happens, who would I have to talk to?"

"Okay, I'll tell you the next time I get a visit from my 'friends', but I refuse to tell them we are related."

"That's seems fair. Good luck speaking with Beth and I love you."

"I love you too" and I hang up the phone.

I gather my thought to try and come up with a good way to open a dialogue with Beth. She and I do love each other, well at least I love her and I hope she still loves me after what we said to each other. I try to come up with the right words, but I can't find them so I figure I'll just call and hopefully the right words will come to me. I hit the connect button on my mobile to Beth's number and I get her voice mail, "Hi, this is Beth. I will be taking a leave of absence and travelling over the next two weeks. I may not be able to answer your call, however please leave a message on my voice mail and I will call when I get back. Thanks, and have a great day."

I decide not to leave a message as I want to come up with the right words. If all I can get is a few moments on voice mail, the words need to be right…perfect. After my discussion with Uncle Al, I am exhausted and I figure I'd relax and watch a little TV and hopefully gather my thoughts. I turn to the local cable news channel as the anchor is finishing a story about corruption in Albany and how the governor and legislature seem to be doing nothing to stop it except perhaps raising taxes. I think to myself, the voters are powerless if they don't vote these clowns out of office.

The anchor begins to read the next news item and a photo of Tom Houston appears on the screen, "We have just received this press release. It was announced today that Dr. Thomas Houston, presidential candidate of the Socialist Liberation Party will be presenting a check for $47,000,000 to Dr. Spencer Price, founder and head of the Price Institute for Cancer Research. You may recall that the contributions were raised at a black-tie event that took place at Dr Houston's Garden City Mansion just a few days ago. It was also announced that Tom Houston will be extending his trip to Florida to include campaign appearances and fundraisers in support of his campaign. He is expected to be on the campaign trail for about two weeks before returning to his Long Island home. In other news…"

The anchor went on to another news item, but I stopped listening. Two weeks? Beth will be gone for two weeks; Tom Houston will be gone for two weeks, that's some coincidence. I now abandon all thoughts of leaving a voice mail message for Beth. Two weeks… 'she may have a totally innocent explanation'; so much for Uncle Al's totally innocent explanation.

I am seething and I can feel the anger and pain coming back in waves. Beth is gone from my life and it looks like I'm alone. I don't know what to do, but I know I can't stay here. I feel the irresistible need to go out, I need a drink, I need to get plastered. I take a quick shower, brush my teeth and shave. I put on a pair of jeans, a sweater and my leather jacket, I am about to look for my wallet when the doorbell rings.

I call out, "I'll be right there" and I walk to the door and open it up and I am in shock.

Amanda Sellers is standing there, smiling, as she says, "Hi, I thought you could use some company."

CHAPTER 17

*J*ohn *of Patmos has ensconced himself in what he believes is his place of visions; a tiny stone hut in Ephesus. John has been instructed by the "one like a son of man" to write all that he hears, all that he sees and all that he is given from the prophetic visions to the Seven Churches of Asia.*

Angels, messengers sent from God and the Son have visited him to reveal what must be told to the faithful. John has not had a vision in many days and he has reconciled that it is the will of God. During the quiet time, John has written down all of what he has been told, all of what the Lord wants him to tell the faithful who suffer greatly from persecutions. Many of the faithful have been martyred and John's words are meant to sustain the believers during this time of great peril and sacrifice.

He has put much of what he has been told by the Heavenly messengers in epistles that he has sent to the Seven Churches. These epistles, letters of great import, are being sent in hopes of renewing and sustaining the faithful in their belief in the Son of Man. John is aware of the enormity of his task and he is careful to craft each word with reverence in that they are the words of God.

As John continues his work, the room becomes filled with light and the angel sent from heaven appears with a new vision. In the vision there appear four living creatures as foretold by Ezekiel. The prophet speaks of these creatures as Cherubim, the bearers of the Throne of God. These Cherubim appear as a lion, an ox, a man, an eagle and have six wings. John is puzzled as Ezekiel's four living creatures are described as only having four wings. John continues to write the verse where he says that Cherubim have eyes all over, front and back and thus are alert and knowing and that nothing escapes their notice. Having read these words written in the Judaic tradition and scripture, John is also aware these living creatures are said to be Angels of Fire. They hold up the Throne of God and are said to hold up Earth itself. John is mystified by this declaration of the angel, but continues to write what he is told. The messenger continues to speak of many things as John envisions what miraculously is shown to him.

"After this I looked, and there before me was a door standing open in heaven. And the voice I had first heard speaking to me like a trumpet said, "Come up here, and I will show you what must take place after this." At once I was in the Spirit, and there before me was a throne in heaven with someone sitting on it. And the one who sat there had the appearance of jasper and ruby. A rainbow that shone like an emerald encircled the throne. Surrounding the throne were twenty-four other thrones, and seated on them were twenty-four elders. They were dressed in white and had crowns of gold on their heads. From the throne came flashes of lightning, rumblings and peals of thunder. In front of the throne, seven lamps were blazing. These are the seven spirits of God. Also, in front of the throne there was what looked like a sea of glass, clear as crystal. In the center, around the throne, were four living creatures."

John has written what he was told of in the vision and is eager to send both encourage and admonish those who are the faithful of the Seven Churches. John is about to put down on parchment, the vision he has seen when the messenger of God warns him of the storm that is to come. John knows better not to ask what the messenger speaks of, but somehow John also knows he will soon find out the meaning of the Seven Seals and he laments that it portends something dire to come.

CHAPTER 18

"What are you doing here!?" Amanda is the last person I expected to see. "Some greeting, aren't you happy to see me?" Amanda is smiling at me knowing that my face is turning red.

"Sorry, but you were the last person I expected to see."

"No problem, I guess I should have called you, but I am a girl who likes surprises." Amanda eyes me up and down and says, "Hey, you've got your coat on; were you going somewhere?"

"Yeah, I was going out to get drunk and I was just about to call a cab."

"Get drunk?"

"Yeah, it's a long story."

Amanda smiles at me, "I love long stories, I'm an actress remember? I've got a few interviews in the city and the studio hired a car and driver to get me around. You're in luck because now we can both get plastered so what say I come along? If you want you can tell me this long story or not, it's your call."

I had intended to make this a party of one so I could drown my sorrows in peace, but I am glad Amanda's here. We hit it off from the start and I'm open to the idea of having someone to talk to about Beth. "Sure, sounds like I could use a friendly ear to talk to."

Amanda says, "Great, come on let's go!"

We walk to the car where our driver, David is standing outside waiting to open the car door for us. I was going to tell him that we want to go to the Huntington Bar and Grill, but I had second thoughts; you can't take a superstar like Amanda to an ordinary neighborhood bar so I tell David to take us to Prime. Prime is on Huntington Harbor and it's an upscale place to eat or have a drink or both.

In less than 15 minutes, David pulls up to the front entrance of Prime and Amanda and I get out and walk up to the front desk. We are about to turn into the bar area when a young woman at the front desk immediately recognizes Amanda. The girl is overwhelmed and is barely able to speak, "Are you Amanda, I mean are you like Amanda, I mean are you the sellers, I mean are you Amanda Sellers?"

Amanda smiles at the young girl as this must happen to her a lot, "Yeah, that's me alright. What's your name?"

The wide-eyed young girl manning the front desk, "My name is Annie. Miss Sellers, I 'm a huge fan; welcome to Prime."

"Well Annie, it's a pleasure meeting you. My friend and I are here for drinks so can you show us where we can sit. We'd like a quiet spot so we can talk."

It is late on a Monday so the bar area in not too crowded. The girl is thrilled that Amanda is actually speaking to her so she says, "Oh, Miss Sellers, I would be happy to show you to a very nice spot by the fire pit. We don't usually get a big bar crowd late on Monday so it should be very quiet and private."

"Thanks Annie, you're a real peach!" and Annie takes Amanda and me over to a couple of very comfortable looking chairs where Amanda gets right down to business. "Annie, should we order drinks from you or will we be served by someone else?" Annie is over the moon at the thought of serving Amanda Seller and she says, "Miss Sellers…"

"Annie, please call me Amanda."

Now Annie breaks out into a huge smile and tells us, "I would love to serve you, umm Amanda, what would you both like?"

"Chris, I know you're a vodka guy, but are you up for tequila?"

"Sure, sounds good to me."

"OK Annie, we will have two shots of Barrique de Ponciano Porfidio."

"I'll be right back with your drinks!" Annie turns and walks to the bar and places the order with the bartender.

We both watch Annie walk away and Amanda says, "Okay, before we get down to why you want to get drunk, I need to ask, 'Do you know the proper way to drink tequila?'"

I answer, "Yeah, in a margarita!"

Amanda laughs, "Very funny. Well, you are about to have a shot of one of the best tequilas in the world. So, in order to fully appreciate the experience here's the proper etiquette for drinking tequila. You're a righty, right? So first, you lick the skin between your thumb and forefinger on the back of your left hand, hopefully your hand is clean."

I had taken a shower earlier and I told Amanda, "I not only have clean hands, but my entire body is clean and my heart is pure."

Amanda answers, "Well that is certainly nice to know given what I have heard about the personal hygiene habits of bachelors, including their hearts. Anyway, after you lick your skin, you need to sprinkle a small pinch of salt onto the area. The saliva will help the salt stick. Now you need to hold one slice of lime with your thumb and index finger, using the same hand that contains the salt. Finally, you need to breathe out, lick the salt, down your tequila shot and bite the lime."

"Amanda, I appreciate the lesson however at this rate, I'll never get drunk because it takes too long just to drink one shot."

"Don't worry, Chris, I'll be sure you get plenty of liquid amnesia."

Before I get a chance to comment Annie comes back empty handed, "Umm, ahh Ms. Sellers, I mean Amanda, the bartender told me that we don't have Barrique de Ponciano Porfidio. It seems that it is only served on special order and we will need a day or two to get it in. I am so sorry. He said that you obviously know your tequilas and he suggested that you may like to try Tres-Quatro-Cinco."

I look at Amanda, "What the heck is going on?"

Amanda says, "It's no big deal, Annie, tell the bartender I like his style and Tres-Quatro-Cinco is perfect."

I am puzzled and I ask Amanda, "What was that all about?"

"Well, Barrique de Ponciano Porfidio is generally considered one of the top three brands of tequila in the world and a bottle costs around $2,000 plus and a shot generally runs between $250 and $350 or more…of course that depends on where you drink it. Tres-Quatro-Cinco is less expensive, but it is very good tequila. I remember this one time…"

I can't believe what I'm hearing, "WHAT! $2,000a bottle! $300 a shot! I can maybe afford half a shot and that's for both of us!"

"Just calm down Chris, I wasn't going to let you pay for this. It was my treat as I think you could use a little pampering."

"Listen Amanda, I appreciate your generosity, but I can't let you pay for such an expensive drink. Maybe we should call it a night and I'll go home where there's a cold six pack in the refrigerator."

Amanda looks at me and smiles, "Chris that shows a lot of integrity. Generally, if I offer the same deal to some actor or producer or whoever is my date they would jump at the chance for free drinks. Some might even try to get me in the sack after getting me drunk on my dime. But let me tell you something my father told me, and I believe he told you too; when someone wants to give you a gift, you should learn to accept is graciously. He told me that when I was a young girl and I'm telling you now, in case you forgot."

I'm not comfortable with this, but Amanda's good-natured admonishment left me with no option, "Thanks Amanda, I really appreciate your kindness, thanks for your generosity and I do remember that Harry told me the same thing."

"Good, now that that's settled, here comes Annie with our drinks with all that is needed to exercise the proper etiquette for drinking tequila."

Annie sets down the shots of tequila along with the salt and limes and Amanda tells her to keep the shots coming.

"Well Chris, looks like you're all set so what do we toast to?"

"How about to your visit, the only good thing that is sure to come out of the hangover I will have tomorrow morning."

"Now that's an original toast; here's to pleasant hang-overs!" and we go through the entire accepted etiquette for properly drinking tequila, lift our glasses and down our shots in short order.

"Wow, that is fabulous tequila! What's it called again?"

"Tres-Quatro-Cinco. It's a special family blend of 30% three-year, 40% four-year and 30% five-year aged tequila. That's how it got the name; Tres-Quatro-Cinco 3-4-5."

"You're like a tequila savant, aren't you? Harry's is a wine aficionado and it seems like you have the same passion for tequila and, for those who are about to get drunk, we salute you!" I am starting to feel a wonderful glow after my first shot.

We pick up the second round and down it with the same enthusiasm as the first. Annie is already there with the third round and that seems to go down as smooth as silk. As I sit there in the lounge, the heat from the fire pit and the effect of the tequila put me in a very mellow mood. Amanda seems to be entertained by my increasingly relaxed demeanor so she asks, "Well, I assume the long story is about a problem you have, do you want to talk about it or do you just want to sit here and drink?"

I feel myself losing control a bit, but I say it anyway. "Well to tell you the truth, you are the problem. I mean you are part of the problem. I mean that you…"

"ME…part of the problem? How can adorable, innocent, lovable me be part of any problem, least of all yours."

"You forgot beautiful."

"Oh, that's right I forgot, I am beautiful!"

"Well, remember that little incident at the Chicago airport?"

Amanda pretends she is searching her memory, "Nope, I can't remember a thing, least of all something that could be remotely considered a problem." She bats her eyelashes and smiles an innocent looking smile that actresses are trained to do.

"Well, let me refresh your memory. You drove me to the airport and before we said goodbye, you gave me a kiss that is now trending on Facebook, Twitter, Google and even the Home Shopping Network."

Amanda teasingly dismisses the incident and says, "Oh that silly kiss. How could that possibly be a problem?"

"Well that silly kiss caused a horrible fight with Beth and me, now it's over between us. We both said some terrible things to each other and…"

I now pause, looking around and ask, "Can I get another drink?" It is as if I have magical powers, because at that exact moment Annie brings over two more shots of tequila and set ups and I throw back my shot and the glow I'm feeling gets even brighter.

Amanda turns serious and she says, "Chris, I am so sorry for getting you into trouble with your girlfriend. I don't know if it will help, but I can call her and tell her I was just kidding." Before she speaks gain, Amanda takes a deep breath, "Chris, I could tell Beth that I was kidding, but I want you to know I wasn't kidding. I really like you and when I kissed you, I felt something, and I was hoping you did too."

I look at Amanda and even in my drunken state I can see she is one girl; well, I'm starting to see double now, so two of the most beautiful women that any man would be over-the-top happy to have in love with them. I don't know how to feel or to react to what she just told me so I try to change the subject. "No, calling her won't help; it seems that she was having a fling while I was with you and Harry."

Amanda is puzzled, "Fling? What kind of fling was she having?"

I explain, "Well to put it as politely as possible, it seems that she and Tom Houston are now a couple. She slept over his house, sorry I mean mansion, after a fundraising event he had and the next day, the whole tender moment of her departure was captured in all its glory in photos. I saw her kissing Tom and she saw you kissing me and both kisses were broadcast to the entire world. …can I have another drink?"

Amanda signals Annie, who is standing at attention at the bar, and she rushes over with what has to be our fifth or sixth round, I've lost count. We both now decide to sip the latest round instead of drinking it in one swallow, and I just lay back in my seat emotionally exhausted, but feeling no pain.

Given our discussion, Amanda appears to have sobered up a bit and is just staring at me with a look on her face somewhere between pity and guilt. She looks as if she has something to say, but she just stays silent and continues to look at me.

"Why are you just staring at me?"

"I don't know, I just feel bad for you about Beth, but I am not sorry about being here with you now."

Chris tries not to slur his words when he says, "Amanda, what do you want me to say? You are beautiful, glamourous, bright, rich, talented, and you can have your choice of any man you want."

"I don't want a man, I want you." Now Amanda starts to laugh and I just crack up at the joke and we both go into convulsions of laughter. Annie is watching us from the bar and she doesn't know what to make of our hilarity and she decides that we need another shot. She walks over to the table with another round and says, "Amanda, Colin our bartender wants to buy you a round and I want to thank you for being so nice."

Amanda is touched by the gesture and says, "Annie, thank you and also please tell Colin thanks from both of us."

I feel the need to express my gratitude to Annie and Colin. "Exsqueeze me, I want shhanks Annie and shhanks to you and Colon and the shpepcial One-Three-Seven-Twenty whatever tequila. Dis was very good drinking and tequila and I am fine." With that, I am told that I passed out.

Amanda looks at the drunken heap next to her and looks up at Annie and says, "You know, I think I'd like the check now."

Annie looks down at me and tells Amanda, "Coming up."

CHAPTER 19

The tribes, out of necessity, have grouped together so that they can cross the central plains of Africa in search of food and water. Samburu, Kalenjin, Oromo, Maasai and more find some small comfort in banding together, but each day their numbers diminish; the living must bury the dead, but traditions of the tribes have little meaning anymore.

For the past three years the gods have been unkind. Drought has parched the land dry and all that has sustained these peoples is gone. Now less than two thousand members of all the tribes of the plains and beyond are left. They cling together in hopes that their common purpose will serve them all and that they will endure this hardship in hopes of survival.

The decision to leave his ancestral lands was not an easy one, but it seems to him there is little choice but to depart. In the past months the Maasai warrior has seen more dreadfulness than he could have ever imagined. For many days the man has walked the plains when he and his people hear a great blast, as if from a horn. The peoples look around in great fear not knowing what may come. It is then they are rained upon by hail and fire mingled with blood. The fear of his people is now all consuming and they try to run, but the terrible downpour follows. For what purpose are these horrors being visited upon them he could not hope to understand.

It is weeks later, when in the first light of day, a second horn can be heard. The horn is so loud that his people cover their ears and scream in terror. It is then they witness a giant ball of fire crash down from the sky. It lands in the sea and upon the sun rising there is a great multitude of dead sea creatures washed onto the shore. The overturned boats and hulls of fishing vessels caught in the great crash can also be seen jutting out of the water. It was at that moment the peoples of the Maasai move beyond their villages onto the plains. During the journey many other tribes have joined them, all marching in fear of the unnamed dread, hoping for some respite and some relief from their suffering.

The Maasai warrior now stands on a small rise overlooking the flat plain, hoping for a sign of green. Green is the sacred color of the land that has nurtured his people through the ages. He bends down and grabs a dry heap of barren soil. It is so lacking in moisture that the earth easily crumbles at the mere touch of his hand. The winds swirl all around and he blinks the dust from his eyes looking for the elusive green, but all that can be seen is the brown of scorched earth. The warrior tries to hold his hands over his ears, but he cannot silence the cries of the children in the night. They hunger for food that no longer grows; they thirst for milk that no longer comes from cattle that have long since died. His people share what little water can still be found, but it has been days since the last watering hole has run dry.

For a period, the men could still hunt for food, but now no animals can be found and for this reason alone they must move from the lands of their ancestors. The elders have decided that the people must move on as they have no choice but to search for whatever sustenance they may find, wherever they may find it.

As the heat of the day abates and night settles in, the small and rickety shelters they carry are set up so that women and children may be afforded some measure of warmth and safety here on the central plains. The warrior thinks that he and the men of the tribes would guard against all manners of beasts that once roamed the landscape; the lions, cheetahs, hyena, rhino, elephants, gazelle, wildebeest, zebra, buffalo, even black rhino; all could be dangerous, but all are gone now. In the morning, at first light and before the extreme heat of the day slows the journey, the people will pack whatever they can carry and continue their move south. The Maasai warrior does not know why the tribal elders chose to journey south, but the warrior seems to believe that it would make no difference what direction is taken, it just seems important to move.

At first light the people gather what they can and continue to shadow the leaders who urge them forward. It is near nightfall when they see a river that is nearly dry. Still, what little water is left would be a gift from the gods and help to keep those that are left among them, alive. As the tribes rush to the river to drink, a great star can be seen by all appears. It crosses the night sky leaving a trail of dust-like particles that settle on the ground and in the river. The star passes over the horizon and the people look at one another not knowing what has just happened. But thirst overwhelms them and many of the first to drink, cup their hands, and swallow the water until sated.

In mere moments the first screams can be heard, and the faces of those who had drunk from the river are covered in blood and all who have drank from the river fall to the ground, dead.

The elders scream a warning to their people who had been waiting to drink. "DO NOT DRINK, THE WATER IS POISON! DO NOT DRINK!" The people that are left alive back away from the river for fear of being poisoned. As they stop to survey the dead that are scattered all over the river's bank, a fourth deafening blast from the unseen horn shakes the terrified throngs to the core. At that exact moment all turns black; a blackness that cannot be imagined; darkness like none before it. The stars are blotted from the sky, there is no horizon, there are no shadows and not one among the people can see their hands in front of their faces. Many call for their loved ones; some answer the call, but many others do not. It is then that a barely visible pin point of light can be seen very high up in the completely black sky overhead. Slowly the light becomes larger and brighter in heavens above.

The people cannot understand what is happening, but they know that they must run, as the bright object descends, believing it will land near where they are standing. It is then that the great horn bellows its hideous explosion of sound and all cover their ears. The people of the African Plains run in all directions away from the falling star and stop only to turn around as it smashes into the earth on the other side of the river. The star creates a large opening in the earth and smoke can be seen rising from the fissure. The smoke is as if coming from a gigantic furnace, and the heat is so powerful that many are burned and, all that watch in fear, are forced even further away.

The Maasai warrior can be brave no longer for he knows that this is not from man, but a horrible punishment from the gods. He stands there in stunned amazement until he hears a sound coming from the abyss. The sound is familiar, but he can only guess what he believes it to be and knows it is not good. He yells to all, "RUN!" and along the way he tries to help those who appear to be in a stupor and cannot find the courage to move. "RUN! RUN!" he continues to scream, but he stops and turns to only to see the source of the noise being emitted from the abyss. The Maasai warrior is now frozen in place as he watches in terror at what appears crawling from the fiery hole. He stands, disbelieving, as the first of the beasts emerge from the abyss.

The beasts are not unlike locust. They have a tail that is much like a scorpion, but they are much larger. The locust creatures are human in appearance, with faces and hair, but with the teeth of a lion, and they are wearing breastplates of iron. There are thousands upon thousands that crawl from the blazing chasm and immediately begin to flap their wings. The warrior covers his ears as he cries out in pain. He now knows the sound; it is like the thundering of many, many horses and chariots rushing into battle.

The remaining people still alive are completely overwhelmed by the locust beasts and frozen in fear. These once brave men and women are powerless to save themselves as they are ripped apart by the hordes of flying beasts. The warrior tries to fight off the locust creatures, but he knows that it is useless and he dies screaming in unbearable pain.

When all the people of the African Plain are dead, the locust creatures carry the remains of the tribal dead into the abyss.

CHAPTER 20

During the drive on his way back to Huntington Hospital, all Chief Barese can think of is the dreadfulness of the crimes and events that seem to be growing day-by-day. The conversation with Chris has not given him any comfort, but rather it makes him feel even more powerless. He grows more and more despondent given the likelihood that these crimes have their roots in evils that, before now, he thought existed only in scripture or in the imagination. Al Barese has been the beneficiary of a miracle and he believes that The Sainted exists and that Chris can actually communicate with them. However, without their guidance, Chief Barese's expectations of ending this mass slaughter and violence seems beyond all hope. Still, he tries to maintain his faith as he hopes Aiden recovers, as he hopes that Chris and Beth can reconcile, as he hopes that there are answers to questions, but his hopes are fading fast.

The chief's thoughts occupy his time as he drives back to the hospital to see Fr. Aiden Langford. The last time he spoke to his friend's physician, Dr. Paul Simonelli, he was told that Aiden's condition was unchanged and he was still in the ICU. It is then that the phone rings in the chief's car and Al sees it's from Dan Orello and he connects via Bluetooth.

"Hi chief, Dan here."

"Hi Dan, I am just on my way to the hospital to see Aiden, what's up?"

"I just want to give you a quick update of the lab reports that have come back. We have the results of the various tests of the evidence that we found at the crime scenes taken from the 'Lamb of God' scrawls written in blood. It seems that the entire blood samples we took on the sites of the crimes were of the human variety and in all cases, it was proven to be the victim's blood, except for one."

Al is puzzled, "Except for one? Which one?"

Dan says, "The one that was written in the confessional where Aiden was hearing confession and where he had…" Dan's voice trailed off.

"Dan, I know you don't want to mention Aiden's heart-attack and thanks for being kind and a good friend. What did the report say on the sample?"

"Well chief, the report says that, and I'm reading right from the report, '…the blood sample as tested does not conform to any type that we have on file even when compared to the rarest of blood type samples on record. The tests determine the antigens that should identify the blood type were used, but the samples tested do not meet any of the normal composition that one might expect to find, human or otherwise.' Chief, the report goes on to say that they'll run more tests, but it seems that the lab folks are as puzzled as you and I."

Chief Barese ponders what he has been told and asks Dan, "Do these people even make a guess as to what it might be?"

"No, nothing I can read in the report. If you want, I can call the lab and ask them to take a guess as to what it might be."

"No, Dan, don't do that, those guys are busy enough and I think I'm just grasping at straws anyway. Do you need me back at HQ?"

"Not now chief, if there is any material change in the status of our investigation, I'll call you and you can decide. In the meantime, just go and visit your friend, and try to relax, all this shit will be here when you get back."

"Thanks Dan and call if you need me."

Dan ends, "I will" and the phone goes silent.

Chief Barese turns into the hospital parking lot and exits his car. He walks through the lobby where he sees Dr. Simonelli. "Hi doc, any change in Aiden's condition?"

"Hi chief, no nothing new as of now. We continue to run tests and monitor his heart and brain function and all results are about what we would expect in a patient that has suffered a myocardial infarction as well as the shock he experienced. Don't worry we are keeping a very sharp eye on any change and we'll react accordingly."

"Thanks doc. Have I told you he is my best friend?"

Dr. Simonelli smiles, "About a thousand times, so go see your best friend, but be quiet and calm. Maybe you could read to him. He will not be able to react, but on some level, he might respond to you speaking, and hearing a friend's voice is always good therapy."

"That's a good idea, he loves poetry, and maybe I'll read him some poetry. If he hears me read in my Bronx accent, he may get so pissed off he might wake-up just to have me stop. Confidentially I hate poetry, but the sacrifices I make."

Both men laugh and shake hands and go their separate ways.

On his way back to the ICU, the chief stops at the hospital's gift shop and sees a book titled, "America's Worst Poetry Written by America's Worst Poets" and he thinks this is just perfect, then again, he thinks it might cause Aiden to have another heart attack so he puts the book back on the rack. Al combs through the rack when he spots a book titled "William Shakespeare…Poet for the Ages" and he quickly grabs it. He thinks this is a perfect gift, given that Aiden loves Shakespeare, and given that Shakespeare is a fellow Englishman, and given that when he hears the beloved Bard of Avon being spoken with a classic 'Bronxese' lilt, he is sure to wake up!

Al walks up to the counter to pay and thinks to himself, "Nineteen Dollars and Ninety-Five cents! For a paperback! And they do this all without a gun!" So, he just sighs and buys the book to take back to the ICU. The chief rides the familiar elevator to the familiar fifth floor and walks to the familiar ICU and goes to his familiar chair by Aiden's bed.

The chief grabs Aiden's hand, "Hey buddy, I'm back. Things are getting pretty serious out there and maybe you'd like to stay in a coma until this is over, but you can't. I need your help and I need it badly. There are things happening that would curl your hair, if you had any. Oh, by the way, I got you a present! It's a book, if you can believe it! The book is filled with poetry by your favorite author, Billy Shakespeare! Did you hear what I called him huh? 'Billy!' Now that should really piss you off, and wait till you hear me read it! That should really make you pissing mad!"

The chief looks through the index of poems that are printed in the book and comes across a title that he is familiar with. He can't recall where or when he heard it first, but he seems to remember the poem so he says to his unconscious friend, "Aiden, I found a poem for you, it's actually a speech, and I think you will like it. As a matter of fact, you've probably committed it to memory."

Chief Al reads a bit of the preface and says, "I think I'll need some background for context so let me familiarize myself with the poem or speech or whatever you want to call it. It's the St. Crispin's Day Speech from Henry V. You know I think I might even remember this from my high school English Lit class! It says here in the forward notes that 'The St Crispin's Day speech' is from Shakespeare's play Henry V. It says here in the notes that in the speech, Henry V commended his men, who were vastly outnumbered by the French, to remember how the English had previously inflicted great defeats in battle upon the French."

The chief clears his throat and begins, "Here it goes Aiden, "St. Crispin's Day Speech from Henry V by William Shakespeare."

WESTMORELAND. O that we now had here
But one ten thousand of those men in England
That do no work to-day!

KING. What's he that wishes so?
My cousin Westmoreland? No, my fair cousin;
If we are mark'd to die, we are enow
To do our country loss; and if to live,
The fewer men, the greater share of honour.
God's will! I pray thee, wish not one man more.

Chief Al Barese takes a moment to just ponder what he has read. "Sorry Aiden, I didn't realize that these words could be so powerful." What the chief reads is having an unexpected impact on him as he continues to read aloud the words of the Bard of Avon,

That he which hath no stomach to this fight,
Let him depart; his passport shall be made,
And crowns for convoy put into his purse;
We would not die in that man's company
That fears his fellowship to die with us.

Al has to put down the book again to ponder even more of what he's read. "Whoa, Aiden, did you hear that? King Henry V is telling Westmoreland that he'd rather stand and die with heroes and send home those too cowardly to fight. Henry will even send them off with money in their pockets rather than die in their company." Chief Barese continues to read, now more to himself than to his friend.

This day is call'd the feast of Crispian.
He that outlives this day, and comes safe home,
Will stand a tip-toe when this day is nam'd,
And rouse him at the name of Crispian.
He that shall live this day, and see old age,
Will yearly on the vigil feast his neighbours,
And say "To-morrow is Saint Crispian."
Then will he strip his sleeve and show his scars,
And say "These wounds I had on Crispian's day."
Old men forget; yet all shall be forgot,
But he'll remember, with advantages,
What feats he did that day. Then shall our names,
Familiar in his mouth as household words-
Harry the King, Bedford and Exeter,
Warwick and Talbot, Salisbury and Gloucester-
Be in their flowing cups freshly remembered.

This story shall the good man teach his son;
And Crispin Crispian shall neer go by,
From this day to the ending of the world,
But we in it shall be remembered-
We few, we happy few, we band of brothers;

The chief is still staring down at the pages of the poem that he has just read and he is overcome with emotion. He imagines himself as a soldier facing odds so bleak in winning a battle that most will die. Al marvels how William Shakespeare can create such poetry as to move one's heart and soul. Henry V was able to inspire *'his few, his brave, his band of brothers'* and imbue in their being, the courage to face their fears, and living or dying they are always, and will always be, a band of brothers.

Chief Al Barese, a hardened veteran of the Police Force, a man whose bravery has been proven countless times, sits there staring at the book and finds tears welling up in his eyes. Al wants to finish reading, but the chief is stopped as the quiet is broken by Fr. Aiden Langford, who speaks,

For he to-day that sheds his blood with me
Shall be my brother; be he neer so vile,
This day shall gentle his condition;
And gentlemen in England now-a-bed
Shall think themselves accursd they were not here,
And hold their manhood's cheap whiles any speaks
That fought with us upon Saint Crispin's day.

Fr. Aiden stares at his friend saying, "Spartaco, are you alright, you look dreadful?"

Chief Barese jumps up in shock and says, "Aiden, what the…"

"My dear Spartaco, even you cannot butcher the Bard. I am very touched that you are here and that you are my most loyal friend

CHAPTER 21

The terrorist leaders have been on their march for a number of days now. The going has been very slow as they must avoid being seen as a great company. The plans for their mission have been laid out by Al-Masih ad-Dajjal, and although many of the heads of the terror groups have questions, they are much too afraid to ask as it might betray their cowardice.

For six days now no one has seen the one they call Masih, the beast he rides or any of his army of bizarre appearing warriors. While there are quiet whispers, any concerns are suppressed as the terrorists march on through the ancient region named Khorasan through Iran. Their group makes camp on the outskirts of small village nestled in the mountains.

In the evening of the seventh day the tribal leaders of all the groups sit around the campfire in awkward silence not daring to speak what is on their minds. The fire that cooks their food and warms their bodies suddenly bursts and out from the flames comes Al-Masih ad-Dajjal, The Deceiver. The men all scurry backwards on their haunches away from the flames as the Masih steps onto the ground that surrounds the fire.

The terrorist leaders are frightened beyond their ability to cope with what they are witnessing. The Masih walks the perimeter of the campfire gazing at each of the men sensing their fears, doubts and their lack of courage to sustain them for what is to come. Al-Masih ad-Dajjal appears angry and he knows that he must steel the spines of these men against the ravages of a disease called cowardice.

Once the Deceiver has circled the campfire he admonishes the men, "Have I not told you that Allah has sent me? Have I not provided all you need to assure his victory? Have I not shown you miracles that only I can perform? If you have witnessed this and more, then why are you so cowardly when I have shown you the way of victory over the infidels?"

As if out of nowhere, there now appears on the hills and crevices surrounding the terrorist camp the bizarre warriors dressed in ancient robes with their faces that are as before having the appearance of hammered shields. The warriors stand in complete silence until Al-Masih ad-Dajjal urges them.

"Who is that you fight for?

"ALLAH AND HIS PROPHET MOHAMMAD!"

The shouts of the warriors' echo through the camp and the terrorists and their leaders are frozen, I fear. Al-Masih ad-Dajjal continues to exhort the group.

"Who is it that must be vanquished?"

"THE INFIDELS AND ALL NON-BELIEVERS!"

"What is expected of you?"

"MUCH!"

"What are you willing to do?"

"TO DIE IN HONOR OF ALLAH!"

"What is to be your reward?"

"ETERNAL PLEASURES!"

"Where do we go?"

"MEGIDDO!"

The terrorists can no longer betray their fears knowing the power of the man that commands them. They must supplicate themselves before the Masih. One sheik, who has lowered his head to touch the ground speaks, "Our lord, oh messenger of Allah, we have allowed fear to shroud our goal and the will of Allah. We will do all that is required to honor Allah and his prophet Mohammad, as we will do all to honor you. Please forgive us our spinelessness and allow us to redeem ourselves in your eyes and in the eyes of the Almighty!"

The Deceiver knows that the fear they are feeling will serve him best if they are told of the consequences of their cowardice. The camp remains in complete silence as the Masih surveys the group. He begins by speaking slowly and deliberately to the group comprising of the leaders of al Qaeda, ISIS, Boko Haram, and the Taliban as well as their men. "I am saddened by what I sense. Your fears have made you weak and your fears may fail you in the battle to come. Hear me and hear me well; if I sense that this instinct will cause you to falter, your punishment will be greater than any you will suffer in battle."

All terror leaders remain supplicant as they bow their heads to touch the ground. They will not show their faces for fear it will betray the shame they feel at their cowardice.

Al-Masih ad-Dajjal is confident that his words are enough to assure his commands will be obeyed. If not, the cowardly among these men will learn to know a pain that has never been visited on a human before.

* * *

The small village named Masuleh is in the Gilan Province of Iran. It is where the terror leaders have chosen to take pause in their journey. It is a small village with no more than 400 people, but it will serve well to rest their men. Al-Masih ad-Dajjal has provided more than the terrorists need to sustain themselves and, as night falls, they settle around the warm fires to eat and talk of victory over the Christians, Jews, Buddhists, Hindus and all enemies of Islam.

The men are restless and in need of a release for the pent-up nervous energy that is now coming to a head. Each man looks around, but no one can say what is truly on their mind. It is then a voice that can only be heard in the minds of each terrorist speaks. It is a familiar voice that declares, "You are the holy warriors of Allah! You are here to fight for the victory over the forces that would defend the bastard infidels."

The men look at one another with questioning glances not knowing if the words in their minds have been heard by others in the group.

"I have given you all that you need to sustain you in battle. I have given you riches and weapons, both ancient and new, to assure you are victorious and now I have given you commands that I expect you to obey. You are not aware, but there is a purpose as to why you are here, now, in this village. I have directed you to this place you have stopped to rest as it is filled with those who profess to believe in Islam, but are unbelievers, enemies of Allah. They hide behind the mask of the faithful, but deny Allah and debauch in the name of all that is evil. This cannot continue; this is why you must purge the land of this abomination!"

The men now are looking all around at the others in their group and beyond. They now know that, even though there is no voice other than in their minds, this is a message all can hear. It is a message from the stranger among them, the Masih sent by Allah and Allah's messenger must always be obeyed.

"You are to rid the land of all men, women and children! Not one is to be left standing! You may do what is the will of Allah and take what pleasures you must, but leave no one alive to spread the profanity of the non-believers!"

The terrorists rise as one and shout and roar as they hold their weapons high. The men run through the village entering each of the huts that line the dirt paths and surrounding hills. Screams and cries of the villagers' echo throughout Masuleh as the warriors wreak terror on the unsuspecting innocents. Children are ripped from the arms of their mothers and fathers and many are brought out to the center of the village. Many of the women are left behind as they implore the terrorists. They plead for their children, but for their impudence they are raped and brutalized. Their cries are only met with the razor-sharp cutting edge of the antique yataghan Turkish ottoman dagger blades that each of the terrorists have been given by The Deceiver.

At the far end of the village, the rickety door to the small hut crashes opens and a lone terrorist enters. He looks around and sees a man and young boy cowering in the corner of the hut. Jawad Mobassari and his son Ashem are frozen in fear as the fanatic points his AK47 at them and screams, "Get up you cowards and do not say a word, DO YOU UNDERSTAND!!!"

The man and his son do not move fast enough so when they try to get up, the terrorist smashes the butt of his rifle against the father's head knocking him down. His son, Ashem screams and rushes to help his father. Blood is flowing from the older man's head, but as his son tries to help, the terrorist lifts his hand and punches the boy sending him flying across the room. The half-conscious Jawad cries out begging the terrorist to stop, but his only answer is to have the rifle smashed into his ribs.

The fanatic's face is twisted in rage as he grabs Ashem by the neck and kicks his father demanding the he get up. Jawad is in extreme pain, but he musters up what energy he has and tells his son not to worry and just be quiet. The terrorist just smiles and thinks that it is good advice for a father to give his son.

Jawad and Ashem are brought to an open area that serves as the small village's town center. Their hands are bound behind them and they are both thrown to the ground and ordered to line up, on their knees, with others of those remaining alive. The villagers assembled are made to kneel in a perfectly straight row. Among those left are men and children, all lined up, and a terrorist stands behind each one.

Ashem speaks through his pain and tears, "Father, I am scared!"

"Shush, Ashem do not do anything that will anger these men."

"But father…" Ashem's words are cut off when the terrorist hits the boy in the back of his head.

"DID I NOT TELL YOU TO BE QUIET?" The shout becomes a hellish shriek. The boy cannot wrap his hands and arms around his head so he closes his eyes as he prepares for another blow and it comes, this time harder than before.

Jawad throws himself over the body of his unconscious son as the terrorist now pummels the man in a maniacal rage. He kicks Jawad off the unconscious young boy and lifts Ashem off the ground by his hair. In one swift motion he removes the dagger from its sheath and holds it to the child's throat.

The father screams and cries as he begs for mercy.

"You have blasphemed against Allah…you have blasphemed against Islam…you have condemned yourself and your bastard child!"

The razor-sharp edge of the dagger slowly pierces the skin and in one, long deliberate motion cuts along the neck and through the jugular vein. The father thrashes as he tries to reach Ashem, crying for the son he loves so much. The terrorist takes the severed head of the boy and throws it to the ground next to Jawad who is losing all sanity. Through his tears, Jawad kisses the lips of the young Ashem and in calmness awaits to be reunited with his son in heaven.

In an instant, the men of al Qaeda, ISIS, Boko Haram and the Taliban use their daggers to cut through the throats of the villagers. As the knives penetrate the skin and bones of the poor unfortunates, their horrific shrieks echo through the mountains until there are no more screams, only silence once more. In the span of less than one hour all of the villagers have been killed. The blood of the dead now covers the hands, arms, faces and clothing of the terrorists. The minds of the fanatics have been made numb by the carnage. No one speaks, no one dares to speak; they remain in deafening silence until Al-Masih ad-Dajjal appears and breaks the quietness. It is then that a voice is heard, "You have done what I have ordered and I am pleased. You are to place the severed heads of these traitors of Allah in front of their bodies. When this is done, I have one more task for you before you can rest."

The men now stand at attention as each hears a voice in their heads that they must begin the last task of this day. Once all that has been asked is done, the dazed and weary group of terrorists makes their way back to camp and collapse into a fitful sleep by the campfire.

The Masih is alone as he makes his way through the empty village of Masuleh. He wishes to see that his command has been carried out as he surveys the homes of the dead. A smile crosses his lips when he sees that the men have done what they have been told to do. The words, "Lamb of God", are painted on the walls of every hut in the blood of those who have been sacrificed.

CHAPTER 22

The limousine pulls into the driveway of Beth's townhouse and the driver rings the front doorbell.

Beth is sitting on the couch obsessing over the trip she is about to take with Tom and the consequences of what it could mean. She knows that she would have many regrets, one of them being that it will permanently end her relationship with Chris. She thinks to herself; does she really want that? After all Chris is a piece of shit, but on some level, she knows that she still is in love with him and that conflicts her. Now that Tom is in her life more than before, she is more confused than ever.

Beth is so lost in her thoughts that she doesn't hear the doorbell ring at first. The driver waits a while as he doesn't know if his passenger has heard the doorbell at all. After the third try he continues to press the doorbell a number of times in a row. Beth is startled and finally runs to the door and asks the drive to come in.

"I am so sorry; I must not have heard the bell. Please come in."

The driver tells Beth, "No problem, Ms. Della Russo. Are you ready to leave? Just tell me where your luggage is and I will load it into the car." Beth shows the driver to the kitchen where she has placed her luggage. She's packed enough clothing to last for the two weeks she will be away and the driver sees the luggage and knows it will take two trips, so he immediately picks up the first load and takes it to the car.

Beth looks around to see that all is secure and that the home's alarm is set. She has arranged for her mother to come over to check the house and to water the plants so that is a relief, but she is still very depressed over what has happened between her and Chris. Beth considered cancelling out at the last minute, but she feels that is not an option as a promise is a promise.

The driver comes back to pick up the last of the luggage and asks, "Ms. Della Russo, are you ready to leave?"

Beth takes one last look around and says, "Yes, I'm ready" and she and the driver walk to the limousine parked in her driveway.

Tom Houston's private jet is housed in a hangar at Long Island's Islip/MacArthur Airport. The trip to the airport is a short 30-minute drive from Northport where Beth lives and the car enters the airport proper and pulls up to a gated and guarded entrance. This is a restricted area that caters to clientele that house their private aircraft at Islip/MacArthur and, after a cursory glance, the limo is waved in. The car drives on the runway and parks next to the very large, sleek and what looks like to Beth as a very expensive jet aircraft.

The driver gets out and opens the car door for Beth to exit. "Ms. Della Russo, I will take your luggage and have it stowed for take-off. Please be careful when you climb the stairway leading to the main cabin." Beth thanks the driver as she carefully climbs the stairway and enters the cabin.

On entering, she is flabbergasted at the beautiful interior and the spacious accommodations. There is a flight attendant to greet her, "Welcome aboard Ms. Della Russo, we are so pleased that you will be flying with us today. My Name is Sherry Temple, don't laugh, my actual name is Shirley, but I couldn't stand the teasing so I changed it. That's a true story." Sherry and Beth share a laugh.

Beth looks like a tourist staring at the lobby of some very fancy hotel when she says, "Wow, I just need to tell you that this is about the most beautiful interior of a plane that I could have ever imagined."

The flight attendant smiles and says, "It certainly is. There are twelve captain chairs set up in pairs facing each other with tables' in-between for working in-flight. The aircraft is equipped with high-speed Wi-Fi capabilities and each seat has their own power access to plug in a laptop or earphones if you prefer music or to watch TV. Each seat has its own digital screen so you can watch movies in flights. We have a library of more than one thousand full length feature films to choose from. Towards the rear of the aircraft, there is a conference table that seats eight. This is important for Dr. Houston as he and his staff have little time to waste and so much work gets done during these flights. There are sleeping quarters in the aft-cabin for Dr Houston. It's equipped with its own lavatory complete with a shower and it is always ready to accommodate him on longer flights, like when he flies overseas." Sherry is taking delight at telling Beth about the luxurious accommodation on the plane and she continue, "There are two other lavatories for guests and staff fore and aft, a full galley as well as a fully-stocked bar with wines, liquors and beer, whichever your preference. May I get you something to drink? Perhaps I can get you a glass of champagne or something else if you prefer?"

A wide-eyed Beth is still looking around, but she smiles at the attendant, "Thanks Sherry, but it's a little too early for me." Beth still remembers how drunk she got at the party for Spencer Price at Tom's fundraiser. Then she thinks, "Wait, maybe I'll have a glass of water if that's okay?"

Sherry smiles at Beth, "Sorry, we have no water."

Beth is a bit startled, "Oh, then nothing for me."

"Ms. Della Russo, I was just kidding. Of course, I will bring you a bottle. Do you prefer still or sparking?" Beth thinks for a moment and tells Sherry, "I think I'll have sparkling, after all, I'm on a private jet." They both laugh and the attendant escorts Beth to her seat. Sherry is back in a moment with the water and tells Beth that Tom will be arriving shortly and they will take off soon after that. Sherry tells Beth, "Please let me, or one of the two other flight attendants, know if you need anything."

Beth thanks her and sits down in one of the very comfortable captain's chairs and she turns to look out the plane's window. She watches the commercial aircraft taking off and landing and thinks that she could have been on one of those planes with Chris and that makes her sad. A shadow distracts Beth as she turns to find someone standing next to her and smiling. "Good morning, Ms. Della Russo, I am Captain Larry Sommers and I will be in charge on the flight to Florida."

He holds out his hand and Beth shakes it and smiles, "You have some airplane Captain Sommers, it is just beautiful."

"That it is Ms. Della Russo. It has all the safety advances and creature comforts that you would expect in an aircraft of this type, but please call me Larry."

"Then you must call me Beth."

"Alright Beth, Dr. Houston is coming on board even as we speak so we will need to prepare for takeoff and the copilot will let you know when you should buckle up. It was a pleasure to meet you."

"Same here Captain…I mean Larry!"

The captain leaves to go to the flight deck and Beth looks up when she hears a number of voices in conversations and she recognizes Tom's voice as he walks through the hatch door.

He looks around and immediately spots Beth and smiles. He walks up and kisses her on the cheek, "Boy, am I glad to see you."

"Really? Why? You did invite me, didn't you?"

"Yes, I did, but I thought that you might chicken out, but hey look, you are here and I am very happy about that."

"I'm glad to be here Tom, though I must admit that you were nearly right. I almost did chicken out, but here I am. I have to tell you that this is the last place I ever expected to be; private jet, sparkling water, Sherry, Larry and South Beach with Spencer."

Tom feigns that he is insulted, "Hey what about me? America's most eligible bachelor, don't I deserve some recognition."

Beth laughs out loud, "I hate to keep correcting you, but you are only one of America's three most eligible bachelors and, yes, you do deserve some recognition." Beth motions with her finger for Tom to come closer and when he does, she kisses him on the cheek and smiles.

Tom smiles back and touches his cheek and says, "Guess that will have to do, as I don't expect that I will ever wash my cheek again."

Beth and Tom share a laugh when the copilot comes over the speaker and tells everyone they should buckle in as their plane is next in line for takeoff, "The flying time to Miami will be three hours and 15 minutes and there are clear skies all the way down to Florida. The temperature in Miami is a balmy 81 degrees so please sit back and enjoy the beautiful day and, as there has been no reported turbulence, we can expect a very smooth flight."

Tom takes the seat directly opposite Beth and smiles, he motions to Sherry to bring him a bottle sparkling water. The plane taxis to the runway and waits for a few moments before the jet thrusters propel the aircraft down the runway and into the clear blue skies over Long Island. Beth looks out the cabin window as the plane heads south. She sees the coastal beaches, inlets and towns that overlook the beautiful Atlantic Ocean and she feels herself relaxing for the first time in days.

Tom sees that Beth seems to be enjoying herself and asks, "So Beth, what do you think of the plane?"

Beth looks at Tom; her deep brown eyes seem to sparkle with life. She jokingly says, "Amazing! So much more than an Italian girl from Huntington deserves."

"Beth, you deserve all this and more."

Beth's face turns red as she looks away from Tom and back out the window. She doesn't know how to respond to Tom, but he speaks before she has a chance. He leans over the table that separates the two. He holds out his hand in hopes that Beth will reach out and hold his. She looks back at him and she reaches for his outstretched hand. "Listen Beth, I think you are a wonderful, beautiful and kind person. I didn't mean to embarrass you, but if someone pays you a compliment you should accept it graciously and, for what it is worth, and from where it came."

Beth considers she should take Tom's good advice and accept the compliment gracefully. "I'm sorry Tom; I didn't know how to respond, but thank you for your kind words and sentiment. I'm not sure what I deserve or don't deserve, but I am very grateful for your kindness and friendship" and with that she squeezes his hand and gently sits back.

Tom smiles at her and says, "You're welcome."

Tom excuses himself once they are in-flight. "Beth, I'll just be a few minutes as I need some time to work with my team, you know, those guys over there in the pin stripe suits. I brought them along for the trip and at a combined $9,000 an hour I want to get my money's worth."

Beth says, "You gotta do what you gotta do, so don't worry about me."

Tom leaves and Beth stares out the window occasionally looking up at Tom and the men around the table. They seem to spend most of their time at the conference table discussing various aspects of the itinerary and agenda for the meetings and fundraisers. When Tom finishes, he goes back to sit opposite Beth. "Sorry for all that, but I need to get some things done with my team and now that it is taken care of, we can spend the rest of the flight talking!"

Beth teasing says, "Good idea, we land in 15 minutes so it's good we have all the time in the world to talk" now Beth laughs.

Tom seems puzzled and he looks at his watch, "My word, I can't believe that I spent nearly three hours working! I'm so sorry Beth, this was supposed to be a fun and relaxing flight, but I got distracted. I'm really sorry."

Beth now smiles and let's Tom off the hook, "I was just teasing you. If you are this busy now imagine how busy you'll be if you are elected President."

Tom considers what Beth said and responds, "Maybe I can change direction and run for Vice President! Those guys seem a lot less busy." They both laugh when Captain Larry Sommers comes back on the speaker and says, "Ladies and gentlemen, this is the captain, we are cleared for landing at Miami Executive Airport so please be sure to fasten your seat belts. We should be on the ground in 15 minutes."

The plane lands and taxis to the private terminal reserved for the special clientele. Once the plane comes to a complete stop, the captain and crew walk down the aisle to say their goodbyes to the passengers. Beth says good bye to Captain Larry Sommers and thanks him for the smooth and safe flight. She turns to Sherry and says, "Your secret is safe with me" and Beth hugs her and they share a laugh. As she and Tom walk down the stairway, Beth can see her luggage, and what she assumes is Tom's luggage, being unloaded and put into the trunk of a stretch limousine. The driver holds open the door and holds Beth's hand as she enters. The driver also has a big hello for Dr. Tom Houston and they shake hands and chat for a moment before he gets in the car. In a matter of minutes, the car leaves the airport and heads east towards South Beach and Tom's art deco townhouse overlooking the ocean.

The distance is not very far and the traffic is light as Beth and Tom talk all the way. The limo passes the historic art deco district with its beautiful architecture and water views that give this place its unique character. The limousine pulls up to a wrought iron gate which opens automatically to let them in. There is a circular driveway leading to the front door and when the car stops the staff is there to greet their boss.

The head of the staff has a big smile and a warm greeting for Tom, "Dr. Houston, it is so good to see you! When we heard you were coming, we were thrilled as we don't get to see you too much these days."

Tom smiles and embraces the man, "Phillip, it's great to see you to. As you can imagine things are pretty busy at my end, but to get down here to South Beach and see you all again is a real pleasure for me. I would like to introduce our guest, Ms. Elizabeth Della Russo."

Phillip extends his hand to shake Beth's, "Ms. Della Russo it is a pleasure to meet you and welcome to 'Escapar por el Mar', Dr. Houston's home away from home."

"Thank you so much and please call me Beth. 'Escapar por el Mar', if my high school Spanish doesn't fail me that's 'Escape by the Sea' correct?"

Phillip seems delighted to tell Beth a bit of the story behind the name. "Ah, very good and that is why it is aptly named as Dr. Houston has so little time to relax, his escape by the sea is something to savor. Dr. Houston has done an amazing job at restoring the building to its original glory and he has added much more, but perhaps Dr. Houston can be persuaded to show you around while we take the luggage to your rooms."

Beth looks around and is very surprised to see how private the property is. She turns to Tom and says, "This property is truly beautiful and it seems so private. I'd love a tour."

Tom relishes the idea of spending time, one-on-one with Beth, "That's a great idea Phillip, then we can have lunch, what do you say Beth?

"Sounds, good to me" and with that Tom extends his arm for Beth to take and they begin to walk. There is a path that meanders through the grounds and Tom explains, "I purchased the properties on both sides and in the rear of my home. South Beach can get pretty crowded and loud, especially during spring break, so I thought I would insulate myself from the noise and have the space to enjoy myself. I kept one of the homes intact which I use to house guests or some of Actelect's staff when they are down here."

Beth is wide-eyed as she looks over the grounds. There is so much to see and Tom continues, "I demolished the other homes as they had been falling apart and in need of extensive repair and with all the extra space, I've added a pool and spa, greenhouse for specimen plantings and for growing the vegetables that we eat. I'm a collector so I added garage to house some of my antique autos."

Tom then walks Beth back to his main house. He takes her on a tour of the various rooms on the ground level including the sun room, parlor, library, formal dining room and his private office. They walk up to the second floor of the townhouse and he says, "This is the master suite." Beth is overwhelmed by the sheer size of room. The master bath is amazing and she loves the beautiful way it is decorated. Even though she wants to tell Tom how magnificent it is, all she can say is say, "I think I could live in this room forever."

Tom smiles answers, "You can! All you got to do is…"

Beth laughs, "Don't press your luck buddy!"

Tom pretends to be crestfallen, "Alas, unrequited love. What have I done to deserve such a fate? But let us move on; there are seven bedrooms, each with their own bath, fireplace as well as balconies where you can enjoy morning coffee or tea for that matter. Now let me show you to your room."

Tom takes Beth down the hallway to a corner suite and opens the door. Beth is amazed; it is a carbon copy of Tom's master suite. Beth stares in disbelief, "You've got to be kidding? You mean this is where I'm staying?"

"As much as I'd rather you stayed in my suite, I guess this will have to do."

Beth smiles, "Tom this is a truly amazing place and I can see why you love it here."

Tom takes the time to look around and admits, "I do, I do love it here, but I have to remind you that we are about to have lunch and once we've eaten you can get settled in. The presentation of the check to Spencer is taking place this evening and we should leave here around 5:30P so that should give you enough time to get ready."

Beth says, "Sounds like a plan."

She and Tom walk downstairs to the patio where lunch will be served. Phillip and a woman named Martina are there to serve them and to attend to their every need. Beth is thinking, I could get used to this, but she turns sad and Tom notices the change. "Beth, is something wrong?"

Beth looks up from her plate and says, "No, no nothing's wrong. I just must be tired from the flight."

"Well, when we are finished, you can go to room and relax a bit. You can let Phillip or Martina, or anyone of the staff, know if there is anything you need."

Beth and Tom finish lunch and she thanks Phillip and Martina, "That was delicious. I think I'll go to my room and rest a bit. Can someone show me to my room and wake me up at 4P in case I really fall asleep?"

Martina says, "I will be sure to let you know when it is time."

Tom hugs Beth and says, "I'm glad you're here."

Beth smiles and answers, "So am I." and they say their good-byes and go their separate ways.

CHAPTER 23

I am lying in bed and the world around me is spinning out of control.

I can only imagine how I got home last night, given the condition I was in. I'm sure that David, the limo driver, and Amanda had something to do with this and I am grateful. I try hard to recall what happened before I passed out, but for the life of me I just can't remember. All I want to do is pass out again when I am overcome by the familiar light and I find myself in a vision.

> *The family sets out for another day in the field. They work hard to support themselves after the husband and father of the house had died. The mother has left their young 12-year-old daughter home to cook, sew and clean, while the young girl watches her youngest sister.*

The vision changes and I am observing the same young girl sitting on the steps in front of her home in the small town of Corinaldo, Italy. The sun is bright and she is sewing a tear in her older brother's shirt that he has torn while working in the fields. Maria's younger sister is sleeping and the girl is enjoying the peace and quiet of the day.

A young man, who appears to be about eighteen years old, approaches the girl. He smiles at her and tries to engage her in conversation. They appear to know each other, but the young girl seems frightened and is trying to ignore him, still he persists.

"You are looking very lovely today, Maria."

"Leave me alone Alessandro."

As Maria tried to concentrate on her sewing, Alessandro grabs her from the front steps of her home and drags her inside the house. He yells at the young girl and forces himself on her in an attempt to rape her. Maria cries out that it is a mortal sin against the will of God. She struggles to break free of his grasp, but he is too strong. Maria screams at him saying, ""No! It is a sin! God does not want it! You will go to hell if you do this!" When Alessandro hears Maria say this, he begins to choke her.

The young girl fights Alessandro's advances and screams that she would rather die than commit this sinful act. Alessandro then pulled out a knife he has concealed in his pants and stabs the girl eleven times. Still alive, Maria tries to reach the door, where Alessandro stabs her again three more times then flees.

As with many of my visions, I am stunned by what I see. The vison changes and I am in a hospital room. There is the poor girl, Maria, lying in bed covered in bandages. Her distraught mother is holding her daughter's hand and weeping. There is a doctor standing alongside the bed and he appears to be despondent.

Her family has taken her to the hospital where Maria under-goes surgery without anesthesia. In enormous pain, Maria turns her gaze from her mother to the doctor and speaks, "Doctor, am I going to die."

The doctor knows her wounds are beyond his ability to help so he tells her, "Maria, think of me in Paradise."

As she lay on the table, she looks up at him and says, "Well, who knows which of us is going to be there first?" She does not realize how terrible her wounds are, but all becomes clear as the surgeon replies, "You, Maria."

Maria becomes thoughtful and smiles as she tells the doctor, "Then I will think gladly of you."

Maria has only two thoughts. She looks at her mother and says, "I do not wish you to be sorrowful and to grieve for me, I am going to be with the Lord my God and I am at peace. As she lay dying, she tells her mother she forgives Alessandro and says she wishes to see him in Heaven with her.

In the young girl's last moments, she holds a cross to her chest while looking at an image of the Virgin Mary.

The vision dissolves and I am standing next to St. Maria Goretti. I am at a loss to understand the vision and its meaning. I am trying to come up with the words, any words, to say having witnessed such a tragedy, but it is unnecessary as St. Maria speaks.

"Christopher, it is important that you understand many things; above all, the power of evil to corrupt. When Alessandro sought to rape me, I saw the face of pure evil. He became outraged; it was as if he was possessed."

I question her and ask, "How is it you can forgive someone so evil after what he did to you? He took your life; he took you away from your family, away from all that you loved."

The Sainted Maria Goretti looks at me and tells me, "One of the rewards of heaven is that you are at peace. You are given complete understanding, and for me, the understanding that Alessandro was overcome by the forces of evil, perhaps Satan himself, it was a revelation. I was able to forgive Alessandro because my faith called for nothing less. In life he repented, and while in prison he changed his ways and redeemed himself and now he has earned his heavenly reward too."

"What are you telling me?"

"I am here to tell you that for you that the face of evil no longer hides behind a mask. It is an ever-growing menace and it has become so pervasive that soon it will encompass all of humanity."

Given what I have seen and learned from my uncle, I am not surprised, but I am very fearful of more horrors to come. "All humanity; what do you mean all humanity, what will happen, when will it happen, where will it happen?" Questions just keep pouring from my mind and out of my mouth. I have no idea what the answers might be, but I am afraid that I may not want to hear them.

The vision of St. Maria begins to dissolve, however before she is called back to Heaven she says, "You have seen certain signs, but there are many more to come. You are to fight this evil and to help those in need, that is your purpose here, but you will never need to rely on your faith more than at this time."

"How can I fight such and evil? All humanity, what can I do?"

The vision of St. Maria is nearly gone, but she ends by saying, "Much, you will be called on to do much. The Lamb of God is with you."

CHAPTER 24

Al is holding onto Fr. Aiden's hand for dear life. His friend is alive and it is, for him, a miracle.

Fr. Aiden Langford squeezes Al's hand and in a voice that should sound weak, but does not, says, "Spartaco, you are a sight for these sore eyes."

Al finally gets over his initial shock, "Aiden, I thank the Lord that you are awake. Do you know what happened to you?"

Fr. Aiden thinks for a moment, "The last thing I can accurately remember is collapsing outside the confessional. I am assuming that I had another myocardial infarction event and this is the reason I am so encumbered by wires, needles and monitoring devices."

"Good guess Aiden, you're right." All I can say is that this has got to be the work of the Lord that you are alive and I am able to speak to my friend. I might have to rethink that whole praying, Bible and Sunday Mass thing."

Father Aiden chuckles at the inside joke between the friends and say, "Alas, my lifelong wish has come true! I can't wait to hear your confession Spartaco!"

Al smiles and says, "Let's take this one step at a time."

Now both men laugh.

The door to the ICU bursts open and Dr. Simonelli and the critical care unit comes rushing in. The doctor speaks first, "Fr. Langford, we saw the remote monitor that keeps track of your condition and I have to say that we are surprised and thrilled to find you so alert! This is very good news and now chief, you're going to have to leave the room while we give Father Langford a complete examination."

A very serious look comes over Father Aiden's face. "Dear doctor, I need to converse with Spartaco in private, so the examination will, of necessity, have to wait."

Dr. Simonelli smiles and says, "Father, when I am in church, you call the shots, but this is my church and you are my, how shall I it put it, my flock; that's it, my flock, and you need to do what I say. Understand?"

Fr. Aiden protests, "But, dear doctor, you do not comprehend. I have some very grave and compelling information that I must convey…"

Dr. Simonelli is used to having to deal with difficult patients and tells the priest, "If, and this is a big 'if', after I examine you and determine that you are not in danger of another heart attack and that you are strong enough, I will allow the chief in to speak with you…"

"My dear doctor, I am fine! Fit as a fiddle I assure you, as I am fully in tune with my bodily idiosyncrasies. All I am asking for is a few moments to converse with my dearest friend…"

Dr. Simonelli looks at his patient and, in as eloquent a manner as he can summon up says, "Father Langford, I understand that you are a devotee of the Bard."

Fr. Aiden immediately brightens up, "Ah! England's gift to the WORLD! Yes, yes I am his most devoted fan…still alive that is."

"Yes, England's gift to the world. Well, I am also a lover of Shakespeare and I remember quotes that I've had to use on patients like you. *'A fool thinks himself to be wise, but a wise man knows himself to be a fool'*, how about *'Wisely, and slow. They stumble that run fast'* or *"How poor are they that have not patience! What wound did ever heal but by degrees?'* Which are you Father, an impatient, fast fool or a slow healing, wise man?"

Fr. Aiden looks downcast at his doctor and says, "Alas, as it written in the Bible, Job 10:15, *'Woe is me'*; you have turned the words of my beloved Bard against me, but I cannot deny, *'How sharper than a serpent's tooth it is to have a thankless child!'*

Dr. Simonelli relishes having the upper hand. "So, does this mean I will have your full cooperation?"

"Yes, of course, I know when I am beaten…like a rented mule as you in the colonies like to say."

"Now again, we will give you a complete examination and if I, and only I, think you are healthy enough to speak to your best friend, then I will allow you to speak for 10 minutes."

Father interrupts, "In private?"

"Yes, in private, for 10 minutes. Are we in agreement?"

"Yes, dear doctor, we are in complete agreement." Father Aiden Langford then turns to his friend, Chief Barese and says, "Spartaco, I have much to tell you and I am sure you will be interested."

The chief has a feeling about what Aiden will want to say and he replies, "I am looking forward to it Aiden, but please listen to the doctor, I don't want to lose you again."

Fr. Langford smiles and says, "You honor me, my friend and I will leave my health and wellbeing to the splendid physician standing by my side."

Chief Barese says, "Good, I'll be in the waiting room."

Al Barese leaves Aiden's room in the ICU and goes to the main waiting room to call the office. Al is concerned with all that is going on and he needs to speak to Aiden to find out what he may know as a result of what happened in the confessional. He finds a seat in a quiet corner of the waiting area and calls his next in command, Dan Orello.

The phone rings and Dan answers, "This is Dan Orello."

"Dan, this is Al I wanted to call for an update."

Dan takes a deep breath, but before he speaks, he asks, "Hi chief, how's Aiden?"

"You're not going to believe this, but he came out of the coma and seems to be in good spirits. The doctor is examining him now, and if his doctor approves, I can have 10 minutes with him. Hopefully that will give us some more information to work with."

Dan is relieved, "That is good news."

"Yeah, it is, now what do you have to tell me."

Dan takes a deep breath and says, "Chief, you're not gonna like this."

CHAPTER 25

Tom Houston's limousine pulls in front of the Price Clinic for Cancer Research and the driver opens the door to let Beth and Tom exit the car.

The parking lot is full of cars, mostly those of the employees of the institute, but there are a number of other cars and vans with logos of the local media. Tom assumes that the word is out that he will be presenting Dr. Spencer Price with a check for $47,000,000, and it will be a good thing to have the press their to publicize this event and further elevate his profile.

Beth looks especially beautiful tonight and Tom smiles at the thought of making a grand entrance into the clinic with her. He holds out his arm, inviting Beth to take it, and they walk into the reception area of the building. The media has taken up a position just inside the entrance so that when Tom and Beth walk in, they are greeted with cameras, video equipment and a gaggle of reporters screaming questions at them.

Speaking over one another, reporters try to get Tom Houston's attention, "Dr. Houston! Dr. Houston!" but not one individual is acknowledged. Instead, Tom takes the opportunity to speak, "Please, please tone it down would you." The reporters become quiet and he tells them, "I am delighted to be here to make this presentation; donations from some very generous people who want to give something back to Dr. Price for his unwavering devotion and tireless work on behalf of a cause that is worthy of our highest praise. As many, if not all of us here, have lost someone close to them due to the scourge of cancer, we can now take comfort in the hope that the work of the Price Clinic for Cancer Research can continue for years to come. Now if you will allow us, I am being summoned to present this to Dr. Price."

A reporter yells out, "Who's the pretty lady with you?"

Beth turns red in the face and Tom answers, "None of your business" and he smiles and waves as he walks through the crowd. There is someone waiting who will escort Tom and Beth to the lecture hall. In the hall there is a large group of attendees gathered and all are engaged in conversations and everyone seems in a very happy mood. When Tom and Beth come through the entry, there to greet them is Dr. Spencer Price who seems genuinely delighted to see them both.

Dr. Price is effusive in his greeting to both Beth and Tom. "Beth, I am so happy that you are here at the presentation to celebrate this wonderful and most generous gift. Tom, I can't thank you enough…that's all the gushing I'm going to do!" Now Beth, Tom and Spencer laugh and Beth embraces Spencer.

Beth looks radiant and she kisses Spencer on the cheek and smiles, "Dr, Price I am so honored to be here, you know I'm your biggest fan!"

"Hey, what about me?" Tom pretends to be insulted at not being appreciated. "I'm the one with the $47 million and you both seem to only have eyes for each other."

Dr. Price laughs, "Ah! that I was only 50 years younger, and then I would give you a run for your money with this beauty, Tom."

Now Beth is laughing, "Spencer, you will always be my hero and you will always have a very special place in my heart." Spencer smiles and sticks his tongue out at Tom and the three of them laugh again, this time out loud.

A podium has been set up on the stage in the lecture hall and because it is time for the presentation, a spokesman for the clinic announces that everyone should take their seats as the presentation is about to begin. All there in attendance jockey for the best seats and the loud conversations simmer down to low volume chatter.

The spokesman begins the ceremony by introducing Tom, "Ladies and gentlemen, thank you for being here on this very special occasion. As you are all aware, the Price Clinic for Cancer Research is a pioneer in finding effective treatments that will ultimately result in finding a cure for this deadly disease. We are indeed fortunate to have the world's renowned authority on cancer research, Dr. Spencer Price as our leader." At the mention of Dr. Price's name, the entire audience erupts in applause.

Once the applause dies down, the spokesman continues, "Now I would like to introduce our very special guest who will be making a presentation to the good doctor. Dr. Thomas Houston is an American success story. He has achieved what few men have ever achieved. He now heads ACTELECT, the largest think tank in the world and if that were not enough, he is running for the nomination of the Socialist Liberation Party for president." On hearing this, the audience jumps to their feet and cheers.

Again, the spokesman allows for the cheers to subside. "Through his generosity, Dr. Houston has donated many millions of dollars to the Price Clinic for Cancer Research and this largesse has allowed us to continue our work in hopes of one day finding a cure for cancer. Ladies and gentlemen, please join me in giving a warm and much deserved welcome to Dr. Thomas Houston!"

Now all in the audience are on their feet, thunderously applauding and cheering Tom as he walks out on the stage. Tom shakes the hand of the spokesman and steps up to the podium to make his remarks. The heartfelt show of appreciation from the crowd makes Tom smile as he waves to all.

"Thank you…thank you so much…what a wonderful and greatly appreciated welcome you've given me." The applause is allowed to subside and Tom continues, "I want you all to know how excited I am to be here and how much I love your boss, Dr. Spencer Price!" The crowd takes the cue and gives a standing ovation at the mention of Spencer's name.

"For those of you who know Spencer well enough, I am sure that you can relate at least one story that will live on in your memory and I have one, actually one of many I'd like to tell you. Now let me see, where should I begin? Oh, yes! All of you in the audience know how infinitely patient and understanding Spencer is." Now everyone bursts into laughter at the mere thought of the words, 'patience', 'understanding' and 'Spencer' being in the same sentence.

"Well Spencer and I were at a wonderful restaurant in New York. I won't mention the name, but the food, service and ambiance were perfect and to put it in proper perspective, it is rated 3 Stars by Michelin. At any rate, it was an extraordinarily busy evening for the restaurant and when we arrived, we had to wait a few extra minutes before we were seated; this requires patience. When the maître d' seated us, he tried to apologize for the wait; this requires understanding. The waiter came with the menus and, in welcoming us, he took his time handing the menu to Spencer; this requires patience. The waiter now asks if we would like something to drink, you know cocktail or wine, and I said we would like to look at the wine list; this requires understanding. The waiter said that he would have the sommelier bring over the list...this requires both patience and understanding. We were asked our preferences by the sommelier and we were given an extensive dissertation on the various wines offered...this requires patience. I placed our order and the sommelier had the temerity to ask, 'Shall I bring two glasses?'; this requires both patience and understanding. With that, Spencer gave one of his special 'Harrumphs' as only Spencer can. We now are in a relaxed conversation with each other and the waiter returns with the bottle of wine I had selected. He carefully places a glass in front of both Spencer and I and we wait in eager anticipation. Now, it was a very expensive bottle of wine and there is a ritual associated with drinking fine wine; you know, looking for color and clarity, swirling the wine, taking a small sip...again, this requires both patience and understanding. Now here's the first mistake the waiter makes by pouring a small amount of wine into Spencer's glass. Spencer looks at the wine and looks up at the waiter; he looks back down at the wine and backup at the waiter and says, 'What the fuck am I supposed to do with this?" The audience now convulses into uproarious laughter at the mere thought of Dr. Price cursing at the waiter, who was surely in shell shock.

Tom is now laughing out loud himself at the story he's telling and concludes his tribute, "The story of my dinner with Spencer does go on and on. There's the ordering of the dinner itself, the renowned chef who is ready to quit or slash his throat and the unexpected dessert, but I think I've embarrassed Spencer enough. I am also sorry to report though, as far as I know, the waiter is still in therapy." The crowd continues to laugh out loud themselves and bursts into applause.

Tom looks to the side of the stage where Spencer in standing, smiling and laughing at himself. "Spencer, come out here, come on." Spencer walks out on stage and embraces Tom and he is still laughing when Spencer turns to the audience and says to the assembled crowd, "I don't want that story to leave this room, make sure you don't tell that story to anyone"; there is more laughter and applause.

Tom now puts his arm around Spencer's shoulder and speaks, "Dr. Price you are about the most original man I know. You are dogged about getting it right, you are unrelenting on achieving excellence, you keep finding ways to motivate your staff, you are tireless, you are brilliant and the most determined man I know." Tom reaches into the inside pocket of his jacket and pulls out and envelope. "Dr. Spencer Price, I am so proud to present you this check made out to the Price Clinic for Cancer Research for $47,000,000 so you may continue to achieve what we know you are determined to achieve; a cure for cancer."

There is a tear coming from Spencer's eye as he hugs Tom. The audience is overcome with emotion as they do not often see Dr. Price showing such a reaction. These men and women are all dedicated to the mission of the clinic and they are most grateful for the donation that will help them to continue their work.

Spencer is overcome with emotion and he wants to say a few words to the crowd. "Friends, I am truly overcome with gratitude for this remarkable and meaningful gift to our clinic. For those of you who have worked tirelessly by my side, exhibiting dedication to our mission, I cannot thank you enough. Just a few decades ago cancer was thought of as a death sentence for so many. This dreaded illness not only affects the patient, but it impacts the lives of his or her family and friends. Thanks to our initiative we can give hope to so many and the chance for a cure that will change the world. I want to close by expressing my heartfelt gratitude to Dr. Thomas

Houston who was instrumental in raising this extremely generous donation. Thank you from the bottom of my heart!"

The audience erupts in thunderous applause as Tom and Spencer turn
to the crowd and wave to the cheering mass.

Spencer continues, "By the way if you see me in the hallway, ask me
to tell you the story about Dr. Houston and the schnauzer that tried to
kill him!"

The audience erupts in laughter. Beth is on the side of the stage looking
out at Tom, Spencer and at the crowd. She doesn't know how she feels,
how can she have feelings for Tom and be in love with Chris? Tom is
smiling as he looks over to where Beth is standing and winks. She smiles
back at Tom and winks.

CHAPTER 26

The vision of St. Maria Goretti seems to sober me up a bit, but I when I return to present day reality, I am not spared the awful hangover from the amount of tequila I consumed. During any vision I have, I always feel well, even if I am sick or even hung over, but that is short lived as I return to the present, my hangover is still there.

I try to remember how I got home and how I managed to get undressed and into my bed.

I look at my watch and see that it is nearly 12 Noon so I drag my ass up and out of bed. I look at my phone and I see its Sunday and I missed Mass. Now I think that I need to add that to a list of my sins that seem to be growing exponentially. I make my way around the condo looking for someone who can tell me what I missed last night, but there is no one here.

My last stop is in the kitchen where I see a note on the table. I pick it up and start to read the note out loud, but that just makes my headache much worse so I silently and slowly go over what is written;

Hi Chris,

Well, we certainly tied one on last night...thank goodness one of us can hold his, I mean her, liquor. In case you were wondering, David took us home and he was the one who got you undressed and into bed.

I must say that you are a very expensive drunk. You must have had at least 8 or 9 shots of some very expensive tequila and I don't know how I'm going to explain this on my expense account. I would have stayed at your place, but I had an early interview in the city so David drove me to my hotel.

I should be back by about 2 o'clock in the afternoon and then we can figure out what to do for the rest of the day.

By the way, nice underwear!

Love,
Amanda

I look down at my underwear and I have to say that I think Amanda is right, my underwear is nice. My head continues to pound in spite of my underwear, and I am hoping that a cold shower would have a mitigating effect on the throbbing going on in my head. I head for the bathroom and take a long hot shower and end it by turning on the cold water to be sure that I am fully awake. I exit the shower and brush my teeth trying to get rid of the sour taste of tequila and the accompanying array of trappings that come with consuming tequila shots. I finally have the courage to look in the mirror and see that I am a bit less for the wear, but not as bad as I expected. A quick shave and I put on my robe before I make my way back to the kitchen.

I put a pod of regular Columbian coffee into the machine and I wait for the water to get hot. The aroma of a freshly brewed cup of coffee is welcome and finally I am able to have a cup and sit down to try and make sense of the vision, my night with Amanda and what this all means. Although I am disturbed by the vision and its meaning, I cannot help, but continue thinking of Amanda and Beth and the dilemma of it all. I have no appetite so after a second cup of coffee I go back to my bedroom and get dressed. I am usually fastidious about making my bed and cleaning up after myself, but I think that maybe I'll put it off. Then I remember Amanda will be coming back, so I push through it all with a throbbing headache. When I'm done, I take two aspirins and go into the living room and collapse on the sofa. While there I turn on the TV and lie down on the couch, close my eyes and just listen to the local news channel.

The announcer is telling viewers, "...as the Palestinians rain down Iranian rockets on the small Israeli town, the prime minister vows that the Israeli defense forces will take swift and appropriate action in response." Being a consumer of news, it seems to me as if this type of bulletin is becoming all too common and it's very depressing.

The news anchor continues, "Our next item has to do with presidential contender, atheist and billionaire socialist, Dr. Thomas Houston." I immediately jump up to a sitting position to see a stock photo of Tom Houston. The photo quickly changes to a video of Tom on stage handing a check to Dr. Price. "Dr. Houston was in Miami to present a contribution of $47,000,000 to Dr. Spencer Price of the Price Clinic for Cancer Research. The money was raised at a celebrity and star-studded event at Dr. Houston's Garden City mansion." The mere mention of the fundraising event conjures up such bad memories that I feel my anger returning enough to eclipse my hangover. As I am watching, the scene changes to Dr. Price and Tom Houston talking to a reporter. They are telling the reporter what the donation means to the clinic and how the funds will be used. I then notice that, standing behind Tom is Beth. At the sight of Beth with Tom, my heart sinks and I find myself falling into an even deeper depression.

The announcer concludes that Tom Houston and his entourage will be making appearances in Florida over the next two weeks to meet and greet donors and voters alike in his bid for the Socialist Liberation Party nomination for president. When we get back LI News Network will have a story about a new theme park opening..." I shut off the TV and sink even lower into the cushion. My worst suspicions and my deepest fears have been realized, Beth is with Tom and I am out of her life for good.

Still seated on my couch, I continue to stare at the blank screen on my TV no longer interested in watching any program. My emotions are so mixed that I find myself wallowing in such self-pity that I fail to hear the doorbell ring. Finally, I am shaken out of my catatonic state by a pounding at the front door. I jump up realizing that someone wants to get in and I make my way to the door and open it.

"What does a girl have to do to get you to answer the door?" A beautiful, smiling Amanda Sellers stands there and says, "Well, aren't you going to invite me in?"

I look around to be sure that I'm at home, "Uh, huh? What?"

"Can I come in?" Amanda doesn't wait for an answer as she enters my condo. She brushes up against me and gives me a kiss on the cheek.

I look down at my wrist and I realize that I'm not wearing my watch and I don't have my phone to tell me the time. "What time is it?"

"It's a little before 2 o'clock. We hit some traffic on the Long Island Expressway, but I'm still here on time." Amanda takes one look at me and she appears like she is about to burst into laughter, "By the way, how are you feeling on this glorious day?"

For some reason I don't share Amanda's exuberance over this glorious day and I mumble, "What glorious day?"

"The one outside silly…come on, let's do something! We can't let this day go to waste; what would you like to do?"

I consider what I'd like to do and I say to Amanda, "I'd like to crawl into a hole and die, thank you. I hope that meets with your approval."

Now Amanda looks at me in a thinly disguised of look of shock and confusion, "Why Christopher, please don't tell me that you are in any way, shape or form, hung over? I would be very upset if I thought that our overindulgence in the fruit of the agave has in any way contributed to this morose outlook. Come on, get dressed so we can do something." Amanda teases me and says in a singsong voice, "I've still got the limm-mmo! David can drive us anywhere you want to take me so what do you say? I've got a big surprise for you!"

I look questioningly at Amanda, "Surprise? What surprise?"

"I'm not telling you until you get dressed and take me somewhere on this glorious day."

Reluctantly I agree to get dressed. I put on my clothing and shuffle my way back into the living room where Amanda is waiting. "Does this meet with your approval?"

"It does, so where do you want to go?"

"Back to sleep."

"Come on, where do you want to go?"

I seem to perk-up a bit and tell her, "Okay, I know when I'm beaten. By the way, how did the interview, or whatever you did in the city, go?"

Amanda looks at me in surprise and says, "I can't believe that you remembered! It went great and they absolutely love me!"

I smile at Amanda and tell her, "I'm happy, I really am. Well, let's get back to the glorious day and what to do. I know a really great place out in Montauk Point. They have the freshest, most delicious lobsters and clams and a beautiful view of the ocean."

"Sounds great, but we have to be back in the city at 6 PM."

"6 PM? Why?"

"That's the surprise, but I'll tell you anyway; I am taking you to a black-tie event at the St. Regis Hotel. The studio is having a party around the release of my latest film and it will be a lot of fun. Plenty of stars, plenty of food, plenty of fun...The Rolling Stones will be performing a private concert just for us!"

"The Rolling Stones?" I am a classic rock mega-fan and just hearing the name 'Rolling Stones' makes my eyes pop. "THE Rolling Stones?"

Amanda knows she has hit a home run with me. "Yes, 'THE Rolling Stones'. They wrote and recorded the theme song for my new movie and I'll even get you into the green room to meet the boys!"

"Amanda, I can't believe this! But there are a few logistical concerns; first, Montauk is too far for us to go and come back to be in the city by 6 PM, second, I have no tuxedo and third, given the way I feel, I may never drink again."

Amanda laughs, "First, we'll do Montauk another time, second, Harry told me your size and I have your tuxedo waiting at the hotel and third, well, you have to figure that out for yourself. So, what do you say, we can do something local if you want or we can do a tourist thing in the city?"

I figure that given Amanda's popularity, walking around New York City would be series of photos with fans, autographs and not much fun. I tell this to Amanda and she agrees so I suggest that we rent a small boat, some rods and reels and go into the bay and fish.

"Wow, that sounds perfect, but I've never been fishing and you're going to have to bait the hook for me."

I agree to the bait issue and tell Amanda, "No problem, but before we go, give me a chance to pack the cooler with something to drink and maybe some snacks or something to eat, what do you say?"

Amanda seems happy and she says, "Works for me!"

I get everything ready and we leave the condo. David is waiting by the limo and he opens the door and we get in the rear. The marina is very close so I give him instructions on where to go and we are off to Huntington Harbor and what I hope will be a relaxing few hours.

When we arrive, I get out and walk to the office and speak to Jack Trent, a friend who owns a marina in the harbor. "Hey Chris, long time no see, how have you been?"

"Fine Jack, fine."

"How's Beth?"

I don't want to tell him, but I realize I'm with Amanda and he'd probably figure it out. "Uh, we kind of broke up."

"Wow, I'm so sorry to hear that."

I want to get off the subject, so I start to ask Jack about renting a boat for a couple of hours when I feel a tap on my shoulder. I turn and it's Amanda smiling at me so I introduce her to Jack, "Jack Trent, this is Amanda Sellers. I want to show her around our beautiful waters."

Jack immediately recognizes Amanda and says, "Wow, you're Amanda Sellers, the movie star, aren't you?"

She smiles and says, "Last time I checked; pleased to meet you, Jack."

"Well, there's only one way that I'll rent you a boat Chris, it's that Amanda here has to sign the papers so I can frame it and plaster the contract on my wall. I'll also need an autographed photo that's signed, 'To Jack, the one that got away! With all my love, Amanda.' This is sure to piss off the other guys who rent boats around here. What do you say Amanda?"

"With pleasure, I like nothing better than pissing off the other boat rental guys."

We laugh and Jack gets all the paperwork while Amanda goes to the limo to get a photo to sign. Jack fills the boat with fuel and asks us if we need rods, reels and bait.

"We do Jack. What's running?"

"Fluke, there out there in decent numbers and they are really good eating."

"Great."

Jack turns to Amanda who hands him her photo and he is smiling from ear to ear. He asks Amanda, "Ever been fishing before?"

"No, I haven't"

"Well Chris is a good fisherman and he'll show you the ropes…" now Jack winks at Amanda, "…and maybe more if you let him."

I cringe at the comment from this idiot friend of mine, "Don't listen to this jackass Amanda."

Amanda gives me a puzzled look and flirtatiously bats her eyelashes, "I don't understand, Chris, what does he mean when he says, maybe you'll show me more than the ropes?"

Now Jack and Amanda are cracking up and I can't wait to get on the boat and out of the marina.

CHAPTER 27

The fundraiser for Tom Houston's presidential campaign is in full swing and the ballroom of the Four Seasons Hotel in Miami is filled to overflowing.

Tom Houston's limousine pulls into the parking lot entrance to avoid the crush of onlookers and media. As they enter the garage though, Beth notices a small group of perhaps 80 people holding signs protesting Tom's views on illegal immigration, euthanasia, the police defunding, his atheism, and many more controversial positions he has taken during his career and on the presidential campaign. The demonstrators scream as they see his limo coming and shout out in protest. Beth doesn't know what to make of it, other than she is a bit disturbed.

"Tom, it seems that not everyone here is friendly to your campaign."

"Yeah, I get this all the time and I just try to ignore them because I'll never get their votes anyway."

Beth has a serious question, "Do you judge a person solely based on whether they will vote for you or not."

Tom thinks about it for a moment, "I guess not, but I'll never be able to convince these people of my position and they can't convince me of theirs, so why bother."

"It would seem to me that if you are going to be president you should want to try and have a dialogue with people even if they don't agree with you."

"When I'm president I will make sure that the government provides every citizen those things that they need and this way they are taken care of. Having the ability to control how tax dollars are spent makes it much easier for people, even those who don't vote for me, to set aside their concerns and let government handle it all."

"Sounds a little scary to me."

Tom smiles, "Don't be scared, I'm really a sweetheart!"

Tom and Beth exit the limo and walk towards the ballroom where the event is taking place. As the guest of honor arrives, he is immediately besieged by celebrity well-wishers and the mega donors that have received his personal invitation. Beth finds herself shoved aside as Tom is swept away by enthusiastic crowds looking to merely have a chance to greet the man who could become his party's nominee for president.

Beth seems a bit relieved as she does not want to find herself anywhere close to the center of attention, so she walks over to the bar for a drink. She decides to stick with sparkling water for fear of a repeat of what happened at the fundraiser hosted by Tom for Dr. Price. The memory of the night she spent at Tom's mansion also conjures up recollections of the last time she spoke to Chris. The horrible things they said to each other and the way that phone call ended with seemingly no chance for reconciliation. She is still angry, but she is conflicted over her feelings for Chris and pangs of regret that are somewhere in the back of her mind.

Beth starts to walk through the crowd when she gets a tap on her shoulder. She turns around and she comes face-to-face with Hamilton Cargill.

"My dear Beth, what a joy it is to see you again. I have had time to think about our last meeting when I proposed to you."

Beth laughs, "I think you took back your proposal and offered me a house with a pool instead."

"Ah yes, you are absolutely correct! Now, however, I have a very different proposal this time."

Beth looks questioningly at Hamilton, "You do? This I'd like to hear."

Hamilton smiles and says, "I'm sure you will! How about an all-expense paid vacation and grand tour of Italy? After all, you are of Italian descent! I am looking at a six-to-eight-week tour as that is the time I have before filming my next feature film. When we complete our tour, and when we have had a chance to fully evaluate my proposed convivial, pseudo-connubial co-habitation experience, I am sure that we will blissfully conclude we are meant for each other and ride off into the sunset to live happily ever after! What say you to my magnificent offer?"

Beth thinks for a moment, "Not a bad idea, I'd like to hear what Tom would have to say about all this?"

Now it seems that Hamilton is questioning his most recent offer to Beth and says, "On second thought if he becomes president, I may have to cloister myself from the forces that will seek to avenge him. This may not be the opportune moment. I've got it! What's say I buy you an even bigger house with a bigger pool than in my original proposal!"

They both laugh and Beth says, "Done!"

Beth and Hamilton continue to talk and are having a good time when Tom is able to break away from the crowds of donors to join them. Tom joins the conversation, "Well I see you two caught up with each other. Beth, has Hammy been bothering you?"

"Not at all, as a matter of fact, I was just asked to join Hamilton on a grand tour of Italy, but when he thought better of it, we entered into negotiations and he decided to offer me a bigger home and larger pool than before!"

Tom immediately chimes in, "I hope you said 'Done'?" Their small group laughs and continues to speak to each other as onlookers stop by to shake both Tom's and Hamilton's hands. Beth is happy to step aside and let the famous men take the spotlight.

The staff of the hotel announces that the dinner is commencing and invited guests work their way towards the dining room. "Well Hammy, they are calling us to the banquet hall and I'll be escorting Beth who will be sitting with me on the dais. We'll see you inside and don't get too jealous."

"What! Beth, please sit with me! Did you know that Tom is a very sloppy eater? I once saw him try to swallow an entire Chilean Seabass, alive!"

Tom now tries to set the record straight, "It wasn't an entire Chilean seabass, it happened to be an entire Grouper."

Hamilton feels the need to clarify the facts, "Beth if you could have seen the size of the Seabass or Grouper or whatever, you would never want to be seen with this man. I'll tell you what; I'll make it a small mansion, with a pool and tennis court as well as a brand-new automobile of your choice. What do you say?"

Beth looks at Tom and Hamilton and says, "I see Dr. Spencer Price, I think I'll eat with him" and she turns to walk away when Tom grabs her arm. "Okay, I'll give you a larger mansion and use of my private jet as many times as you want."

Now they all burst out into laughter and Beth reaches over to Hamilton and pats him on the shoulder. "You almost had me with the offer of a car, but it was the private jet that closed the deal for me." Beth took both their arms and they walked into the banquet hall in a very festive mood. All the tables in the dining room are filled with those who spent $100,000 plus for a table of ten. There are very lively conversations taking place at the tables and all seems to be going well.

Tom escorts Beth to the dais where she is seated a few seats away from Tom. He explains that he needs to make a speech at some point and there are major party dignitaries and donors that were promised a special place of honor next to him. "Sorry about that Beth, but you will be sitting next to Stephen Kindslow, the famous author. I'm sure he will keep you entertained."

Beth smiles, "I'm sure he will. Good luck with your speech."

The dinner, speeches and evening's entertainment went on until well after 1AM and the excitement and rigors of travel start to take their toll on Beth. Tom and Hamilton Cargill are speaking to each other and laughing at some private joke when Tom looks over to see Beth yawning.

"Hey, you look beat."

"I am."

"Listen Beth, I have to stay and mingle, press the flesh, you know how these things are. I can have my limo take you home so you can get a good night's sleep. What do you say?"

Hamilton butts in, "I can go with Beth and make sure she gets tucked in! What do you say Beth?"

Beth tries to smile, "No thank you Hamilton, I can tuck myself in. Thanks Tom, I would appreciate it if your driver can take me back to your home."

"No problem." Tom calls over Nancy McGrath, his chief-of-staff and asks her to escort Beth to the limo for her drive back to his estate. Nancy's pasted on smile remains and Beth follows her out the door.

Beth kisses both men on their cheeks as Hamilton and Tom watch Beth exit. Hamilton sighs out loud and turns to tell Tom, "You are one lucky son of a bitch."

Tom, still looking at Beth, says, "I know I am. You are looking at the future Mrs. Thomas Houston and the next First Lady of the United States."

CHAPTER 28

Chief Al Barese is waiting in the visitors lounge to hear the results of the doctor's examination of Fr. Aiden Langford.

Al is immensely happy that his friend has come out of the coma and appears to be conscious and lucid although weak from his heart attack. The chief is anxious to hear the details of the incident at Immaculate Conception Seminary, what happened in the confessional and the knowledge he may have relating to the crimes of violence and murder ascribed to the Lamb of God. The chief is pacing back and forth when his phone chimes.

"Chief Barese here."

"Hi chief this is Dan. How are you holding up?"

"Much better than I was. Aiden is out of his coma and the doctors are examining him right now. "

"Wow! That is great news."

"Yeah, it is. I'm hoping to have a few minutes with him so I can get any information he may have."

Dan goes quiet for a short moment when the chief says, "Dan, you still there?"

"Sorry chief, I was just handed the latest update on the investigations currently being handled and I am at a loss. There are so many crimes that it is almost impossible to keep up. Our team is up to their eyeballs in this mess and many of the new cases that have been reported are being sidelined. It is a real shitstorm and I need to have some help with all this."

"Dan, can you patch me in to the Suffolk County Police Commissioner's office. I want approval to reactivate some retired detectives with experiences in violent crimes and homicides. I'll also request adding some civilian personnel to take over clerical duties. Hopefully this can free up officers to assist in the investigations, both new and old."

"Sounds good to me chief, hang on and I'll call and see if she's available and I can conference you in."

A few seconds pass by and the conference call is connected, "Good morning chief, this is Commissioner Petry; I am painfully aware that we have a real shitstorm going on."

"Good morning commissioner, yes we do, that's why I'm calling."

"What do you need?"

"As you know there are so many current investigations that any new incidents being reported have to be set aside. I think we may need to contact some detective retirees and ask them to come back in to help out. Also, if we had civilian administrative assistants to relieve officers on desk duty, we can redeploy the officers to help out. We need this to happen as fast as possible."

The commissioner is silent for a moment when she says, "I'll call the County Exec and get the ball rolling at our end, budget and personnel wise. Meanwhile contact those retirees that you think are best suited and put them on standby."

"Thanks Commissioner. We'll keep you posted and let us know if there is anything we can do or if there are complications at your end."

"I will and keep me in the loop." and the commissioner hangs up

Al then asks, "Dan are you still on?"

"Yes, chief. I heard what she said and I'll make some calls to guys that I think can get involved immediately. If we have them onboard that would be a big help."

"Listen Dan, I need to be here a while longer as I've got to speak with Aiden. You can reach me at any time and if I can't answer, I'll call you back as soon as I can."

"Thanks chief and send our best wishes to Aiden for a speedy recovery."
"I will."

Dan and Al disconnect and Al goes back to pacing the floor of the visitor's lounge. He knows that he will have only about ten minutes with Fr. Langford so he's trying to collect his thoughts. Al makes notes of some of what he wants to ask his friend and is looking them over when Dr. Simonelli comes into the waiting area to speak to the chief.

"Well chief, we examined Fr. Langford and determined that he is no longer in any immediate danger, but he is in an extremely weakened state. We will keep him in ICU until tomorrow morning, if he remains stable and continues to improve, we will move him into another room. I will allow you to speak to Fr. Langford only for a short while, say ten minutes, after which I want him to rest. Is that understood?"

"It is doc and thanks for taking care of him."

"You're welcome, but he could conceivably have another attack and I don't want him to become agitated or excited in anyway, agreed?"

"Yes doc, absolutely. I'll be sure to keep it short and as low key as possible."

"Good, I'll check back with you both after about ten minutes." Dr. Simonelli and Chief Barese walk back to Aiden's room together and they shake hands and part ways.

Al opens the door to Fr. Langford's room to find the priest deep in thought. "Aiden, you do look a lot better. I'd like to speak with you about the incident at ICS, but your serious demeanor tells me you're already thinking about it."

"Ah, Spartaco, dear friend, I have been contemplating how I can find the words to tell you of my experiences and what they all mean."

"Listen Aiden, before we speak, I need you to remain calm, cool and collected. Dr. Simonelli said any agitation can result in another heart attack and I don't want to be responsible in any way for that."

"I totally understand my dear Spartaco and I assure you that I wish the same thing for myself. Now where do I begin?"

Al smiles, "How about the beginning?"

Fr. Langford laughs, "Ah, very droll Spartaco, very droll. Well, each Thursday ICS opens its chapel to hear confessions from the general public. I was assigned duty that day and I made myself comfortably ensconced in the Centre Compartment awaiting the first penitent. The chapel was empty at the time and, as I am wont to do, I spend time reading. My choice of a book is a fascinating study by a former…"

Al interrupts, "Aiden, I've got maybe ten minutes and I think that we should focus on the important aspects of the incident."

"Of course, I often do tend to diverge from the subject at hand. Alas, as it turns out, I heard the curtain pull aside as the penitent knelt on the stand behind the screen. I tried to engage the person requesting him to begin the act of reconciliation, but he was silent."

"Are you sure it was a male?"

"Yes, the timbre and distinct voice pattern pointed in no other direction. Once I was able to engage the penitent, we began a long and often disturbing dialogue."

"Disturbing, what do you mean disturbing?"

"Spartaco, the man started to confess to sins of such horror, such magnitude that initially I thought him to be greatly disturbed; disturbed to the point of insanity. I, of course, told him that he was delusional and that he needed the services of a mental health professional. I attempted to point out that he could not have possibly committed such atrocities. If he indeed had committed such sinful acts, his identity would have eventually become widely known and there would have been severe repercussion from a number of authorities."

"What happened when you confronted him with that logic?"

"That was when he stated to me that he, in the company of a cadre of accomplices, committed the carnages that have become known as the Lamb of God murders."

"No wonder you thought that he was insane."

"Yes, as priests we are instructed on how to deal with certain instances of people who have become psychiatrically disordered. At first, in my estimation, this person appeared to be well beyond that clinical designation."

"What did he say, or do, that caused you to come to that conclusion?"

Fr. Aiden stops to consider how he might answer the question. "Spartaco, the man, I cannot even refer to him as the penitent, told me that he had communicated many horrific acts. He gladly took complete responsibility for these crimes to the degree that it was beyond my ability to even consider."

"I am very glad that you didn't confront him in a way that could have made him violent. What happened next?"

"At this time the man indicated that he wanted to debate the nature of good and evil. He also indicated that he already knew I was a biblical scholar; he even had knowledge of my heart condition."

"You're kidding?"

"Trust me; I do not kid in such matters. So, when I acquiesced to his challenge, so to speak, he used quotes from the Old Testament scripture to validate his point of view. What he ascribed to these quotes from scripture was the implication that these were God's word."

"Huh?"

"Spartaco, this man said that God condoned murder, rape, incest and genocide. He held that the Bible was the source for this. I told him that these quotes were written, as scripture, by the men at the time, perhaps inspired by Satan, but surely not of the Lord. The man then paused as if to reflect on what I've said, and he responded in these exact words, 'Inspired by Satan, not a bad conclusion on your part.' He told me that he has seen much evil, especially from man, and that he, in fact, was the inspiration for such evil."

"He said that? It's certainly clear why you thought he was insane."

"Ah, but it was then that he issued a warning of such ferocity and import that it shook me to the core."

"What! What did he say?"

Fr. Aiden tells the chief, "He said, again his exact words were, '… neither God nor His Son can stop the horror I will wreak on mankind; do you understand?' Upon hearing such a vile declaration, I immediately rose from my seat and rushed from my confines to tear open the curtain to his side of the confessional. It was then I saw the words 'Lamb of God' inscribed in the interior wall."

"Who the hell was this man?"
"Spartaco, I was hearing the confession of Satan."

CHAPTER 29

John of Patmos senses darkness in his visions that have become a constant source of wonder and dread.

The Revelations that he has been instructed by his Lord, Jesus Christ and the angelic messengers, has been written down. Now he must try to understand the meaning of the words and what they foretell.

His vision is of Seven Spiritual Figures that they prophesize events leading to the Third Woe. John is troubled for he must attempt to tell the faithful in the Seven Churches. They have suffered greatly, martyred for their faith and the holy man needs to allow what he has learned to be shared with the believers.

Much of what he has learned has been made evident. The Woman clothed in a white robe, pregnant with a male child. She is wearing a crown of twelve stars. The next figure John is told of is the Dragon. The Dragon looks to pursue the Woman in an attempt to devour the child, but she is given aid to evade him. The Dragon is infuriated, prompting him to wage war against the rest of the Woman's offspring, who keep the commandments of God and have the testimony of Jesus Christ.

John knows this heralds the battle between the third figure, St. Michael, and the forces of Heaven against Satan and the forces of Hell and Satan and his demons are vanquished to spend eternity in the Lake of Fire.

John has been told of the Beast. The Beast has seven heads, ten horns, and ten crowns on his horns and on these heads are the names of blasphemy. The

Beast emerges from the Sea to the wonderment of the peoples of the world. The peoples choose to follow the Beast and the Dragon grants him power and authority. The Beast of the Sea, blasphemes God's name and all who dwell in Heaven, wages war against the Saints, and overcomes them.

Then, in an ensuing vision, a Beast emerges from the Earth having two horns like a lamb, speaking like a dragon. He directs people to make an image of the Beast of the Sea who was wounded yet lives, breathing life into it, and forcing all people to bear "the mark of the Beast", "666".

John sets aside the parchments of Revelations that he has written. He has been told that the spiritual figures are a prelude to events leading into the Third Woe. This is most distressful to John and he looks to try and find the meaning of this vision, but he knows that this may not be revealed until later.

CHAPTER 30

"I got something on my string! I got something on my string! Chris! I got a fish on my string, come here quick!"

I rush over to Amanda as she struggles with her rod and, sure enough, given the way the rod is bending it appears that she has caught something other than a water-soaked log or the boat's propeller. I caution her, "Amanda, don't reel the line in too fast, take it slow, you don't want the fish to somehow slip off the hook. Here let me help you."

"No way, I want to bring the fish in myself."

"OK, by the way it's not called the string, it called the line."

Amanda is still struggling, trying to concentrate on the fish she's got on her hook, but she finds a way to put me in my place, "Semantics, by the way, where's your fish, huh, where's your fish Mr. Big Shot fisherman."

I smile at Amanda's delight at having caught a fish for the first time in her life and I concede, "Well I'm sure he or she's out there somewhere."

After about five minutes of trying to get the fish up out of the water and onto the boat, Amanda and I look over the side and see a really nice size fluke break the water and stare up at us. I grab the net and place it under the fluke and lift the fish out of the water. It's pretty heavy and I am as excited as Amanda.

"Wow this is a keeper!" I take a quick measure and it seems the fish weighs in at more than four pounds and is over 25 inches long. I tell

Amanda, "Hey girl, let's record this for posterity and The New York Post. Hold your rod up and you and the fish need to smile."

I take a great shot of the flopping fluke and a smiling Amanda with my phone and tell her that we will have fish for dinner for tomorrow.

She says, "What! You want to eat the poor thing? How cruel can you get; I want you to throw it back."

"You're kidding, throw it back? What for? It's a keeper; totally legal."

"I don't care, I've already named it and I can't eat anything that I've named."

"You named a fish? You've got to be kidding me. What did you name it; Moby Dick?"

"No, I named it 'Chris' because he's cute, just like you. Now throw him back in the water."

I just shake my head and take the fish off the hook and throw it back. "Cute? You think that fish is cute?"

"Just like you." and Amanda reaches over and kisses me on the cheek.

I touch my face and ask, "What was that for?"

"It was for taking me out fishing, being there when I caught my first fish, not eating it and for being so nice."

I know I blushed, "Well uh, thanks. We still have an hour before we have to leave for the city so what do you say we cruise around a little and we can anchor somewhere and have a drink?" I had brought a cooler with some bottled water, ice tea, sodas, two beers and a bag of Doritos, just in case we get stranded. I check the cooler to make sure the drinks are still cold and the Doritos are still there.

Amanda smiles and says, "Sounds good to me."

We spent the next half-hour cruising the bay and the waters in and around Lloyds Neck. I'm at the helm motoring around the shores of Lloyds Neck when spot a beautiful home overlooking the Long Island Sound and recognize it as the home of Beth's parents. Just the sight of their house makes me sad and I think about Beth and our last call.

I don't notice that Amanda is looking at me and turn to her when she asks, "Chris, is everything okay? All of a sudden you look kind of down, is something wrong?"

"Sorry, I think that last night is still catching up on me. I'm fine; hey how about anchoring off this small inlet that leads to the Coast Guard Station on Eaton's Neck. It's a bird sanctuary and it's very calm and relaxing."

"That sounds wonderful!" So, Amanda and I motor off to the inlet and I anchor the craft. We get comfortable and Amanda asks for an ice tea and I stick with water looking to counteract the tequila and hoping it will do my liver and kidneys some good.

Amanda knows something is bothering me when she asks, "Chris, when you had that sad look on your face, what were you thinking about?"

I'm a lousy liar and I don't want to lie to Amanda so I tell her, "When we were cruising around Lloyd's Neck, we went past Beth's parent's home and I just felt bad about all that's gone down between us."

Amanda doesn't say a thing. She just gets up and sit's next to me and puts her head on my shoulder and I put my arm around her. It's funny that we are able to have a comfortable silence after knowing each other for such a short time. I keep thinking to myself, how can I possibly still be in love with Beth and have such feelings for Amanda?

* * *

We return the boat to Jeff Trent's Marina and David is waiting for us in the parking lot. We climb into the limo for our ride into the city.

Amanda explains more about the event we are attending. She tells me that it's to celebrate the completion of her last movie which is just about to be released. She seems very excited about the film and tells me that she relishes the part she played.

Amanda tells me, "In the movie I portray this woman that suffers from hallucinations. She believes she is hearing voices and seeing apparitions of a ghostly figure that is making her go crazy. She doesn't know what do so she decides to get away from her home and the hallucinations she's been experiencing. The woman decides to take a trip to a spa located at some ski resort out West. But no matter where she goes, the ghost is there. While she is becoming traumatized by all that is happening to her, she meets this real hunky guy who is attracted to her and there is something starting to happen between them."

"Gee, I can't understand why? "

"Don't be such a wise ass. Anyway, she is very troubled and after a number of incidents that guy realizes that there is something very strange going on and he is tries to find a way to help the girl find out what's behind it all."

"Well, don't leave me hanging, what's behind it all? "

"Sorry, you have to buy a ticket! Or maybe, if you're nice to me, I'll let you attend the preview as my date."

"Hmmm, will there be free food?"

"Yep!"

"OK, it's a date."

We arrive at the hotel and exit the car. Amanda has reserved rooms for each of us. "I didn't want to seem forward so I reserved two rooms for us, adjoining of course, in case you want to show me more than the ropes."

I refuse to blush again so I say, "Ah…ummm…huh…ahem" and Amanda laughs.

"Oh, by the way your tuxedo and all that you'll need are in your room and we should try to get to the Grand Ballroom before the crowds arrive. The event starts at 7:30 PM so how about you call me at 7:00 PM and we walk in together?"

"Sounds good to me."

Amanda goes to her room and I go to mine. I find that everything that I'll need is there and more. I've got to tell you that this is really the life. I take a shower and put on my tux it fits perfectly and I smile thinking of Amanda's dad, Harry and how he could guess my size just looking at me. I have about 15 minutes before I need to call Amanda, so I sit down on the sofa and turn on the TV. The television is preset to the NY Cable News Channel and I start to watch a reporter telling the viewers about the fundraiser being held in Miami for the Houston for President Campaign. The camera pans over the audience and there's a close up of Tom along with a few of his sound bites. The reporter continues speaking when the camera now focuses on other dignitaries and guests seated at the dais and

I spot Beth immediately. She's smiling while speaking with someone who looks familiar, but I can't place his name.

I now find myself confronting the realization that I have lost Beth forever and that she is with Tom. I turn off the TV and sit there for a moment. I want to eliminate any thoughts of being morose about this and thankfully I am determined not to let this spoil my evening with Amanda.

I look at my phone and its 6:30 PM and I call Amanda's room, "You ready?"

"Yep, meet you outside in 30 seconds."

I check myself in the mirror once more and I'm satisfied that I look fine. I open the door to find Amanda standing there looking about as beautiful as I've ever seen a woman look. At first, I am at loss for words, but I finally have the nerve to tell her, "Amanda you look strikingly beautiful. I mean it, you look amazing."

Amanda smiles and gives me one of those Hollywood air kisses. "I would have kissed you full on the mouth, but it took me long enough to get my make-up and lipstick right. Thanks for the much-deserved compliment Chris!"

I laugh as Amanda looks me straight in the eye, "...and thanks for being here with me."

"I should be thanking you. I'm escorting the most beautiful actress in the world, I get to stay in this fabulous hotel, by the way, just to be sure, are the food and drinks free?"

Amanda laughs, "Yes, they're free."

"I get to eat and drink for free and I get to meet Mick Jagger, Keith Richards, Charlie Watts and Ron Woods! You are my heroine!"

I hold out my arm and Amanda takes it as we walk to the elevator for the trip down to the grand ballroom. The door to the elevator opens and we walk into a large open space that leads to the grand ballroom. There are various tables set up with covered chafing dishes that I'm guessing contain the food that I intend to eat at some point. There are also open bars strategically placed so that no one is more than ten feet away from a drink. Amanda sees someone she knows and takes me over to meet him.

He is a middle-aged man with an ample stomach, a big bald head and a wonderful smile.

"Amanda, I am so happy to see you. I haven't seen you since the last edit and I miss that beautiful smiling face telling me that I am a piece of shit."

"Well, the truth hurts." She kisses him on the cheek and they both laugh.

Looking at me the man says, "Who is this guy Amanda, someone else whose heart you will break?"

"Mitchell Kapps, please meet Chris Pella."

"Mr. Pella, it is indeed a pleasure to meet you, however, you do have my sympathies as Amanda is so beautiful and so wonderful that she will spoil you for every other woman you will ever meet. Just look at me, would you, just look at me. Who would think a few short months ago I was the world's most perfectly built man? My physique graced body-builder magazines; I was even asked to play stunt double for Brad Pitt. Now look at me, and this all happened because Amanda shunned my advances. Alas, that same thing is in store for you, and I take pity on you, as it is destined that you will become a miserable wretch all because of her!"

"Chris, Mitchell, is one of the producers of my latest film, 'Reflections in the Haze', and who I most affectionately call a 'piece of shit', so don't tell anyone, but he is actually a very nice man."

Our small group talks and I find out some of the inside stories behind various Hollywood stars. I won't mention their names, but you'd be surprised, or maybe you wouldn't, about some of what Mitchell says goes on among the denizens of the motion picture industry.

The lounge area is now getting crowded as the guests make their way to the buffet tables and bars. I get Amanda a sparkling water as she doesn't want to drink before she has to introduce the Rolling Stones. I decide that I will also stay with club soda and cranberry juice, just until I get to meet the Stones.

Amanda grabs my hand and says, "Chris, follow me."

"Where are we going?"

"We're going backstage to meet the Rolling Stones before they have to perform."

"Really? Now?"

"Really! Now! Get your ass in gear because they are leaving for the airport right after they perform. They're leaving for the next stop on their tour and we only have a few minutes with them."

I am getting nervous now as Amanda drags me through the hallway backstage to where they are setting up. I think to myself, what's a nice Italian boy from the Bronx doing getting to meet the Rolling Stones! "Amanda, I'm getting nervous…I mean what can I say to one of the greatest rock groups in history?"

"Just tell them you're a big fan and it's a pleasure to meet them."

"I may get tongue tied, if I do, just kick me in the shins and get me going."

Amanda doesn't miss a beat and she kicks me in the shins.

"OW! What the hell was that for?"

"That was for being such a candy-ass. Now get some starch in that spine and don't be a little girl groupie about this."

She leads me by the hand and when we reach their dressing room Amanda knocks on the door to the green room. The door opens and standing there is the Stone's drummer, Charlie Watts. I am speechless. Amanda looks over to me and she kicks me in the shins again.

"OW! That was harder than the last one."

Charlie kisses Amanda on both cheeks and says, "Amanda what a wonderful surprise. So glad we could see you before we go onstage."

Amanda gives Charlie Watts an air kiss, "It is so good to see you too. This coward beside me is Chris Pella, a huge fan."

I stammer as usual, "Ah, Mr. Watts, umm, ah, Amanda ah,"

Now Charlie and Amanda are laughing out loud and he said, "Chris, don't be such a candy-arse, come on in and call me Charlie."

Amanda and I walk into the dressing room and I get to meet all the members. I even get to call them by their first names and I am in Rock 'n Roll Heaven. They tell Amanda and I about their tour and how excited they are about the music they've written for her movie.

We talk a bit and I get to call Mick Jagger, Mick! Mick tells us, "Keith and I wrote the music and lyrics and we are very happy with the way it turned out. Amanda, what did you think of the final mix?"

"I was blown away. I really love the movie and the music makes it so much better. I can't thank you enough for doing this. I know you need to leave after your performance and you'll miss the preview, but the studio has arranged for you all to get copies and I'd love to know what you think."

Amanda and the Stones talk a bit when she says, "Well, you boys are on in a few, so we'll leave you now." Amanda takes time to air kiss the individuals in the group and we leave.

Chris is slack-jawed, "I can't believe I got to speak with the Rolling Stones in person, and they called me Chris! I can't believe that I got to call Ron Woods, Ron, and Keith Richards, Keith!"

Amanda looks at me with some of distain, "Well at least you didn't faint or pee in your pants."

"Ha, ha, very funny! You get to meet these people all the time, but I am; what did you call me? Oh yeah, I'm a peasant and this never happens to peasants."

"Well come on Mr. Peasant, we need to get to the stage so I can introduce the Rolling Stones."

Amanda and I walk through the hallway backstage and into the lounge area. There are camera crews, photographers and reporters lining the carpet on the way to the Grand Ballroom and the camera shutters and video crews are working overtime trying to capture the perfect image of beautiful Amanda. I am walking about ten feet behind her not wanting to intrude when she stops and turns towards me. She walks back to where I am standing and smiles, "May I take your arm?"

I look her in the eyes, smile at her and say, "I'd be honored" as we walk arm in arm past throngs of adoring fans and reporters.

CHAPTER 31

"Satan?!"

"Yes Spartaco, Satan. I am certain that the entity was not of human origin and although it may have been a demon from hell, I do not ascribe to that possibility. I cannot tell you how I know this; I know it was Lucifer himself."

"Aiden, I'm not saying that I doubt you, but how is this possible? Why now?"

The priest is circumspect in this reply, "My dear friend, I have thought this over and the realizations of the horrors that have transpired likely point to this being an undeniable fact. Let us examine what has happened; crimes are rising at an unprecedented rate worldwide, it appears the use of the term Lamb of God as a metaphor for our Lord and Savior Jesus Christ, is being exploited in connection with these heinous crimes. Upon investigation of the murderous rampages, you have discovered the ancient symbols conjuring evil made use of at the scene of a number of crimes. Spartaco, when I exited the confessional to confront the entity within, it could not have been more than three seconds at most. In three seconds, there is no way that the person could have gone unnoticed by either myself or anyone of a number of persons present. Spartaco, there was no one present; all that remained was the blasphemy on the penitents confessional wall."

"Aiden, this is more than I can comprehend."

"Spartaco, there is one more incident that I believe is crucial in drawing the conclusions that I have arrived at. I have told you of my episode in the Bonaventure Room in the ICS Library during the early morning hours. Initially I discounted the possibility of some divine intervention when I was performing my research. I was rereading biblical scriptures from Revelations when I heard sounds emanating from the Bonaventure Room. When I sought to determine the origins of the sounds, again, mysteriously appearing in the oldest Bible in our collection, were the same quotes from Revelations pointing to coming of the antichrist. It seemed far-fetched to me at the time, now the connection seems all too possible."

Al is at a loss for words. What Aiden is surmising seems so astonishing.

Fr. Aiden Langford continues, "Finally, when the demon in the confessional told me that, again, in his exact words, '...neither God nor His Son can stop the horror I will wreak on mankind; do you understand?' This must be taken in the context of the eternal struggle between good and evil and the battle for the souls of men and women."

Al is silent. He needs to contemplate what Fr. Aiden has told him and he is becoming more and more disheartened. "Aiden, how are we supposed to stop the slaughter of people all over the world? How can we fight this scourge, if it is what you think it is?

"Spartaco, you fight fire with fire. Remember when we discussed this possibility when we had lunch with Christopher. At that time, I expressed that you will need to confront the possibility that the source of this evil could be otherworldly?

"Yes, I do"

"Well, I believe this horror emanates from Satan and it is with hellish intent that he will strike against humanity. The forces of heaven are what are needed now to stem the torrent of evil that persists in destroying mankind."

Chief Al interrupts, "Do you think that this is a sign of Armageddon?"

"I do."

"Holy shit!"

"I believe that expletive is proper at this moment in our discussion."

"Listen Aiden, our time is just about up, I need to ah, speak to someone and I'll be back as soon as the doctor tells me it's okay for us to talk again."

"I understand; I do have one last item to relate."

"What's that?"

"I have a close friend and associate, actually mentor, whom I may wish to consult with concerning the subject at hand."

"Who?"

"I prefer to keep his identity concealed for the time being. I am, however, going to consult with him, but I need to have some time to think of how to explain this theory of mine. I am hoping he will have insights into these matters and thoughts on how to confront this evil."

"That sounds like a very good idea. Maybe we should keep this to ourselves for the moment. I may also have someone who can help with all this."

Fr. Aiden is curious, "Ah, whom may that be?"

"I'm not at liberty to confide in you at this moment, but I will let you know once I can speak with this person."

At that moment Dr. Simonelli enters and says, "Well gentlemen, times up, as a matter of fact I gave you an extra five minutes."

In his typical grandiose manner Fr. Aiden looks towards the Heavens and responds, "To quote the beloved Bard, 'O Lord that lends me life, lend me a heart replete with thankfulness!"

Dr. Simonelli responds, "Very clever Father, but I would have preferred 'You great benefactors sprinkle our society with thankfulness. For your own gifts, make yourselves praised.' I think that sums up my beneficence."

"Ah, you are quite right" and the three men laugh at the battle of the Shakespearean quotes.

Chief Al asks that doctor, "When will I able to visit Aiden again doctor?"

"Well, we'll keep monitoring his recovery and if you call me in the morning, I'll give you an update, and if I approve, you can meet with Fr. Langford for a bit longer. Does that meet with your approval Father?"

"Approval granted!"

"Good, then I'll talk to you tomorrow chief."

"Goodbye Aiden, please get a good night's sleep and we'll talk in the morning if the doc says it okay."

Chief Al Barese leaves Aiden's room in the ICU and as he leaves the hospital lobby, he runs to his car and gets on his mobile. The phone call is put through and a recorded message is played. When Al hears the beep he says, "Chris, you've got to call me as soon as possible, we need to speak."

CHAPTER 32

Tom arrives home from the fundraiser at 4 A.M. He walks to Beth's room and opens the door to look in. Beth is sound asleep and Tom takes time to look at her, but he doesn't have much time

He quietly closes the door to Beth's bedroom and makes his way to the gym and spa on his property. The door leading to the sauna opens to reveal a seating area surrounding the lava rocks. Tom walks into the cold space and it melts away into the hellish landscape he has become familiar with. Tom walks through the jagged rocks into a large open area and, as always, the noxious smell of Sulphur permeates his surroundings. A short walk from where he is standing is prostrate Al-Masih ad-Dajjal and Tom joins him in supplication to their master.

"What is it you have to tell me?" declares a booming voice that seems to come from all directions.

Al-Masih ad-Dajjal is the first to respond, "O lord, the seeds of terror continue to be sown among the Islamic tribes. Many of the weak, the non-believers and ignorant have died at our hands. The warriors and terror seekers under my command have created much fear as we make our way through the territories. In the journey to Megiddo there is little or no resistance from the hapless humankind encountered."

"Are your forces ready for battle?"

"Yes, my lord, they are. At first there was the need to steel the resolve in many of the terrorist leaders, but I have made it clear to them that cowardice will not be tolerated. All who do not bend to your will, are to suffer and be eviscerated; beheaded or disemboweled by the Warriors of Isfahan as you have ordered."

"Ah, I like that word; eviscerated, I think it is the proper term. These fools will join my demons as they experience everlasting torment."

With his head still touching the ground of the hellish underworld, Al-Masih ad-Dajjal, simply says, "Your command is our vow, my lord."

"Now let us hear from the one whom too much is never enough, what is it you have to tell me?"

As with Al-Masih ad-Dajjal, Tom Houston is also prostrate for fear of looking at Satan in the eye. He wants to protest how Satan has defined his efforts, but he knows that is not an option. "Oh master, I have executed our plan with great success. The world continues to deny the existence of God in greater numbers each and every day. My labors in achieving the nomination for President of the United States are bearing fruit. Many people have come to support my initiatives and those numbers are also growing daily."

"And what of the woman you so blatantly covet?"

"My lord…"

"Quiet, do you not know that I am aware of all that you both do every moment you are in my service. Do you not think that I can detect danger when it is forthcoming? Your careless fawning over this pitiful creature is a flaw that can prove fatal to my plans and failure will wreak havoc on both your souls for time unending."

"My lord, the woman will be helpful as a means to our end. I am hopeful that she will become my wife and help to assure my election. It was my…"

"MUST I KEEP TELLING YOU TO BE QUIET?"

Satan roars and Tom trembles in fear. "Your vanity, hubris and your penis will cloud your ability to carry out my wishes and this cannot be tolerated. Remember what I have told you both; there is a special place in my kingdom for those who betray my will. It is a place of eternal torture and a fire that never dies. I now feel compelled to remind you both again for it needs to become indelibly etched on your feeble minds. You will feel pain as never before and it will be that way for every moment of every hour of every day for eternity."

Tom wants to speak. He wants to assure his lord and master that he is committed to the battle ahead, but his fear far outweighs his need to explain himself.

"Here is what you are to plan for in the coming days and weeks. The battle for the souls of humans is to begin shortly."

Satan addresses Al-Masih ad-Dajjal, "When it is that you have reached the Jerusalem Plain and stand in the shadow of Megiddo, I will open the portal and you and your warriors will enter. It is there; on the ethereal third level of the Jerusalem Plain you will assemble for the battle and wait for my command. Is that clear to you?"

Satan is sneering at Tom Houston who is still bowed with his head to the ground. "Now Dr. Thomas Houston, by the way, what kind of a doctor are you?"

"My lord I am…"

"Shut up you idiot, I could care less what kind of a doctor you are. Look at me; I want you to see me when I tell you this."

Tom is exceedingly fearful of looking up at Satan. He has seen the face of pure evil before and it is beyond frightening, but he has no choice. Tom lifts his head slowly up off the ground and, while still kneeling, he stares at the hideousness of the prince of hell.

Satan speaks, "Here is what you are to do. When it comes close to the time, you are to fly to Israel. You will say it is a trip to meet the foreign leaders of the cursed Jewish state. When you are there, you will find a pretext to visit the Jerusalem Plain. Once you are there you are to go to Megiddo and I will guide you to the portal and you will enter and stand by the side of The Deceiver. Is that understood?"

"Yes, my lord."

"Oh, and there one more thing, as long as you are going try to fuck that bitch you have coveted, take her along. Chris Pella will be sure to follow and I want him very badly to pay for the blasphemy he has shown to me and my demon generals. Is that clear?"

"Yes, my lord."

"Now I want you both to rise and look at me." Satan takes a moment to slowly and deliberately speak to his slaves, "Do not make me regret my choice of either of you for this task. You have my commands and you have my promise of what will come to pass if you fail. Is that understood?"

Both Tom Houston and Al-Masih ad-Dajjal answer in unison, "Yes, my lord."

Satan disappears and Al-Masih ad-Dajjal walks away through a cloud of noxious gas and disappears without saying a word. Tom is alone and he has to hold himself back from vomiting.

CHAPTER 33

The Rolling Stones performing the theme from Amanda's movie was incredible and the audience loved every minute of it.

Following the Stones was the preview of Amanda's new film, 'Reflections in the Haze.' Judging from the cheers and applause it seems the movie was a smash hit with the crowd too. The famous people that assembled for the preview are industry big shots, financial backers, sponsors among others. They seem thrilled by the reaction and the studio execs and the actors are patting themselves on the back and the after-party begins in earnest. Amanda is laughing and speaking with a number of people from the media and some of her friends from the studio; all-in-all, everyone seems to be having a great time.

I cozy up to one of the stations and fill a plate up with some of the delicious foods they're serving. I grab a drink and find a table where I can eat and do some stargazing. As I put what seems like an entire lobster tail in my mouth, I take a look at my phone and I see I got a voicemail message from Uncle Al. His message sound very urgent and he is anxious to speak with me as soon as possible.

I need to find a quiet corner so I can call him back to see what the problem is so I leave my food and drink, figuring that it will be taken away by the wait staff. I think to myself there's plenty of food so I'll just have to make another plate. I am standing beside the entry way that leads to restrooms when I dial Uncle Al.

Al picks up the phone on the first chime, "Chris, we have to speak."

"Hi Uncle Al, this is the first opportunity that I've had to call you. We had to shut off our phones before watching the movie."

"Huh, where the hell are you?"

"Oh, I'm with Amanda Sellers at this very fancy hotel. She invited me to a screening of her latest film. There's food and drinks and I even got to meet the Rolling Stones. Did you know that Ron Woods is…"?

"Forget about Ron Woods, we have something very important to talk about."

I immediately get upset, "Uncle Al, what is it? Are you okay? Is something wrong?"

"Listen Chris, I'm going to tell you something that you are not going to believe…well, maybe you will believe it."

"What is it Uncle Al?"

"Aiden has had another heart attack, but seems to be getting better."

"That is good news but what is it that I'm not going to believe

"He had the heart attack while he was hearing confession, but that's not the main problem. Chris, this is something that we need to talk about in person, not over the phone. I'm sorry about having to ruin your evening, but this can't wait. Do you think you can come and meet me at the hospital?"

"Of course, just let me say goodbye to Amanda and I'll grab a car service. I should be there in about an hour and a half."

"I'll be waiting."

Uncle Al hangs up, no 'I love you' not even a good bye. I look around the room and I spot Amanda talking to some fans. She's scanning the room, but stops when she spots me and waves. I wave to her and motion for her to come over to where we can speak. She excuses herself and walks over to where I'm standing.

Even after an evening like this, Amanda is radiant and she smiles at me when she says, "Hey, Mr. Coward, you having a good time?"

"Amanda, I am so sorry, but I just got a call from my uncle and there seems to be a very serious problem."

"Really? Is he okay? What's wrong?"

"I don't know, he won't discuss it over the phone, but it is very serious and he never exaggerates. He told me that we need to meet in person as soon as possible and I'm so sorry Amanda, but I need to leave right now."

"I totally understand Chris. I'll ask David to drive you to where you need to go."

"Thanks so much Amanda, I was going to call a car service, but this will save some time."

Amanda looks at me and asks, "Can I call you tomorrow?"

I smile and give her a hug, "You better!"

Video lights are blazing and cameras are now clicking overtime as Amanda holds me close and kisses me long enough for all the folks nearby stop talking and just look at us.

When our lip's part, I smile and say, "What about your make-up?"

She smiles back, "Screw my make-up."

* * *

I tell David, Amanda's limousine driver, where I need to go and he puts it into the GPS. All the way to Huntington Hospital I tried to conceive what Uncle Al possibly wanted to talk about in person that can't be said over the phone.

In less than 70 minutes I arrive at Huntington Hospital. I thank David for getting me to the hospital so fast and I rush into the lobby to see Uncle Al pacing the floor of the waiting room. He looks up when I enter and he rushes over to greet me. It's well after 1 AM and there is no one in the waiting room, but he still drags me to a quiet corner.

"Chris, sit down we have to speak."

"Okay, but you are kind of scaring me. Are you alright?"

"Yeah, I'm fine, but I need to tell you about my discussion with Aiden."

"How is Father Langford?"

"He still in the ICU and sleeping now, but the hope is that he is on his way to recovering from his heart attack. Chris, he told me something that, if I didn't know better, I'd think that Aiden suffered more than a heart attack; I'd think he lost his mind."

"Lost his mind?"

"First let me tell give you some background. When we had lunch in town with Aiden and you were gone from the table, I told him some of what we are confronting in terms of the incredible increases in the most violent of crimes. Aiden told me that he would do research and that if he found anything he would let me know. He told me that while I had to consider all the physical facts of the matters being investigated, he had to consider that there may be some kind of a spiritual connection and he would look at things from that point of view. He also made it a point that I had to keep an open mind."

"Was he able to find out anything?"

"I think he told you and Beth about the incident in the library and the weird events related to the passage from Revelations."

"Yeah, I remember. Aiden didn't seem to think it was nothing more than a strange series of coincidences. He even said that he couldn't conceive that God would choose him to reveal the connection to scripture."

"Yeah, that's pretty much what he told me, but he did tell me something that is so far out of the realm of possibility that I believe it to be true."

"What? What did Fr. Langford tell you?"

"He told me that he heard the confession of Satan."

"WHAT" I said it so loud that the security guard at the front desk looks over and tells me to "SHHHHH!"

I look back at him and silently mouth, "sorry" and continue to speak with Uncle Al. "Do you think that this could have been some sort of a hallucination? Maybe his having the heart attack clouded his abilities and comprehension. Maybe Fr. Aiden only thought he heard what he heard."

"Chris, I've interrogated hundreds of people in my career and this was no false memory or whatever you want to call it. Aiden said he heard what he heard, and saw what he saw and I believe him."

"What did he see?"

"Well, at first Aiden felt this was a person estranged from the church and he hoped that he could help bring him back. It was when this person confessed to some of the most horrific crimes, Aiden rushed out of his place in the confessional to confront him. He tore open the curtain to where this guy was sitting and he was gone; in a matter of three seconds, he was completely gone. There were a number of witnesses in the chapel at the time and none of them saw anyone leave the confessional. But here's the kicker, when Aiden opened the curtain written on the wall were the words 'Lamb of God' written in blood."

I am silent, not knowing what to say next.

"I know you're at a loss for words, but we took a sample of the blood and the lab ran the tests and guess what?"

"What?"

"The blood was of a type that could not be identified, it wasn't human or animal. The techs at the lab said they have never seen a blood sample of this type ever and there are none on record."

"My God."

"Yes, Chris, it seems that there is a strong signal that the evil we are witnessing worldwide is being fomented by hellish forces. The last thing that the demon told Aiden was that neither God nor Christ can stop what is going to happen to mankind. I don't remember the exact words, but Aiden came to the conclusion that it could mean the final battle between Heaven and Hell was to come. Chris, I have to say that after what I and my team have seen, I agree with him. I am hoping that Aiden is well enough to get out of ICU and he will be sent to his own room."

What I am being told is incomprehensible and I look at my uncle and ask, "What are you going to do then?"

"There's only one thing, but I can't do it, you have to."

"Wait, listen Uncle Al, I've told you a million times I have no control over the saints when I interact with them."

"I know, but I'm not asking you to call on the saints, I want you to tell Fr. Langford about your gift."

CHAPTER 34

Zhang Yong Liu has been having dreams and they are so much more wonderful than he could have ever imagined. In his dreams he is a brave warrior who kills and destroys the enemy! It seems altogether natural to him as his name, Zhang Yong means brave and his surname, Liu means kill or destroy.

Zhang Yong wakes from his dream and sits up in his bed. He keeps very still as his roommate; Liang is fast asleep and he does not want to wake him. Liang is a good person, a pain in the ass, but a good person. Zhang Yong knows if Liang wakes up, he will keep talking and talking and that is not what he wants. Quietly Zhang Yong gets out of bed and stealthily opens the door to his room and steps into the hall. It is late at night and the dormitory is quiet and the hallway lights are kept low so as not to disturb the students who are fast asleep. Tianjin Normal University is located in a heavily populated urban area of Tianjin and the city is getting more crowded by the moment. The university has nearly 34,000 students so finding time to even think has made Zhang Yong aggravated beyond measure.

Zhang Yong is so happy to be here as a student. He could not wait to leave the small village that he came from and he is grateful to get away from his peasant parents. His mother and father still live there and what they can earn from their small farm is barely enough to keep them alive. His mother and father foolishly adhere to a belief in Christianity and they still attend a weekly service is secrecy. His parents must keep their belief secret out of a fear of retribution by the Communist authorities. The party has burned down many churches in China and Zhang Yong thinks that if the Communist Party of China ever finds out, his parents could become martyrs, but this may be the best thing that could happen to them.

The thought of his parents dying should have bothered the student, but he was surprisingly calm at the prospect of their death. His parents were always urging him to come to the weekly mass, but he was old enough to make his own decisions and he wanted no part of their religion. After all, there is no God so what's the point.

"What fools!" Zhang Yong thinks to himself. He knew that once he was able to leave home, he would be free of their incessant nagging. He tells himself that once he attains full membership in the Communist Party of China, he will consider what he should do about his parents. One of his options would be to turn them both in at Party Headquarters and let the leaders deal with his parent's sedition.

Zhang Yong is one of the most fortunate ones. He attends the university on a full academic scholarship and receives free tuition along with room and board. He is enrolled in one of the hundred majors offered by the Tianjin Normal University's Psychology and Behavior Research Center. He has always been interested in politics and humanistic social science and he knows that if he is to become a member of the Communist Party of China, his area of study could serve him well; it is also a requirement of his scholarship. Zhang Yong has been tested and the results indicate that he is considered to be at a genius level, academically.

At Tianjin Normal University he also became very interested in learning more and more about the internet and social networks controlled by CPC. Because of the cheap labor to be found in Tianjin, the city has become the censorship capital of China, and that could also help him deliver the message of socialism to the masses. Funny, he used to care a lot, but he doesn't care as much as he used to. Zhang Yong has been able to circumvent the tightly controlled internet in China and gain access to the world of wonder available to all online. Actually, it was pretty easy for him.

The vast expanse of the web is filled with glorious things of all types; sex videos, Islamic terror, gay pornography, Hollywood celebrities, books of all types and his favorite video games. The student loves to play all the best and most violent video games; Bulletstorm, Sniper Elite, Call of Duty, DOOM, Halo and his beloved Manhunt 2. He has become proficient in many games that reward competitors by virtue of the number of enemies eviscerated. He enjoys competing against other players around the world and the one thing that he has learned is that winning is all that really matters. The student has been told that there is a new world to be discovered and Zhang Yong will lead the way. He is told this in his dreams and today his dreams will come to life.

He walks down the corridor to the exit and onto the path that leads towards the center of the campus where his journey will end. It is a starlit night which is very rare in Tianjin where the air quality is very bad. He would normally wear a mask, but he figures that he does not need one now. It is 3AM as Zhang Yong takes the path toward the library. The only persons out at this hour would be the security patrol or the crazy medical students obsessed with their studies. If he meets up with the security guards, they will probably ignore him, but if they ask, he will tell them that he is on his way to the library to study; sometimes the truth works best.

In his dreams Zhang Yong is told to select the optimal vantage point in the heart of TNU central campus and he has found the perfect spot; the library. It is a point high above all others and it is there he has been promised to find all that he wants and all that he will need. All will be waiting for him and his anticipation is growing, making him smile every step of the way. The building he has chosen looms very large in the distance and Zhang Yong figures to be there in about 10 more minutes. That will give him plenty of time to enter the building, find his way to the top and ensconce himself where he was told the package will be waiting for him.

The student arrives and opens the door that leads to the main lobby and the corridor that further leads to the halls of study. The rooms contain thousands of books, periodicals and other materials and, given the early hour, he sees only a small number of other students around tables with their heads buried in the volumes available to them. The technology center is also open and Zhang Yong can see a few students gazing at images, their faces lit by computer screens, oblivious to all that is going on around them. He knows that no one will bother to take notice of another crazy student who has chosen to punish himself or herself by being there as opposed to being in their dorm rooms sleeping.

Zhang Yong walks toward the elevator and presses the 'UP' button. The door opens and he presses the button for the 12th floor. This is the highest floor that he is able to access however the floor is closed off to all students at this hour and the lights have been turned off. The student knows there are another four floors above him and he will need to find the emergency exit to access the stairs for the rest of the way. The student is in very good shape and he makes the climb in short order not even breathing heavily. He finds the exit door unlocked as he was told he would and walks out onto the roof and into the dark night. The student looks around and sees where he was told he would need to be; a small cement and cinder block equipment hut in one of the corners of the roof.

He walks to the hut and turns the doorknob and again, as he was told, it is unlocked. He enters the dark small space and tries to find the light switch. The student finally finds the switch and turns the light on. It is a single low wattage bulb, but it throws off enough light for him to see the interior of the space. There is a generator that takes up most of the room which Zhang Yong assumes becomes operational in the event of an emergency. He thinks this is clever in that it may be of service today and he pats the generator saying to himself out loud,

"Your services will be in great demand today."

Located behind the generator is what he was told would be waiting for him; a large black canvas duffle bag. The student opens the bag and in it he finds what he was told he would. Zhang Yong stroked the long barrel of the sniper rifle. He was told in his dreams that this was the latest and most effective weapon available to the Chinese military. He already seemed to know all about the rifle even though he had never fired a weapon or even held a gun or rifle in his life.

He wonders to himself, "How do I know that this is a Qbu-88 sniper rifle?"

As he picks it up, he immediately notices how light it is and Zhang Yong credits the Chinese People's Liberation Army for creating this perfect weapon. All in all, this seems far more exciting than the last time he spent playing the video game, Murder 2. The duffle bag was also filled with many clips of ammunition; lots of ammunition. The student instinctively knows that the Qbu-88 uses a 10-round detachable box magazine for 5.8-millimeter rounds, but instead the clips contain 7.62-millimeter rounds. He also knows that this is the more popular sized ammunition that is used around the world because of their higher impact and accuracy.

"How do I know these things?" Zhang Yong doesn't really want to know; all he cares about is that he just knows.

Holding the rifle in one hand and the bullets in the other excites him, and the student feels his penis growing harder. He stokes himself and in mere moments he ejaculates and the tension he initially felt immediately subsides. He takes a few moments to relax and allows his heart beat to moderate.

A voice that no one else can hear calls out, "Zhang Yong, is it not all that I have told you it would be?"

The student has heard this voice many times and he says, "It is as you said it would be and more. I am grateful."

"Greatness comes at a steep price, are you willing to pay the price?"

"I am."

"That is good and I will remain with you until it is done."

"I am grateful."

"Now you must ready yourself for what you have started. Need I remind you that your reward is more that you could have ever imagined. Zhang Yong, you are destined to be seated among the greatest legends of China; Pangu, The Jade Emperor, The Dragon Kings, The Great Yu, The Yellow Emperor. They await your arrival and all that remains, all that is required now rests with you."

Zhang Yong feels his excitement growing. He wishes to pleasure himself again, but there is little time and much to do as he tells the voice,

"I will not fail you and I will take my place among the other great legends of the Chinese people."

The voice goes silent as the student positions himself in the perch on the library roof, high over the central grounds of Tianjin Normal University. He sets up the rifle and tripod on the spot he was told to and he surveys the entirety of what can be seen. Zhang Yong looks out over the central campus and he realizes that this is the best view he could have hoped for. Next, he peers through the rifle's scope and he is amazed how sharp the focus is. He has no knowledge of how to adjust for the various distances, but the voice has told him that all is set and he would merely have to point and shoot.

The hazy first light of dawn appears at the horizon in the eastern sky. The weather report has predicted this to be a beautiful day with clear skies, clear at least by Tianjin standards, and the student continues his reconnoiter of the campus grounds. Given the early morning hour, he is able to see the first students walking towards the cafeteria for breakfast and then off to the first of their classes. Zhang Yong knows that by 9AM the central grounds of the campus will be filled with students and that will be the opportune moment to achieve the greatness he has been waiting for.

The student looks at his phone and sees that it is nearly 9AM and his excitement grows. He looks through the scope and he sees someone familiar. It is his roommate Liang and Zhang Yong smiles thinking, that this is as good a place as any to start. It is the first time that the student has ever fired a gun, but he was told by the voice that he should get the victim in the rifle's sight and squeeze the trigger, and he does.

As he looks through the scope, he sees Liang's head explode. All that remains is half of a skull as Liang's body collapses. The people all around him that freeze in place. There is a girl standing next to Liang, frozen in fear when the student's next shot severs her arm and the next shot blows through her chest. At first no one realizes what is happening, but then the realization kicks in. The students all try to run in different directions and as they do more and more shots ring out.

Zhang Yong has exhausted the ammunition from his first two clips and he has determined that at least twelve students are dead. The student ejects the clip and then slams in a third one and thinks,

"Funny, how do I know how to do this so well?"

Pandemonium has taken over the central campus and students are running in every direction. Zhang Yong smiles knowing he can take advantage of this confusion as he continues to fire 7.62-millimeter rounds to inflict the greatest damage. It seems like only seconds go by when he needs to eject his fifth clip and replace it with his sixth. The student also realizes that no one has bothered to notice where the shots are coming from and this allows him to consider other options. The rifle has a range of between 500 to 1,000 meters and this allows Zhang Yong to take aim at students far across the campus. At first the students just stand there watching the chaos far away, but the next shot has found its target as it rips through the bowels of a coed holding her books tightly to her chest. Before she has a chance to fall to the ground, five more shots ring out and panic ensues as more students fall to the ground, dead.

Zhang Yong quickly reloads and is pleased with the outcome. So far, he estimates that there have been at least 35 confirmed kills and at least thirteen or fourteen wounded. The student considers finishing off the wounded that are lying on the ground, but if he were playing the video game, he would be looking for the kill. He is also pleased that his perch high above the central campus grounds has not yet been discovered, but he assumes that soon it will be found.

"You do not have much longer", the voice warns the student. "It will require that you redouble your effort and continue your path to take your place among the legends."

Zhang Yong chooses a group of students that are running for safety, but they cannot realize that they have been marked for death by the student. Before the group can reach what, they hope is safety, the student releases a burst of rapid-fire shots and the group, he estimates as eight all fall to the ground.

"You have done well, Zhang Yong"

"Thank you."

By now pandemonium continues to rule and the police have taken over crowd control. Using the rifles scope, Zhang Yong follows heavily armed troops that are now seen moving from building-to-building attempting to determine where the sniper is hidden.

"You know that the time is near" The voice tells the student

"Yes."

"Then you must prepare for the climax. Do you know what you must do?"

"Yes"

Zhang Yong Liu reloads the rifle. He has a number of other clips, but he only needs one more. The student reaches into the black canvas duffle bag and pulls out the one remaining item that he was promised would be there. The bomb appears to be a complex system of explosives, wires, a timing device and a simple switch. He holds the bomb in his hands and stares at it as if he can't conceive its purpose.

"I see you have found what I have placed there for you."

"Yes. Am I still to do what you have asked me to?"

"Yes."

Zhang Yong stands next to the wall that has previously concealed his position and he looked through the opening from which he had been firing the weapon. He surveys the grounds and he no longer sees students running in all directions. The student can only see the movement of armed soldiers quickly moving from place to place and taking cover long enough to assess where the shooter may be hiding. One group of soldiers has taken cover by the corner of library right under the corner of the roof where he is hiding.

The student knows that this is the moment and he is ready to do as he was told. Zhang Yong opens the door to the generator hut on the library's roof and exits. He is holding the rifle in his left hand and the bomb in his right hand and he flicks the switch. A smile comes on the student's face and he hurls the explosive in the direction of the soldiers.

The bomb lands in the midst of the men and before they realize what has happened an enormous blast takes place and the soldiers are ripped apart. The student observes that body parts have spread over a large patch of the campus grounds in front of the library. There appear to be no survivors and Zhang Yong takes satisfaction that perhaps as many as 20 soldiers have perished in the explosion.

The police and remaining soldiers are shouting directions and firing shots in all directions still unaware of the sniper's exact position. The student avails himself of the opportunity to take advantage of the chaos and begins to fire his rifle at the police. Each shot brings down another security office, but now it reveals his location. A number of military have taken a position at the opposite end of the central campus grounds, among them an expert Chinese sniper. The soldier is in an excellent position to see where the shots are coming from. His hands are steady, his eyes focused, as the soldier sniper adjusts the rifles scope. He takes aim at the man firing a rifle from the library roof and holds his breath as he has been taught to do.

Zhang Yong continues to fires his weapon, oblivious to any danger when a bullet rips his arm off at the shoulder. The Chinese soldier sniper takes aim again hoping the next shot would kill, but Zhang Yong drops to the floor behind the short wall that surrounds the roof. Zhang Yong is slipping in an out of consciousness waiting for the end to come. He is losing much of his blood from the wound when he hears a familiar voice,

"You have done as you were told, Zhang Yong."

"I…I have. I am…ready to take my…" but the student stops speaking as his eyes seem to gaze into nothingness.

"Ah, do not leave me just yet as there is one more thing you must do."

"I…what I…what am I to do?"

The voice tells Zhang Yong to use his one good hand and dip it into the blood coming from his severed shoulder. "You are to mark the wall exactly as I tell you."

The student tries to reach over to dip his hand in the blood puddling the floor of the roof. He is next to the roof's wall and does as he is asked. He lies on his back as the pain he feels becomes agonizing and he stares up to see the image of Pesado, the keeper of chaos.

Zhang Yong does not understand what he is seeing, "Who are you?"

"Ah, Zhang Yong, I have some good news and I have some bad news."

"Bad news?"

"Oh, you want to the bad news first. Well, no; I think I will tell you the good news first. You are to take you place among the legends very soon!"

Zhang Yong smiles "Tha...thank…you."

"We have made a special place for you within our domain where you will spend eternity with the legends, but perhaps not the legends you had hoped for."

"...not hoped for?"

"Yeah, but I'm sure you will get along with them anyway. There's Stalin, Pol Pot, Osama bin Laden, and a personal favorite I'm sure, Mao Tse-Tung. I would have included Hitler but, well, he's got his own special place."

"Why can I not see you?"

"Oh, here, let me help." Pesado merely stares at the student and for a moment all becomes clear. The demon is hovering over Zhang Yong and it

becomes evident what awaits him. He tries to turn away from the hellish figure, but he chokes on his own blood and dies.

The military now surrounds the library and carefully make their way to the roof. They find the body of Zhang Yong, the student, and the cryptic message written in his own blood, reading Lamb of God.

CHAPTER 35

I am staring at Uncle Al, not knowing what to say.

"Listen Chris, I know you have kept this secret for so long. I feel privileged that you told me and I have never spoke to a soul about your special gift, but this defies all logic. Confronting an evil such as Satan, and what Aiden says this demon has sworn will happen, leave me no alternative, but to ask you to please let him know about the saints."

I want to consider all of what I have been told before I answer my uncle. I have seen the ultimate evil as represented by Julian and I have seen hell and the prospect of an apocalypse scares me beyond what I could have imagined.

"Uncle Al, I need to think about this, can I go home and sleep on it before we speak to Fr. Langford?"

"Sure Chris, I understand how difficult this is, but I know that Aiden will believe you no matter what. Aiden is supposed to be examined first thing in the morning and, if he is given the okay then they will take him out of the ICU and they will give him a room of his own. Why don't we meet in the lobby here at 11AM, we should know Aiden's medical status by then?"

"Sure, can I get a ride home? I came here by limo so I'll need a lift."

Uncle Al says, "No problem, my car is out in the lot."

We walk together not saying much to each other. For the entire time in the car going home Uncle Al and I are silent. I am in a very confused frame of mind and I need to seriously consider what I've been asked to do. When we reach my condo, he parks and looks at me, "I have the feeling that things are going to get a whole lot worse and without The Sainted intervention it could mean doom for us all. Chris, please think this over carefully before you make your decision and get a good night's sleep."

"I will Uncle Al, and thanks. I'll see you at around 11 A.M. in the hospital lobby."

We hug each other and I go to the door and enter my condo when the world goes still and I am transported to a place and time long ago.

> *The holy man has been standing in the bramble bushes for nearly forty days…the saint stood motionless for forty days and forty nights with only water and without food and little sleep to sustain him. He awakens only to become immersed in prayer as the faithful surround him. Many who have witnessed that, the man suffering such as he is, have come to believe that he is touched by the hand of God. The man has journeyed to many holy places so as to become close to leading a monastic life and he striving to preserve the grace given him during Baptism. The holy man took a vow of silence, and as part of the life he has chosen, he partakes of food only once a week.*

The scene changes and I find myself overlooking a large area of what was then Ancient Egypt. The man is there with a number of others. It is then I witness the miracle.

> *The Wonderworker, as he is called, stands before a large on vast expanse under the open sky in prayerful solitude. The people are fearful, but hopeful that their prayers will be answered. There has been a drought for many, many days and the land is parched and the hunger grows and the multitude is on the verge of starvation. The man does not speak, but merely looks*

to the heavens, closes his eyes and prays. As if in answer to his prayers, the skies open up and rain begins to fall steadily, and the barren ground now absorbs the water and the people fall to their knees to thank the Lord and to praise the Wonderworker.

Again, the scene changes and I am taken to the banks of the Nile River. The holy man is standing by the water's edge.

The holy man gazes across the river to see a multitude of disciples waiting on the other side. They are there to see the man, to pray with him and to seek the peace and grace that have become part of his being. Without hesitation, the man takes a step into the water and begins to walk to the other bank of the Nile River. Neither his feet nor the hem of his cloak is wet; nothing is wet and all those who witness this miracle bow, knowing that they have seen the power of the Lord.

Upon reaching the shore, a demon in the guise of a man, screams epithets at the holy man. The demon knows that the forces of heaven are at play and he curses the holy man.

With one word the Wonderworker says "Depart" And the evil spirit bursts into flames.

I wait for Saint Bessarion, the Wonderworker of Egypt, to leave his earthly body and to have his spirit appear before me. He stands looking at me straight in the eye before he speaks, "During my life, I had taken the vow of silence, but now I must speak to you."

"I know; I am more confused than ever before. I have seen evil take hold all over the world and I do not even know where to begin. My uncle is overwhelmed like others that do what he does. I was told by The Sainted that my purpose in life is to fight evil and help those in need, but what can I do against the evil that is now taking place."

Saint Bessarion knows, "You are now being asked to do something for which you have kept hidden for so long."

"My Uncle Al wants me to reveal that I have communicated with you and all The Sainted for more than twenty years. I have kept it a secret because I was afraid no one would believe me, but then when I told Uncle Al, of the miracle that saved his life he believed."

"Your uncle has now asked you to reveal this to the priest, Father Aiden Langford, out of a helpless feeling he has."

"Yeah, helpless is the right word. What he is confronting and the fear of what else is about to happen has made him even more fearful. What should I do Saint Bessarion? Please help me."

"Christopher you will know the demon before you as I knew him when I cast him back to the hell from which he came. You must do all you can to defeat this evil and if it is ordained that your secret is the means to this end, then you must follow your purpose."

I consider what he is saying and on some level I'm sort of relieved to share this with Father Langford because of his knowledge about the teaching in the Bible. On the other hand, I fear I won't be able to convince him, even with Uncle Al on my side.

"I'm going to share my secret with Fr. Langford and I hope he will understand."

"That is wise. Look to the home of the Pope."

"Do you mean Vatican City?"

"As the Lord gave me the power to cast out demons, He has given that power to the Church. Look there for guidance."

"Thank you, Saint Bessarion, please pray for us."

"We among The Sainted always do Christopher, and know that we are with you always and the Lamb of God is also with you."

Saint Bessarion bows his head in prayer and blesses me in the name of the Father and the Son and the Holy Spirit and disappears into the heavenly glow.

I am exhausted by all that has happened and all that is ahead of me. I take off my tuxedo and crawl into bed and immediately fall fast asleep.

* * *

I get up early enough to take a shower and stop for coffee. When I arrive at Huntington Hospital, Uncle Al was waiting in the lobby as we had arranged last night.

"Morning Uncle Al, how did you sleep?"

"I barely slept at all."

"Sorry to hear that."

"Yeah, so am I. Have you thought about what we discussed last night?"

"I did. I'm going to tell Father Langford about The Sainted."

Uncle Al seems surprised and relieved at the same time. "I think that's the right thing to do. What made you decide?"

"I had another vision; this one was from St. Bessarion. He was a recluse living in the fourth century. He was known as the 'Wonderworker' because of his many miracles. I think I had this vison because The Sainted knew what a difficult decision this is for me. He spoke very little during his lifetime on earth, but he spoke to me and told me that I am following my purpose in life by letting Fr. Langford know my secret."

"Well, Chris, I believe you and I know Aiden will too."

"I only hope so."

We sat in the hospital lobby and spoke for a while. We were anxiously waiting for Dr. Simonelli to tell us if we could see Fr. Langford. It wasn't until 11:30 AM when the doctor arrived and came over to talk to us.

"Good morning chief."

"Good morning doctor. I'd like to introduce you to my nephew, Chris Pella. Chris and Aiden are good friends and he was keeping me company while I waited for you. I was hoping that he would be able to visit with Fr. Langford too."

Dr. Simonelli extends his arm and we shake hands, "Pleased to meet you Mr. Pella."

"Doc, please call me Chris."

"Ok Chris. Well gentlemen, I've got some good news and I've got some bad news. First the good news; Father Langford is feeling much better. We've examined him and determined that he can leave the ICU and recuperate in the critical care unit until he's strong enough to leave here."

I think of Beth as soon as I hear Critical Care Unit.

Uncle Al must have known what I was thinking because he said, "That's where Chris' friend, Nurse Beth Della Russo works. "

Dr. Simonelli seems pleased knowing this. "That's really nice. Beth is a superstar around here and we all love her. Unfortunately, she is on a leave of absence at the moment, but the staff here is among the best and Father Langford will be well taken care of. Well, now for the bad news."

"Uh, oh." Uncle Al cringes as he waits for the bad news.

"I know you were hoping to see him regarding your investigation, but we are fearful that Fr. Langford could still be in danger of another heart attack, and this time it could be much more serious. I would like him to rest for today and reevaluate his condition tomorrow. Hopefully he will be strong enough to have visitors and then you can see your friend, but only for a short time. I don't want to see him excited or agitated; understood."

"Doc, can we just see him for a few minutes just so he knows we are here and thinking of him? I really believe it would make him feel better."

Dr. Simonelli considers the chief's request for a moment, "Well, I agree, it may help, but I think that it should only be you chief. Chris will have to wait until tomorrow."

"But doc…"

"No buts, its either you or you'll both have to wait until tomorrow if he's up to it."

Uncle Al looks dejected, but he knows it's a losing battle to fight the system so he says, "I understand; can I see him now?"

"In about a half-hour, we want to be sure he's settled in and comfortable enough for you to visit." We all shake hands again and the doctor heads back to the elevator.

"Chris, I was hoping to give Aiden an update, but you need to be the one to tell him. Let's hope we can meet with Aiden tomorrow and you can tell him about your saints."

I am a bit dejected because I have put my hopes on speaking with Fr. Langford. "I was hoping too, Uncle Al, but I understand what the doctor was speaking about and it seems the right thing to do."

"Yeah, I know that too, but what about this whole Armageddon thing, Satan the murders, genocide and crimes that would crush even the most hardened investigators. My team and the whole of Suffolk County's Police Force have so much on their plate that they can't keep up."

"I don't know what to say, but I know this horror has to stop."

"How?"

"By the Lord, the forces of Heaven and The Sainted."

Uncle Al sighs, "I hope you're right. Want to go for a cup of coffee?"

"As long as you're buying!"

Uncle Al smiles for the first time in a long time, "Some things never change."

CHAPTER 36

The next morning Beth wakes up and for a moment she doesn't realize where she is, but then it all comes back to her. The memory of the evening with Tom, Spencer, and Hamilton Cargill at the fundraiser comes back and she smiles. Beth checks her phone to see that it is 9AM and she is glad to see she slept through and had the rest she craved.

There is a knock on her door and someone calls out, "Good morning, Ms. Della Russo, may I come in."

"In a moment" Beth puts on the robe that was there for her to use and she opens the door.

Martina is standing there with a big smile. "Good morning, Ms. Della Russo, it is another beautiful day here in South Beach!"

Beth smiles at Martina and confesses, "I wouldn't know, I just got up."

"I hope you had a good night's sleep."

"I did; I guess I was a lot more tired that I realized."

"Well, would you like a cup of coffee and perhaps some breakfast? I can have the chef prepare you some eggs and toast or something else if you prefer. I can bring it to you and you can sit on your balcony and enjoy the view."

"That would be lovely. Is Tom, I mean is Dr. Houston, up?"

Martina laughs, "Oh, yes Ms. Della Russo, he's been up since 7 AM. As a matter of fact, he got home at 2:30 AM, so you can say that he slept in. He has meetings most of the day today, but he wants you to enjoy the pool and spa or any of the other parts of the grounds. If you prefer, there is wonderful restaurants and shopping on Lincoln Road or you can enjoy the beach; its right outside. Dr. Houston also asked me to invite you to join him for a dinner that he is hosting here."

"Wow, this is the life! Thanks Martina, and please call me Beth. I'd like eggs and I think I will sit out on the balcony and enjoy the view."

"Wonderful, I'll be back in a little while with coffee and breakfast." Martina leaves and Beth takes a peek to look outside and sees that it is a beautiful day as Martina said. She is looking forward to sitting on the terrace and enjoying the day and the spectacular view of the ocean. The beaches are already getting crowded, but there is no one in front of Tom's mansion. People are just walking by, staring at Tom's house, hoping to get a glimpse of the next president of the United States.

Beth doesn't want to go outside in her robe so she turns on the TV while she puts on a pair of jeans and a tee-shirt. The Florida News Network features local news and one of the items being shown is a video taken at Tom's fundraiser. She sees the images of Spencer and Hamilton mingling with the crowds and she sees herself in the background as the reporter questions Tom about one thing or another.

The anchor then moves onto the next story featuring another item. "In entertainment news, there was a star-studded event to celebrate the release of Amanda Sellers latest film, 'Reflections in the Haze'. The premier took place at the elegant St. Regis Hotel and our cameras were there. Kate Berra was also on the scene and she had the chance to catch up with Amanda Sellers.

"Amanda, Kate Berra from the Florida News Network. Do you have a moment?"

"Sure."

"Amanda, can you tell us a little about your newest film."

"Well, I can say that this is a bit of a departure from my usual roles. 'Reflections in the Haze' combines elements of horror and suspense with a bit of the romantic thrown in. Some very strange things happen along with a surprise ending, but I'll keep your viewers in suspense about that.

I will say that I loved working with the cast and crew on the film and I think moviegoers will be pleased with the results."

Kate Berra smiles and says "I'm sure they will."

The cameraman pans over the crowd of notables as Kate tells her viewers that The Rolling Stones will be appearing at the premier of the movie and singing the theme song they wrote for the film. As the camera moves across the crowd, Beth sees Amanda walking up to Chris and she puts her arm threw his and keeps talking to some of the guests.

A tear comes to Beth's eye and she reaches over and turns off the television. She sits back in her chair and becomes depressed and faces up to the realization that it is over between her and Chris and she puts her face into her hands and cries. On some level she had hoped that she and Chris might have been able to work it out, but seeing him with Amanda made that seem impossible. Beth wipes the tears away, trying to regain her composure when there is a knock on the door.

"Come in."

The door opens and Martina is carrying Beth's breakfast and coffee. Beth, who forces a smile, asks her, "Martina, I'm thinking of doing some exploration of South Beach, got any suggestions?"

"Well, I have heard that people love to tour the various Art Deco buildings that are all over the area. Some are wonderful examples of the architecture and there are so many interesting stories that go along with them."

"Really?"

"Yes. There is one hotel that has certain insets in the tiles on the floor that direct you to either to a well-hidden gambling parlor or a probation era speakeasy."

"Wow, that sounds very interesting and a lot of fun." Beth gets little somber thinking that she could have been doing this with Chris, but she doesn't want to ruin her day

Martina tells her, "I'm sure you will enjoy your adventure! There are a number of tour guides and if you like I can find you one that comes highly recommended and I'll make a reservation if that is okay with you."

"That sounds wonderful"

"Good, I'll go and make all the arrangements."

"Martina, you are a gem. Thank you."

"You're very welcome."

Beth spends quiet time enjoying the beautiful morning. After finishing breakfast, Beth takes a shower, gets dressed and decides that she wants to begin exploring South Beach. Martina has made arrangements with a tour guide and offered to have the limo take her to the address. It's only a few blocks away so Beth declines and says that she would prefer walking. In about 15 minutes Beth finds herself in front of the address that she was given. There are a few others waiting for the tour and all the people exchange pleasantries.

One older woman asks Beth, "Where are you coming from?"

"I'm down here on vacation, but I call home Northport on Long Island."

The woman gets very excited, "I'm originally from Malverne! I love it, lived there for years until the income taxes, real estate taxes and crazy fees and regulations drove me out. Anyway, I've been down here for a few years now and this is home now."

Beth smiles, "You look happy and that's what counts."

The guide arrives and introduces himself to the group, "Good morning, I am so happy to see so many of you are here for the tour. Now let me tell you some of what you will be seeing today." The entire group huddles around him to hear about the South Beach Art Deco tour and the sights. His name is Jack Marcus and he tells everyone that there are certain architectural details that are unique to art deco and can be found all over the historic district. He assures the group that he will be pointing out these details as they come into view and answer any questions the people in the group may have.

"We will also be going into some of the buildings so I can reveal certain of the secrets that were purposely hidden from view, most likely because they were illegal." There is laughter and a general murmur of approval from the people and the guide continues.

"I also have a special surprise for you! Is there a Ms. Della Russo present?"

Beth is stunned to hear her name. "Uh, I'm Beth Della Russo."

"Well Ms. Della Russo, my good friend, Martina, told me that this is your first trip to South Beach and that I must make the 'Haunted Manse of South Beach', or as it was originally named 'Damian's Retreat', a special stop on the tour!"

The entire group seems delighted and applauds a very embarrassed Beth. The woman who was speaking to Beth earlier asks a question of the tour guide,

"Who haunts the house?"

"Ah, well let me save that story for when we arrive at the Haunted Manse; so, let's begin our sightseeing excursion at The Colony Hotel. Now, the Colony Hotel is famous for its shimmering blue neon sign that lights up Ocean Drive. This art deco treasure was built in 1935 and is one of the most photographed art deco hotels in all of South Beach." Jack points to all the special features that make this hotel a prime example of art deco design and structure. The tour continues for more than an hour and the group is treated to some very interesting facts about the architecture and the beauty of the art deco buildings that have survived the major redevelopment that has been taking place all over Florida.

Jack Marcus points out, "The art deco district now comes under the landmark preservation codes that require all renovations or construction need to follow strict adherence to the rules and guidelines in order to preserve the beauty and character of South Beach."

The group stops for lunch and while they are eating, Jack tells them the story of the haunted mansion. "In the 1920's, the mansion was built as a vacation home by a very wealthy gentleman for his family. His name was Damian Forsythe and he was quite a character. He had earned his fortune in a, well let me just say, unconventional and unlawful way."

One curious tourist asks, "What way was that?"

"He bought and sold rare and endangered species of animals and birds."

Many in the group seemed upset about this, but Jack tried to assuage their anger. "Don't fret as I think that you should also know that Damian got his just desserts!"

A number of people in the group raise their hands and ask the same question, "What happened to him?"

"Well, I am sure you will be happy to learn that one of the rare species of tiger that he smuggled from India did not appreciate being confined. So, one night when Damian went to admire the beast, it seems that door of the cage had been left opened and the tiger got to have his revenge. It was never determined if the door was left opened by accident or if it was left opened by someone with a score to settle. You can make your own determination draw your own conclusion."

A collective gasp went up from the group and Jack ended the story by saying, "Poor Damian was hardly recognizable as the tiger made a meal out of a good portion of the man. Unfortunately, the tiger needed to be put down and the family left the mansion never to return. The beautiful mansion was left unattended for a number of years and, given the Florida climate and lack of maintenance, it soon fell into ruin. Over the decades the house has been restored by the local historical society and it is pretty much safe to explore. There are certain areas that are off limits so I must ask that you stay with the tour group and I will guide you through the mansion and show you the highlights."

The group anxiously lines up waiting to go in when the older woman in the group asks again, "Who haunts the house? Is it the ghost of Damian Forsythe that haunts the mansion?"

"Well, that is open to some debate. Some believe it is the ghost of Damian, but others who claim to have seen the spirit say that, based on an early photo, it's not him. They say it is a demon that haunts the house."

The tour guide does a poor, but funny, imitation of Dracula and ushers his group through the front door. The entrance hall is quite large and decorated in period furniture pieces, artwork and photography. "As you can see the historical society tried to stay true to the form and function of art deco architecture and features. The furniture and art work, although some are not original to the home, are all from the 1920's and early 1930's and are faithful to what would have graced such a home as this. Next let us go through to the library on our way to the main lounge and ballroom."

Beth is intrigued by what she sees and stops to admire the statuary and photographs of the Forsythe family. She appears to linger while the tour moves on ahead. As Beth explores the surroundings, she sees a dimly lit, large alcove where a number of niches hold some very unusual sculptures. She enters the alcove and stands in front of a very strange looking animal, more like a mythological beast than a statue of an actual animal and it sends shivers down her spine. Beth becomes very uncomfortable and she quickly turns away to look for the exit out of the alcove. As she does, Beth becomes disoriented, she looks around, but there seems to be no exit and she becomes very frightened. She stops hoping to calm down and prays that this bewildered feeling will pass when she hears a voice that makes her blood run cold and she collapses in a chair in the alcove.

"Ah Beth, it is so good to see you again."

Beth hears a voice speak in her mind and recognizes that it is Julian and she suppresses the urge to scream. Beth frantically looks around the alcove to determine where the voice is coming from.

"I hope you are enjoying your tour."

"How…"

"How am I? Oh, thank you for asking, I am fine, couldn't be better! I must say that you are looking quite lovely."

"What are you doing here? I…I thought you were…"

"Dead? Oh no dear lady…well, strictly speaking, actually I am dead; not in the way you humans think of the term, but rather in a more metaphysical sense of the word, you know in a kind of abstract way. At least that is the way God thinks of me."

"God? I…I…I need to leave…"

"Oh, you will leave, but not before you help me with one, small, tiny, teeny, wenny, itsy, bitsy, trivial, insignificant, little task!"

"Task…?"

"Yes, spread your legs and get fucked, by me of course, and give birth to the heir to my kingdom. The way I look at it, once the souls of so many have been damned to hell, I'll need some more help and a son, or a daughter for that matter, will work just fine! Oh. I just thought…maybe TWINS!"

"What!"

"Oh, it will be such fun. I think that I might send you roses and candy before our sexual encounter, after all I am an incurable romantic."

Beth tries to scream, but she can't. She is in a state of paralysis and her fear is driving her to the brink of insanity.

"But until the time comes, I think that I will have you watched over by a particular favorite demon master of mine, Verrine! Say hello Verrine!"

The amorphous Verrine says, "Hello Verrine!"

"Ah, ten thousand comedians out of work and Verrine thinks he's funny. Anyway, you will come to know him well and he will, how shall we say, assure that you will be more compliant...that's it more compliant! Then, when I am ready, I will take you, plant my seed and you will carry the next demon master or masters of hell. How do you like them apples, you lucky woman, you!"

Beth feels like she is going to faint and she gets up from the chair and leans against the wall to keep from falling. She tries to take one small step, but collapses unconscious to the floor. Julian gazes at Beth, as demon master Verrine takes delights in the mission he has been given by his master.

The tour guide, Jack, finally notices Beth is missing and goes back to try and find her. He sees her lying on the floor of the alcove and rushes over to help. Jack kneels at her side and calls for the security guard to assist in getting her up and sitting her down. Jack asks the guard for water and tries to waken Beth from her fainting spell,

"Ms. Della Russo? Ms. Della Russo, are you alright? Can you hear me?"

Beth's eyes suddenly open wide; she has no recollection of the encounter with Julian and Verrine. At first, she appears not to know where she is, but then she comes to life and tells the tour guide, "I spotted the statues in the alcove and I went in to look at them. When I did, I felt a dizzying spell coming on so I was looking for someplace to sit down and when I got up, I fainted. I am sorry to put you through this trouble, but I am much better now."

Jack, the tour guide is much relieved, "It is no trouble at all Ms. Della Russo, but I am worried about you. I think it would be better if you let me call the paramedics to be sure all is well."

Beth tries to assure Jack, "No, that's not necessary at all. I'm fine, really, please don't worry. I would love to continue the tour."

Jack doesn't seem convinced when he asks, "Are you sure?"

Beth smiles at him, "Yes, I'm positive!"

With that settled, Beth rejoins the group and they continue the tour for another hour. At the end everyone acknowledges that the excursion had been a wonderful experience and Jack got a round of applause and generous tips from all those on the tour.

Beth was the last one to approach Jack and she tells him how much she appreciated his concern and hands him a $100 bill. "Please take this and let's keep my little fainting spell a secret between us, okay?"

Jack is flabbergasted at the $100 tip and says, "Of course Ms. Della Russo and I can't thank you enough for you extremely generous tip."

"You deserve it and I will remember this excursion for a very long time."

Beth and Jack shake hands and she walks back to Tom's mansion. When she enters the townhouse Martina is there to greet her. "Hi Ms. Della Russo, I mean Beth, how did you enjoy the tour?"

"It was really wonderful…especially the surprise visit to the…" now Beth changes and speaks in a ghostly voice, "Haunted Manse of South Beach!"

Martina laughs and says, "I'm happy you enjoyed it. I know Jack was happy to do it. He's a bit of a ham, but I knew you would enjoy the experience."

"I did. Is Dr. Houston around?"

"Not at the moment, but he did ask me to tell you that his guests would begin arriving at 7 P.M."

"I will be sure to be ready. In the meantime, I think I'll go to my room and rest up a bit."

"Can I get you anything?"

"No Martina, I am fine…you've done enough already!"

They both laugh and Beth goes to her room. Once inside, her room Beth sits down in a chair and for the first time she feels fatigue coming on. She doesn't know why, but she feels that something is not right. The chair is comfortable and Beth's eyes begin to close and in a few moments she is asleep.

Julian and Verrine gaze at Beth sleeping when Julian says, "I will wait until the battle commences and I will take her as my own. She will be part of my revenge against God and I will screw the bitch in front of Christ and The Sainted and Chris Pella. Until then you are to watch over her and keep her from harm."

Verrine continues to look at Beth, "What of your groveler, this Thomas Houston? He letches after the woman."

"I will deal with him. Under no circumstances is he to defile her in any way. Is that understood?"

"Yes, my lord."

Julian leaves and Verrine thinks to himself that it will be a long night and he causes Beth's body to float in the air and rest on the bed. He smiles thinking that for all that is to come, she will need her sleep.

CHAPTER 37

Al-Masih ad-Dajjal stands before the leaders of the terror groups he has assembled. He proclaims, "We must be prepared for the End of Days to come and the final defeat of the bastard infidels; the Jews, Christians and all non-believers. The Gog and Magog are increasing in numbers and the signs of the end are appearing in all corners of the earth. They will lead the armies of the non-believers against the best of the nation of Islam. They who will come from Medina where, it is so prophesized, we will witness the apocalypse on the Jerusalem Plain in the shadow of Mount Megiddo."

There is urgency in The Deceiver's proclamations as he tells the terror group, "Hear my words, the signs have begun to appear and the end is near."

The terror leaders look at one another and there is consternation among them. "Oh, Masih, what are these signs you speak of?"

"There are many. The coming of Fitna is near. You will see many tribulations sent by Allah and because of the removal of Khushoo; the fearfulness of God, taqwa, reverence and piety have been abandoned. Allah has commanded that we destroy the Gog and Magog. They ravage the earth, and kill all believers in their way. They break their covenant with Allah and His Messenger and God enables their enemies to overpower them."

Al-Masih ad-Dajjal's voice rises to a deafening crescendo. "Look and listen! Have you not heard of the loss of honesty among the infidels? The spread of riba; of usury, the spread of zina; adultery, fornication, the drinking of alcohol. Sexual immorality appears among people to such an extent that they commit it openly. They will reap what they sow and are even, at this moment, afflicted by plagues and diseases unknown to their forefathers. They blaspheme and reject Hadith and so much more. They laugh in the face of Allah!"

Al-Masih ad-Dajjal has sensed the anger in the terrorist leaders who hang on to his every word.

The Masih then lifts his arm and passes it over the crowd of terrorists. "Be aware, that you will be witness to more signs that speak of the end of days. There will appear a huge black cloud of smoke that will cover the earth, the sun will rise from the west and the blasphemy spoken by liars will be believed, honest people disbelieved, and faithful people called traitors. There is more you must know…"

The Deceiver waves his arm over all those present and all the signs are immediately revealed all to them in their minds. "I have given you knowledge of the many signs that are coming to pass and you will need to put an end to this blasphemy against Allah and his prophet Mohammad, praise his name, by all non-believers."

The men of the terror group look at each other knowing that they each have now been given the knowledge of the signs; the signs that foretell the coming of the apocalypse. They know this is a gift to them and they shout in unison, "All praise and thanks are due to Allah, and peace and blessings be upon his Messenger Muhammad!

* * *

The army of terrorists has been making their journey for a number of weeks and one evening they stop to rest for the next day's march. They camp at the summit of a high hill overlooking the city of Halabja, Iraq. The camp has been hidden from view at the command of Al-Masih ad-Dajjal and where he calls for another gathering of the terrorist group leaders. As darkness fall over the city, he takes them to a vantage point where all can see the expanse below.

"I have brought you here so that you may see Allah's will being done. The city below is infested with infidels. You have listened; I have enlightened you with the signs of prophesies fulfilled and the battle that will come before the apocalypse."

The Deceiver considers the group and assesses that they will need to further steel their resolve for the battle ahead. He eyes each leader individually along with some of the men that are standing guard over the perimeter of the camp. The group numbers 68 individuals and Al-Masih ad-Dajjal orders them to follow him to the edge of a precipice behind the hidden encampment. Smoke from the chimneys and lights from the homes can be seen as families, most likely, are eating their suppers.

"You see the city below."

There is a quiet murmur as all there acknowledge the city at the base of the mountain. "Yes Masih."

"I have told you of the non-believers that have blasphemed Allah and his Prophet. They live in this place, an unholy place, a place that only exists because nothing is being done to eliminate its existence."

Each of those in the group look at one another not understanding what is being told to them. "Yes, oh Masih, but there are many thousands and we are but a few. How can we hope to gain this victory for Allah, all praise His name?"

Al-Masih ad-Dajjal says to the men, "Silence! Do you not believe that through Allah all is possible? Look at the precipices above and surrounding where you stand."

The terrorist leaders and their soldiers turn around and look up and there, through the darkness, all can see the Warriors of Isfahan lining the cliffs. The faces of the warriors are like hammered shields that cast an unearthly glow in the moonlight. They stand at attention and await the words of Al-Masih ad-Dajjal. The Deceiver looks up at the warriors as he extends his arms and shouts to the assembled warriors above,

"Warriors of Isfahan, why are you here?"

"TO DO THE WILL OF ALLAH!"

"What is the will of Allah?"

"TO DESTROY ALL THE INFIDELS AND NON-BELIEVERS"

"What are you willing to do for Allah?"

"TO FIGHT...TO WIN...TO DIE...WE DO THESE FOR ALLAH...ALL PRAISE HIS NAME AND PEACE UPON HIS MESSENGER MOHAMMAD!"

The Deceiver exhorts the warriors, "The lights of Halabja shine bright. The people believe themselves to be safe and they go about their lives as if there was no retribution for their sinful ways."

Al-Masih ad-Dajjal shouts, "Is there to be retribution for breaking the laws of Allah?"

"YES!"

"Who shall carry the sword of retribution?"

"THE WARRIORS OF ISFAHAN!"

Al-Masih ad-Dajjal lowers his arms and closes his eyes. The warriors that line the precipice dissolve into a dense fog that stealthily moves its way down the mountain, past the frightened terrorists and their leaders. The Deceiver and his minions watch as the dense fog settles at the base of the mountain and slowly creeps along the roads that surround Halabja. Once completely surrounded, the fog creeps its way into the city.

At first the lights on the huts and homes on the outskirts of the city go out and only faint muffled screams can be heard. The fog surrounding the city continues to cover a larger, sprawling number of homes as the menace looks to coalesce in the center of Halabja. The screams of the terrorized men, women and children grow louder and louder. Even the terrorists must hold their hands to their ears so they do not have to hear the cries of the people being viciously slaughtered by the Warriors of Isfahan.

In less than ten minutes the cries stop, all the lights in all of the homes in Halabja have been extinguished. The dense fog that covered the whole of the city now disperses and steals its way back up the side of the mountain. Once settled on the cliffs above the campground, the warriors magically appear.

"You have done well and Allah is pleased" declares Al-Masih ad-Dajjal. The Deceiver then turns toward the terrorists and says, "This is the power that I have been granted and this is the power I will use to defeat the infidels. Do not disappointment me in our most holy quest for if you do, it will incur the wrath of Allah, praise be his name and his prophet Mohammad all blessings to him. Is that understood?"

The terrorists declare in unison, "Yes of Masih, we are united as one in the holy war against all non-believers. We only await your command as we march toward battle and to victory."

Al-Masih ad-Dajjal smiles, "And where do we march?"

"MEGIDDO!" answers the terrorists in a cry that echoes over the mountain and down into the valley where the dead city of Halabja lies in darkness.

CHAPTER 38

I didn't sleep well that night and I woke up early and I went into the kitchen to make breakfast and have a cup of coffee.

I told Uncle Al that I would meet him at the hospital at 11AM as that's when we should be able to learn if we can see Father Aiden. My thoughts are focused on a number of things that are very troubling. I keep thinking of my visions and the messages I've been given by The Sainted. I'm very disturbed by their predictions of a coming apocalypse and the truth of the saints that I need to reveal to Fr. Aiden. I am also troubled about all that has come between Beth and I and my new found feelings for Amanda.

I'm about to place a pod into the coffee maker when the world stands still and I am swept into another vision.

The Archangel St. Gabriel is kneeling before the Blessed Mother Mary. She is seated as he speaks in reverent tones announcing:

"Fear not, Mary: for thou hast found favour with God. Behold, thou shalt conceive in thy womb, and bring forth a son, and shalt call his name JESUS. He shall be great, and shall be called the Son of the Highest: and the Lord God shall give unto Him the throne of His father and He shall reign over the house of Jacob forever; and of His kingdom there, shall be no end."

The vision changes and I am transported to a surrounding of light and mist. St. Gabriel is looking beyond the distance and I can't conceive what he is experiencing.

> *St. Gabriel stands with wings spread looking through the light and the mist. The Archangel is clothed in blue robes and he is holding a trumpet in one hand and a scroll in the other. He hears words that no one else can hear. He kneels before the unseen, unheard voice and bows his head in worship.*

My surroundings change and St. Gabriel stands before me. The look on his face betrays deep and distressing visage. I am at a loss and I don't want to speak first, so I wait until The Archangel is ready.

The Sainted speaks, "I am greatly troubled."

"I am also troubled. I have been shown things and told things that are very frightening and I don't know how to react."

"Do you know why I am holding this trumpet?"

"I am not sure."

"At the command of the Lord our God, I am to blow this trumpet to signal the coming of Christ. It will signify the end of times and the judgment of God on mankind."

"Why now St. Gabriel, why is this all this happening now?"

"The armies of hell are assembling. They look to do battle with our Lord Thy God and the forces of Heaven for the souls of mankind."

"What…"

St. Gabriel holds up his hand and I become silent. He turns and points at the distance and when he does the vision changes to a large, dark and forbidding vastness.

> *The mist melts away and St. Gabriel is overlooking a great expanse. The skies are dark grey and the plain is bare and foreboding. As far as the eye can see there is not a tree nor path nor blade of grass nor a breeze to disturb the stifling atmosphere*

that seems to permeate this place. There is only one anomaly in the barren vastness that looms large, Megiddo.

St. Gabriel turns to me and asks, "Do you know what this place is?"

I am taken aback and say, "I know this place, St. Gabriel! I was shown this place by Julian at the fundraiser for Tom Houston."

"This is the third ethereal parallel of the Jerusalem plain in the shadow of Megiddo. This is where the great battle, foretold to all by St. John in Revelations, will take place; the forces of Heaven and the demons of Hell will clash for the souls of mankind so coveted by the fallen angel, Lucifer. It is, for Lucifer, his revenge against God for casting him into the inferno."

"Is this why all the horrors taking place around the world are being done in the name of the Lamb of God?"

"Yes."

"…in preparation for the great battle?"

"Yes."

"I am going to tell Fr. Aiden about my visions, the messages and my times with The Sainted."

"There is much danger to come and you must assure him of your gift. Once this is done, he will know what can be prepared to meet the evil. It will all begin at the Church of St Peter, and without intercession, all will end in the shadow of Megiddo."

I am at a loss for words and I watch the vision close as St. Gabriel the Archangel spreads his wings and flies into the light.

* * *

Numerous of thoughts are running through my mind when I snap back to reality as I hear my phone chiming.

"Uh, hello."

"Uh, hello? What kind of greeting is that?"

"Oh, sorry, good morning, how may I help you?"

"Tell that adorable Chris Pella, that Amanda Sellers is on the line."

"Does Mr. Pella know what this call is in reference to?"

"Yes, please tell him that I want him to show me more than the ropes."

I laugh out loud and say, "Hi Amanda, sorry I wasn't able to stay for the rest of the event. How did it go?"

"It went great. Judging from the initial reviews and comments I think we have a winner with "Reflections in the Haze."

"I am so happy for you, but I could have told you it was a winner without even seeing the movie, even though I did see it. I thought it was great!"

"Glad you liked it, but I wanted to call to see how you are and find out about your uncle. Is everything okay?"

"Not really, Uncle Al's best friend, Father Aiden Langford, is in the hospital. He had a heart attack and the incident has something to do with the Lamb of God murders. Are you familiar with the Lamb of God murders?"

"Are you kidding, who isn't? Everyone knows about the murders and some of the other horrible things that have happened all over our country and other countries around the world. Chris, is your uncle, okay?"

"Well to tell the truth, he's not. He is under so much pressure that I am very worried for him. I told you that he's Chief of Detectives here in Suffolk County and there are so many crimes being committed that his team can't even keep up."

Amanda now seems concerned for me, "What are you supposed to do about that? Chris, you aren't a detective; as a matter of fact, didn't you tell me that you almost got him and yourself killed by that gang?"

"I know, but after what happened at the drug house with Tina being held captive by MS13, he seems to like to bounce things off of me. I try to help, but I think he uses me as sort of a sounding board, more like hearing himself talk and going through the facts of whatever he's working on. He has been a surrogate father to me after my dad passed away, and I will always be there for him."

"You are a really good guy Chris and I'm glad to know you, I really am. I was going to call and see if we can meet later on, but I'm guessing you're busy."

"Wow, Amanda, I would have liked to see you today, but I really am busy. Uncle Al and I are going to visit Father Langford and I am sure my uncle will want to talk to him about his experience."

"I understand, but can I call you later to see how you're doing?"

"Are you kidding? The most talented, glamorous, beautiful, tequila loving, fish catching goddess in the world wants to know how I'm doing? Well, I think I just died and went to heaven!"

Now Amanda laughs out loud and says, "I'll call you later" and she hangs up.

I am smiling when I hang up the phone, but then I become sad as I think of Beth and how we broke up. I am still in love with her, but now I am starting to have strong feelings for Amanda and that has me very confused. I make myself another cup of coffee when my phone rings and I see it's Uncle Al.

"Good morning, how are you feeling?"

"Chris, I didn't get any sleep last night. I was kept awake with worry over what is going on Chris; I mean the end of the world. How does anyone cope with something like that?"

"Uncle Al, I had another vision last night and it frightened me beyond my ability to cope with it."

"What! Another vision, tell me about it."

"It was a vision of St. Gabriel the Archangel."

"This sounds bad."

"It is. St. Gabriel told me of the great battle to come; the apocalypse, like the one prophesized in the Bible. He said that there will be the great battle between the forces of Heaven and hell. The battle will be the one that will be fought for the souls of mankind. St. Gabriel warned me of the signs that will be made known once the battle has begun. He showed me the great trumpet that will use to signal the coming of Christ and the final judgement and he took me to the place where the final conflict will take place."

"You're not kidding are you, where is the place?"

"St. Gabriel said the battle will take place on something called the third ethereal parallel of the Jerusalem plain in the shadow of Megiddo. Uncle

Al, Megiddo is a place as foretold in Revelations and where Armageddon will take place."

"Holy shit."

"That about sums it up…holy shit is right."

"We need to see Aiden as soon as possible."

"Have you heard from the hospital about Fr. Langford's condition? I told St. Gabriel that I was going to tell him about my visions and he told me that Fr. Langford will be able to guide me and help."

"What did he say Aiden could do?"

"He didn't say anything specific, but he told me that answers would be found at the Church of St. Peter."

"You mean at the Vatican?"

"Yes, that what I believe St. Gabriel meant."

"Chris, I haven't heard from the Dr. Simonelli yet, but I'm thinking of going to the hospital so I can be there when we get to know if we can see Aiden."

"It's 9:30A.M. I'll meet you at the hospital at around 10A.M."

"Okay, Chris, I'll see you then" and Uncle Al hangs up the phone.

Chris finishes getting dressed and ready to leave. He gets into his Mustang and puts the keys into the ignition, but he doesn't start the car. He thinks to himself about all that is ahead of him. He tries to think of the right words to tell Father Langford about The Sainted and his visions. Will he be able to convince the priest that he is telling the truth? Will he be able to make him understand? And lastly, will Father Langford be able to show him the way to help stop the horror that is about to be unleashed on mankind?

CHAPTER 39

Tom Houston concludes his meeting with the various wealthy donors and supporters of his campaign. He has invited them all to a dinner party that he will be hosting at his mansion in South Beach.

At the end of the meeting, Tom shakes hands with all the people in attendance; after all they have pledged to raise tens of millions of dollars for his run for the party's presidential nomination and ultimately for the presidency itself. Tom tells Nancy McGrath, his chief of staff, that he wants to make some calls and that he will retire to his office and that he does not want to be disturbed.

"Nancy, is that clear? I have some confidential discussions ahead and I must prep. I need no interruptions what so ever."

Nancy McGrath is used to these private sessions of Tom's and replies, "Of course Dr. Houston, I will alert the staff and all calls will be routed to me. If there are any emergencies that require your attention, I will schedule call-backs at a time when you are available."

"Thank you, Nancy." Dr. Houston enters his home office and closes the door. He takes the extra precaution of locking it just in case someone tries to enter and find him gone. Tom walks to a bookshelf in a dark corner of the office and it disappears and becomes a portal into Satan's hellish domain. He has become quite familiar with this place and he knows where he must be. He navigates through the razor-sharp rocky protrusions and when he gets to where he must be, he prostrates himself on the ground and awaits his master.

"Ah, glad you could make it. It is a last-minute thing, but you know how impatient I can be when I don't get my way."

"I am here to do your bidding, my lord."

"Of course, you are and I am especially glad as I have some good news and I have some bad news. What would you like to hear first; the good news or the bad news?"

Tom Houston is at a loss for words. What could this possibly mean? He can't imagine what the good news is and he's afraid to ask what the bad news could be.

"Oh, cat got your tongue; well, I'll give you the good news first. I have been keeping track of your progress and it appears that you have made great strides in securing the nomination for president that I have determined is necessary to put my plan into high-gear so to speak. I am pleased."

"Thank you, my lord." Tom now feels a sense of relief and pride over the compliment that was paid to him by the Prince of Darkness.

"Now for the bad news"

"Bad news?"

"Yes, you know that woman you lust after?"

"Beth?"

"Yes, that's right, Beth Della Russo! Well, I have some bad news; actually, bad news for you and good news for me. I have decided that she will become the vessel that will give birth to my child and that child will hold sway over the demons of hell, you know, help me run things. Of course, you needn't worry; I'll still be the top dog."

"Master I…"

"I know you are disappointed, but as the old saying goes; 'There are plenty of fish in the sea!'"

"But master I…I…"

"Oh and, as this will be a very special tryst between good old Beth and me, I don't want you to defile her in any way, is that understood?"

"Master I have…"

"You have feelings for her, I know, but this is most important to me and if you in anyway disobey my orders you will find yourself as a guest in a part of hell that you cannot ever even hope to imagine. Is that clear?"

"But my lord…"

An angry Satan now grows to an enormous size and screeches, "IS THAT CLEAR?"

Tom cowers in fear knowing that it is useless to argue, "Yes, master."

"Now just to show you that I am not totally heartless, well I guess I am totally heartless; I am going to allow you to marry Beth and for you to become president. She will of course be pregnant with my offspring, and you will have the honor of raising he, she or them and no one will know better, least of all Beth. See, aren't you happy now!"

"Yes, my lord."

"Good, now that it is settled go and do what must be done. The hour approaches." Those are the last words of Satan to Tom and the demon disappears leaving Tom alone.

* * *

The limousines are lined up along the streets that border 'Escapar por el Mar', Tom Houston's South Beach estate. The invitations to the dinner have been extended to select billionaire businessmen and women, Hollywood elites and dignitaries from the world of finance, fashion and the technology industry. The notables exit their cars and are escorted into the mansion where they assemble in the open-air courtyard for cocktails.

Tom has a wonderful way of ingratiating himself to his very well-heeled supporters and he is there to greet each guest personally, "So glad you could make it Stan…", "I was hoping you would be able to come, Sally…", "Let's be sure to set up a tee time Matt…" The greetings go on and on and Tom always finds a way of making everyone feel special.

While Tom is talking to Campbell Fredrick, the global online shopping magnet, he spots Beth coming down the steps. She looks absolutely beautiful in a long, shimmering light blue silk gown. Tom stops talking to Campbell and they both turn and smile.

Beth smiles back as she walks up to Tom and gives him a kiss on the cheek.

He says, "Beth you look beautiful"

Tom smiles as he stares at her in silence for a moment. He seems to snap out of his silence and says, "Sorry, Campbell Fredrick, may I introduce Ms. Beth Della Russo. Beth is my guest and she is here to celebrate with me and Dr. Spencer Price on his receiving very generous donations from friends and admirers for the ongoing work at his cancer institute.

Campbell is infatuated and takes Beth's hand and kisses it in grand style. "Ms. Della Russo, it is a pleasure to meet you."

"Thank you, Mr. Fredrick, and please call me Beth."

"Well then you must call me Campbell."

Tom notices that a number of guests have been staring at him and Beth and he decides that it would be a very good maneuver to work his way through the crowd and introduce Beth to the invitees. Everyone seems to be enthralled with Beth and speculation has already begun about Tom's latest romantic involvement.

Drinks are being served in the garden and everything seems to be going very well when Phil, head of the house staff, announces that dinner is being served in the dining room. The guests stroll through the garden and back into the mansion where the staff directs them to the dining room. Even though there are nearly thirty people, all can be seated very comfortably at the table and the wine, along with conversations, flow freely and all is going splendidly. Tom is seated at the head of the table and Beth is seated between Hamilton Cargill and Spencer Price. When making plans for the party, Tom did this seating purposefully as he wants to be sure no one has a chance at Beth…but that was before and now he has the very real responsibility of keeping her for Satan himself.

Tom rises from the table and tells all that he would like to make a toast. "Dear friends, new and old, I want to thank you all for being here. I hope you are all having a good time…" The guests all around the table applaud, "…and I personally want to thank everyone for their unwavering support for my campaign. When I began my quest for something to give back to our country for all that it has given me, I was thinking along the lines of maybe a new student center at some university or sponsoring an initiative to clean up the plastic water bottles that litter our beaches, so how the hell did I ever get sucked into running for president?"

The guests burst out into laughter and Tom continues, "Well, I did get sucked in and I've never been more committed to anything in my life. If given the chance, I hope to change our country and maybe even the world in order to reflect the socialist values and wants of everyone at this table. Together I know that we will change what we can as destiny calls us to action." Tom lifts his glass, "Let us toast our future and what awaits us!" All raise their glasses and take a sip in celebration as the first course of dinner is served.

Spencer, Hamilton and Beth are engaged in a very pleasant conversation and Beth can be heard laughing at Hamilton Cargill who is proposing marriage to Beth once again. He now has just upped his initial offer to her of a new car, house with a pool plus a six-month vacation in Europe and now he wants to include a 105-foot luxury yacht complete with captain and crew.

Beth thinks for a moment, "Well Tom told me that he has a 140-foot yacht that I can use anytime I want."

Hamilton says, "That son of a…tell you what, I'll add a helicopter and that's my final offer!"

Beth, Hamilton and Spencer are laughing hysterically when Tom walks up and asks, "What's so funny?"

Hamilton pretends to be crestfallen, "Tom, I offered her a yacht and helicopter and she turned me down, again!"

"Hammy, let's face it, Beth has too much character to fall for your bribery. Now if Spencer were offering her these things, then we'd both be out of the picture."

Beth, who is sitting next to Spencer, puts her arms around him and, mimicking Spencer's classic line, says to Tom and Hamilton, "You're damn right!"

The party goes on for hours and it is after midnight when the guests leave. Tom and Beth take a moment to relax outside on the patio. It is a moonlit night over South Beach and they both are happy to just relax a bit.

"Did you have a good time tonight?"

"Thanks Tom, I really did. Hamilton and Spencer kept me in stiches most of the time and the other guests I met were very gracious and friendly to me, I really feel at home."

"I'm glad you do."

Beth and Tom are looking into each other's eyes until they both realize what is happening. Beth cannot understand the feeling that she has for Tom, but when she saw Chris with Amanda on the news that made her come to the realization that it's over with Chris. What is even more puzzling is that, even though she is now free of that entanglement, it makes her very sad.

As for himself, Tom is more confused than ever before. He knows he cannot go against Satan for that would mean punishment well beyond damnation.   He has his whole plan laid out before him; he would get the nomination, marry Beth and get elected President of the United States and now that plan is shattered. He thinks to himself, do I love Beth or is she just a means to my end.

The awkward moment, brought on by confusing emotions seems to pass. It is late and Tom says, "Beth, what do you say we turn in?"

"Yeah, I am tired."

Tom holds his hand out and Beth takes it and rises from the chair. She is standing close to Tom as Beth brings her lips close to his. She gives herself to him in one passionate kiss and he holds her close as he basks in the heat emanating from her body.

Suddenly Tom pulls away and appears be very disconcerted, "Beth, I don't know what made me do that I am so sorry."

"Tom, don't be there is nothing to be sorry about."

"I...I just don't want to; I mean I can't."

"I understand, maybe we should go to bed now and we can talk in the morning."

"I think that's a good idea."

Tom and Beth walk through the mansion and into the foyer and the stairway that leads to their rooms. When they get to the top of the stairs they look into each other's eyes,

"Good night, Tom."

"Good night, Beth."

As Beth lies in bed, she tries to understand what just happened. She knows that Tom wants her and she knows that she would have been willing to give herself to him, but she can't understand what just happened. Beth closes her eyes and tries to fall asleep, but the questions keep turning around in her mind until sleep finally takes over.

The next morning Beth hears a knock on her door. She checks the time and sees that its

9 A.M. and figures that it's Martina waking her up.

"Martina, is that you?"

"Yes, Beth, I just wanted to wake you up for breakfast. Dr. Houston has asked that you join him on the garden patio."

"Sounds wonderful, do I have time for a shower?"

Martina laughs, "Of course you do. You will probably want to wash all the dirt and grime away from last evening's festivities. Shall we say 9:30 for breakfast?"

Now it's Beth's turn to laugh, "That's right, I am filthy from all that elegance. See you down there at 9:30 A.M."

It is another beautiful day in South Beach. Beth has finished getting dressed and ready as she makes her way down to the patio where Tom is waiting. He gets up and gives her a big hello and kisses her on the cheek.

"You look none the less for wear after last night's dinner party."

"Well, it is exhausting, having to be treated like a celebrity. Cocktails in the garden, a dinner party where you get waited on hand and foot, and to top it off getting proposed for, what was it, the fourth or fifth time by one of Hollywood's most popular actors? And, to top it all off, I have to stay at this dump you call 'Escapar por el Mar'. You know Tom, I thought you liked me."

Tom turns serious, "Beth, I do like you, as a matter of fact I do like you more than I can say. Beth, I'd like to explain about last night…"

"Tom, you don't have to explain."

"I think I do. I have done everything to pursue you and try to get you to like me as much as I like you."

"Tom, I do like you…"

"Please Beth; I need to say this to you. I know you like me, but I want you to like me enough so that someday you may even learn to love me."

Beth is silent as she stares into Tom's eyes. She believes him to be sincere and that scares her.

"Beth, I didn't want to push myself on you last night because I want this to be real for both of us. The last thing I want to have been some awkward moment come between us. I want you and me to have something special like I believe we can."

Beth is confused and she tries to find the right words. "I don't know what to say to you; how to react to what you've said. I like you, Tom; I really do like you very much. You have been generous of yourself and your time, you've shown me that you are a total gentleman and for that I thank you. This has been a very confusing time for me, breaking up with Chris and all. I suppose you could have played me and gotten what I assume you want, but you didn't and that means a lot to me."

Tom smiles for the first time since he and Beth met for breakfast. "Listen Beth I would love to spend more time with you. You know, take time for us to get to know each other better to see if what we have is real and maybe even a chance at falling in love. I'm not pushing it, but I hope that you can see that I am being sincere."

"I can Tom, I can see you are sincere, but this is a lot for a girl to handle."

"I know it is. I have been thinking of something, and I don't want you to give me an answer now, but I do ask you to take time to think of what I am suggesting before you let me know your answer."

Beth can't imagine what Tom is going to ask. "Tom, what are you saying?"

"Beth, I am planning to go on an extended tour of the Middle East. It has been in the planning stages for a while and I will be gone for a little more than three weeks visiting a number of places and beginning with my trip in Israel. The trip will help me to get a better understanding of the issues that conflict both sides. I really want to know what I may have to confront if I am elected President…"

Beth smiles at Tom, "You mean *when* you're elected President."

Tom laughs out loud, "Yes, *when* I'm elected President. In this way I can have the important background information to make an impact and hopefully jumpstart the peace initiative...again!"

"Wow, you've got it all planned out, don't you?"

"Well, everything except for you."

"Me, what do I have to do with peace in the Middle East?"

"Beth, I want you to accompany me on the trip."

"What!"

"Beth, I want you to come along with me. You can have a front row seat to some of the most interesting and provocative topics that countries have to confront on a daily basis. We will even take time to see some of the most historically and culturally significant places in the world."

"Tom I can't possibly..."

"Of course, you can. This is a wonderful opportunity for you on a number of levels: most importantly it will give us time to be together to really get to know each other."

"Tom, I have a life back in Huntington. I have family, I have a career, I have..." Then the thought of Chris comes into her mind and she pauses.

Tom realizes what Beth may be thinking and continues, "I know you have a life, family, career and I'm not asking you to give it up. This could be a defining moment for us, even if we find out we can only be great friends, it will be the trip of a lifetime for you."

Beth goes silent.

"What do you say Beth? Please promise me you'll at least think over."

Beth doesn't know how to answer, but finally she says, "Alright, I'll think about it."

"Promise?"

Beth smiles, "I promise I will."

CHAPTER 40

I meet Uncle Al in the lobby at Huntington Hospital and we sit in the waiting area and wait to hear from Dr. Simonelli.

Uncle Al has a very concerned look on his face. "I am hoping we can see Aiden soon. You know that all that is happening is eating away at me and my whole team, as a matter of fact I heard from Dan this morning and that he is already reporting an increase in the murder rate in the overnight and it seems that the crimes committed are becoming increasingly more violent…as if they could get any more violent."

"Uncle Al, I am going to speak to Fr. Langford and tell him about The Sainted, but I am afraid he won't believe me, as a matter of fact, if someone told me they've experienced what I experienced, I would gracefully exit and run for my life."

"Well, we should be grateful that Aiden is so wired up that he can't get out of bed, let alone run after you. Chris, I wouldn't worry about him believing you. He's confronted evil first hand so it doesn't seem out of the realm of possibility that he would believe you have seen the face of goodness in The Sainted, first hand."

"I hope you're right."

Uncle Al and I just sit there in silence for a short while and look up when we hear Dr. Simonelli greet us. "Good morning gentlemen, I have good news for you, Father Langford seems to be making great strides and he appears to be recovering nicely after his last treatment and a good night's sleep. I am allowing you to see him if you agree to follow one simple rule."

Uncle Al doesn't like to be told what to do, but he keeps his opinions to himself and says, "What rule?"

"The rule is this and it is designed to keep the patient comfortable and in good spirits. The rule says you are not to agitate him in any way. I know you need to ask him questions regarding what he witnessed, but remember what he witnessed caused him to have that heart attack. If you see that he is getting nervous or disturbed in any way, stop and let us know. We will monitor his condition from the nurses' station and if we see his condition change, we will be in the room stat. Get it?"

Uncle Al tells the doctor, "Yeah, we get it. The last thing I want to happen to my best friend Aiden is for him to have another heart attack. I want to thank you for taking such good care of my friend doctor."

Dr. Simonelli smiles and says, "You're welcome. Now that he's out of ICU, he's been settled in room 446."

We both say goodbye to Dr. Simonelli and wait the requisite 30 minutes before make our way to the elevator and push the button for the fourth floor. We exit and walk past the nurses' station and I'm relieved that Beth is not there, then I remember that she's in Florida with Tom Houston. We stop at the door to room 446 and Uncle Al opens the door slightly and peaks though. Immediately he is greeted by an unexpectedly chipper Father Langford who looks like he's in good health considering he's had a heart attack.

He seems to have been waiting for exactly this moment as he greets Uncle Al, "Spartaco! What a joyous sight for these sore eyes! Please, please do come in and sit for a while. I am most thankful you and I are finally able to speak!"

Uncle Al enters the room and I follow behind him. When Fr. Langford sees me, he seems genuinely happy, "Christopher! What a wonderful surprise I am so glad you have come to see me! I fear however, that your uncle and I have some rather important items to discuss and I am sure he would want them kept confidential."

Uncle Al interrupts, "Aiden, I've asked Chris to join us as I think that you will want to hear something very important, he has to tell you."

Fr. Langford looks to Al and then turns to Chris and asks, "Christopher, what is of such import of which Spartaco speaks?"

I take a deep breath and begin to tell him of The Sainted. "Father, I am going to tell you something that I have not told anyone, except for my uncle. It is something so unbelievable that I can only hope you will understand."

"Unbelievable? What is so incomprehensible that I cannot possibly understand?"

"I guess I'll just blurt it out because I have no other way of letting you know what I've experienced…I can communicate with The Sainted."

Father Aiden smiles, "Christopher, I know of your devotion to the Saints and I know you have taken an enthusiastic interest in their lives…"

"No, Father, that's not it. I actually see, hear and speak to the saints and I have been having visions since I was 14 years old."

"What!?"

"It's a long story, Father."

Father Aiden smilingly says, "Well Christopher, I seem to be incapacitated at the moment and I've got nothing much else to do, so please commence."

I start from the beginning and tell Father Aiden everything I can. I tell him of my first experience when I had a vision of Sts. Cosmas and Damian. I tell him of many of my visions where I was taught my purpose in life and where I was witness to events in the lives and deaths of The Sainted. I tell him that through these visions I have been told of the warnings of evils that I would confront and that I would need to withstand many of the horrors that emanate from the hellish domain of Satan. I also told Fr. Aiden that my faith had been tested in the past and that the saints told me it would be tested again in the future.

After nearly an hour I end my account by telling the priest, "Father I know that this sounds incredible and I would understand if you thought that I had lost my mind, but I assure you that it is the truth."

Father Aiden looks up at Uncle Al who has been patiently listening and he nods his head signaling to the priest that I am telling him the truth. Father Aiden then stares back at me. I believe the priest is trying to assess my truthfulness or at least looking for signs of insanity. "Christopher, yours is a remarkable tale and, would that I had not experienced my own manifestation of evil, I would politely suggest decades of intense psychotherapy. Alas, I can only submit in that your uncle has vouchsafed belief in your truthfulness."

"Father, Uncle Al told me that you believe you have heard the confession of Satan, is that true?"

"I believe this to be true. The person I initially assumed to be a penitent appears to be, in actuality, the Fallen Angel, Lucifer. The demon, as I think him to be, was in possession of information that led me to believe he was in fact Satan. The last words he spoke to me are indelibly etched in my mind; 'Listen priest and listen well, neither God nor His Son can stop the horror I will wreak on mankind; do you understand?' When I realized whom, I was speaking to, I rushed from my place in the confessional and I tried to confront this evil visage, but regrettably my heart was not in it."

As Father Aiden relates his experience, I am becoming anxious and I tell him, "Father, recently my visions of The Sainted point to exactly that same outcome. I am constantly being warned of a great battle, the battle of Armageddon that will take place."

Father Aiden is silent, deep in thought when he asks me, "Where is this battle to take place?

"I was told by St. Gabriel…"

"The Archangel, St. Gabriel, what did he say?"

"Yes, he told me that the battle will be fought for the souls of mankind and now I quote, 'On the third ethereal parallel of the Jerusalem plain in the shadow of Megiddo.' He held a trumpet in his hand and told me that when he sounds the call, Christ will appear in judgement of all mankind."

Father Aiden speaks in a soft voice, almost to himself, "As foretold by St. John in Revelations."

"I also should tell you that I have met Satan too."

"What!?"

"Yes, I have met Satan who has appeared to me, in human form, as a man I only know as Julian. I've seen the horrors he has done so far; gang violence, drug dealing, child prostitution and the murders he has caused to be committed. I have also seen his true face, the face of a demon so terrifying that I will never be able to forget it."

"What else can you tell me?"

"I have been to the ethereal parallel plain to where I was taken by Julian. Although I didn't know what it was at the time, St. Gabriel revealed this to me in the vision."

"My word, Christopher, you have had quite an awful time of it for any one person." Father Langford appears to be deep in thought as he tries to comprehend what I have told him and of the visions that point to the impending battle.

"Christopher I am almost afraid to ask you, but is there something else that you wish to tell me?"

"Yes Father, there is something else."

"Something else? What is it, Christopher?"

"St. Gabriel told me that I must prepare myself to confront the evil to come and that it will begin at the Church of St. Peter."

"The Vatican?"

"Yes, at least that's where the only St. Peter's I know is."

"That does make sense in that it is St. Peter's Basilica, one of the holiest temples in all of Christendom and home of the Holy Father."

"Father, when I mentioned that I was going to tell you about The Sainted and my vision, the Archangel Gabriel said that I should and that you would be able to help me."

"Help you? St. Gabriel told you that I could help you?"

"Yes, I was hoping that you could."

"Christopher and Spartaco, please give me a moment as I must ponder the meaning of what the saints have told you and what I may be able to provide in the form of assistance, however, at the moment, I am at a loss." Then Father Langford leans his head back on the pillow and thinks to himself.

While we are sitting there waiting for Father Langford to speak, the door to his room opens and in walks Nurse Diane Breuer, Beth's good friend. She looks around to see if all is well and when she sees me, she smiles and says,

"Oh, hi Chris, I forgot you knew Father Langford; how have you been?"

"I'm fine, I hope you're well. I do know Father Langford and we are having a nice visit, but I hope that we didn't set off any alarms at the nurses' station. Dr. Simonelli warned us to adhere to the rule."

"So far, so good: we are monitoring the situation and all seems well on our end. By the way, I heard about you and Beth and I'm sorry, I really am."

"That's really sweet of you to say that. I'm okay; just sorry that we ended it the way we did, she's a wonderful person and I miss her smiling face."

Nurse Breuer says, "Well you take care." Now turning to Father Langford, "You should get some rest so I'll ask you guys to leave in 15 minutes, okay."

Uncle Al says, "Not a problem, we were boring Father Langford anyway and I'm sure he wants to get rid of us."

"Okay, good seeing you again Chris; you too Chief" and Nurse Breuer turns and leaves the room.

Father Langford seems to have become energized after his thinking things over. "Gentlemen, I believe that I have the seed of an idea that is taking root and I would like to work it out in my extremely fertile mind. I would ask you take leave and allow me to develop it fully. I would also ask that you both come to visit tomorrow, noontime would be best, when I will reveal the outcome of my though processes and the appropriate actions that I will recommend. Of course, I will do nothing until I have provided you with the details of my findings. Is that agreeable to you both?"

Uncle Al walks to his friend's bedside and takes his hand, "Yes and we'll be here tomorrow. You take good care of yourself and please be careful, for in the words of Billy Shakespeare, 'Hell is empty and all the devils are here.'"

For a man who has the best of comebacks ever, Father Langford just lays there in stunned silence.

CHAPTER 41

The operator at the Vatican executive offices answers the phone, "Good morning, Vatican Executive Office, how may I direct your call?"

"Good morning, this is Father Aiden Langford; may I please speak to Monsignor Amedeo De Marinis?"

"Of course, Father, I will put you through."

The phone rings twice and a voice familiar to Father Aiden answers, "Monsignor De Marinis, may I help you."

"In the words of The Bard of Avon, 'I count myself, if for nothing else, so happy as in a soul remembering my good friends.' Is that not true"

Msgr. De Marinis laughs out loud and says, "Ah, it is most true…most true! Aiden, it is so good to hear your voice."

"Ah! My dear Amedeo, I am delighted to hear your mellifluous voice stalwartly spoken and resonating with your unbounded vitality."

"I am equally delighted to speak to you Aiden; it has been far too long. I have been informed by Father Marcus Teller of your recent heart attack and I was waiting to call until you came out of ICU. Now that I hear you speak, I am profoundly grateful that you appear to be of strong voice yourself and what passes for a sound mind, at least in your case."

Father Aiden laughs at the joke and says, "Ah, thank you my friend, I was just released from the ICU and I am feeling much better both in spirit and in good health both mentally and physically. I am truly blessed!"

Msgr. De Marinis sounds greatly pleased, "As we all are my friend, and I am much relieved to hear. You have; however, aroused my curiosity so please let me know what has prompted this utterly unexpected, but most welcomed call?"

"To be totally candid with you, I have a situation of such profound import that I fear, if left without being challenged, it will lead to dire consequences. My dear Amodeo, I have a daunting task that, by my imposing on you my friend, goes well beyond the boundaries of our attachment."

"Aiden, you know that I can refuse you nothing, so what can I do to help my dear old friend!"

"I fear when I tell you what I must, you may become overwhelmed at the prospect."

"Aiden, you have now got my undivided attention."

Father Aiden begins to confide in his friend by telling him of recent events. "I should begin by informing you that my recent heart attack was not caused by a general lapse in my health. It was exacerbated by an incident whose roots lie in the Lamb of God horrors that have been heaped on us."

"How dreadful!"

Father Langford continues to explain to Msgr. De Marinis of the experiences that have prompted him to make this call. He explains his exchange in the confessional and how he came to the conclusion that the penitent was, in fact, Satan himself. Father Langford then continues by relating the experiences of Chris and the Saintly visions he has experienced over the years.

Msgr. De Marinis listens intently and comments, "I have known many supernatural events in my ministry, but this is most extraordinary."

Father Langford continues his narrative by telling Msgr. De Marinis of Chris' confrontations with Satan, who has manifested himself in human form. Aiden finishes by telling the Vatican's chief exorcist, "Satan is among us Amedeo, and no one is more aware of this than you."

"Aiden, you say this young man; what is his name again?"

"Christopher Pella."

"Christopher Pella can actually communicate with The Sainted."

"Yes."

"And that the blessed ones have warned him of the impending apocalypse."

"That is what I have been told and, although the entire episode defies credibility, I can vouch for Christopher's character and his sincerity, so I believe it to be true."

"I have no doubt that you believe what he has told you. I can also believe in his saintly visions of the church's holy icons as I have seen the vile and unholy legions of hell and how they possess men and women. As you also know Aiden, in my ministry, I have had to exorcize these demons to try and save the souls of the poor misfortunates, but even I have never seen such a precipitous rise in the forces of evil and their impact on so many."

Father Langford asks the monsignor, "What do you believe is the cause of this precipitous rise?"

"Aiden, it seems to have arisen from out of nowhere. Each week I receive literally hundreds and hundreds of letters in correspondence from churches around the world. The priests who have written entreaties that speak of demonic possessions that are classic in their form, but unparalleled in their extremes."

"That conforms to the murders and violence now being committed in the name of our Lord and Savior Jesus Christ, the Lamb of God."

"Yes. Aiden, I had a recent exorcism where a woman was possessed and had been for years. She was a holy woman who, when she became possessed, murdered her entire family. This caused her to be institutionalized and when we arrived, my assistant Father James Fielding, and I performed the ritual in accordance with our laws and teachings. Both Father Fielding and I attempted to drive the out demon, who called himself Leviathan, with holy water, prayerful invocations and the PYX. When we confronted him, the demon that possessed the woman became extremely violent. I was tossed about and the demon grabbed my assistant, Fr. Fielding, and ripped his beating heart from his chest."

Msgr. De Marinis becomes quiet for a short moment because he is greatly saddened having to repeat the events that took place during the exorcism. When the Vatican's chief exorcist continues, he tells Fr. Langford, "Lastly, the demon took a dagger that seemed to appear from out of nowhere, and slit the throat of the young priest severing his head from his body."

Father Langford makes the sign of the cross and says, "May he rest in the arms of our Lord and Savior, Jesus Christ."

Msgr. De Marinis answers, "Amen" and he continues, "We had failed in all we tried to do to save the poor woman, but before it was over, the body of the woman who was possessed explodes in a mass of putrefied flesh and bones. The demon, however, did say something to us that now seems to be coming to fruition."

Fr. Aiden, who has stayed silent up to now, asks Msgr. De Marinis, "What was said?"

"The demon Leviathan, declared that all was in preparation for the coming of the anti-Christ. He avowed that the great battle will take place on the Jerusalem Plain…"

Father Aiden interrupts, "That is the exact place that Christopher said was prophesized by the Archangel St. Gabriel, on the third ethereal parallel…"

Msgr. De Marinis completes the sentence, "…of the plain of Jerusalem in the shadow of Megiddo. What is it that you would have me do, Aiden?"

"I would ask that you meet with us where all will be revealed to you so we may look to determine what must be done."

"Us? Are you planning to come to The Vatican?"

"Yes."

"What of your recent heart attack, Aiden? Why would you risk such a danger to your health?"

"My dear Amodeo, if what I believe will happen, actually happens, my future as well as the futures of mankind will have been written and my soul will be in the hands of the Lord."

"I see; then let us meet whenever you say."

"Thank you, Amodeo, I will call once I have spoken to Christopher and I will then provide you with details as to our arrival."

"I hope and I pray your journey will be safe."

Father Aiden responds, "Amen."

CHAPTER 42

The flight home to Long Island on Tom's private jet was very pleasant. Beth had a wonderful time in Florida and staying at Tom's estate was like living in a fantasy world. Now, however, she needs to get back home and the reality of her life.

Tom was supposed to fly back with her, but some last-minute meetings and events prevented him from accompanying her so he decided to stay another week. Beth was very understanding and she kissed him goodbye and they agreed to call each other to make sure all is going well.

Beth was driven to the airport in Tom's limousine and when she arrives, she sees his private jet is waiting on the runway. She is welcomed onboard by Sherry, the head flight attendant and Larry Sommers, the captain who both ask if she had a good time.

"Oh, the entire trip was truly fabulous and a much-welcomed vacation from it all, thanks for asking."

Larry told Beth that the weather up the East Coast was pleasant and that the flying time should be about three hours when they land at Long Island's MacArthur Airport. Sherry asks if Beth needed anything, but she declines. Once Beth gets settled in her seat, she realizes she is looking forward to going back home and getting back into her normal routine. She has been away for about two weeks and all went well, but for some reason Beth has had a very peculiar feeling that something is wrong.

The hatch to the main cabin closes and Capt. Sommers taxis down the runway and the jet takes off. When the plane reaches cruising altitude, Beth relaxes a bit as her thoughts turn to the dilemma she finds herself in. Beth recognizes that she and Tom are getting closer and that she finds her feelings for him to be growing, but she finds herself still missing Chris. How can that be?

Beth thinks about the last conversation she had with Tom and the decision that she needs to make. They discussed the possibility of going on a trip to the Middle East and Beth is very confused as to what she should do. Her being a companion on Tom's trip will certainly raise the curiosity that is beginning to mount about their relationship and it will only get more intense. Being gone another three weeks is also asking a lot of Dr. McMasters, her boss and head of the hospital and that is a definite consideration. Tom has suggested that he call in advance to see if it would be okay, after all his foundation is a big contributor to the hospital.

The last time they were together, Beth told Tom, "I appreciate it Tom, but I haven't made a decision yet, besides, it's something that I need to do."

"I know Beth, but it might be a good idea just to feel him out, you know, so he can have time to think it over and make accommodations until you get back."

Beth is starting to feel the pressure and she thinks about it for a moment, "You're probably right. You say that we would be leaving in about three weeks, correct?"

"Yep, I know that this is kind of last minute, but like I told you, it is really the experience of a lifetime and I know that you will get a lot out of it."

Beth sighs, "I know I will, but give please me a little more time to think it over. I am not scheduled to report back to work for another two days so I will serious think about it and make a decision by then."

"Okay, but please let me know as soon as you can because I need to make preparations."

"I will…I promise."

* * *

The plane lands and Beth says goodbye to Capt. Sommers and she gives Sherry a kiss on the cheek and thanks them both for their hospitality. When she disembarks Beth spots the limo driver taking her bags and putting them into the trunk of the car. He opens the door and Beth takes her seat for the short drive to her townhouse. The driver just smiles and he takes his place behind the wheel and closes the window between the driver and passenger compartments. Beth welcomes the privacy and she leans back into the seat to continue the thought process of all she will need to decide.

Beth is considering what the trip would mean and she believes her entire world would change. She would get to meet important people and she could tour many of the counties in the region that she has only read about in books or exposed to online and in news features on cable. Beth also recognizes she would also get to know Tom better. He really likes her and she is getting to like him more than she ever imagined she could… but still. Although she knows that the trip with Tom would be the thrill of a lifetime, she thinks her answer will be no…but still.

In a short while the limo pulls into Beth's driveway and the driver unloads her suitcases and brings them in her home's entryway. She thanks him very much and tries to give him a $20 tip, but her refuses to take it.

"Thank you, Ms. Della Russo, but I cannot accept this."

Beth smiles, "Why, I won't tell if you won't tell."

The driver smiles back at her, "Thank you for the generous offer, but I must refuse for two reasons, first Dr. Houston would kill me and second, well, there is no second, I love my job. It's been a pleasure." The driver smiles and he and Beth shake hands and he leaves. Beth wheels the suitcases into her bedroom and turns on the TV to the LI News Channel. She starts to unpack her bags and she is only half-listening when she hears a news item and the announcer says the name, Amanda Sellers.

Beth immediately looks up at the screen and she watches the actress being interviewed for her new movie. The person interviewing her is telling the TV audience that the movie has received wonderful reviews, but it is her opening question that has caught Beth's attention,

"Ms. Sellers, I want to talk to you about the movie, but first I need to ask you about that photo in the New York Post."

Amanda now laughs, "You mean the one with the fish?"

"Yes! My word, that fish looks like a monster catch."

"It was! It also was my first-time fishing and I had a great time."

"Did you stuff and mount your catch?"

Amanda now cracks up, "No, I made my friend throw it back."

"You did?"

"Yes, I did. He wanted to make me dinner and the fish was to be the main course, but I told him that the fish was the cutest thing I ever saw and I couldn't eat anything that I had already named."

"Really, you named the fish?"

"Yeah, I did."

"What did you name the fish?"

"I named him Chris! Actually, I don't know if it was a girl fish or a boy fish, but it was adorable, just like Chris."

"And may I ask who Chris is, other than the fish."

"Well, let me tell you that Chris is just about the bravest, most handsome, funniest and most down-to-earth guy you would ever meet."

Beth just stares at the screen as the interviewer cuts to video taken at the premier of the movie. She sees Amanda walking down the red carpet when she stops, turns around and walks back to take Chris' arm to be escorted into the theatre.

"WOW! What a scoop. So, are you and Chris an item?"

"Well, I'm not telling, but I will say he's really a great guy."

The interview went on for a few minutes more when the host tells viewers, "Well, be sure to check out Amanda Sellers' new movie, 'Reflections in the Haze' and we'll also continue to chase the breaking news about beautiful Amanda's new boyfriend Chris…"

Beth finds herself crying after the report ends. After the way she and Chris broke off their relationship she should feel nothing, but if that's the case why is she crying? She starts to unpack her suitcase, but she is too upset to finish. She pours herself a glass of wine goes to the living room and sits down to think about what she should do. She has always secretly hoped that there was some slight chance of getting back together with

Chris, but now with Amanda in the picture, she finally believes that any chance to reconcile is over.

Beth pours herself another glass of wine and, given that she hasn't eaten, she feels a bit light headed. After her third glass of wine Beth is feeling better and she thinks that Chris isn't worth her getting upset over. She thinks that this is just the thing that needed to happen in order for her to make up her mind. She pours herself a fourth glass of wine and picks up the phone.

A familiar voice answers, "Good afternoon, Dr. Thomas Houston's office, may I help you."

"Hi Nancy, this is Beth Della Russo, how are you?"

"Oh, hello Ms. Della Russo how was your flight?"

"It was totally uneventful, which is the way I like to fly."

Nancy chuckles and asks, "That is fortunate. How may I help you?"

"Can I speak to Tom; I mean Dr. Houston?"

"He's in a meeting now, but he asked me to put you through in case you called, please hold on."

A few moments pass when Tom answers, "Beth! Great to hear from you; how was your flight?"

"It was wonderful Tom; I could get used to this"

Tom laughs and says, "Well, you know what you have to do!"

"Well, that's why I'm calling."

"Really, what's up?"

"I'm in."

"What! You're in!"

"Yep."

Tom is ecstatic, "Beth, I can't tell you how happy this makes me. I am so excited for you…well I'm also excited for me too."

Now it's Beth's turn to laugh, "I had a chance to think of your very generous offer and the opportunity to visit the Middle-East with the man who would be president and I couldn't pass up the opportunity."

"This is truly wonderful. The itinerary is being finalized now and I'll be sure to tell Nancy that you will be accompanying me and that she should make the accommodations. She'll also send you a list of the places that you and I will be together and those you can visit while I may be indisposed."

Beth teases Tom, "Indisposed? I hope that's with the Israeli Prime Minister or some bearded sheik and not another woman."

"There is no other woman; I hope that you will find that out when we are together during the trip."

Beth is quiet for a moment, but she finally says, "I was just kidding Tom. I look forward to getting the information from Nancy."

"I need to get back to my meeting, but I'll give you a call later and we can talk."

"Okay Tom, speak to you later."

"Goodbye Beth" and the call disconnects.

Beth puts down the phone and she realizes that she's become dizzy and a little drunk. She lies down on the couch and immediately falls asleep.

An undetectable Satan and Verrine are gazing at Beth. "Your plans are falling into place my lord."

"Yes, they are, aren't they?"

"Quite frankly I thought that the lecher would be a problem, but again, my lord, you are correct."

"Ah, Verrine, have you not been cast out of Heaven as I have? Have you not been made a demon master, as I have commanded? Have you not tormented the endless numbers of souls sent to my kingdom much as I have predicted? Verrine, I am crushed that you still have doubts? I think apropos to this discussion I need to paraphrase a quote from the Bible, 'Trust in your lord, *that's me Verrine*, with all thine heart; and lean not unto thine own understanding.'"

Verrine says, "You got me with that one."

A self-satisfied Satan replies, "I know."

CHAPTER 43

Uncle Al and I visit Father Langford in the late afternoon as promised. We peak through the door as he was finishing a call with someone, "Thank you for your understanding, Marcus, I know you are very concerned and I am most grateful, but I assure you I am making the proper decision and I will keep you informed as the specifics become known. Again, thank you for your confidence and understanding."

Father Aiden spots us and motions us to come into his room. We find him sitting up and first thing we notice is that he is looking much better than he had the day before.

"Aiden, you are looking so much better; thank the Lord and the doctor!"

"Ah, Spartaco, I am glad you have given thanks for my recovery to the entities in the order I would place them in!"

"Well, it figures…after all you are a priest."

The three of us laugh, but Father Langford's expression now becomes serious as we are all gathered in his hospital room for one purpose, and that is to consider what to do next.

"Dear Spartaco and Christopher, I have taken the current catastrophe we have at hand and called upon an old friend and confident."

Uncle Al asks him, "Who?"

"He is the Monsignor Amedeo De Marinis and a man of great skills and experience in the supernatural and the forces of evil that permeate our corporeal world. Msgr. De Marinis is the Chief Exorcist at The Vatican and has been for the past 30 years. We spoke for nearly one hour and I gave him sufficient background so that he could have the requisite understanding of the plight of which we have spoken."

Uncle Al and I stare at Father Langford in silence waiting to hear how much he has told his friend.

"Christopher, I know that you are concerned that I have revealed some of your clandestine relationships with The Sainted and it was your mention of the Church of St. Peter at the Vatican that provided the impetus for my reaching out. I gave Amedeo an abbreviated account of what you had told me and he was not at all dismissive. He provided me with insights into what he has experienced of late in the course of his duties."

The group of people who now know of my visions has become larger and that concerns me, but I tell Father Langford, "I know that it was a difficult conversation to have, but I know you had to tell him something as it would be impossible for him to give us whatever help he can. What did he say?"

Father Langford tells Uncle Al and me about how Msgr. De Marinis has seen the precipitous increase in demonic possessions taking place around the world. The numbers of attempts to exorcise these evil spirits has become so difficult due to the lack of priests practiced in the rituals. "Amodeo is fully aware of the consequences of the prophesies as made known in Revelations, and he fears that current events, including the Lamb of God atrocities could foreshadow the end of days."

I am beyond confused and at a loss as to what I should do. "Father Langford, I know that I must do something to help, but what can I do against such forces."

"Christopher, you need to heed the lessons you have been taught by The Sainted. They shall be a constant resource, stalwarts during those difficult times when faith is all that can sustain you."

"I know Father, The Sainted have always been there all the times I've needed them, even at times when I doubted them, much to my shame."

"Then it is settled, we leave for The Vatican in three days. I have notified the monsignor of our arrival time and he has arranged for someone to meet us at the airport. He has also made arrangements for accommodations at The Vatican."

My Uncle Al, who has been uncharacteristically quiet up until now yells out, "What! You've got to be kidding me Aiden. You've just had a heart attack you could wind up killing yourself!"

"Ah, Spartaco, thank you for reminding me!"

"Aiden, for once in your life be serious, you can't possibly think about making the trip all the way to The Vatican. You'll become enmeshed in all the horrors that can be brought about by a battle between Heaven and hell. Oh, and I forgot, how about the possibility of having to confront Satan, huh, have you thought of that…Satan! We're not talking about some common ordinary run of the mill demon, we're talking about Lucifer, the Fallen Angel. You might have heard of him."

"My dear friend, you are always there with sage advice, however, need I remind you of one important fact; nothing will matter if the forces of hell are allowed to succeed in this unholy quest for the souls of mankind. Spartaco, I do not fear death and if it is my fate to make this my last quest then I shall gladly rest in the arms of the Lord."

I interrupt, "Father Langford, I have to agree with Uncle Al, you are in no condition to take on a burden like this. We both can get the monsignor on the phone and I can give him details of my visions and he can ask me any questions he wants. I can then go to The Vatican and meet with Msgr. De Marinis, I am sure that he can give me the guidance that I will need to find my place in the scheme of things and do whatever I can to help."

"Christopher, it seems you are cut of the same cloth as your uncle, but my mind is made up. I have spoken to my boss, Father Marcus Teller, who has also given me the same admonishment, but having on numerous occasions encountered my intransigence, he acquiesced. I must tell you that Father Marcus Teller is far more effective at arguing than either of you. I have also informed my doctor of my plans and eliciting a similar reaction, and providing me with the direst of warnings, he relented knowing that it was my choice. Finally, he conceded and acquiesced under protest."

Uncle Al and I continue to tell Father Langford all the reasons why he shouldn't go on the trip, but it was no use, he is determined to go with me and, on some level, I am glad. He is a priest, a biblical scholar, a friend of The Vatican's Chief Exorcist and if anyone can guide me through what I fear is more than I can handle, its Father Langford. "Well Father, I guess we are a team, and I can't think of anyone, other than The Sainted and my uncle, that I would rather have with me at this time."

Uncle Al turns to me and says, "Chris, you know I can't go with you although there is nothing that I would rather do, but there are so many things happening right here in Suffolk that I must be around to try and help. My mind will be on my job here, but my heart is with you and Aiden."

I hug my uncle and say, "I love you too."

* * *

We stay for a while longer discussing what we will be hoping to accomplish with Msgr. De Marinis. After more than one hour Father Aiden appeared to be growing tired and we all agreed to keep in touch with each other should something need to be addressed. I told Father Aiden that I would make the reservations and pick up whatever else he may need from the Immaculate Conception Seminary.

"Christopher, I am truly in awe of what you have told me and what you have experienced. It seems apparent to me that the Lord has chosen you as the vessel to communicate with The Sainted because you are a human without guile and with the frailties that are embodied in us all. I imagine that the Lord could have given this blessing to His Holiness the Pope or some other religious leader, but He chose you and that is, in and of itself, a miracle. Now I believe we have covered some of what is required in preparation so I shall take this opportunity to bid you goodbye and God Bless."

"Thank you for your kind words and try to get as much rest as you can before we leave for Rome; for some reason, I think you and I will need it."

Father Langford smiles, "Sage advice. Good bye my dear Spartaco and peace be with you and I pray to the Lord for the resolution to the challenges you are facing."

"Thank you, Aiden, and please come back alive and in good health. Tell you what, if you come back intact, I will make my confession, I might decide to leave out a couple of slip ups especially with the ones that include the woman I met when I was 22 years old, but you can give me general absolution for that."

Father Aiden laughs out loud, "That alone gives me the incentive I need to return in fine form and fit as a fiddle."

* * *

We leave the room and Uncle Al and I say our goodbyes and I take the short drive home. When I pull up to my condo, I see a familiar limo parked in front. David opens the door of the limo and Amanda steps out and has a big smile for me. I get out of my car and return the smile. I am happy to see her, especially after my discussions with Fr. Langford and Uncle Al.

"Hi, what are you doing here? Aren't you supposed to be at some public relations event or interview with the media or shopping for fishing gear and a new boat?"

Amanda laughs and pulls out a copy of the NY Post and shows me that article about our fishing trip. "Take a look at this, you're becoming famous and you have me, and the fish, to thank for it."

I read the article and say, "I think I'm a lot cuter than the fish."

"Yes, you are, but he or she does have a certain charm, you must admit."

"I guess so, but the fish would look far more appealing as a fillet broiled in a bit of olive oil, butter and lemon."

"You are a callous beast. Come on, I've got David waiting and we can do something together. Why don't we go out east to Montauk like you wanted to do the other day?"

I think to myself that I should really go to the shop and get some work done, but I have second thoughts about it and decide that, given what is ahead for me in Rome and beyond, it might not matter as God may have other plans.

Having assuaged my initial guilt I tell Amanda, "I really should be working, after all I do have a business to run. With all that is happening, I've let a lot of that slip, but you twisted my arm. We can go to Montauk or is there something else you want to do?"

Amanda thinks a bit, "Well how about this, why don't we go to your shop and work? I can help and you can get caught up. What do you say?"

"Wait, you are a world-famous actress, smart, funny, accomplished, rich…"

"You forgot beautiful."

"Oh yeah, and a beautiful woman and you want to help this lowly peasant that, by the way, looks like a fish…"

"You forgot cute…"

"Oh yeah, cute fish…with his work?"

"Enough with the banter; you can buy me dinner after we get done. Come on let's go."

I am sure David is grateful that he is getting paid by the hour because it's going to be a long day for him. We drive to my shop and I tell Amanda about how I got the name for the shop and what my days are like. I open the door and continue speaking as I see Amanda's eyes start to glaze over.

Amanda yawns and says, "How interesting."

"Ha, ha, very funny; now let's get to work."

I give Amanda the mail that has accumulated and ask her open the envelopes and separate orders and other correspondence. I go to my computer and download the orders from my site and look over the emails received in the overnight. It all seems to be business as usual and I am grateful that all is going as well as it is.

Amanda and I work really well together. After a few hours we are mostly done with the work I had planned to do when I hear the door open and in walks Fred Klein. "Hey, Chris, how's it going?"

"Fine Fred; how are you feeling?"

"Great I'm…" all of a sudden, he stops speaking as he sees a smiling Amanda looking up at him.

Fred seems in shock, "Hey, aren't you…"?

I jump in and say, "Fred, I'd like you to meet the winner of this years 'Amanda Sellers Look-A-Like Contest', Gertrude Miasma. Gertrude, I'd like you to meet Fred Klein."

Fred looks at Amanda and back at me and says, "My word, I can see why she won the contest."

Now Amanda, Fred and I burst out laughing and I say, "Fred, meet Amanda Sellers, Amanda, this is Fred Klein. Fred, I told Amanda about Tina and all that you and she have gone through."

Amanda holds Fred's hand and says, "I am so pleased to meet you, how is Tina?"

Fred looks down at his hand and back up and says, "She's doing really well and we are so thankful to Chris and his uncle." Now he looks back down at his hand and says to Amanda, "I may never wash my hand again."

Amanda scolds Fred, "You better if you ever want to shake my hand again."

I explain to Fred that Amanda and I became friends through her father and that I've fallen behind because of helping my uncle and Father Langford. "She has offered to help me and at the current NY State minimum wage law being what it is, I jumped at the chance for free labor."

We continue to talk when the shop door opens and two of the old guys that I know walk in. "Hey Chris, how are…"

Before they have a chance to drool all over Amanda, I say, "Guys, I'd like you to meet Amanda; Amanda, this is Tom Feldman and Aaron Symington, good friends of mine."

Amanda radiates her charm and practiced smile and says, "Tom, Aaron how nice to meet you." Now Amanda turns to me in all seriousness and says, "Chris, you didn't tell me that you had such handsome friends? Boys, please come in and sit next to Fred over there. I have got some things to show you that you are going to love. Chris, can you please get me some of those coin thingies that you sell?"

I have to stifle a laugh as I know these guys very seldom buy anything and usually just like to come in to sit, drink coffee and talk. "Sure enough." I go to my safe and pull-out trays of some of my recent acquisitions and hand them to Amanda. I tell her, "These are recent finds and the boys here haven't seen them yet."

Amanda acts very excited, "Gentlemen! How fortunate you are here at this exact moment in time. I must admit to you that I have very little experience with money, except on how to spend it, so you are going to have to give me an education and let me bargain with Chris, I have a number of ways of getting you the best deals."

I practically have to hold my breath to keep from bursting out in laughter as these guys fall all over themselves trying to explain to Amanda about the coins and their value to a collector. This goes on for about 30 minutes when the door to my shop opens again, but this time there are a small group of people who have found out that Amanda Seller is here in my shop. Before you know it, my shop is packed and there is a standing room only party going on with Amanda and everyone there having a great time. Someone even ordered enough pizza and soft drinks for everyone and so the fun continues.

Amanda has been sending customers to the counter all afternoon and now she is speaking to a woman when she walks up to introduce her to me, "Chris, I'd like you to meet Helen Ferguson. Helen's husband, Marshall is a passionate collector and she wants to get him something special for his birthday. Now I told Helen that you would select something very nice for him and that you better give her a good price or I will make it impossible for you stand up straight again, is that clear."

"Yes, and thank you Amanda; pleased to meet you, Mrs. Ferguson, do you know the type of coins your husband likes to collect?"

"No, not really; I do know that he likes to collect silver coins, oh and American Coins usually ones that are very old, you know perhaps 150 to 200 or so years ago, something like that."

"I just might have something he will like." I go to my display case and pull out an 1829 US Large Cent with Large Letters, graded a VF 20. "Mrs. Ferguson, I think he would like this one. It is called a Large Cent and it was minted in the US nearly 200 years ago and this one is in very fine condition. Coins of this type are highly collectible and I think he will really like it."

"Oh my, it does look old. How much is it?"

"In this condition, it's valued at $85."

"I had a budget of $100 for his present so that seems fine."

"Here, let me wrap it for you." I put this coin in a plastic shell casing and place it is a gift box. When I'm done, I hand it to her with another coin, "Here is your husband's gift and this is a little something from us to him. It's an 1893 Silver Quarter Dollar in pretty good condition. Tell him Happy Birthday from us."

Mrs. Ferguson seems delighted and says, "Thank you so very much I'm sure he will love these gifts, and I'll tell Amanda not to kick you in the crotch!"

After I finish laughing, I say, "Please tell Marshall that if he already has either of these coins to come back and we'll exchange it for something else." Well, it went on pretty much like this for the rest of the afternoon with Amanda meeting and greeting the customers, laughing along with them and enjoying herself immensely. It was after 6:30PM when we finally were able to close shop and lean back and relax.

"Chris, this was so much fun! I had a wonderful time."

"So did I and I appreciate your 'saleswomanship', I think I may have beaten my previous one-day sales record thanks to you."

"You're welcome, now I'm starving so let's go eat."

I want to take Amanda to my favorite, Mabella's Restaurant, but then I thought that it will be awkward as Frank and Maria are also good friends with Beth. I ask Amanda, "Do you like Steak?"

"Sure, I love steak."

"Great!" We walk to Amanda's limo and I tell David to take us to Mac's which is not far from my shop. The driver pulls up in front of the restaurant and we get out. When the people who are waiting to get in see us, they get very excited and part the way to let us go through. The greeter recognizes Amanda and is delighted to welcome her. We ask for a table and he escorts us to a booth in the corner and we sit down.

In a very short while our server arrives and he seems very excited to be waiting on our table, "Ms. Sellers, I want to welcome you and your escort to Mac's. My name is Hugo and I will be your server this evening, can I get you both something to drink? Wine or a cocktail perhaps?"

Amanda says, "Can we see a wine list?"

The waiter just happens to have one in his hand and he gives it to Amanda. She looks it over and says, "Given that we are having steak, I think a Pinot Noir would go well, what do you think Chris? "

"Well, if your father were here, he would probably choose a Cabernet."

"You're right." Amanda looks up at the waiter and asks, "What Cabernet from the wine list do you recommend?

The waiter reviews the wine list, but you can tell he has already come up with a recommendation in his mind, "I would recommend the Summers Cabernet Sauvignon Calistoga Estate 2014. It pairs well with beef and it has been very well received by many of our guests."

"Well then the Summers it is! Thanks."

"You're welcome, Ms. Seller and I'll be right back with your wine."

I look at Amanda and say, "How come no Tequila?"

"Oh, if you'd rather get drunk again, I can always…"

"NO! Wine is fine. Hey that rhymes."

Amanda and I are settled in and comfortable. Many of the guests are trying not to stare at Amanda, but she doesn't mind and is used to it. I ask her, "Does it ever bother you that you can't go anywhere without being recognized?"

"Not really. These are my fans; I wouldn't be doing what I love without their support and I am really very grateful for what I have.

"Sounds like a very mature attitude given what I've heard about some assholes in your business."

"True, but I don't ever take my fans for granted…ever."

"Well good for you."

The wine comes and the waiter pours her a small amount to taste. Amanda performs the time-tested ritual and approves and we order our dinners. For appetizers, Amanda orders the mozzarella & tomatoes and I have the shrimp cocktail. For the main course, we order the Porterhouse for 2, cooked medium rare, with side dishes of sautéed spinach and potato parmesan croquettes. I say, "Do you think we have enough to eat?"

Amanda thinks and says, "No, we haven't ordered dessert yet."

I've been waiting for the right time to tell Amanda that I will be away. I know I can't tell her the real reason for my trip so I have to make up a story that seems plausible. "Amanda, I have some news to tell you about."

"Really, what is it?"

"Well, I am going to meet a friend of Father Langford's that is attached to the Vatican! Can you imagine, The Vatican! Father Langford arranged this all from his hospital room and I was told that this person has a number of things to discuss and I'm very excited. I'm going to be there for a short while and it's my first trip abroad, so the adventure begins."

"Wow, sounds really exciting. What's it all about?"

I look to the left and look to the right and I tell Amanda in a whisper, "I can't tell you, its super-secret."

She smiles and says, "I wish I could go with you, but I'm going to have a meeting with a major studio about what I hope will be my next project."

"Really, what's the project?"

"Oh, I can't tell you, is super-secret, but when I can let you in on it, I think you will be very surprised, at least I hope you will."

"Super-secret huh, well I'm looking forward to hearing about it when you can tell me."

Amanda reaches over to hold my hand. "You'll be the first to know, well outside of the big shot producers."

The waiter comes to the table with our appetizers and tops off our wine glasses. We spend the next few minutes just enjoying each other's company and the food and are not aware of the many people who are continuing to stare at us. Next the waiter returns with the Porterhouse steak for 2 and it is cooked just right; medium rare as Amanda and I ordered.

Hugo asks us, "May I serve you now?"

Amanda tells him, "Hurry up Hugo, I'm starving and the steak smells delicious!"

Hugo serves us the steak and adds the side dishes to our plates and we both dig in. Amanda and I eat with gusto, approving of every bite. "I do enjoy this, I'm always watching my weight so when I can cheat, I relish every moment."

Well, I'm glad you're enjoying the dinner and again, thanks for your help today; actually, it was a lot of fun."

Amanda smiles, "Yeah, it was."

When we had our fill, the waiter comes back and sees we have some food left so he asks us if we want to take it home and I enthusiastically say, "Yes!"

Amanda looks at me and laughs, "Another meal you don't have to cook huh."

"Well yeah, but I happen to be a great cook. I once made this meal…" and then I think of Beth and the meal I made her. "Anyway, it was fabulous even if I say so myself. I'd like to cook for you sometime, if you'll let me."

Amanda seems very happy and says, "I'd love it if you would cook for me" and we stop speaking and look in each other's eyes when her phone chimes.

Amanda answers, "Hello" and she is quiet while she listens to the voice at the other end. "Can't this wait until tomorrow?" more of the voice at the other end of the line and Amanda sighs, "Okay, okay, I'll be there in about an hour, okay, goodbye."

"Oh, oh, sounds like a problem."

"Yes, there is. There is a problem with "Reflections in the Haze" and the studio in California has a conference call with the production team that is still here in New York. They need to make some changes and, according to my contract, I have to provide input and approval and it has to be done now, tonight, as a matter of fact."

"I am really sorry. I thought it was perfect and got great reviews"

"It did, but there are other issues, some are actually legal issues and the studio could be sued if the changes aren't made before the release which is in less than a week. I'm really sorry Chris I was hoping we could spend some time together."

"Amanda, just you being here was great and I totally understand. I'll be leaving for Italy in less than three days and I'll call you when I get back."

I pay the bill and walk Amanda to the limo. "I'll have David drive you home."

"Don't bother Amanda, I am a short 15-minute walk to my condo and I can use the fresh air. Just get back to your hotel and I sincerely hope the meeting goes well."

I take Amanda in my arms and she puts her arms around me and holds me close to her. Our lips meet in a passionate kiss and when we part, I see tears welling up in her eyes.

"Please don't wait to call me until you get back, call me when you're there in Italy."

I smile at Amanda and hold her tight, "I promise, I will."

CHAPTER 44

Three days pass and I am on my way to pick up Father Aiden who is waiting for me at Huntington Hospital.

I've booked us seats in coach on a non-stop flight with Alitalia Airlines and we need to be able check into international security at least two hours in advance of out flight time. I decided to use a car service to take us to JFK and I ask the driver to drop me off in front of the hospital entrance. I make my way to the elevator and press the button that takes me to the fourth floor. As I get off the elevator, I am hoping that Beth will not be there as I just can't take anymore drama in my life.

I look down the corridor to the nurses' station and I'm relieved that I don't see Beth. I walk towards Father Langford's room and as I am nearly past the nurses' station, Beth comes walking out of the back office looking down at a clip board in her hands. Beth looks up and sees me walking past the desk and we both are silent not knowing what to say.

Beth is the first to speak, "Hello Chris, how are you?"

"Uh, I'm good Beth, how are you?"

"Fine."

"I'm here to pick up Father Langford."

"Listen, we here are all very concerned; Aiden is in no condition to leave the hospital. I can only hope he is going back to the seminary to rest."

"Well, to tell you the truth…"

Beth can't hold it back any longer, "Hah, the truth; that sounds rich coming from you."

"Please Beth, I don't want to argue, I really don't. As I was saying, I am here to pick up Father Langford as we will be leaving on a flight from JFK to Rome in about three and a half hours."

Beth now gets really upset, "Flight to Rome! Are you kidding, Father Langford shouldn't be leaving the hospital, let alone flying to Rome?"

"I'm sure you're right, but he has his mind made up and he won't listen to anything anyone has to say about the trip. I'm going with him and I'll try to make sure he is taken care of."

Beth, in a snarky voice, says, "Anyone else going with you? Perhaps someone from Hollywood."

I am not going to take the bait of Beth's thinly disguised reference to Amanda, so I just say, "No one else, just me and Father Langford. Oh, and how is Dr. Thomas Houston? By the way, what kind of doctor is he?"

Beth ignores my question and answers, "Just fine and none of your business."

"Well, it was good to see you and I'm glad you are well. I'll go get Fr. Langford now."

I turn to leave when Beth calls out. The look on her face has softened as she says, "Chris, please wait a minute. I'm sorry for being so abrupt with you, I really am. I'm also sorry for the way we left it the last time we spoke. Have a safe flight and take care of Aiden."

I smile at Beth, "Beth, thanks for being so gracious about this. I also want to apologize for the way I spoke to you too, you are a fine person and I'm glad to know you. Please take care of yourself and send my regards to your family."

We smile at each other, glad we have turned an awkward moment into a civil, if not pleasant, parting of the ways. I walk down the hallway and enter Father Langford's room. He is already in a wheelchair; his suitcase is next to him and there is an aide waiting to take him down to the hospital's exit through the lobby.

"Good morning, Father."

"Good morning to you Christopher. It seems to be a lovely day for our flight to the Eternal City, does it not?"

"It does! I've picked up your clothes and passport at ICS and your chariot waits!"

"To quote my beloved Shakespeare's, The Tempest, 'I would not wish any companion in the world but you!'"

Father Langford and I, along with the hospital aide, walk past the nurses' desk and Aiden asks to stop so he can say goodbye to Beth, "Ah, I am more than grateful to the wonderful staff here at Huntington Hospital. I count myself among the fortunate to have been placed in the care of such compassionate and capable professionals such as you. Please convey my heartfelt thanks to all as I bid you a fond adieu!"

Beth scowls at the priest, "You know that you shouldn't be leaving here, don't you?"

"Ah, reprimanded by the lovely Beth; I ask you in all sincerity, shall this recrimination be the last words we share?"

Beth knows that she can't stay angry at Father Aiden for long. She walks around the counter and bends down to give him a gentle hug, a kiss on the cheek and a big smile. "Please take care of yourself and come back home to us."

"As you all know I am fond of quoting the Bard and to you my dear Beth I declare, 'I won't say goodbye my friend, for you and I will meet again.'"

Beth smiles at us, "Goodbye and good luck to both of you."

I smile back, "Thanks Beth and stay well."

We leave for the elevator and Father Aiden looks up at me and says, "It seems that, in spite of the cordiality, you and the lovely Beth have much unsettled between you."

"It's a long story."

"Well, it is a long flight and long stories help the time to pass, so we shall talk then."

* * *

We arrive at JFK International Terminal with plenty of time to spare. I've already asked for a wheelchair to be available to make it easier for Fr. Langford to get around the cavernous terminal. After I present our passports, confirm seat assignments and check our baggage, we make our way to the gate where we will board our flight on Alitalia. We have time to relax a bit before the flight so I suggest that we stop for something to drink. I ask, "Father Langford would you like some tea or water or something else to drink?"

"Christopher, you treat me like royalty and I am most appreciative. I would like a bottle of water and here, take this" and Fr. Aiden hands me a $5.00 bill.

"Please Father; I can't take your money."

"Christopher, I insist."

"Father Langford, if I were to take your money, I'd have two groups to answer to; well technically one group and one person. First, The Sainted would frown on my taking money from you plus I've seen what they can do when they are angry and second, Uncle Al would kill me so I'm paying whether you like it or not."

Father Aiden puts the money back in his wallet and says, "Thank you and thank The Sainted and my dearest friend Spartaco for making thinly veiled threats against your life."

I laugh and say, "I'll be right back…"

I get our drinks and I find a corner of the café where we can sit down and talk. "Father, I need to get a bit more background into Msgr. De Marinis and what you think our rolls in all this will be."

"I have been giving this the utmost consideration as it falls well beyond my own experiences and abilities to comprehend. Amodeo is the Vatican's foremost authority on demonic possession and exorcism and in that capacity, he has encountered many demons commanded by the forces of hell. I trust he can provide guidance in terms of the rituals associated with the exorcising of those demons."

"Father, this seems like there is so much more of a threat. The battle that has been predicted will shake all of humanity."

"I understand Christopher. This is a horror that will be visited on mankind and in order to defeat the satanic forces of hell, it is important that we understand the nature of the evil in hopes of routing it and, in that regard, there is no more appropriate advisor than Msgr. Amodeo De Marinis." Father Langford went on to explain the biblical prophesies and the various predictions of the end of days as written in scriptures. He also told me that we will meet with the monsignor, and he will help to establish and guide a course of action.

"I must confide in you Christopher that I have a presentiment of great import, regarding Amodeo. I do not know what that will be, but in concert with the power of God the Father and His Son, the Heavenly Host and The Sainted, I am confident we will prevail."

"So am I."

A short time later the call to board our overnight flight is made over the loud speaker and we both get comfortably seated for the long flight. When we reached cruising altitude Father Aiden turns to me and says, "Now that we are comfortably ensconced, would you like to tell me of the rift that has developed between yourself and Beth?"

I sigh not wanting to relive all that has happened, but I know Father Langford has my best interests at heart, so for an hour I recount all that has gone on between Beth and I and the resulting breakup. I tell him how we said some very hurtful and nasty things to each other and I regret all that happened between us.

"I guess I was jealous and angry at the same time. Being accused of something that I didn't do made me lose my temper and that helped create the rift that either of us could bridge or even try to."

"Very sad indeed Christopher; have you tried to reach out to her in the interim?"

"The first time I've seen Beth since we had the fight and broke up was today when I picked you up at the hospital. I think we left on good terms, but there is still a lot of hurt and I'm sure she is as bitter as I am about what happened."

"So, as you have related, it seems Beth saw you kissing Amanda Sellers which was broadcast over the airwaves and you saw Beth kissing Dr.

Thomas Houston which was also broadcast over the airways. Now let us examine the facts as I perceive them; you say Amanda in fact kissed you and it was not expected nor encouraged by you. In fact, you are as innocent as a new born baby and totally blameless"

"Yes; well actually it was very flattering and I kind of enjoyed it, but I immediately felt guilty. I knew that it could be conceived as cheating and wanted to explain to Beth as soon as I got home from my trip to Chicago."

"Ah, I can see your conundrum; now what of Beth?"

I gave Father Aiden a snide response to his question, "Well, the way I see it, the photos of Beth and Tom Houston certainly looked as if they were enjoying the kiss."

He ignored my being snide, "I see and you both made a logical assumption based on the evidence at hand. You each saw what you wanted to see and this erupted into a war of words and that was the cause of your estrangement."

"I guess that pretty much sums it up. Now it seems that Beth and Tom Houston have gotten really close, as a matter of fact they just spent a couple of weeks together in Miami."

"What of you and the lovely Ms. Sellers?"

"Well, we have also been spending time together. She is really a very nice person and I think she genuinely likes me and I have feelings for her, but nothing really happened between us."

"So, as you have related, Beth does not know that you were accosted by Amanda Sellers."

"Well, I wouldn't say accosted, but yeah, she doesn't know what really happened."

"And you, my dear, conflicted Christopher; as it appears to me you have not an inkling as to what actually transpired between Dr. Houston and Beth."

"Well, what about the photos?"

"Ah, yes what about the photos and what about the video of you and Amanda."

"Well, that was not what really transpired."

"So, it becomes apparent that neither of you took the time to discuss what actually happened and based your apparent anger with each other. What may have been an innocent happenstance now has caused you both to have moved on to other relationships, leaving so much unresolved. You need not answer my next question, but you may wish to ponder it as we fly to Rome; do you still love Beth?"

At 35,000 feet I am confronting the possibility that this all could have been a series of unfortunate assumptions by both of us. "I see what you're getting at and I think that I will take time to think things over."

Father Langford smiles, "I hope you will. Now I am a bit fatigued and I will use this respite in our conversation to take repose in order to endure what I assume will be the unimaginable rigors of the next few days."

I smile and say, "Sleep well Father, see you in the morning" as the priest closes his eyes and falls fast asleep.

The quiet time I had while Fr. Langford is asleep allows time for me to think of Beth and how it all spiraled out of control. What of Tom Houston? He and Beth obviously have developed a very close relationship and I don't know how I should feel about that. Are they in love; am I still in love with Beth?

The introspection also gave me time to consider the warm feelings that I have for Amanda. It seems startling to me how a woman of such fame and beauty could possibly be in love with me. Can she take the place of Beth in my heart? I think that maybe she can, but I am not sure. As I consider all that has happened my thoughts turn to Fr. Langford's premonition, our meeting with Msgr. De Marinis and what may be ahead for us. The impending battle between the forces of Heaven and hell that can spell doom for all humanity and the realization that I have been called as a participant in it all weigh heavy on me.

I am abruptly roused from my thoughts by the captain announcing that the attendants will be coming around with dinner and soon after he will be turning off the lights in the main cabin. I think to myself what I really need is a drink, preferably alcohol and as if the saints recognized what I could use in this my hour of need, the attendant stops at my seat with the cart.

"Would you like something to drink?"

Without hesitation I say, "Double vodka on the rocks."

CHAPTER 45

We land at 9 A.M. local time in Rome at Fiumicino International Airport "Leonardo da Vinci." It is one of Europe's largest and busiest airports. Father Aiden and I have a rough time negotiating the Alitalia terminal when we finally arrive at customs. We pass through customs with no problems and I wheel Father Langford towards the exit and tell him that I will look for our ride. As we pass through the doorway, I see a young priest with a sign that reads *Fr. Aiden Langford*.

I wheel Father Langford over to the priest holding the sign and say, "Buongiorno, mi chiamo Chris Pella e questo è padre Aiden Langford."

He smiles at us and says, "Good morning Mr. Pella and Father Langford, I am Father Giovanni Sellisi, I am assistant to Monsignor De Marinis."

"Ah, I see you speak English and that should help make things easier to communicate with Father Langford."

Father Aiden looks up at me and says, "Al contrario, Christopher, sono altrettanto a conoscenza sia dell'inglese che dell'italiano, così come di altre cinque lingue. Buongiorno Padre Sellisi."

I shake my head and tell Father Aiden, "I see you've found another way to illustrate your brilliance" and both Father Sellisi and I laugh.

"Always pleased to be of assistance!"

Father Sellisi tells us, "I am here to drive you to the Vatican where Msgr. De Marinis anxiously awaits you. He has asked that you meet him

"

in the Basilica by the 'Chapel of the Pieta' where he will escort you to your quarters."

The drive from the airport through the streets of Rome is a thrill for me. Rome is such a beautiful city and I can understand why they call it 'The Eternal City.' We pass so many famous sites and historic landmarks that have withstood the test of time and I am the classic definition of a wide-eyed tourist. This is my first trip abroad and given my Italian heritage, I feel like I am coming home.

Father Sellisi occasionally looks at the rear-view mirror and smiles as he observes my gawking as we pass places that I have only seen in books. He tells me, "Mr. Pella, I had much the same reaction during my first trip to Rome and even up until today, I continue to marvel at the architecture, history and beauty of this city."

"Please call me Chris; I can see why. So, you if weren't born in Rome, where did you come from originally?"

"I am from the Basilicata Region of Italy. I was born and raised in Montescaglioso, a small hill town. It has become popular for tourists and it is home to the 11th Century Abbey of San Michele Arcangelo."

I think of Saint Michael the Archangel and I say a short prayer of thanks to him for saving Uncle Al's life.

Father Sellisi continues, "There is a beautiful little church in Montescaglioso built in honor of San Rocco and if you are there in August, the Festa di San Rocco is a wonderful and exciting local celebration. There's a religious parade and incredible fireworks; I hope you can get there one of these days."

Father Aiden says to us, "Ah, I have been to Montescaglioso when I was on sabbatical and travelling through this beautiful country of Italy. I can attest to Father Sellisi's description, it is a truly enchanting place."

"You've convinced me…I'm already hooked."

We arrive at Vatican City and we pass through the service gate manned by the Swiss Guard, a security force that is responsible for maintaining the safety of the Vatican residents, especially the Pope. Father Sellisi pulls to the rear of the Basilica into an area reserved for those who work for the Vatican and off limits to the millions of tourists visiting this holy place each year.

The young priest points to a door just a few yards away and says, "That is the entrance to the Chapel Hall. From there we will walk down the Nave until we reach the Chapel of the Pieta where Monsignor De Marinis will be waiting. It is quite a long way to walk so, at the monsignor's request, I have arranged for a wheelchair for Father Langford."

Father Aiden seems relieved and tells Fr. Sellisi "Thank you so much, that will be most helpful."

As I enter the Basilica of St. Peter's I am literally stunned at the magnificence of the interior. It is so much more than a shrine to the Apostle St. Peter, who is the 'Rock'; the foundation on which the Roman Catholic Church was built. It is the ultimate expression of man's devotion to God and His Son, Jesus Christ. I am awestruck and humbled just looking at all there is to see; the sheer size and scope of St. Peter's is beyond comparison. I make a solemn vow to myself to tour St. Peter's, The Sistine Chapel, the Vatican Library and the beautiful grounds.

Our small group walks past the vaults of a number of Popes from the earliest of times. Throughout the Basilica there are many amazingly intricate mosaics, some of which depict the life and times of many of The Sainted. I find myself stopping just to gaze at the incomparable skill that must have been used in completing such works. When we reach the Chapel of the Pieta, I stop in stunned surprise at the lifelike beauty and passion used by Michelangelo in creating this world-renowned masterpiece. Michelangelo created his masterpiece in such a way that he has carved details using the grain of the marble as the features down to the veins on Christ's hand. I am literally frozen, never wanting to take my eyes off the Pieta, when suddenly the world stands still and I am taken back in time

Jesus is standing on a hill overlooking the throngs of faithful. He is preaching to them and telling them of the way to salvation. When approached by His disciples, they tell Him of the crowd being preached to and of the need to feed them. It is then Jesus performs a miracle; He makes five loaves of bread and two fishes enough to feed the group of more than five-thousand people.

I remain still in reverence as I witness what the Scriptures have recorded as a miraculous event in the life of Jesus Christ. The vision continues,

> *Following the miracle of the loaves and fishes, Jesus tells His disciples to take their boat to the other side of a nearby river. After He bids farewell to the throngs of people, He prays by Himself in the hills. As He prays, the boat the disciples are on experiences rough waves. In the fourth watch of the night, Jesus approaches their boat by walking on the water.*

> *When his disciples spy Jesus walking on the water, they are afraid, but Jesus calls to them and says, "Courage! It is I! Do not be afraid." Peter answers, "Lord ... if it is You, tell me to come to You across the water."*

> *Jesus motions and tells Peter to come and he begins to walk toward Him on the surface of the water and at the Lord's command, he walks on water. It wasn't until Peter becomes aware of the fierce wind that blows that he begins to fear for his safety and cries out, "Lord ... save me!" Because he loses his faith in Jesus' power, St Peter sinks into the waters.*

> *Jesus reaches out and touches Peter and he is saved, but Jesus is saddened and tells his disciple, "Have you so little faith ... why did you doubt?"*

St. Peter steps out of the vision and stands before me. "I have relived that moment of doubt for millennia and I still feel ashamed. I have seen the Lord perform miracles, I have seen Him heal the sick and comfort the dying, but when it came to my believing in Him, my own fear allowed me to doubt what my eyes beheld."

I am at a loss as to what I can say to him, but the vision changes again as I see St. Peter, head bowed, speaking to the Lord,

St. Peter tells his Lord, "I am Your vessel, do with me what You will and I will do all You command."

Jesus tells the Sainted, 'Simon, son of Jonah, you are a blessed man! Because it was no human agency that revealed this to you, but my Father in heaven so I now say to you: You are Peter and, on this rock, I will build my community. And the gates of the underworld can never overpower it."

St. Peter tells me that through the power of Jesus he was able to spread the gospel by performing miracles. The vision changes yet again and I am able to witness the power St. Peter was able to wield for so many…

…to such an extent that the locals even carried the sick out into the streets of the towns and laid them on cots and pallets. This was done so that when Peter came by at least his shadow might fall on any one of them. Also, the people from the cities in the vicinity of Jerusalem were coming together, bringing people who were sick or afflicted with unclean spirits, and they were all being healed.

St. Peter tells me that the time is near and that I must do what is needed to stop the evil that seeks to corrupt and ruin the souls of all humankind. He says that all will be held to account once the battle is run and that Jesus will come again to judge the living and the dead.

"Christopher, our Lord, Jesus Christ has already removed the first seal. It speaks of the rider on the white horse. The rider will arrive on the world scene at the beginning of the Tribulation and he will work to pretend to unite the nations. He will be a charismatic leader that presents himself as the savior of the world. But you must beware that his power and authority will come from the dragon, and like Satan he is a great deceiver. This is the false prophet, the Anti-Christ who will set up a confrontation that threatens to destroy belief in the Lord and the damnation of so many souls."

"I have been told this."

"What has not been foretold to you is that there is a second false prophet."

"What! A second false prophet…who is it?"

"The second false prophet is the Muslim anti-Christ. He is the Deceiver, the last of a line of 30 Deceivers and he is known as Al Masih ad Dajjal, the Kafir."

I am trying to grasp all of what I have been told, but I have no words to describe what I am feeling at this moment.

St. Peter continues, "You and the priests will be needed to confront both of the anti-christs pitted against heaven in their alliance with Satan and the forces of evil."

"How can I, I don't even know who they are?

"You already know."

"Know? How can I possibly know who it is?"

"He is already on his journey to The Holy Land. He will be in the company of someone innocent, but who is in grave danger. Evil will consume this being and if possessed, all will be lost."

"Grave danger? What danger?"

"Time is drawing near. You and the priests are to represent man in this conflict."

"This can't be; how can the three of us hope to fight the forces of hell?"

"You can, for you will not be alone; you will have the forces of Heaven and in the words of our Lord, 'the gates of the underworld can never overpower it', but it is for mankind to prove that they are worthy of saving. You three have been chosen and it is only through your faith that you will prevail."

I start to speak, but as I try the vision of St. Peter slowly fades and I am back in the Basilica where Msgr. De Marinis and Father Aiden are greeting each other with a fond embrace.

"Amodeo, it has been too long and I am so please that you are doing well!"

"I am also very thankful that you seem to be in fine health and spirits."

Father Aiden says as he turns to face me, "My dear monsignor, I would like to introduce my…" but he stops speaking when he sees the look on my face.

"Christopher! Christopher, my son, what is it? Why have you turned so pale?"

I am holding my breath and try to speak, but the words will not come. Father Sellisi rushes to my side to hold me up as my legs go wobbly and it seems to them that I might pass out.

Father Sellisi gently slaps the side of my cheeks in hopes that I would come out of my stupor. All of a sudden, I start to breathe in heaves and my legs are like rubber.

"Christopher, please speak to me."

I finally catch my breath and say to Father Langford, "I…I don't know what happened to me, but I'm okay now."

Father Aiden turns to his friend, "Amodeo is there a medical facility that we can take Christopher to? I believe he needs to receive medical attention."

I immediately protest, "Father, please I am fine now. I must have experienced some negative effects from the long flight; please I don't need to see a doctor. I would like to be able to go to my quarters and sit down for a while. I promise if I feel any ill effects, I will let you know and then I will go to the doctor."

I can read the concern on Father Aiden face, "Christopher, I do not feel it wise to neglect your condition, as a matter of fact…"

"As a matter of fact, Father, you did pretty much the same thing by leaving the hospital declaring you were, how did you put it? Oh yes…fit as a fiddle."

"It appears you have taken lessons from your uncle and my physician in turning my own words against me. I am not pleased, but I must accede to your will."

I am already feeling better, "Good, can we all go to my room I would like to discuss something confidential with both you and Msgr. De Marinis, if I may?"

Msgr. De Marinis says, "Of course." He turns to Father Sellisi, "Giovanni, you a free to go about your duties and I want to thank you for taking such good care of my friends."

We all say our goodbyes and watch Father Sellisi walk away.

The monsignor tells us that we should follow him and motions the way.

I look around to make sure that no one is in earshot, and I say to the priests, "Please, before we go, I need to tell you both something."

The priests turn to face me and I tell them, "I've had another vision."

They look at one another and turn back to me to ask in unison, "What? When?"

"Just now."

Father Aiden is taken aback as he asks, "What was the vision of?"

I answer, "Jesus Christ and St. Peter and what I was told is terrifying."

CHAPTER 46

The press gaggle surrounds Dr. Thomas Houston and his entourage as they begin to board the plane. The group of reporters is shouting questions and Tom knows what he needs to do to keep the press on his side. He smiles his practiced smile and points to one of the particularly strident TV newscasters.

"Yes, Chuck, what is your question?"

"Dr. Houston, your opponent for the nomination of the Socialist Liberation Party has called your trip to Israel and the Middle East a publicity stunt, how do you respond?"

"Well Chuck, it seems that Congresswoman Helen De Witt would prefer to stay close to home and not strain herself too much; after all campaigning is a tough grind."

The press corps laughs and Tom takes another question. "Dr. Houston, you will be stopping at some very dangerous places. Are you at all afraid for your personal safety and the safety of your entourage?"

"Of course, I am and we will abide by whatever the security protocols in each of the countries we visit. I also have my personal security staff and they have been given complete access to the various steps taken to assure our safety. Let me say that while I don't wish to put myself or my staff in harm's way, I realize that we live in a dangerous world and I am prepared to face whatever need be to try and stop the violence and establish peace."

The press starts to scream more questions, "Dr. Houston...Dr. Houston...Dr. Houston..."

Tom acknowledges Ronald Bryan from Worldwide Press Syndicate, "Ron, you're next."

"Thank you, Dr. Houston. I've noticed that you are flying to the destinations on a commercial airline flight. How is it that you're not taking you private jet? I understand that it is beautiful and it can travel great distances."

"Well Don, I want to be environmentally conscious and try to reduce my carbon footprint. Taking a commercial charter flight with my staff and others, including you in the press corps, allows us to do our part to fight the scourge of climate change. Next..."

"Dr. Houston, Andrea Williams from National Public Radio. Among your passengers is Ms. Elizabeth Della Russo and it appears that you both are spending a lot of time together. Is there anything to the rumors going around that says you are a couple?"

Tom smiles at the cameras as tape rolls and shutters go off, rapid fire. "You may remember that I introduced Ms. Della Russo at a campaign event. She is one of the members of the great staff at Huntington Hospital that made the valiant effort to save the life of Officer Nicholas Josephs. I have recognized the team at Huntington Hospital for the contribution they made and I've asked Beth to accompany my staff on the trip. Her experience and knowledge of the nursing profession in the US can be helpful in evaluating how patient care systems work in other countries. I've asked that she provide her thoughts on steps that we can take to integrate what are best practices in other institutions with ours. Ms. Della Russo will also be attending certain of the confabs covering various topics relating to medical and health issues. We have become very good friends and I greatly value her time and opinion. Now for one final question...Laura Engelman, you're up."

"Dr. Houston, you are a fervent and avowed atheist. Your planned trip will take you to a number of countries, some of which are Muslim Theocracies and others that have very strong religious roots. How does this comport with your personal beliefs and how will it impact your ability to have a dialogue with their leaders?"

Tom bristles at the question. He has been trying to downplay his anti-religious stance given that many potential voters have deeply held religious beliefs, but he knows he must answer. "I have repeatedly stated that I have no quarrel with people who are religious; they can worship whatever way they wish and live their lives as their faith dictates. What I have always argued is that religion should not be used as an excuse to suppress peoples of all faiths or no faith at all. We are one world, one people with one goal and I intend to unite us all behind the goal; World Peace."

Laura Engelman interrupts, "World Peace? Does this apply to Muslim countries that quash female freedoms, and torture and kill homosexuals among other crimes against humanity? How does that reconcile with your goal?"

"Laura, I condemn anything that suppresses human rights and I will do all in my power as President of the United States to try and change these practices. Now we are getting ready to board, for those who will be coming along, let's have a safe flight, and for those who are staying behind, I'll see you when we get back."

The reporters continue to shout out questions, but Tom ignores them and walks down the ramp and enters the first-class cabin. As he does, he is applauded by many of the staff and guests on board and, as he walks down the aisle, he stops to shake hands and say a few words to each passenger. Beth had boarded the flight earlier and Tom takes his place in the seat next to her.

"Did you hear the press conference?"

Beth smiles, "Yes I did. Good job and thanks for making sure the team at Huntington Hospital got the credit for taking care of Nick."

Tom smiles back at Beth, "I made sure that I did. I figured that's all I need is to have you pissed off at me for the next seven hours and my life will become a living hell."

Beth laughs out loud, "Smart move on your part. By the way, I heard you had a very nice call with Dr. Harold Mc Masters."

"Umm, ah, yes I did."

"Well, he was very concerned about my taking another leave of absence, but it seems he changed his mind. However, did that happen?"

"Umm, I can't imagine."

Beth smirks at Tom, "Well, it seems that another donation of $2,500,000 helped to grease the skids so to speak. Did you have anything to do with that?"

Tom acts in mock surprise at the accusation, "Beth, how can you even think such a thing! That is certainly a generous amount and I am sure the money will be put to good use. You must be pretty special to have elicited such appreciation!"

Beth reaches over to touch Tom's cheek, "Tom, thank you for your generosity. Dr. McMasters told me about your call and the donation. All of us at Huntington Hospital appreciate it." Beth leans over the armrest between the seats, looks over to be sure no one is watching and she kisses Tom.

Tom smiles, "That's a pretty expensive kiss, but worth every penny!"

They both laugh as the captain announces that all passengers are on board and the plane is on the runway and next in line to take off. When they reach cruising altitude the flight attendant comes around to offer champagne, wine and both alcoholic and non-alcoholic drinks. Beth has a glass of champagne and Tom orders scotch on the rocks.

When the drinks come, Tom says, "What shall we toast to?"

"How about a successful trip and good luck with your campaign?"

"Sound good to me; to a successful trip, to my campaign and to us."

Beth answers, "To us" and she and Tom take a sip of their drinks and pause for a moment to look in each other eyes.

Tom is about to kiss Beth when he comes back to the realization that he needs to keep his feelings apart from what he has been commanded by Satan to do. He turns away from Beth and says to her, "Beth, I'll be right back; I need to use the restroom."

Beth shrugs her shoulders and says, "Well when you gotta go, you gotta go."

"Very funny, I'll be right back."

Tom goes to the lavatory reserved for use by first class passengers and he opens the door and locks it behind him. In an instant the interior changes into the familiar hellish cave of horrors and Tom kneels on the ground and waits for his master.

The smell of Sulphur gas is overpowering and the noxious odor nearly causes Tom to pass out. "Ah, I have been following your exploits with the beautiful Beth and I see that you have convinced her to accompany you. Good job Tommy!"

"Thank you, my lord."

"Al Masih ad Dajjal has provided me with complete details on his journey towards the great battle and I am also very pleased. He and the terrorists that follow him have wreaked havoc on their way to Megiddo and the lands of the Middle East have become an even greater cauldron of violence. I must tell you I do love that guy!"

Tom Houston is still bowed in supplication to Satan. "My lord, all is in place. I have made arrangements and set my itinerary so that I will be able to join you on the appointed day at the appointed time."

"Good, now go back to your seat before they think you got sucked into the crapper."

"Yes, my lord."

"Oh, and one final thing…"

"What is that my lord?"

"Keep your pecker in your pants, is that understood?"

"Yes, my lord." Tom looks up to see Satan has gone and he is once again alone in hell.

CHAPTER 47

Father Langford, Msgr. De Marinis and I remain silent as we walk to our quarters in the Santa Martha Residence, a modern Vatican guesthouse for priests and bishops who are visiting the Vatican for meetings and conferences. Msgr. De Marinis opens the door to the apartment Fr. Aiden and I will be sharing during our stay. Father Sellisi has arranged for our luggage to be sent ahead and placed in each of our bedrooms. There is a small area with a refrigerator, microwave and coffeemaker; all in all, a comfortable and simply decorated suite.

Everyone is anxious to hear about my latest vision so we immediately sit down at a small table by the window.

Fr. Aiden begins, "Christopher, I think you may want to explain the genesis of your communications with The Sainted and of your visions."

I agree and explain to the Monsignor my experiences beginning with my first vision, some of the intimate details to many of the other visions in the years following. I also recounted my confrontations with Satan in human form, Julian. When I am finished both priests make the sign of the cross and whisper a quiet prayer.

"Gentlemen, I know how this must sound and I know that you have many questions, but I am grateful you believe what I have told you, but now I have more to say...much more."

Monsignor De Marinis says, "My dear Christopher, as I have told my old friend Aiden, it is not too difficult to believe your visions when I have witnessed the horrors of evil and confronted demons in their many forms for years now. Your Saintly visions are miraculous, and for me, utterly believable and now tell us about your vision in St. Peter's Basilica."

"Thank you, monsignor, you can never know how good it is to hear your words." With that I start to recall my latest vision.

I begin to speak to the priests and for a while I provide additional background into my communications with the saints. I pause for a moment and tell the priests of my latest vision. "I saw Christ speak to the multitudes. In the vision of St. Peter and Jesus Christ, I witnessed the miracle of the loaves and fishes. I saw St. Peter try to walk on water, as Christ did, only to sink when he lost faith. He told me that his loss of faith in Christ still shames him."

The priests remain silent, but they make the sign of the cross.

I also tell them that there is a point in all my visions where The Sainted step out of the past and stand before me so we can speak to one another. "I have already told some of this to Fr. Aiden, but I have now been told by St. Peter that Christ has already broken the first seal. There will be a great battle that will take place and it will be led by the anti-christ."

Monsignor De Marinis is listening, but breaks his silence, "The seal will reveal the rider on the white horse and this is the Antichrist. His arrival will mark the beginning of the Tribulation."

"Yes, but there is something else."

The priests look at one another and back to me and I tell them, "St. Peter told me there is a second false prophet."

Fr. Aiden exclaims, "A second false prophet?"

"St. Peter said the second false prophet is the Muslim anti-christ. He told me that he is called the Deceiver,"

Msgr. De Marinis completes my sentence, "…the last of a line of 30 Deceivers and he is known as Al Masih ad Dajjal, the Kafir."

"Right, that's exactly what St. Peter told me, and he said that we three will be needed to confront the forces of evil. He told me that the rider on the white horse and Muslim anti-Christ is already journeying to the Holy Land."

Fr. Aiden is troubled by this, but he is emphatic when he says. "Then, we three must begin our journey to the Holy Land soon. It is there, God has led His chosen people and where I am hoping we will receive the guidance that we seek."

I take a deep breath and tell the men. "There is one more thing that St. Peter told me."

The monsignor asks, "What? What did he say?

"He told me that the anti-christ will travel with someone that I know and that this person is in grave danger. He also told me that evil will consume this person's being and if he or she is possessed, all will be lost. Monsignor, I think it all seems to be coming together; Fr. Aiden, you and me and my visions, it all seems to be leading us to this."

I continue, "St. Peter also left me with these words; the three of us are chosen to represent humanity and we will not be alone. We will have the forces of Heaven with us, but that for all to be saved mankind must prove they are worth saving and there is very little time left."

All three of us look at each other and make the sign of the cross and Father Langford leads us in a short pray after which we answer in unison, "Amen."

CHAPTER 48

After their long trek though the territories of many Muslim countries, the terrorist army was able to recruit many thousands of men for the battle to come. Al Masih ad Dajjal orders the terrorist soldiers to camp in a remote area west of at-Tayba, a Palestinian village in the West Bank.

The small, isolated town of at-Tayba has a population of about 2,000 inhabitants and the Masih orders that the men keep away and not attract any undue attention. It is not unreasonable to assume that the citizens of at-Tayba would have sympathies toward the terrorists, but as the battle nears all must be done to prepare for what is to come.

The Deceiver addresses the terrorist leaders and warns them, "Due to Allah's blessings, our movements have been hidden from view as we must be ready for the battle. I have given you all of what you need and your men must not waiver."

The terrorists shout, "Oh Masih, we will not betray our destiny and do what we must to assure this victory for Allah!"

Al Masih ad Dajjal gazes over the men as he issues one of his last commands, "Now we march to the final stand against all non-believers; it is Allah's will, praise be his name and the name of his prophet Muhammad."

In unison the terrorists yell, "Praise be to Allah and his prophet, Muhammad!"

The Deceiver surveys the large terrorist army assembled before him. He believes that these men will not waiver as they are blind to the truth and fearful of the retribution, he has promised all who turn coward.

Al Masih ad Dajjal exhorts the group standing before him. "What has Allah decreed?"

The terrorists yell, "To vanquish the infidels!"

"What awaits the faithful who fight and die for Allah?"

"Eternal rewards and pleasures await!"

"…and where do we go to assure our rewards?"

"MEGIDDO!"

CHAPTER 49

The charter flight lands at Tel Aviv's Ben-Gurion International Airport where Tom Houston and his entourage disembark.

Looking like a typical tourist, Beth stares all around and tells Tom, "I can't believe I'm here is Israel. This is such a sacred and wonderful place. I've only read about Israel, but now I'm here! Thank you so much Tom, for letting me come along on this trip!"

Tom smiles and puts his arm around Beth's shoulder and says, "You're welcome, but it is I that should be thanking you."

"Thanking me, what for?"

"For making what I am sure would have been a very boring, working trip into a delightful journey."

They both laugh as they are escorted to an awaiting limousine. Their limo, along with a caravan of SUVs, leaves the airport and travel west, along 461 toward the Jaffa Hotel. The Jaffa is one of the finest hotels in all of Israel and arrangements have been made by Tom's staff for separate rooms for him and Beth. In about 30 minutes they arrive and Tom and his entourage are warmly greeted by the hotel management.

"Welcome Dr. Houston, I am Naftali Peretz, the hotel manager and we are honored that you have chosen to stay with us. All arrangements have been made according to your staff's request and we hope the accommodations are to you satisfaction.

Tom shakes Naftali Peretz's hand and thanks him for his warm welcome. He introduces Beth and the senior members of his staff. "It's been a long flight and I am sure most of us would like to relax a bit before our first meeting and dinner.

"Of course, my staff and I will personally escort you and your guests to their rooms. Your luggage is being sent up to your rooms now and we are at your service should you need anything."

"Thank you very much; may I call you Naftali?"

"Of course!"

"Thank you, Naftali, I am sure all will be perfect during our stay."

The hotel manager leads the way and escorts Tom and his staff to their rooms. When Beth arrives at her room she enters and is very impressed with her accommodations. She reaches for her handbag and offers the bellman a tip, but she is told that all gratuities have been paid and he thanks her as he leaves and closes the door behind him. Beth looks around and from her top floor vantage point she can see the cityscape all the way to the Mediterranean Sea and marvels how truly beautiful the Tel Aviv is. She takes her time unpacking and when she is finished, she sits back to relax a bit before what she has been told will be a whirlwind of lectures, activities, meals and touring. Before Beth can close her eyes the phone rings.

"Hello?"

"Hi Beth, are you settle in?"

"Hi Tom, pretty much, I'm just relaxing a bit. Nancy gave me the schedule and I'm dizzy just reading it. I don't know how you do it."

"Well, you get used to it. Anyway, the reason I am calling is to tell you that I have a surprise for you."

"A surprise? What kind of surprise?"

"Well, I'm going to swear you to secrecy so I need you to promise you won't tell a single soul, do I have you word?"

"That depends on the surprise."

"I have arranged for a special get-a-way for us, just you and I. There won't be any cameras, news people, security, toady's or lackeys. I have reserved a car and you and I are going to do some sightseeing. I have a special tour planned where we will visit some of the sights referenced in the Bible and we will begin the tour with a trip to Armageddon."

"Armageddon? You've got to be kidding."

"No, as the scriptures like to tell us, Armageddon is the place where the battle between the forces of Heaven and Hell takes place. It's said to be located on a plain near Mount Megiddo, north of Tel Aviv and Jerusalem. You're gonna love this and to top it off, we are also going to visit Nazareth and the Sea of Galilee! Is that great or what!"

"Tom, you can't do that! What about security, you could be in great danger to say nothing about me being along with you."

"Oh, come on Beth, where's your sense of adventure?"

"I left it home with my bullet proof vest."

"Very funny, if it will make you feel better, we'll leave very early and we'll be sure to be back before dinner. I'll tell Nancy to cancel my schedule and say that I have an emergency meeting. Come on Beth, it will be fun, I guarantee it and if you don't have the best time of your life, I will give you a complete refund plus 10% for your trouble. What do you say?"

Beth is nervous about the dangers, but she sighs knowing that she would love to see these ancient sites. "I don't know how you do it, but you always manage to talk me into things."

Tom smiles on his end of the phone call, "Ah, you have succumbed to the Houston Charm! It is overpowering and your defenses are useless."

Beth laughs on her end and asks, "Okay, what should I wear?"

"Well, nothing would suit me, but you should dress for comfort; light jacket, blouse, khakis, walking shoes that sort of stuff."

"Tom, I didn't bring any of that so I guess I'll just sit by the pool!"

"Not on your life; there is a wonderful shop on the next street over and you can buy anything you need. I've already called and they have my credit card so charge away!"

"You're pretty sure of yourself, aren't you?"

"Well, I am told that I'm the most eligible bachelor in America."

Beth reacts to their inside joke and corrects him, "You seem to keep forgetting that you are one of the *three* most eligible bachelors in America."

"Ah, yes! Well, I guess I'll just have to eliminate the competition."

CHAPTER 50

The three of us sit in silence in our room in the Vatican apartments simply trying to figure out what we should do next.

Msgr. De Marinis is the first to speak. "We all must assume that your vision requires us to take immediate action. I will consult with my immediate superior, Cardinal Agostino Castelli and ask for time off to pursue research studies and relax a bit. I will need to find a logical premise to take a leave of absence in order to make the trip to Israel with my close friend Aiden. I'm sure Cardinal Castelli will be grateful that I will have a companion. My Parkinson's has been of great concern to him so I am hopeful he will agree and allow this leave of absence."

Father Aiden asks, "Do you have someone who we may rely on to help in our journey to the Holy Land?"

Msgr. De Marinis tell us, "I am good friends with Rabbi Achazyah Ohayon and I am sure, if needed, he will be able to help in whatever way he can."

I immediately get nervous, "Monsignor, I don't want anyone else other that our small group to know of my visions of The Sainted as it will only raise doubts, disbelief and more questions."

"Ah, I see your point. Well, rather than take him into our complete confidence, I will explain that we are in Israel to visit Megiddo as part of an investigation into the origins of Armageddon. I am sure the Rabbi will help in whatever way he can and I believe that the Lord shall forgive our omissions. Now I will take my leave and go to see Cardinal Castelli."

Father Aiden sees this quest coming together and says, "Good then it's settled and we need to prepare for our trip. Christopher, would you be so kind as to check flight schedules and make reservations for all three days hence?"

I am also getting both excited and nervous as I stand up and face the two priests. I say something that is in my heart and I think needs to be said. "Throughout most of my life I've thought my visions were a prelude to something of profound importance. I didn't know what it was, but I believe that everything I've experienced, everything I was told by The Sainted has a purpose and a meaning that will be revealed; I just didn't know what it was…now I know. This battle between the forces of Heaven and Hell is very real and we have been given a most important role. We three are to represent humankind and we must prove that men and women are worthy of God's love and mercy, I can only pray that I can meet the challenge."

Both Fr. Aiden and Msgr. De Marinis are silent for a moment until Fr Aiden speaks. "Christopher, if we must face what has been prophesized in the scriptures, I can think of no man more worthy than you."

Monsignor De Marinis adds, "Christopher, in my role as the Vatican's chief exorcist I have had to deal with so much evil that I can only imagine what Satan may be up to, but what I do know, what was revealed to me as I performed the exorcism of Valentia Trullo confirms much of what you have been told in your visions. The way is being prepared by the forces of Hell for the arrival of the anti-Christ. This was foretold to me by the demon Leviathan who had possessed the woman. It has also been made all the more manifest by the increase in possessions and heinous crimes committed around the world. I do not know you well, but I know your heart and you are brave beyond my ability to describe. For all that is ahead for us, I can think of no man better than you to take the lead."

I am embarrassed by the praise and still fearful for what is ahead, but I know that this is what I am meant to do. "Thank you for your kind words and your courage to join me in this battle. I don't know what will happen, but I do know I am among the bravest men I have ever known.

Now if I can offer a piece of advice to Father Aiden, I think that you will need to get as much rest as possible. Given what is head of us I am sure we will need all our strength."

"Ah, Christopher, your keen interest in my wellbeing is very much appreciated and welcomed. I will take leave now to rest and I leave you with the words on my beloved William Shakespeare spoken by witches of Macbeth; 'When shall we three meet again, in thunder, lightning, or in rain? When the hurly-burly's done, when the battle's lost and won.'

* * *

Over the next three days Monsignor De Marinis, Father Langford and I spent hours in the Vatican Library reading certain scripture and some of the books that speak of the battle of Armageddon. The priests spend hours in discussion of the relevance of the many aspects that we may need to confront and help me to understand what they believe is most important.

I made the reservations for our fight to Tel Aviv on EL AL and according to the schedule we would arrive in Tel Aviv early afternoon. Msgr. De Marinis has arranged for us to stay at Latroun Abbey, the Trappist Monastery of The Silent Monks. The monastic way of life in based on the vow of silence the monks take up themselves. It is a simple lifestyle and Msgr. De Marinis prevailed on his friend Father Luke Rowe to provide us with accommodations.

We meet early in morning to take the short ride to the airport and board the El Al flight to Tel Aviv. Our small group arrives nearly two hours before our flight takes off and I excuse myself and find a quiet corner to call Amanda. I dial her number and the phone rings and she answers, "Chris! I'm so glad you called! How are you? How was the trip? Are you having fun? How come it took you three days to call me? Come on, give it up!"

I laugh because I know she is glad to hear from me and I am glad to hear her voice. "Hi Amanda, sorry it took so long, but I really got bombarded as soon as Father Aiden and I arrived at the Vatican. I met a good friend of Fr. Aiden's, Monsignor Amedeo De Marinis, who has been so gracious and welcoming to us."

I couldn't tell Amanda what we had really done over the past three days. In preparation for the days ahead, the three of us became immersed in biblical scripture and other writings that speak to the end of days. Legends and prophesies that foretell what will transpire and how it will come about and throughout it all I think of The Sainted and their warnings of dire events. I told Amanda that I was given access to the Vatican Library and many of the priceless coins and medals that are part of the Vatican collection. In fact, it is not a total fabrication as the monsignor did give us a guided tour of the museum and I did get to view many of the masterpieces it contains. He even gave me a tour of the vault where I was able to see many of the coins in their collection.

"Amanda, you have to come and see this place, it is truly magnificent."

"Okay, I'll go under one condition."

"What's that?"

"You take me!"

I laugh, "It's a date!"

We continue to speak when I hear an announcement, "Boarding for Flight 469 to Tel Aviv begins in 15 minutes…"

Not thinking I say, "Amanda, there's my flight, I need…" and then I realize I never mentioned that I was going to Israel.

"Chris, where are you going?"

"Ah, ummm, I well, I am going to Israel."

"WHAT!"

"Listen Amanda, this came up at the last minute and I was going to tell you. Msgr. De Marinis was able to arrange for us to go to Israel and meet with some good friends."

"Are you kidding me? My dad is a rock star there. He could have opened any door that you need."

"Amanda, I didn't want to bother Harry and I didn't want you to worry."

"Worry! Worry? What the hell do I have to worry about except for the fact that you might get killed?"

"Amanda I won't get killed; I promise. We are guests staying at a Trappist monastery near Tel Aviv and…"

"You mean Latroun Abbey."

"How the heck…I mean how did you know that?

"My dad took me there a few years back and I loved the place; it is beautiful. There are gardens and vineyards that are tended by the monks and you can buy olive oil made from olives grown there. They also make wine and dad buys a number of cases each time he's in Israel, but you're trying to change the subject, why didn't you tell me."

"Well to tell you the truth I was afraid to tell you because I knew you might react in this way."

Amanda is quiet for a moment when she finally says, "Chris, I really like you and I want you to be happy. If it means going to Rome or Tel Aviv or anywhere for that matter, I only wish that I could be there to share it with you."

I smile to myself and tell Amanda, "Even if I take you on a tour of all the coin shops in Budapest?"

Amanda laughs, "Well, I think in that case I think I'll stay by the pool while you go on your adventure."

"Amanda, look, I'm really sorry for not telling you, but you have to believe I didn't want you to worry. My plane is leaving in a few minutes, but I promise that I will call you once I get settled in Tel Aviv, okay?"

I wait for Amanda to answer, but I hear what sounds like a sob and I ask, "Amanda, are you okay; please don't cry. I promise to be careful."

"You better." and with that, Amanda hangs up the phone

I want to call Amanda back, but boarding has begun and I rush to meet my travelling companions. The flight is nearly full, but I had managed to get us a window seat and two aisle seats directly across from each other. I think he would be more comfortable so I tell Father Langford to take the window seat and I take the aisle seat. Monsignor De Marinis takes the other aisle seat and we relax for the short two and a half-hour flight to Israel.

The flight attendant comes over the loud speaker and announces the all too familiar procedures relating to seat belts, tray tables and the pleasant admonishment that all electronic devices are turned off for the duration of the fight or put into airplane mode. To be sure that all passengers don't go into Facebook or Twitter withdrawal, El Al provides each of us with a personal television at our seats to keep us occupied until we land. Our plane is positioned at the end of the runway and we are airborne in a matter of seconds and reach our cruising altitude in a few minutes. Father Aiden reaches into his carry-on and pulls out the inspirational book, 'The Prayer of Jabez' by Bruce Wilkinson, and begins to read while Msgr. De Marinis takes the opportunity to close his eyes to rest for the long days ahead.

I neither feel tired nor inspired so I decide to plug in my headphones and turn on the TV to the Israeli News Network. I thought I would get caught up in the news of the day and thankfully the network broadcasts in English. Israel is an amazing place and in spite of all they are coping with I remember a story my Uncle Al told me that his friend, Danny told him about Israelis. He told Uncle Al that the Israelis are like a 'sabra' or what they call a prickly pear as it is adorned with sharp spikes. Danny said that Israelis are tough and dangerous on the outside like a sabra, but mushy and soft on the inside and will always remain loyal. I still remember that description. News item after news item come on giving me a perspective on modern day Israel and, aside from the occasional story about the ongoing issues with the Palestinians, there is little in the way of any current conflicts.

I am about to shut the TV off when I nearly jump out of my seat as a newsperson begins his report, "Earlier this week, Tel Aviv welcomed a very special visitor, Dr. Thomas Houston." The video switched to show a group of stretch limos arriving at the front of a hotel.

"Dr. Houston and his entourage arrived at the exclusive Jaffa Hotel and were welcomed by Naftali Peretz, the hotel's manager. This reporter was fortunate enough to get a chance to speak with the charismatic man running to become the presidential candidate of the Socialist Liberation Party."

The reporter interviewing Dr. Thomas Houston then asks why he is in Israel. "I'm here so that I can accumulate firsthand knowledge of the region from all sides. If I am to govern the United States of America as President, I will need to do all in my power to assure that peaceful coexistence can be realized between all parties in the Middle East in order to hopefully achieve a long and lasting peace that has been elusive for so long."

"How long will you be in Israel and other countries and what is on your agenda?"

"Our group will be here for about three weeks and we have a number of meetings planned with government officials as well as various religious and political leaders. In addition, I will be hosting events, dinners and giving speeches on topics that are sure to be of interest to many of the citizens of Israel and surrounding Middle Eastern countries."

"Does that leave anytime to visit and explore our beautiful country?"

"I am hoping there will be some time for that, but there are a number of things I must do before I am able to relax bit. Now if you will excuse us, my staff, guests and I would like to get settled before the whirlwind begins. I also want to thank the government and the peoples of Israel for their hospitality and kindness."

The reporter turns to the camera, "That was Dr. Thomas Houston, candidate for the Socialist Liberation Party nomination for president." The video switches to show Tom Houston and his group entering the hotel. I am frantically searching the screen to see if I can spot Beth and my heart sinks when I see her and Tom entering together.

The reporter continues with his report, "Among those in the entourage is Ms. Beth Della Russo, head nurse of a hospital's critical care unit and a friend of Dr. Houston. There have been rumors of a possible romantic relationship, but according to Nancy McGrath, Dr. Houston's Chief of Staff, Ms. Della Russo is here as an expert on hospital protocols and will be compiling information from the Israeli health authorities that will be valuable to the campaign. This is David Haddad for the Israeli News Network."

I am despondent over seeing Beth with Tom together and I'm growing sadder by the minute, and then I am stunned by the realization of what I have just seen. I needed to share what I have just come to realize with Father Aiden when the plane and all its passengers disappear and I find myself in the midst of a vision.

The exceptionally beautiful woman stands before the emperor
Maxentius who had begun to persecute Christians throughout

the empire. She was there to denounce his cruelty, but instead of putting her to death, the emperor summons 50 of Rome's most skillful orators and philosophers to confront the woman and look to persuade her to deny her faith.

I watch as she challenges the men and one by one annuls their arguments leaving these scholars in doubt of their own beliefs.

The emperor is furious at what he perceives as blasphemy. He orders his guards to imprison the woman and torture her in the vilest of ways. Through it all she remains courageous and steadfast refusing to abandon her faith.

The vision changes once more and the woman is on her knees praying in the cold, dark cell where she is held captive. The door to the prison cell suddenly opens and in walks the emperor Maxentius. His manner and demeanor appear to have changed and he seems to have become kinder and more solicitous towards the woman.

Maxentius looks kindly at the beautiful young woman, but there is lust in his heart. "You have endured much and this has caused me to change my feelings towards you. I am here to offer you all the power and wealth of my kingdom if you will marry me, be my empress and all I ask of you is to deny this foolish faith of yours."

The woman seems to consider how to respond as she looks up at the emperor and smiles. "You cannot ever hope to dissuade me from my belief in my Lord and Savior. Christ is the only one who commands my soul and rules over my heart."

The emperor's features become distorted as he screams for the guards to immediately take the woman and put her to death on the breaking wheel; the torturous device occupies the middle of the courtyard where the executioner awaits. He holds a long and heavy metal rod that will be used to thread the woman's limbs in the spokes and shatter her bones.

As she is brought to the breaking wheel, she closes her eyes and silently prays and merely touches the wheel. In a miraculous occurrence, the wheel itself completely shatters and falls into pieces.

Unable to tempt or torture the woman, the emperor is confounded and cannot understand the power this woman has. In a fit of rage Maxentius orders the guards to behead the woman. In spite of the impact this woman has had on the people of the region, he believes that this will finally rid his kingdom of the profane religion. As he walks back to the palace, however one can see there is foreboding on his face and fear in his heart.

St. Catherine of Alexandria steps out of her past and into my present. I am anxious to ask what I need to know, but afraid of the answer.

"St. Catherine, I think I know what your vision means."

"The Sainted asks, "What is it you believe it means?"

"It means that what you have gone through and what I was told of by St. Peter is going to happen. It will take place in Megiddo and me and my companions will need to confront this evil head on, without fear, only resolve."

"What is it you believe will happen?"

"The battle for the souls of mankind will take place and it can only be won if our faith prevails."

"What else do you think will occur?"

"I think there will be temptations and the horrors of hell will be unleashed."

"Who will unleash these horrors?"

"Satan, the forces of hell and the two anti-christs that were prophesized to me by St. Peter. He also told me that Fr. Aiden and Msgr. De Marinis and I are the only ones that stand in the way of overcoming the prophesy of the end of days."

"Did St. Peter foretell of other events?"

"Yes, there is something else."

"What is it?"

"St. Peter told me that the anti-christ will be in the company of an innocent person; someone who is in very grave danger. He told me that if evil is allowed to consume this being and if this person is allowed to become possessed by Satan, all will be lost."

"The visions of my life, in some small way, were meant to show you that the battle of good over evil can be fought and won. Even a single person can stand up to the forces of evil and win. There is little time left. Search your heart to find the one you must save and be brave against what you fear the most."

I call out, "St. Catherine…" but the vision fades and is gone. I am back in my seat on the plane when I suddenly realize what I need to know. I turn to Fr. Aiden who had fallen asleep and I gently wake him up.

"Father Langford, wake up. Father, please wake up I have something very important to tell you."

A bleary-eyed Father Langford looks around and turns to see me practically jumping out of my seat. "Christopher, you look extremely distressed. Have you had another vision?"

"Yes Father. I think I know who the other anti-christ is."

"Whom, may I ask?"

"Dr. Thomas Houston."

"WHO!"

"Dr. Thomas Houston, the socialist party candidate for President of the United States. Don't you see; it all fits; rich, powerful, handsome, an atheist and he holds sway over a large and devoted following. He is now in Israel and I have to believe it is much more than a coincidence."

Fr. Aiden stares at the back of the seat in front of him and says, "You may be right Christopher, you may be right."

"…and Father, remember I told you that St. Peter said the anti-Christ is traveling with an innocent person and this person is the key to whether evil or good will triumph."

"Yes."

"That innocent person in danger is Beth."

* * *

The EL AL flight to Tel Aviv arrives on time and taxis down the tarmac to the assigned gate.

The moment the plane lands I turn on my mobile phone and call Beth. The phone rings and I hear Beth's familiar voice mail greeting. "Hi, this is Beth and I'm not available, but just leave a message after the tone and I will call you back as soon as I can. Have a wonderful day…"

The entire time I am saying to myself "Come on Beth, come on and pick up the phone…", but she doesn't answer so I leave her a message.

"Beth, this is Chris. I don't have time to explain, but you are in great danger. Don't go anywhere alone or with Tom. I know it sounds crazy, but I beg you, don't go anywhere. As soon as you get this message, please give me a call and I will explain everything. I end the call and leave a short, "Good bye and…um good bye."

I was on the verge of saying I love you, but I thought better of it and I disconnect the call. I look over to Msgr. De Marinis who was staring at me. I look around and no one seems to be paying attention so I say, "Monsignor, I don't want to discuss this now, but I have just had another…uh, vision and I will talk about it when we get through customs and into our car."

Msgr. De Marinis looks concerned and asks, "Christopher, are you alright?"

I want to tell him what has happened, but all I can say is, "No."

CHAPTER 51

Beth is awakened from a deep sleep by the loud shrill of the phone in her suite. She groggily reaches for the phone and it falls from her hand. She feels around the covers and finally find the phone.

"Uh, hello?"

"Beth; hey sleepy head, time to get up for our adventure."

"Tom? What time is it?"

"It's 5AM!"

"5 AM? Are you kidding? No civilized human being should have to get up at this hour."

"Come on Beth, the land of Israel awaits, so many of those places that you've only read about are there just waiting for us. Come on Beth, you should be so excited to go!"

"I am, but 5AM, you've got to be kidding."

"Listen, if we leave early, we'll beat the traffic out of Tel Aviv, we'll get to the sites I have planned and we'll be back in time for cocktail hour, what do you say?"

Beth just sighs and says, "Okay…alright. I'll get dressed. Where do you want to meet?"

"That's my girl. I'll pick you up at your room at 5:30; this way you'll have plenty of time to get ready."

"Oh, sure, that leaves me a whole 15 minutes, you're more than generous."

"Thanks for noticing, see you in 15!" and Tom hangs up the phone.

Beth slowly gets out of bed and she is thankful that she took a shower before she went to sleep. Beth did not bring the kind of clothing that would be appropriate exploring for the ancient sites, but Tom had been gracious enough to offer to pay for her purchases of the items she would need. He even gave her directions to the store that had the clothing perfect for this excursion and Beth was impressed how everything was taken care of. She walks over to the closet and looks through some of the appropriate attire she purchased and selected something suitable. No sooner has she finished dressing there was a knock on her door.

Beth looks through the peephole and sees that it's Tom, so she jokingly says, "Who is it?"

"It's me."

"Who's me?

"Come Beth, times a wasting!"

Beth opens the door and Tom is standing there looking handsome as always and he is holding two coffees. He hands one to Beth and kisses her on the cheek.

"Thought you would need this; black with one sugar, right?"

Beth smiles, "You certainly know how to mollify a very sleepy and grumpy girl."

"Hey, aren't 'Sleepy' and 'Grumpy'; two of the seven dwarfs?"

Beth takes a long sip from her coffee and says, "Funny."

"Okay, enough with the levity, princess, your chariot awaits!"

"Okay, I just need to get my phone."

"You don't need to take your phone; it won't work anyway. When we get to the plains and hills around Megiddo you won't be able to get a signal."

"You're kidding; what if we get into trouble, how do we call for help?"

"Got it all taken care of." Tom reaches into the interior pocket of his jacket and pulls out a satellite phone. "This is a sat-phone, I can call from anywhere with this baby so we will always be able to contact anyone in an emergency. Come on, let's get going."

Beth frowns and looks at Tom, "I'm not sure, for some reason I've got a bad feeling about this."

"You're safe with me. Where's your sense of adventure?"

"I left it home along with my bullet proof vest and my sense of humor."

"Come on, I'll protect you!"

"Alright, alright, I'm coming." Beth just resigns herself and she and Tom take the elevator to the basement level. When the elevator doors open, Beth and Tom step into the corridor that leads to the kitchen and beyond. Other than a few workers moving about and preparing for the day to come, the basement seems deserted.

"Why are we down in the basement?"

"I thought it would be better if we snuck out early to avoid any of the media folks that have camped out looking for a scoop. I've arranged for a great vehicle to get us around in."

"I hope the seats recline because I'm going to sleep."

"No, you're not going to sleep because on our drive we're going to see so much that you won't have time to sleep."

Beth and Tom work their way through the labyrinth of corridors and tunnels that make up the basement of the Jaffa Hotel. As they exit the door leading to the back alley of the hotel there is a vehicle parked a few steps away.

Beth stares incredulously at the car and asks, "Is this a tank or what?"

Tom laughs, "No, it a Hummer H1! What, you've never been in a Hummer?"

"No, I also never have eaten sheep's brain either."

"Well after you exhibited some reticence about going sight-seeing with me, I wanted you to feel comfortable and safe…I can't attest to how comfortable you'll be as it is built for the off-road, but I can tell you that you will be secure and safe."

Beth continues to stare at what looks to her as some sort of military vehicle when the driver's side door opens. Her attention turns to a very tall, extremely muscular man who looks to be about 40 years old. Her eyes follow him as he crosses in front of the car and he stands before Beth and Tom. The driver is dressed in what looks like a camouflage uniform of the type what soldiers would wear for desert warfare.

"Beth, I'd like to introduce you to our driver."

"Tom, I thought you said that we were going alone."

"I know I did, but I had to tell Nancy that I was sneaking away and she insisted that I have a driver 'slash' bodyguard accompany us. You expressed the same feelings and I finally thought that it is better to be safe, so here is our companion."

Beth turns her stare from Tom to the driver. She doesn't know how she feels about him. On some level he looks very scary, but she guesses that bodyguards need to look frightening to scare away trouble, so she just smiles and tells Tom, "Well, that seems like a good idea to me."

She then faces the bodyguard and asks, "Now, what should I call you, Mr. Muscles?"

The driver smiles back at Beth and says, "Just call me Verrine."

* * *

Their small group takes the road leading north and Beth is excited to see the countryside and the small towns and villages they pass along the way. Occasionally Beth would look upfront and often notices their driver Verrine, staring at her through the rearview mirror. She quickly turns away as a slight shiver passes through her making her very uneasy with both him and the situation. She considers telling Tom about her misgivings when they are alone, but she decides not to and blames it on her nerves.

After about three hours of driving, Tom tells Verrine to stop at the next place where they can stop for breakfast.

"Are you hungry Beth?"

"I'm starving."

"Good, then let's take a short break to eat and stretch our legs."

Tom explains to Beth that in a few miles they will pass through Hadera, a city along the coast. "It's a really beautiful city and we should be able to find a nice place to eat and relax a bit before we continue our trek."

Beth seems excited, "Sounds great, but can we find a place that the locals like, you know, the kind that serves traditional Middle Eastern dishes?"

Tom turns from Beth and asks Verrine, "Verrine, do you know the kind of place that Beth would like?"

"Yes, I do."

"Good, then take us there, we're starving."

Verrine looks through the rearview mirror and smiles directly at Beth and says, "I know just the right place."

About a half hour later, they stop at a wonderful local café called 'Abu Salem' that specialized in Middle Easter cuisine. The place was nearly filled with both Israeli and Arab customers, and there are a number of conversations going on in an atmosphere makes you feel like a local yourself.

Tom opens the door on Beth's side and helps her out of the vehicle. He turns to Verrine and asks him if he wants to join them, but Verrine bows his head and thanks to Tom saying, "Thank you Dr. Houston, but no, I will wait for you here."

Tom and Beth enter the café and find one of the few remaining open tables where they sit down. There is no menu that they can find so they have to wait for someone to come and ask what they want to eat. Soon an old man comes over to their table and welcomes them in what sounds like Hebrew. The old waiter smiles knowing neither Beth nor Tom knows what he is saying.

Tom is forced to admit, "I am sorry, but I do not speak your language."

The waiter laughs and says, "Ah, then you are most fortunate that I can speak English! What would you like to eat?"

"What would you recommend?"

"Ah, that is a dangerous question in Israel. Do you trust me?"

Beth and Tom look at each other and say in unison, "Is there a reason why we shouldn't?"

"Of course, there is, I'll be right back; by the way, coffee? Tea?"

Beth orders tea and Tom orders coffee, but before the old waiter leaves to bring breakfast to their table and he asks, "You have money?"

Tom is a bit confused by the question, but answers, "Of course."

"Good because you will need it" and the old man leaves.

Beth and Tom now find themselves laughing at the waiter and she is relishing this time. Beth is wide-eyed as she looks around at the people in the café while talking and eating adding to the charm of this local custom. A short time later the waiter returns with the coffee and tea and a large tray filled with food.

The waiter feels the need to educate us so he begins, 'Well, I'm glad you are rich because I've brought you all different kinds of yogurt, this is labane; it's like a type of yogurt cheese, and I've also brought you some white cheese; very tasty. We just pressed some juices and I've brought you only four kinds to save you some money, but I've got more if you want. Now this is cottage cheese, but not like any other you've ever tasted. You'll also need salads and this is my favorite made of a combination of tomatoes, cucumbers, herbs, and olive oil."

Tom and Beth just stare at all the food before them and the waiter says, "Oh, I see you want more, so here's a plate of small omelets along with olives; they are very salty, roasted peppers, flat breads, and of course, marinated fish. Now you see this here; it is a small dish of red peppers." The waiter looks at Beth and says, "You are a very pretty young lady; don't these peppers look pretty too?"

Beth stifles a laugh, "Yes, they look very pretty."

"Ah, good, I'm glad you think they are pretty. Don't eat them; they will burn a hole in your tongue. I can't stand around and talk all day as I have other customers, but don't worry, if you want more, we'll make it. Any questions?"

Tom looks at Beth and then he looks at all the food and says, "You've got to be kidding, do you expect us to eat all of this food do you?"

"Yes" and with that the waiter walks away.

Tom and Beth laugh out loud again, but the food looks delicious and they dig in. It is a very pleasant time for both as they enjoy the beautiful day, great food and each other's company. When they are done, more than half of the food is untouched.

The waiter returns to the table and has a very somber look on his face. "What! You don't like my mother's cooking? I would rather slit my own throat than have to tell her that you didn't like what she made. How can you do this to such a wonderful old woman who probably doesn't have much time left on this earth?"

Now Beth stares at him looking very suspicious. "What is your name?"

"You should have asked me earlier; my name is Yossi."

"How old are you Yossi?"

Yossi tries to stand taller and says, "I am a very young, virile 83 years old."

"So let me see; you are 83 so if your mother gave birth to you when she was, let's say, 18 at the youngest, then she would be at least 101 years old."

"That is correct! She tells everybody she is 101 years old, but just between us; I think she's really 106. The fact you didn't finish her meal will probably take at least 20 years off her life. I don't want to say you could be the cause of her premature death, but you and I know the truth."

Beth jumps in and tells Yossi, "Why don't you pack up all the delicious and untouched food and give it to some of those who are less fortunate. I am sure your mother would approve and it could prolong her life."

"I don't know if that will be enough to save her life, but I will try."

Tom interrupts, "Ok Yossi, how much for the breakfast?"

The waiter looks at the bill and starts to read all the items, "Well let me see. There was the yogurt, and don't forget the cheeses. You must have liked the olives because they are all gone..."

Tom interrupts, "Just tell me the number."

"Well, we're talking about uh, 350 shekels, and maybe I should add some money for the shiva I will need to hold for my mother. She has so many friends; I will probably need to rent a hall for to hold the crowds that will come. I remember one time..."

While Yossi goes on and on, Tom reaches into his pocket and pulls out a roll of bills. He asks Yossi, "At the current exchange rate of $.30 US for one shekel, the total should come to comes to around $105. Do you accept US currency?"

"US? Of course!"

Tom peels off six $100 bills and hands them to Yossi. "This should cover the charges and there's a little something extra for you and your mother, be sure to buy her a nice present."

Yossi looks at the $600 and then back up at Tom and asks, "Are these real?"

"Yes, they are…very real. Thanks for making this such a memorable meal and providing the entertainment Yossi. You are a very funny guy!"

"I know; momma and I thank you!" Beth, Tom and Yossi all laugh, say goodbye and leave the café.

On the way out they spot the Hummer parked a short way down the street and begin to walk toward the vehicle. As they are walking Beth is pushed into Tom and they both fall as a thief grabs Beth's shoulder bag and runs past them toward Verrine. Tom quickly picks Beth up off the sidewalk and asks "Are you okay?"

"I…I seem to be fine, no injuries, but that man stole my bag."

Tom looks towards the Hummer and Verrine who is standing there. As the thief is running very fast and passes him holding the bag, Verrine very calmly gives chase after the man who turns and runs down a narrow alley.

Beth stares in disbelief, "I can't believe a man the size of Verrine can run so fast! The bag is not that important Tom, please tell him to stop before he gets hurt."

Tom does not seem at all concerned, "Take it from me Beth, Verrine can handle himself. Its's the thief you should be worried about."

After a few minutes Tom and Beth see Verrine come out of the alley holding Beth's shoulder bag. He walks up to Beth and hands it to her the bag and says, "Here is your bag, I hope you were not harmed in any way."

Beth takes the bag from Verrine, "Thank you so much. What happened to the thief?"

"I was able to wrestle the bag from his clutches and I am sure he regrets his decision to steal from you. Now, may I suggest that we resume your tour?"

Tom jumps in and says, "I think that's a good idea. Beth, what do you say we first go to the 'Sea of Galilee' and after that we can have lunch and stop at Megiddo on the way back to Tel Aviv?"

"Sounds like a plan!"

Verrine then opens the door so that Beth and Tom can enter and he gets behind the wheel for the next leg of the journey.

The next day it will be reported in the Times of Israel that a man with a long criminal record was discovered dead in a Hadera alleyway. His eyes were wide open and 'terror filled' as the reporter described the dead man. It was also reported that his spine was broken, literally bent in half, backwards. When questioned, the police said they had no suspects and the investigation is ongoing.

CHAPTER 52

When we disembark, Fr. Aiden, the Msgr. De Marinis and I rush through customs and find our way to the car rental counter. I had reserved an all-wheel drive compact SUV for our time in Israel. I load the back with our luggage and take the wheel as we three drive toward Latroun Abbey. While driving I tell Msgr. De Marinis about my vision of St. Catherine of Alexandria and how I know that Tom Houston is the anti-Christ and Beth is the innocent victim that I was told of in a previous vision.

Both priests make the sign of the cross and are silent for a short while. Msgr. De Marinis is the first to speak, "All the pieces of this puzzle seem to be falling into place; the visions, the revelations, your sacred duties and now Armageddon begins. Christopher, it seems apparent to me that Beth was sent to lure you to Megiddo as an added incentive so that you would not be deterred from this sacred undertaking."

"I am not so sure this is all there is monsignor, I don't know why they need Beth. Satan and his demons had to know that I was going to be at Megiddo and nothing would stop me. Besides, Satan has always been aware of my visions."

Father Langford interrupts, "Christopher, perhaps Satan has different plans for Beth, something of which you have not become privy to as of yet."

I am at a total loss, "Plans? What kind of plans related to Armageddon would the demon want to carry out that could possibly include Beth?"

We are at a loss for what to say next, so the three of us remain silent for the remainder of the trip. When we arrive at Latroun Abbey. Father Luke Rowe rushes out to greet Msgr. De Marinis and they embrace.

"It is so good to see you my dear friend."

Father Luke smiles and returns the compliment, "It is so good to see you again Amedeo, and you are looking well."

"Ah, 'well' is a relative term, but I am rejuvenated by being here in the Holy Land and I am so very grateful for your hospitality."

"Nonsense, it is I who delights at seeing you again!"

"Father, let me introduce my travelling companions. This is Father Aiden Langford and like you, is a very dear old friend."

Father Langford and Father Rowe shake hands and Msgr. De Marinis then introduces Chris. "And this is my other companion and newfound friend, Christopher Pella."

I smile at the priest, "It is a pleasure to meet you father, thank you for letting us stay at your beautiful monastery."

"It is our pleasure; the monks have nearly completed their days work and we will be gathering for vespers. Once vespers are over, we will be gathering for dinner and as our members have taken the vow of silence, I have made arrangements for you all to have dinner in a small dining room near the kitchen. If you don't mind, I would like to join you and we can catch up then."

Msgr. De Marinis is happy at the suggestion and says, "That sounds wonderful Luke, we would welcome spending some time together."

"Then it's settled. Let me show you to your rooms and we will meet at 7PM for dinner."

Father Luke then escorts us up to our rooms. The room is sparingly furnished, but it is very comfortable and I take the time to just lay back and consider all that has happened. I am deep in thought considering all that we will be confronting when I hear a knock at the door.

When I open it, I see a very concerned Father Aiden. "Christopher, I believe that we have a serious conundrum."

I'm puzzled when I ask, "What's the problem?"

"As Amedeo and I see it, Father Rowe will be curious to know why we are here in the Holy Land and I fear that we have already stretched the truth in what we have told Cardinal Castelli. Both Amodeo and I are concerned as to what we shall tell Father Rowe if he asks why we have journeyed to the Holy Land."

I think for a moment and suggest, "Father, I can tell Father Rowe that I am a devoted follower and student of The Sainted, which in truth I am. I am currently learning 'Revelations' and I have wanted to visit The Holy Land and the place that St. John foretold of in the scriptures where Armageddon will take place, this is in fact the truth. Our trip will take us to Megiddo and you have asked to accompany me, again the truth. The monsignor is your dear friend, another truth, and we invited him to join us and he accepted, again the truth."

"Ah Christopher, so many truths albeit, tortured ones, but truths none the less. I believe we shall need to partake in the sacrament of reconciliation once this is over, assuming the battle is won."

Now it's my turn to say, "Amen."

* * *

Before I get ready to meet with Father Rowe for dinner, I try to call Beth's mobile again, but there was only the same voice mail greeting. I leave another message, pleading with her to call me and I warn her again not to go with Tom Houston until she speaks to me.

After I disconnect, I call Amanda as promised and wait for her to answer, but I also got her voice mail greeting, "Hi this is Amanda, I'm glad you called, please leave a message and I will get back to you as soon as I can. Much love!"

I smile as I think of Amanda recording that message, "Hi Amanda, nice greeting! This is Chris. Well, I got to Israel in good shape and spirits. Me and my entourage made it through customs in short order and we just arrived at Latroun Abbey and it is everything you told me it is. We are having dinner with Father Luke Rowe who is making us feel right at home. Tomorrow we will be touring some areas north of here and hopefully I can learn something about ancient coinage…you're probably laughing right now. Anyway, hope you are well and I'll try you again later."

I take a shower to wash some life back into me after our day of travel and the latest vision. I am frightened for Beth and what Satan has in store for her. The shower rejuvenates me and I dress in something more appropriate than jeans and a sweatshirt. It is nearly time to go to the small dining room where Father Rowe said we would meet and I go into the hallway to join my friends so we may walk down for dinner together.

Father Rowe is already seated and rises up to greet us. "Ah dear friends, welcome to what I hope will be a memorable dinner,"

We all sit down and I am overwhelmed by the wonderful scent of freshly baked bread. There are bowls filed with steamed, sautéed and roasted vegetables, green olives, savory cheeses and a wonderful variety of wines that I remember Amanda telling me about. There is a small saucer by each plate to hold the delicious olive oil made from the olives grown on the monastery grounds and pressed on site.

Father Rowe can see the delight on my face and he tells me that the Trappist Monks abstain from eating meat and only on occasion will eat fish, but that doesn't bother me. "Father, who needs meat and fish when I can enjoy the feast before me! Thank you so much for your hospitality."

Father Aiden and Msgr. De Marinis wholeheartedly concur. Father Rowe leads us all in saying grace before the meal and ends the prayer by saying, "…and Lord please watch over my friends while they are here in this, Your Holy Land, and help guide them in whatever they have set about doing. Amen." Father Rowe gives us all a penetrating stare and asks, "By the way gentlemen, what is it that you have set about doing?"

There is an ominous silence among us as we look to each other to see who will answer Father Rowe's question. Monsignor Amedeo holds his hands up as I am about to speak and tell Father Rowe my tale filled with 'tortured half-truths' as Father Aiden calls them.

"Christopher, please allow me to answer. My dear Father, we have known each other for…how many years is it, Luke?"

"I believe we have known each other nearly 30 years."

"My, my time does fly. During that time, you have come to know the holy work I have been put in charge of by the Vatican do you not?"

"I do; you are the Holy Roman Catholic Church's chief exorcist."

"That is correct. Father, can I trust your discretion?"

"Of course, Amedeo, you can rely on it."

"I am here on a sacred mission with my friends. This requires the utmost care and secrecy as it involves the forces of darkness. I can say no more, but I implore you to trust us and know that we are engaged in doing what God has willed us to do. I can tell you no more, but I know that you would bless our undertaking if you knew what it entailed."

Father Rowe is silent for a moment, "My friends, old and new, I would like to lead us in a prayerful exaltation to the Lord that he may guide you to successful completion of your mission in His name."

We all bow our heads and pray, but all I can think of is what lies ahead of us.

CHAPTER 53

After leaving Hadera; Beth, Tom and Verrine make their way toward the Sea of Galilee. Along the road from Hadera towards Galilee, Beth notices a sign that points north toward Megiddo.

"Tom, I just saw a sign for Megiddo; it's early so maybe we should stop there now."

Tom, says, "It's a little too early and we have plenty of time. It can get crowded with tourists who flock to the Sea of Galilee later so it's best if we get their early. I've got it all planned!"

"You usually do; I guess that's why you are one of the three most eligible bachelors in America."

Tom and Beth take a moment to just look into each other's eyes and they seem to forget Verrine is in the car with them. Beth moves towards Tom and they are about to kiss when the car suddenly swerves and Verrine blasts the horn.

"Ant kataa minn al-qaraf!"

Tom and Beth are tossed around the back seat and grab onto the side of the vehicle.

Tom yells, "What the hell happened Verrine? You almost got us killed."

"I am so sorry to have frightened you both, but that car that just passed almost hit us. I apologize for the vulgar way I spoke."

Beth looks back at the road behind them, but she doesn't see a car. She doesn't think much of it and she doesn't want to upset Verrine, "Don't worry about cursing; we didn't understand a word of it anyway" and she smiles at the driver and he returns her smile.

The trip from Hadera doesn't take long and when they arrive it is early enough. There were no crowds to speak of, but Verrine says there would be many people coming later.

"See, didn't I tell you would be a lot less crowded!"

Beth just smirks, "You're always right, aren't you?"

Tom turns to her with a big grin and says, "Yep!"

Verrine finds a parking spot near the port on the shore of Galilee and he gets out and opens the door to help Beth exit. Beth is staring in wide-eyed wonder at the beautiful expanse of the Sea of Galilee and she turns to Tom and is so excited.

"Tom I can't believe we are here. The Sea of Galilee is where Jesus walked on water; this is where He fed the multitude with just 5 loaves of bread and two fishes at Tabgha. I want to see Magdala, I want to tour the Church of the Twelve Apostles, we should walk the streets of Nazareth, let's have lunch right near here, look how beautiful it is with the restaurants right on the water. Oh, and we must leave time to See the Ashkenazi HaAri Synagogue and the House and Church of St. Peter, the…"

"Whoa Beth, calm down. We don't have years to see all that stuff; we only have a couple of hours before we need to head out to Megiddo. Question; where did you learn about all those places?"

"I read a lot before we came."

"I see. Well, why don't you pick a few places to tour near the harbor and we can come back for lunch. When we're done, we can then head off to our final stop, Megiddo. What do you say?"

"Party pooper. Okay, I guess you're right, but hurry up we have a lot to do. I see the sign for the Tomb of Maimonides; let's go there first. On the way back we can visit St. Peter's Church and then have lunch and then Verrine can drive us down to Aqua Kef to see Hamat Tiberias. Then we can drive back north to Magdala." Beth grabs Tom's arm and yanks him towards the sign that point the way to the Tomb of Maimonides, "Come on, and let's get cracking' you heathen!"

Tom has to stifle a laugh, "Okay, okay, but we might have to cut a few hundred items off of your must-see list" and they head out on their tour.

* * *

About two hours have passed. Verrine has been waiting patiently by the Hummer trying to ignore the gawkers looking over the large camouflage colored Hummer H1 vehicle. As he is standing there, Verrine spots Tom and Beth walking down the street. They are-in-arm laughing and they seem to be enjoying themselves immensely.

When Tom spots Verrine he says, "We are going to stop here for lunch, would you like to join us."

Verrine smiles and says, "Thank you, but I am not hungry. Dr. Houston, I would like to remind you that we will need to leave soon so that we have enough time to visit Megiddo."

Tom acknowledges, "I know Verrine; I think we still have plenty of time, but we will be sure to leave enough for our trip to Megiddo." Then Tom turns to Beth and, in a mockingly scary voice, says "BWAHHAAA Armageddon!"

Beth laughs at Tom's poor attempt at humor and they walk a short way to a beautiful restaurant right on the water overlooking the Sea of Galilee. For nearly an hour they relax and enjoy the beautiful day. They eat fresh fish, hummus with grilled lamb, and a delicious Israeli vegetable salad called 'salat yerakot'. By the time they were finished, Tom and Beth have stuffed themselves full and walked back to the car.

Verrine was standing in the same position that they had left him in and Tom says, "Verrine, do you think we have time to go to Aqua Kef to see Hamat Tiberias and the national park?"

"I think not Dr. Houston. We are on a tight schedule if you are to be back at your hotel. Besides, you asked me to remind you to leave enough time for Miss Della Russo's surprise."

Beth stares at Tom, "Surprise? Tom what surprise, you have already done enough."

Tom glares at Verrine, "Verrine, you should have kept this a secret like we discussed., but now that the cat's out of the bag…" turning to Beth, Tom says, "it's something that was last minute and was planned for once we are at Megiddo."

Beth gets really close to Tom and puts her hand on his arm and kisses his cheek and, whispering in his ear, says, "Can't you just give me a little hint about what the surprise is?"

"Not on your life…you're just going to have to wait."

Beth pouts, "You are a party pooper."

Verrine "Ms. Della Russo, I apologize to both you and Dr. Houston for spoiling the surprise."

Beth says, "No worries, I'll be sure to thank Dr. Houston personally tonight back at the hotel. Now let's get going I can't wait to see my surprise!"

CHAPTER 54

After dinner and before we turn in, the three of us agree to get an early start for the trip to Megiddo.

I set the alarm for 5AM and I told both Father Langford and Msgr. De Marinis that we would meet outside my room and walk to the car together. I am exhausted when I say goodnight to the group and retire to my room. I am just about to fall into a deep sleep when my bed and the room disappear and I am transported into another vision.

> *It is the First Century AD. A young boy sits in the great library at Alexandria. His father was determined to provide his son with a classical education that challenged the boy's curiosity and love of learning. The young boy had been named after the god of the grape-harvest, winemaking and wine of fertility. He had not pondered why he, being such a serious person, could be named after a god who relished ritual madness, religious ecstasy, and theatre in ancient Greek religion and myth.*

The scenes change as the young boy is seen taking a walk into the desert on a beautiful spring day. It is in this place where he witnesses an event of supernatural origins.

The sky above went completely dark. The darkness lasted for three hours and the young boy had never witnessed anything like it. The color of the sky had taken on the deepest and darkest azure he'd ever seen. It seemed to the boy that there was a miraculous intervention involving God's heart in this mystical occurrence. The boy took care to write down the time and date of this occurrence. He also wrote what he inwardly sensed from the remarkable event, "God suffers or is always despondent."

The vision changes yet again and a number of years have passed. The young boy has grown into a man, and he is among an increasing number of people who have come to hear the holy man.

The holy man stood before the crowd assembled beneath the Parthenon. He surveys the many learned who have assembled there to hear him speak. The boy, now a man, was among those who gathered and it was there he heard the preaching of the Apostle Paul in the Areopagus Hill in Athens.

It was there the Apostle Paul described to all, in the greatest of detail, the day of Jesus' death. "…and as He was left to die on the cross for our sins, it was written in the gospel of Mathew, 'The sun suddenly went dark from noon 'til three in the afternoon.' The Apostle Paul went on to describe the day of Jesus' death, when the sun went supernaturally dark for three hours. The man, remembering the miraculous event from his boyhood, asked Paul how many years ago this was. When Paul told him the date and time, the man was shocked with astonishment…he came to find out that God had indeed suffered terribly as this was the same day His Son has died on the Cross for the sins of mankind.

St. Dionysius the Areopagite and his family were baptized that very day by St. Paul the Apostle.

St. Dionysios the Areopagite and St. Paul the Apostle step out of the vision and stand before me.

St. Dionysios is the first to speak, "The sky going dark and remaining so for three hours was an omen. It was the time and date of the death of our Lord and was revealed to me for a purpose. The darkness has haunted my soul, and now by God's good grace, this mystery was being revealed through Saint Paul's teaching."

St Paul says, "As I have written to all the faithful, I can do everything through Him who gives me strength. You are about to face an evil that can overwhelm, but it will never sap the strength that God can and will provide."

I am humbled, "I will never deny my faith and I will never allow the forces of hell to declare victory over mankind no matter how many demons I may face. If I should die, my only regret would be that I did not succeed, but my faith will help to sustain me"

St. Paul smiles knowingly and says, "That will always be a power you will wield; Remember, we walk by faith, not by sight."

St. Dionysios then tell me, "Christopher, we are here to reveal to you the time of the battle that must be won if humanity is to endure."

"Time? What time is that?"

The vision starts to fade and I call after Sts. Paul and Dionysios, "Please, tell me when the battle will take place?"

St. Dionysios speaks, "This day the battle will commence at noon and last for three hours. You must enter the third ethereal level through the portal. The sky will grow dark over the Jerusalem Plain, and in the three hours that darkness will last, the battle will be fought and the outcome will determine the fate of all."

St. Paul' last comment, "May the Lord bless you and keep you."

I awaken from the vision to find The Sainted have gone and I am alone. I lie in bed feeling my heart beating faster and faster and I try to calm myself down, but my mind is going a mile a minute.

I jump up and look at my phone to see that it is 6AM and that leaves us only six hours to get to Megiddo and to find the portal that St. Dionysios spoke of. I quickly get dressed and I go to Father Aiden's room and knock on the door. I hear a Father Aiden ask "Who is it?"

"Father, it's me, Chris we need to speak."

He opens the door and I am surprised to see he is already dressed. "Father, I had another vision."

He looks at me and simply asks, "Who?"

"Saint Paul the Apostle and St. Dionysius the Areopagite."

"What did they tell you?"

"The battle will begin at 12 noon and last for three hours."

"When?"

"Today."

Father Aiden says, "I will collect Amedeo and meet you outside your door in ten minutes. We will need to leave immediately."

"I'll be ready, just knock."

Ten minutes later there is a knock on the door to my room and I open it to find both priests waiting and ready to leave. We try to be quiet as we exit the abbey, but as we find out, the monks have been up for about an hour. We make our way toward the exit only to find Father Rowe standing there.

"Gentlemen, it appears like you are early risers like our monks."

Msgr. De Marinis says, "Ah Luke, not intentionally I must admit, but it appears that duty calls at the moment and we are forced to commence on our sacred mission."

"Then you all must take coffee or tea and our baked bread for your journey." Father Rowe walks us to the kitchen and loads a basket with coffee, baked bread and homemade jams.

Before we leave, Father Rowe offers to bless us by saying, "Dear Lord, bless and protect these loyal servants of Your church. Give them the strength and the wisdom to do good in Your name and to withstand the evils that abound in this world. If it is Your will oh Lord, return them to us safe so that they may continue to serve in Your holy name." He blesses us by making the sign of the cross and we all say, "Amen."

CHAPTER 55

The Hummer turns onto the main road leading toward Megiddo.

Beth and Tom are gazing out the vehicle's windows hoping to see the location where, according to Biblical scripture, Armageddon will take place. As they look over the landscape, they drive past a kibbutz located on the valley floor below Mount Megiddo. There are a few workers going about their daily chores and it all seems very serene.

In spite of the peaceful surroundings, Beth is incredulous as she says, to herself, out loud, "You've got to be kidding! This is Megiddo?" She then turns to Tom and tells him, "You know the old expression don't make a mountain out of a mole hill? Well, this is the mole hill! I was really expecting something much more…well, grandiose."

Tom agrees, "As a matter of fact, so was I. Verrine, are you sure this is the place that is mentioned in the Bible?"

Verrine answers, "Yes, Dr. Houston, this is Mount Megiddo. Even though it may not appear to be as majestic as you had hoped, it is steeped in historical relevance and there is much that can be learned here. In Christian apocalyptic literature, Megiddo, the hill overlooking the valley where kibbutz we just passed is located, has been identified as the site of the final battle between the forces of good and evil at the end of days. This is the Armageddon as mentioned in the New Testament in Revelation 16:16 as written by John the Apostle."

Beth and Tom look at each other in surprise at the level of knowledge Verrine appears to have. Tom tells him, "Verrine, we are both surprised at your knowledge of Megiddo."

"Thank you doctor, I have made obtaining knowledge of this, and other places as mentioned in scripture, as sort of a pastime of mine. I look to understand the various aspects of the region. I could go on and on about Megiddo, but I fear that I would bore you with the historical, political and Biblical references to this place. It should be noted though; Megiddo is one of the most ancient settlements in the Middle East. May I suggest that we find a proper vantage point where we can park so you may explore the area?"

Tom smiles, "Verrine you never cease to surprise me."

Verrine smiles back, "…and I hope I never will!"

They drive a short distance and arrive at a clearing where there is an area that they can park. Tom opens the door and helps Beth exit and they stand there for a moment and look over the valley, fields and plains."

"Is the name of this valley also called Megiddo?"

Verrine tells them, "No, it is named the Jezreel Valley. It is beautiful is it not, and very fertile I might add. Much is grown here…you can see in the distance there are fields of wheat, cotton, sunflowers and corn." Verrine points to the west and says, "Look a bit closer and you will see patches of watermelon and other types of melons, oranges groves, gardens growing rows of white beans, cowpeas, chickpeas, green beans, as well as grazing tracts for flocks of sheep and herds of cattle."

Beth and Tom crack up, "Verrine, you are a virtual fountain of knowledge."

"I am happy to oblige. Ms. Della Russo, do you see that large hill in the distance?"

Beth looks around as Verrine points in the direction of the hill and she tells him, "Yes I do."

"Ah That is Mount Tabor, although not as majestic as you may had hoped Megiddo would be, it is still very beautiful, is it not?"

Beth smiles, "Yes, it is." Beth turns to Tom and holds out her hand, "Come on; let's walk up the incline to get a better view."

"Sounds good to me."

Tom and Beth walk up a small incline where they have a better view of the entire valley and the surrounding plain. Tom turns in front of Beth and block her view of the valley. He puts his arms around her and looks into her eyes.

"Beth, I can't tell you how much it means to me to have you here. I hope you have enjoyed the day, I wanted you to enjoy this day more than anything else."

"I did Tom; it was so good to have time to spend with you. You said that you wanted to have me along so we could get to know each other better. All I know is that you are about the most kind and generous person that I have ever met. Thank you for all this and thank you for treating me like a, well, princess."

Tom and Beth are about to kiss when they hear a voice, "Doctor, you and Ms. Della Russo should see this."

They both turn around and in back of where they are standing is a vast multitude of what appear to be armed fighters. There are thousands upon thousands of men dressed in traditional middle-eastern garb from different places. Behind where the fighters' stand, there are an even greater number of soldiers whose features strike terror in Beth. Their faces are distorted, they carry ancient weapons and they are clothed as warriors would have dressed in past times. The number of terrorist fighters is so great that Beth cannot see any of the plain and valley beyond where she and Tom are standing.

Beth is stricken with fear as she clutches at Tom's arm, "Tom, who are these men? Where did they come from?"

Tom himself is taken aback by the multitude until out from the center of the vast lines of soldiers steps The Deceiver. Tom stares at his counterpart and whispers loud enough for Beth to hear, "Al Masih ad Dajjal."

The grotesque features of Al Masih ad Dajjal are no longer hidden as he speaks, "Good afternoon, Dr. Houston, it is so good to see you again."

Beth is repulsed by the hideousness of the man and she looks at Tom, "Tom, you know this man?" Beth is confused and terrified. She is looking around for some miraculous way that she might escape, but she can't seem to move as she is frozen in place.

Verrine speaks to Tom, "The time is near. We are called to the battle and the master is waiting." Verrine now morphs back into the demon he has always been and Beth gasps in horror. He grabs hold of her and she is powerless to move. The demon looks into the distance and out of nowhere appears what seems to be a portal, a gash torn in the horizon before them that opens to allow all those who have gathered to enter.

Beth manages a scream that is completely stifled as she attempts to beg Tom for help. Tom knows he cannot do anything for Beth to avoid her fate at the hands of Satan. "Beth, it will be over soon, don't fight it. When it is done you will forget all this and we can be happy, I promise."

A silently screaming Beth pleads with crying eyes, "Tom! Tom! Help me I'm frightened, please make him stop."

Tom looks grief stricken and as he sees Beth being dragged away by Verrine, but all he can manage to say is, "I…I'm sorry Beth."

Verrine grabs hold of Beth's arms and she is powerless to break free. The more she struggles the stronger the grip that the demon Verrine, has on her. Beth is terrified as she looks back at Tom trying to scream and pleading for help. It is then that Beth is made to float in air next to Verrine who follows her into the portal.

Tom just stands there, incapable of doing anything as he watches Beth being taken through the portal to become the vessel for Satan's spawn.

CHAPTER 56

I try calling Beth's number again, but all I get is her voice mail message so I leave her another message saying the same thing I've already said at least three times before.

After we say goodbye to Father Rowe, Msgr. De Marinis, Father Aiden and I get into the car and consult the map. Megiddo is north of Latroun Monastery and, not knowing the roads or any issues with traffic in Israel, I can only estimate that it could take a couple of hours.

I am silent at the start of the trip just sipping my coffee and taking a bite of bread and jam we were given by Father Rowe. Father Aiden is also quiet, taking time to contemplate whatever he is contemplating; I think I have a good guess what it is.

"Father, do we have a plan or 'do we march into hell for a Heavenly cause?' Wait, let me see if I remember something from my high school English Lit, 'From this day to the ending of the world, but we in it shall be remembered; we few, we happy few, we band of brothers'

Father Aiden just smiles, "…For he to-day that sheds his blood with me shall be my brother." That quote is the part of the magnificent soliloquy; St. Crispin's Day Speech from Henry V. Spartaco read the entire speech to me when I was in a coma. I sincerely believe it is what awakened me from my unnatural slumber. It is foresight that you have thought to invoke the same and for this I am truly heartened. Thank you, Christopher."

I smile at Father Aiden and say, "You're welcome and thank you and the monsignor both for your friendship, bravery and most of all your unwavering faith."

Msgr. De Marinis has been quiet just listening to us while he sips his coffee, but he feels the need to contribute with a quote from Jesus, "I would like to add these words of the Lord to our ruminations, 'Henceforth I call you not servants; for the servant knoweth not what his lord doeth; but I have called you friends; for all things that I have heard of my Father I have made known unto you.' I believe the Lord has chosen us and He trusts us to do what we must to save mankind and that is the will of God." Father Aiden and I look at each other and smile with Aiden saying, "Those words are enough to eclipse even the Bard."

We continue to drive while discussing what we might do when we enter the portal and what we might encounter when we get there. There was little else to conclude as the only consensus is to allow things to happen in whatever way the forces of Heaven will allow. A short while later we turn down the road leading to Megiddo.

The nice weather betrays what we all know we are in for and I tell both priests. "When I was taken to the ethereal plain by Julian, the ground under my feet felt very strange."

Father Aiden asked, "Strange, in what way?"

"It's hard to describe. It wasn't solid yet it wasn't soft; I don't know any way to tell you other than it was very strange, weird; you know what I mean."

The priests look at each other and just say, "No, I fear we will need to experience it for ourselves."

We drive past the kibbutz and look up to the mount that the sign tells us is 'Megiddo' and scan the area for any sign of activity. The surroundings are eerily quiet; there are no tourists, farm workers, even the stirrings and calls of small animals and birds; all activities that one would expect are non-existent making it all the more surreal.

I look ahead and spot a clearing where I park the car. We all get out of the car and take an initial look around. I look down at the ground and say to Father Aiden and Msgr. De Marinis, "What do you think of all these footprints on the ground?"

Father Aiden says, "It appears that these footfalls are relatively recent and judging from the sheer numbers, many, many people have assembled here."

"I agree and it seems not too long ago."

Each of us decide to head off in different directions to see what we can find, but there is no sign of Beth or Tom or anyone else for that matter. It is not long after that I spot a vehicle parked at a spot further down the road that overlooks the valley. The vehicle looks like it is painted camouflage and I start to walk toward the car hoping to be able to find the owner. The closer I get I can see that it is a Hummer, but there is no one in or near the vehicle. When I get to the vehicle, I find that the doors are open so I yell out, hoping someone will hear me and come back to their car, but there is only the same eerie quiet.

I take a look inside to the car's front seats and there is nothing there. When I check the back seat however, I spot a shoulder bag in the rear seat on the passenger's side. I take a look around hoping to see someone coming toward the car, but there is no one to be seen. I reach into the car and pull out the shoulder bag and take a look inside and immediately I recognize that it is Beth's. I see her wallet, I see her favorite pair of sun glasses, I see a scarf she always takes with her and I smell the perfume she always wears. I run over to the edge of the ridge that overlooks the valley trying to see if I can spot her down there, but it is totally void of any life.

I scream out, "Monsignor De Marinis, Father Aiden, come quick! Hurry I found something!"

I look down the road and I spot both of then hurrying to meet me where I'm standing. A concerned Father Aiden, breathing heavily, says, "Christopher, what is it?"

Monsignor De Marinis, also out of breath says, "What is it? What have you found?"

"Look" and I hand over the Beth's license from the wallet that I found in her shoulder bag.

Father Aiden looks at it, "It's Beth" and he asks me, "Christopher, have you searched the area to determine if she is anywhere in proximity of the vehicle.

"Yes, I looked around here, I've looked over the ridge, but there is no one, nothing, not even a bird or a cat or a squirrel, nothing."

"Then, Christopher, I fear Beth is in the clutches of Satan and the anti-christs. They must have entered onto the ethereal level of the plain through the portal. The time is near and we must find the doorway or I fear all will be lost." The three of us have no idea where to begin to look for the portal. We frantically search around for a sign, any sign, that would point the way, but to no avail.

It is Monsignor De Marinis who first observes a small ripple, a disturbance in the air at the edge of the ridge overlooking Megiddo. Cautiously he calls us over, "I believe that this is the portal we are looking for."

We stand a few feet from the ripple and watch it expand. It is now large enough for all three of us to enter. We look at each other and, never at a loss for the right words, Father Aiden says, "Once more unto the breach, dear friends, once more!"

CHAPTER 57

Beth does not need to walk; she floats over the surface of the ethereal plain. Verrine has been commanded to bring Beth to Satan and he guides her towards where they will meet.

Beth cannot speak, she can only look at the surroundings in horror. This is a place like none she has ever seen. The sky is a dark grey, the surface is a dark grey, there are no trees or clouds or buildings or plants; there is just a conglomeration of nothingness except for one thing. In the distance there is a mountain of enormous proportions that casts an ominous shadow over all; Mount Megiddo.

Verrine, Beth, Tom and Al Masih ad Dajjal, as well the legions of terrorists and the Warriors of Isfahan, steadily make their way to the base of Mt. Megiddo where Satan has established a strategic position in advance of the battle between the forces of Heaven and Hell.

Along the way certain of the terrorists become frightened. They look around and cannot comprehend the meaning of this place. They have been told it is Allah's will to be here, but they cannot understand its meaning. Dutifully, however they will go to their death and their reward of eternal pleasures have been guaranteed, at least that will make it all worthwhile.

The closer they get to their rendezvous with Allah the more doubts seem to arise, but they have not been told the truth. The group scans the horizons and the base of Megiddo and find that the entity before them is alone.

Verrine is the first to speak to Satan. "Lord, I have brought you your concubine as you have commanded."

"Ah yes! Thank you Verrine; good job!"

Turning to Beth, Satan says, "Welcome, welcome my dear! So good of you to come"

"Julian?"

"Yes, you remembered, how sweet! Yes, it is I Julian. I felt that my current form would be far less unnerving for you than to see my true, how shall I say it, nature so I decided that I would take a more pleasing visage; by the way, how about these pecs, huh?!" Satan unbuttons his shirt to reveal a muscular chest with sculpted pecs and abdominal muscles which he is able to move up and down.

Beth is repulsed by the demon that tried to kill her, but she is powerless to do anything to break free as she is forced to look on in disgust.

"Master" Al Masih ad Dajjal bows his head and speaks.

Satan looks over the vast group of warriors assembled and he seems delighted "Ah, welcome! I see you've come and look at who you've brought! I am very pleased. I went food shopping and I picked up a lot of provisions, but I didn't realize there were so many mouths to feed, but don't fret, I'm sure we can make due. Anyway, I've made bacon, lettuce and tomato sandwiches, I have a huge pork roast with baked apples, I've baked mom's original ham hocks recipe and I've grilled enough pork sausages to feed an army. Oh, and I'm sure the boys are thirsty from their trip so I've filled the cooler with beer, wine and for those who want something stronger, I've made pitchers of Mojitos! It's my very own special recipe and I bet you'll never guess what the secret ingredient is!"

The Deceiver smiles and says, "That is most generous of you master."

"Oh, think nothing of it."

The Muslim terrorists now are beginning to come under the realization that they have been deceived. They look around at each other hoping someone has an answer, but their blank stares betray a growing concern.

One terrorist has the temerity to speak, "Oh Masih, what is it that you have done? Is this the will of Allah and his prophet Mohammad, bless his name? This man cannot be Allah, this cannot be his will!"

"Oh, Al Masih, let me take it from here." With the wave of his hand, Satan commands the Warriors of Isfahan who immediately surround the terrorists. The Muslim fighters are terrified trying to retreat in fear for their lives, but they are surrounded and there is no retreat. The terrorists attempt to defend themselves, but the Warriors of Isfahan have taken the form of a deadly fog and they swoop down on them to tear them apart, limb by limb. The carnage along with the cries and screams of the dying men are so hideous, so pitiful that Tom clamps his hands over his ears and shuts his eyes.

The base of Mt. Megiddo then opens to reveal a massive entrance to a cave that is radiating blistering heat. The body parts of the terrorists reconnect themselves in the most haphazard of ways and the condemned are dragged by some unseen force into the cave.

"Ah, now that they are out of the way, we have plenty of food for everyone! Isn't that great?"

Al Masih ad Dajjal does not want to betray his fear, but it is palpable. He can only respond, "Yes, master."

"By the way, what did we promise them? 72 demons or 72 virgins, I forget?"

"It was 72 virgins, master."

"Whoops, I think I made a mistake. Oh, well, you can still get fucked by 72 demons, or was it the other way around, I forget. Anyway, you can't always get want to want."

Satan turns to tell Beth who is still floating near him, "Beth, it is so good that you are here to share my bed!"

In an instance a large bed complete with a canopy surrounded with flowers along with an end table with an enormous box of chocolates on it appear. "See didn't I tell you I was an incurable romantic? I can't believe how excited and nervous I am! Before we consummate our union, I need two things to make it complete. Verrine, would you please bring my adorable Beth over here to me? Just lay her on the bed, will you? Ah, how alluring you are my dear."

Verrine does as he is told and Beth is virtually incapable of doing anything other than move her head. She looks down as she sees her clothes coming off and they are replaced by a very flimsy negligee. Satan leers at her saying, "Hubba, hubba!"

Satan then takes his eyes off Beth and points out to a place in the distance. He seems delighted at what he sees and beckons Beth to look. "Beth, I have a real surprise for you, I promise you're going to love this!" She turns to face the direction Satan in pointing, but she can't make out who or what it is. Beth keeps staring at the people as they move closer then her eyes go wide.

Satan lies down on the bed next to her and whispers in her ears, "I invited someone that I want to witness the consummation of our blissful encounter." Satan's hands find their way up and down Beth's leg and she tries to scream, but can't.

"What cat got your tongue?" Satan smiles

Now the horror of the moment wells up inside and Beth can't believe what he sees as she is able to scream, "CHRIS!"

CHAPTER 58

The three of us are alone as we take our first steps through the portal and onto the third ethereal level of the Jerusalem Plain. The monotone grey of everything matches our mood as we take tentative steps forward. The surface beneath our feet is as inexplicably bizarre as it was the first time I was here with Julian. We three look down at our feet and then up at one another and Father Aiden says, "I now see what you mean about the odd inconsistency of the surface."

It is obvious to us that there is some sort of gathering in the distance so we make our way toward them not knowing what we will find.

I first hear someone scream my name and then I see Beth.

She is lying on a huge bed and by her side lays Julian. I get ready to run to where they are, but I am stopped by Father Langford.

"Christopher, you must resist the temptation to try and rescue Beth from the clutches of Satan, which appears to be exactly what he would like you to do."

"But Father, he will certainly kill her."

"I do not think that is his intention. I believe he has a far more sinister purpose."

"Christopher" Msgr. De Marinis interrupts, "I believe as I believe Aiden does, that Satan is looking to impregnate Beth and have her carry his spawn. Apparently, Satan wishes you to witness this and have you react violently."

"But Father, Monsignor, I can't let this happen. What can I do to stop this?"

I am looking past the priests only to see Beth trying to struggle and hearing her screams. I can see Julian continuing to stroke Beth's legs while smiling at me.

"Ah Christopher I see your priests have finally figured out what I'm up to. You see Beth will become the vessel that will carry my offspring. I am going to need help with caring for the vast numbers of souls that will be damned for eternity. Eternity! That's a long time and having the help will be an immense relief in my golden years."

I scream at Julian, "You bastard! Leave her alone!"

"What are you some kind of nut? Just look at that body! Can't you see this prime example of feminine pulchritude laying here next to me. I used to suffer from erectile dysfunction, but I ordered something from the online shopping network and now think I'm cured and Beth will be the first lucky recipient of my newly reclaimed virility!"

I attempt to run to where Beth and Julian lay in bed, but again Father Langford and Msgr. De Marinis hold me back. Father Aiden says. "Christopher, remember why we are here. We are here at our Lord's beckoning and we must fulfill our calling."

Julian calls to me and says, "Oh Christopher, given the importance of this union, I think I should invite some of my close personal friends to witness to the consummation; what do you think?

Satan doesn't wait for an answer. At that exact moment, out from the fiery cave pours millions upon millions of demons. Satan is flanked on both sides by the princes of hell and behind them many demon masters that will command the legions of demons. The hellish creatures spread out all over the ethereal plain to the point where the horizon is totally obscured as they also surround the bed. Beth witnesses the dreadfulness of the demonic hoards and she feels her sanity slipping away.

I realize the truth behind what the priests have said and I reply, "It's okay father, I'm okay." Father Aiden and the Monsignor let go of me and we three just stand, side by side, and stare at the spectacle unfolding before us. We can feel the heat emanating from the entrance to cave leading to hell.

I look around and see Tom Houston just standing there and I feel my anger growing.

Julian knows my hatred for the man so he goads me into reacting. "Christopher, you know that after my tryst with the lovely Beth, I am planning to have her wed to Dr. Thomas Houston. She will make a lovely First Lady, don't you think? Oh, and I just thought my offspring will get to play in Oval Office!" Satan then turns to Tom and says, "Be sure to send me photos!"

Msgr. De Marinis reminds me, "Christopher do not let these feelings of revenge and anger consume you. Do not give in to the temptation."

I tell both priests "Don't worry. I know my purpose and I realize how Satan is trying to manipulate my emotions and what I now know is my true love for Beth."

Satan sneers, "You know, I really love getting to damn priests to hell? Well, you know, some of them have done very bad things and I get to punish them. What a kick!" Now Satan turns to Father Langford, "By the way, I really enjoyed the time I spent in the confessional with you. It was truly enlightening." Father Aiden stares back at the demon with equal intensity, but does not engage him in any way.

The Monsignor then tells me, "Demons know the power of prayer and they fear it. I know a wonderful prayer that I have adapted to praise the Lord; 'A Prayer of Light.' I will lead us so let us pray together." Father Aiden, Monsignor De Marinis and I get down on our knees and he leads us in prayer.

Light, dear Lord
Dissolve this night.
Dark is it
Cold is it.
Yet dear Lord You are here.
Your presence is my beacon.
Your warmth dear Lord is my hope and my refuge.
Light, dear light.
Dissolve, this night.

Ignorant and restless spirits roam here
Let them rest in your grace, dear Lord

Julian howls with rage and now transforms himself into the demon he always is; Satan. Beth sees him and she lets out a scream from the bottom of her soul as Satan crawls on the bed towards her. I can no longer stay calm and I am about to get up and run to rescue Beth when an all-encompassing light emanates from behind us and its glow completely surrounds all the ethereal plain.

I look over to see Satan staring at the vast expanse behind where we are kneeling. He is frightened, very frightened as he climbs off the bed to stand amidst his minions. Beth is now able to move and she climbs off the bed and looks past the three of us in wide-eyed wonder. Father Aiden, Monsignor De Marinis, and I slowly turn and see something so beautiful, so divine it takes our breath away.

CHAPTER 59

It is very early in the morning and Chief Al Barese is sitting at his desk deeply immersed in the large pile of recent crimes and criminal stats that have been occupying most of his time. The chief's sleep has become increasingly fitful and he has grown accustomed to getting to work in the early morning hours. He is using the time to catch up on all the horrors happening around Suffolk County and the whole world for that matter.

As chief, he and his team have been actively involved in the investigation of increasingly violent crimes taking place in his jurisdiction. The daily meetings where he gets regularly updated have become so disheartening that he often feels powerless to keep up the morale of his team. Lately he has also had a very hard time concentrating on police work since Chris went to Israel with Aiden. The chief is growing more and more concerned that he has not heard from his nephew for three days and when he tried to call last night all he was able to get was Chris' voice mail.

There is a knock at the chief's door and he gets up and opens it. Standing there is his second in command, Dan Orello and his entire team.

"Good morning, Dan, come on in. I didn't know you were going to bring the whole gang.

"Thanks chief, I wanted the team here to be part of this." They both walk towards the small conference table in the corner of Chief Barese's office.

"Coffee?"

"No thanks, I had my ration of 30 cups so far."

The chief smiles at Dan and asks, "So what's up? As if I didn't know."

"Well chief, we have a situation."

"Oh no, not another situation, what is it this time?"

"I think you should sit down for this."

The chief gives Dan a questioning look, but he takes a seat and Dan explains, "If you can believe it, this is a good situation, really good, but really weird."

"Good and weird? You know I've had it up to here with just weird, but a little good and weird can't hurt; tell me about it."

"Well, like you, I get in early just to get caught up on the crime reports from the day and night before. As you know better than anyone, these reports of crimes have been building up day after day and it can get pretty depressing."

"Tell me about it, so what's happening?"

"I checked the reports this morning and you could have knocked me over with a feather. The incidents of incredibly violent crimes have dropped so dramatically that they have virtually disappeared."

"What?"

"You heard right, virtually disappeared. I thought that I had gotten only a small amount of the usual reports I get, but when I looked, the numbers of precincts reporting were complete and nothing seemed to be out of order.

"I hoped you double checked all this."

"I did chief. I called each of the precincts and spoke to my counterparts there. Each and every one of them had the same reaction; they were dumbfounded by the dramatic drop in crimes."

"Wait, you can't tell me that there are no crimes being committed."

"Well, no there are still crimes out there, but they are being committed by the usual scumbags, I mean suspects. You know; the guys we know, all with arrest records and all committing the same kind of crimes that they've done in the past. What is also weird is that those people who have committed the truly horrendous crimes that have baffled us for so long are all gone…every crazy psycho nut job criminal that we would normally expect to find is gone."

"Gone?"

"Gone!"

CHAPTER 60

The three of us stand up not able to take our eyes off of what we are seeing. The divine light is emanating from the glorious presence of God and the powers of Heaven now totally obliterating the grey sky above. The assembled spirits are arrayed among the glowing light and Father Aiden, Monsignor De Marinis and I immediately fall back down on our knees once more.

I am in awe as I look to see so many of The Sainted that I have come to know and love. Without turning my gaze from the heavenly vision, I whisper to the priests, "I can see all The Sainted are among the spirits." For me, it is just like the gathering of Saints that I experienced in my very first vision of Sts. Cosmos and Damian. In the vision is now there appear more than 10,000 of the holiest men and women appearing among the divine spirits. These spirits are assembled and in the forefront of The Sainted appear the twelve apostles; Sts. Mathew, Mark, Luke, John, Jude, Bartholomew, Thomas, Peter, Paul, Andrew, Phillip and Thaddeus.

St, John the Apostle looks over at me and he smiles. In my mind I can hear him tell me,

"Christopher, God is love. Whoever lives in love lives in God, and God in him. Our love should not be just words and talk; it must be true love, which shows itself in action. This is the time to affirm your faith, your belief in the Lord of God, His Son Jesus Christ all by the power of the Holy Spirit. You have

been chosen to stand firm against the forces of hell and the evil as manifested in Satan and The Sainted pray for you every minute of every day."

I silently answer St. John in my thoughts and tell him, "I will not fail you."

Father Aiden's attention turns toward another apparition, and he is wonder struck. He excitedly points out an assemblage of Major and Minor Prophets of the Old Testament to the monsignor. "Look Amodeo there is Isaiah and Elijah, Abraham, Eli, Ezekiel." The priests are overwhelmed by what they are witnessing. Father Aiden instinctively knows who each of the prophets are as he continues, "I cannot believe what I am allowed to behold; Moses, can you imagine, Moses!" Father Aiden excited points, "Amodeo, there's Jeremiah, Daniel…" Aiden goes on and on naming each of the nearly 60 prophets who are standing near the center of the vision.

Monsignor De Marinis becomes entirely absorbed in the vision of prophets and exclaims, in as reverential a tone he can muster, "Aiden… there is St. John the Baptist." We three are astounded by the heavenly revelations before us.

St. John the Apostle now comes forward for me and my companions to hear. "Christopher, this is the fulfillment of the Revelation that was revealed laid bare to me by the messenger of God. At once I was in the Spirit, and there before me was a throne in heaven with someone sitting on it. And the one who sat there had the appearance of jasper and ruby. A rainbow that shone like an emerald encircled the throne. Surrounding the throne were twenty-four other thrones, and seated on them were twenty-four elders. They were dressed in white and had crowns of gold on their heads. From the throne came flashes of lightning, rumblings and peals of thunder. In front of the throne, seven lamps were blazing. These are the seven spirits of God. Also, in front of the throne there was what looked like a sea of glass, clear as crystal. In the center, around the throne, were four living creatures."

St. John then expands his arms and what he has said would be revealed is now shown to us. In the center of the divine glow a figure now grows to great proportion and before us ascends the vision of Jesus Christ. He is dressed in magnificent white robes and hovering above His head is the

Holy Spirit in the form of a white dove. I behold the vision of Jesus and am so absorbed and I find myself overcome with the miracle appearing before me. In the foreground of the vision of our Lord, a new apparition appears; it is the vanguard of Archangels.

St. Michael the Archangel is in the center holding the shield and a sword in much the same way I saw him when he saved my uncle's life. On one side of St. Michael appear Sts. Gabriel, Rafael, and Selaphiel and on the other side of St. Michael appears Sts. Jegudiel, Barachiel and Jeremiel. They are the fearless protectors of the Father and of His Son, Jesus Christ.

As the vision continues to multiply, it is then the Heavenly Host overtakes the entire land and skies surrounding all the forces that have assembled on the ethereal plain in the shadow of Megiddo. Fr. Aiden, Monsignor De Marinis and I are motionless as the entire manifestation unfolds before us. Father Aiden cannot take his eyes off what he is witnessing and whispers to himself a quote from Revelations, "Then I looked and heard the voice of many angels, numbering thousands upon thousands, and ten thousand times ten thousand. They encircle the throne and the living creatures and the elders."

Satan shrieks a hideous stream of blasphemies as he sees the forces of Heaven materializing in front of him. The demon masters are screaming their own stream of obscenities as the glowing lights engulf ethereal plain and the demon hoard. There is fear among all the hellish forces and they begin to move backwards toward Megiddo and the entrance to hell. Satan turns to see this and senses their fear. He causes himself to grow to enormous proportions, turns toward these monstrous beings and with the swipe of his hand eviscerates a huge number. The demons that have not incurred Satan's wrath are frozen in their tracks. They cower in fear of the master of hell who has turns to face Christ and the forces of Heaven.

Satan orders the demon masters, "This is the moment. Our time is now as we must achieve victory before we may claim the souls of humankind. Take your legions into battle at my command."

Satan exhorts The Deceiver, "Al Masih ad Dajjal prepare the Warriors of Isfahan."

Al Masih ad Dajjal himself is trembling at what he is seeing. He tries not to betray his fright, but he is only able to reply a weak, "Yes master."

Satan then turns to Tom, "Ah, Dr. Houston! I am so glad you came. Here's something useful you can do to pull your own weight as they say. Take the lovely Beth and put her in front of me so that Christopher may see me screw her brains out."

Tom himself is so frightened by what he sees that he doesn't immediately respond.

Satan roars, "HAVE YOU NOT HEARD WHAT I HAVE SAID?"

Tom trembles in fear as he walks toward the bed, never taking his eyes off the forces of Heaven and hell that are about to do battle. Tom grabs Beth by the arm and pulls her off the bed. She struggles to break free, but she cannot and Tom drags her toward Satan. Just before he gets to where he was told to bring her, Beth kicks Tom in his groin and he bends down in pain and he lets her escape from his grasp.

Beth spots Chris and she runs to him frantically. He rushes toward her and he brings her back to where Father Aiden and Monsignor De Marinis are standing.

Satan sees Beth in Chris' arms and he will not suffer this outrage. He looks at Tom Houston with such evil malevolence that all Tom can say is "Master I..." before Satan casts him into the inferno.

Saint Michael moves toward where Satan is standing. There is fearlessness in his demeanor as he is holding his sword and shield. Satan takes steps backward in fear of the retribution that will rain down on him. The prince of hell remembers being cast aside by his brother angel, Michael, and the rout has never left his consciousness.

Before Satan is able to begin the battle, however, the prophet Isiah steps forward and stares down the demon saying, *"How you have fallen from heaven, morning star, son of the dawn! You have been cast down to the earth, you who once laid low the nations!"*

For Satan to hear these words, makes his anger grow. He tries to summon the courage to begin the battle, but he is somehow unable. It is then that Jesus appears in front of Satan and stares down at Lucifer who now cowers in fear. The Lord speaks as thunder when He demands the fallen angel, *"Again it is written, you shall not put the Lord your God to the test. Depart from Me, you who are cursed, into the eternal fire prepared for the devil and his angels."*

Slowly the millions upon millions of demons retreat into the cave followed by the demon masters as well as Al Masih ad Dajjal and the Warriors of Isfahan. Satan is left alone of the Jerusalem Plain in the shadow of Megiddo. There is no false bravado, no shrieks of outrage, no forceful threats; nothing to provide even a small measure of resolve.

Satan knows the battle is over before it even began.

CHAPTER 61

The mouth of the cave leading to hell at the base of Megiddo closes and all is quiet on the Jerusalem Plain.

The forces of Heaven and all that have been blessed with eternal life in the arms of God slowly drift toward the light that comes down from the skies above. We all stare as the apparitions as they fade, leaving three spirits in our midst.

I immediately know who they are; St. Raphael the Archangel, St. Margaret of Antioch and St, Agrippina of Mineo. Father Aiden and Monsignor De Marinis are silent, not knowing who these saints are, look to me to understand what they should say or do. Beth is also by my side, but she seems to be in the state of shock after what she has been through and what she has witnessed.

I tell the priests, "These Sainted before us are St. Raphael the Archangel, St. Margaret and St. Agrippina."

St. Raphael is the first to speak, "You have done what your faith commanded and you have saved humanity. Satan and his minions could not withstand the power of God and His Son. He knew this yet his pride was so great he believed himself to be more powerful than the Maker of the Universe."

"We did nothing. We were only here and we did nothing, our faith was always foremost in our minds, but we did nothing."

St. Margaret said, "Your faith is all we ask of men and women. The Lord wished to determine if there was hope for humankind; He now knows there is hope."

St. Raphael continues, "He will now heal the earth from when it was defiled by the sins of the fallen angels. You have given hope to the world."

"Christopher," St. Agrippina says, "We among The Sainted are very grateful that your faith never wavered and that you were able to overcome the fear that evil always evokes."

I don't know what to say, how to respond. I manage to say, "Thank you. I would never have been able to even hope to survive if it was not for…"

St. Margaret smiles and says, "Father Aiden Langford and Monsignor Amodeo De Marinis. We Sainted are most grateful that you accompanied Christopher on this perilous journey. May the Lord always bless you and keep you in His heart for the rest of your days."

Both priests bow their heads and say, "Amen."

I am still holding Beth up, but she starts to collapse unconscious. I put my arms around her trying to keep her conscious but it is no use. I look up at my friends, The Sainted, and I ask them, "What can I do to help Beth? Will she be alright?"

The images of the Sainted are fading slowly and they tell me, "She will be fine, but she will have little or no memory of these things."

"Are you leaving me? Will I never see you again?"

St. Agrippina smiles at me and says, "I believe that the correct response to that query, in your colloquial, is 'fat chance'".

I laugh at St. Agrippina's attempt at humor and I look over and see both Father Aiden and Monsignor De Marinis smiling from ear to ear.

CHAPTER 62

At the exact moment The Sainted disappears, we find ourselves next to a ledge overlooking the Jezreel Valley near the base of Megiddo…the Hummer is gone.

Beth is still unconscious and in my arms. I take my handkerchief and soak it with bottled water that I have in my jacket. I wipe her forehead and softly say, "Beth, it's me, Chris. Beth are you okay, please speak to me?"

She doesn't respond so I keep wiping her forehead and cheeks hoping to revive her. Father Langford and Msgr. De Marinis are watching me care for Beth and they are as concerned as I am.

Father Aiden says, "Christopher, we must make haste and transport Beth to the nearest healthcare facility for medical treatment. I fear she may be suffering some form of mental collapse after witnessing the events on the Jerusalem Plain."

"You may be right father; I'll go get the car and drive back to pick you all up." I get up from beside Beth when she opens her eyes. She looks at me and breaks down is a torrent of tears.

She opens her arms, "Chris! I can't believe you are here. Hold me, please hold me, Chris."

I take Beth in my arms and she sobs uncontrollably for a few minutes. As she tries to calm herself, I ask, "Beth are you alright?"

Beth is silent for a few more minutes, but she will not release me from her embrace and I hold her as tight as I can without hurting her.

I don't want to probe her memory to find out if she has any recollection. I know that The Sainted have assured me that she will have little or no memory of the events that took place at Megiddo, but I want to understand what she may remember about Tom.

"Beth, what happened?"

"Chris, Tom…Tom…"

"What about Tom?"

"He brought me here. He changed; became someone that I didn't know. He had a driver or bodyguard or something that dragged me out of the car. I thought that I was going to be raped or killed. It was horrible and Tom just stood there, it was like he was another person. Oh, my God! Tom and that man, I think I remember his name; Verrine! That's it Verrine! They may still be here!"

"Don't worry Beth. When we arrived, we spotted the car and saw them standing there. We rushed toward them, but they escaped and left you here. Father Aiden, and Monsignor De Marinis and I looked around and there are no signs of anyone else."

Beth looks into my eyes, but she will not let go of me, "Where could they have gone? Chris, it was so frightening I thought I was going to die. I also have a faint memory of some sort of evil thing, some weird place, but I don't remember anything else. But you are here, how did you know where to find me?"

"It's a long story and you've got a hundred messages from me on your phone. I was calling to warn you about Tom, but you never answered."

"Tom told me to leave my phone in the hotel and I just did. Why did you call me? What did you want to warn me about Tom?"

I had to think fast, "Listen Beth, when you started becoming attached to Tom, I was jealous. I tried to find out something, anything that I could use to turn you against Tom. It wasn't until I met Amanda and she gave me some insights given her father's relationship with Tom. It seems Tom has a very dark side; sort of a split personality that comes out when you would least expect it. Amanda never said so, but I think she might have seen him display this trait."

"Amanda really told you that?"

"When Father Aiden and I went to Rome to visit Msgr. De Marinis I had just found out that you would be in Israel and I was frantic to let you know that he could be dangerous. Let's forget Tom for now; you are safe and he can't harm you anymore and that's all that matters."

Beth hugs me again, tighter this time and she stops to stare at Father Aiden and Msgr. De Marinis, she lets me go and tries to get up, but she is still wobbly. "Father Aiden, can you come over here?"

The priest smiles, "Of course, dear Beth."

Beth embraces the priest and whispers to him, "Thank you so much Aiden. If you, Chris and…" Beth then looks over to the monsignor and asks, "It's Monsignor De Marinis; did I get it right?"

"Yes, my dear."

"Can you please come over here?" Msgr. De Marinis walks over to Beth and she embraces him and tells the three of us, "If you three hadn't been there to save me I don't know what would have happened. I can never thank you enough."

Our group gets in the car and we drive back to the hotel where Beth has her clothing. She is still frightened and wants me to stay with her while she packs. When she finishes, I reach down to pick up her luggage, but she puts her hand on my arm to stop me.

"Is it too late for us?"

I was not expecting to have to deal with our relationship at this time. I stare at her and I realize that I am, and always was, in love with Beth.

"I hope not."

Beth puts her arms around me and we kiss. I look into her eyes and smile and tell her, "Let's go home."

EPILOGUE

Worldwide News Consortium – Brussels, Belgium – A great number of reports are coming in from around the world with news of a remarkable turnaround. For many months now local, national and international sources have been reporting an enormous surge in violent crimes including the most horrific murders, rioting, arson, mass shootings and knifings, beatings, torture and rape among many other vicious criminalities.

In a number of instances these violent episodes have taken place in many different locales around the globe including, college campuses, and prisons; in large cities, small towns and villages, in remote desserts or frozen tundra, among places. The enormity of the human carnage cannot be overstated with victims numbering in the hundreds of thousands worldwide. One element that has been common to all these events is the scriptural context of the "Lamb of God" referencing Jesus Christ.

We spoke to Dr. Theodosius Clureshnicous, a representative of the United Nations for World Order (UNWO). He appears to be at a loss to explain the precipitous, but welcomed drop in crimes around the world. "We at the United Nations World for Order are as baffled by this outcome as are most governments and law enforcement officials around the globe."

When asked to explain the connection between "Lamb of God" and the horrors that have been visited on humanity, Mr. Clureshnicous said, "Many of the leaders and senior officials of the UNWO do not hold any religious affiliations or beliefs so they have discounted any possible other-worldly connection. It was probably some loose affiliations of radical religious cults who saw this as an opportunity to exert control over weak people. This is why the UNWO was formed so that people can have our organization take control to provide structure and security for member nations and their peoples"

In contrast, religious leaders had their own points of view, but all seemed to recognize the extreme depth of horrific violence that can only emanate from the singular source of all evil.

Christians believe it is 'Satan or Lucifer', Muslims believe it is 'Iblees', Jews who believe in a nameless evil that occurs from the actions of man, nature or personal failings, or as Hindus believe, evil comes from violating dharma, the natural force of order that permeates the universe. There are other religious teachings that point to various sources of evil, but there is universal agreement that what has transpired has been committed by men and women, but rooted in the ultimate evil.

Given the Christian connection of the 'Lamb of God' to the vast horrors that have befallen so many, we asked Cardinal Richard Collins of the Western States Diocese about what he thought. "To connect this evil in any way to our Lord, Jesus Christ, is not only a blasphemy, it is an insult to over 1.3 billion Christians around the world. As we believe evil comes from one source, one vile beginning which is the root of all immorality, sinfulness and corruption and that source is Lucifer."

The dramatic drop in crimes and the resulting relief of so many have caused a startling uptick of those women and men who seem to have been reborn in their faith. Another new phenomenon has been observed as a number of serious memes have been posted all over the internet on social media sites. These memes showing the published photos of "Lamb of God" written in blood at various crime scenes have been overwritten with the words "He Is Risen."

Among all those we have talked to, whoever are correct, remains to be seen, but it is apparent that there is a great sigh of relief that can be heard from around the world.

* * *

Lake of Fire – Hell – The lone soul of the damned floats over the razor sharp-edged crags, the protruding outcropping of sarsens and massive pillars of fire that line the floors of Hell.

As he floats over the vast expanse, he can see countless numbers of souls below being tormented by demons and the deafening screams that accompany their torture. He can't remember much except that the Master was not happy with what transpired at Megiddo. It wasn't his fault, he's sure it is all a mistake and he is anxious to speak with Satan to get this all straightened out.

Why do these demons take such delight at making people suffer like they do? He can't explain why so he tries to close his eyes, but he can still see. He tries to close his ears to the sounds, but he can't make the screams go away. It seems like he has been floating over the hellish domain for a very long time while his senses have become overwhelmed with the noxious fumes of Sulphur infiltrating the atmosphere all around. The damned wants to choke, but he can't open his mouth. It seems he was meant to inhale the sulphuric fumes…and to feel the heat; the unbearable, scorching heat, driven by flames that shoot up at him as he floats past.

There is no true sense of time like there was before he came to this place. Before this place you knew when to eat or work or sleep, but here there is no consciousness, no real awareness of time itself, except that it is interminable. It could have been minutes or it could have been centuries, who knows, who cares all he can think of is his suffering, but he can resolve it all once he can speak to the master.

Even if he tries to hold his breath, he can still smell the poisonous fumes and feel the intense flames that lap his body. The flames have caused huge blisters to form on his skin; his pain is even greater when the blisters burst and new one's form again. The pain is unbearable, but he believes all will be well once he can speak to the master.

As the damned floats he comes dangerously close to the edge of the cavernous hollow. He cannot move his arms or legs so he really can't keep himself from being impaled or ripped apart by the jagged edges. There is a horizontal, very smooth, almost polished looking stone pointed straight at him, but he cannot change the course of his journey, so he collides into the stone and it rips much of the skin where the blisters had formed. There is no outlet for his agony; he can't scream, he can't cry, he can yell, he can't do a thing to stop the suffering and that makes him even more anxious to speak with Satan to get this all straightened out.

The damned floats over the surface of Hell for what seems to be an eternity and he sees that some things have changed. There are no longer countless numbers of souls being torn apart and tortured by demons. All he can recognize are vast lakes of fire as far as the eye can see, but as he floats over one lake, he sees only a lone soul in the center. On the surrounding edge of the lake of fire there are legions of demons and hovering over the lone soul is a demon master of enormous proportions. The soul of the being in the lake is undergoing pain of such enormity that the damned wants to look away, but he can't. He starts to consider; 'Is this what I must endure?' He puts such thoughts out of his mind because believes all will be well once he can speak to the master.

It seems as if it takes many years to fly over each lake, but how can it take so long? One after another, vast lakes of fire loom over the hellscape and the damned can see only one soul in each of the lakes and that soul is tormented by the many demons and their demon master. The damned then thinks, that one looks like Mao Tse Tung, and that one looks like Stalin, oh and that has to be Hitler. There are a number of others that he recognizes and the damned knows they each deserve their fate, but not him. He will surely straighten this out once he can speak to the master.

The damned floats past another lake of fire and suddenly he plunges down toward the demon master in the center. It appears that the demon master is torturing Usama Bin Laden, but as he dives closer the hideous demon looks up and he slashes at the body of the damned with razor sharp nails that rip open a huge tear in the abdomen. The guts do not drop out, but the pain is horrific and the damned floats back up to continue his journey. The damned continues to believe this is all a big mistake and he will have to straighten it out once he sees the master.

He is sure that centuries perhaps millennia have past when he finally stops floating. He is in the middle of a lake of fire every bit as big as the ones he has floated over there is no one he can see; no demons or demon master just unbearable heat and noxious fumes arising from the sulphuric stench. Then it happens…he is no longer floating…he is plummeting down into the fire and he can see the flames lapping his body and feel the skin melting off his bones.

"Ah, Dr. Houston, glad you could make it, how are you?"

The silent screams coming from the damned can only be heard by the damned himself.

"Well, I see you have arrived safe and sound. I must say that it is quite hot here. I will be sure to call maintenance and have them check the AC. By the way, that was some battle back about three thousand years ago, huh? Oh well, no use crying over spilt milk. As the old saying goes, win some, lose some right? Anyway, now that you are firmly ensconced in your own personal hell, I wanted to be the first one to welcome you."

More silent screams, more unimaginable pain as the skin that has melted grows back only to melt once again. It is far more suffering than can ever be imagined in the worst of nightmares and it is then Tom Houston realizes what his eternity will be.

Satan has one last word, "Oh and I know that you hoped we could straighten this all out, well we can't. There is a special demon master that will be calling on you soon. He has 30 legions of demons so please be sure to welcome him as he can get a bit testy if he thinks you are not treating him properly. Oh, by the way, guess who your neighbor is! Al Masih ad Dajjal! I knew you would be happy. He may not be able to visit much, but I know you would feel safer knowing he's around…you know, if you need him to water the plants and to be sure the mail is picked up. Well, take it easy, I'll be sure to check back."

* * *

Combined News Services, Washington DC – The Socialist Liberation Party convention was a raucous affair with thousands of the party faithful gathered in celebration of what they assure themselves will be a victory of historic proportions.

Congresswoman Helen De Witt and Dr. Thomas Houston had been in fierce competition for the party's nomination. According to the most recent polls, Thomas Houston had taken the lead and it appeared he was on his way to becoming the Socialist Liberation Party's nominee for President of the United States. That is why it was all the more shocking that Dr. Houston disappeared under what can only be considered 'mysterious circumstances' on his recent trip to the Middle East. His Chief-of-Staff, Nancy McGrath, said she was at a loss to explain where her boss had gone to and she had no idea why he would leave without telling anyone.

The Israeli government instituted an investigation to look into the disappearance and they put their secret service, the Mossad, on alert to determine if the disappearance had anything to do with the terror groups like Hamas and Hezbollah. To date nothing has been found to indicate any foul play was involved.

Since the unfortunate disappearance of Dr. Thomas Houston, the party leaders have coalesced around his opponent, Representative De Witt, as she faces the nominee of the Constitutional Rights Party, Ohio Governor John Paulding. With the election only three months away, Rep. De Witt has a 3-point lead over Governor Paulding in the most recent polls with a margin of error of 4 percent points making it a virtual tie.

* * *

Papal Apartments – Vatican City – Monsignor Amedeo De Marinis is lying in the hospital bed that has been provided to him by the Vatican and placed in his quarters in the Papal Apartments. His condition relating to Parkinson's disease has taken a recent turn for the worse. Tremors, involuntary movement of his lips, hands and legs as well as the stiffness and slowness have increased greatly in the months since he has come back from The Holy Land.

The monsignor is now confined to a bed and, as a result of his illness; he has also become totally blind. Msgr. De Marinis' assistant, Father

Giovanni Sellisi, has been by his side for most of the time reading to his mentor and growing sadder as he witnesses the symptoms of Parkinson's continuing to deteriorate the monsignor's health and vigor.

Amodeo's voice is shaky and he can barely speak above a whisper, "Giovanni you are most kind to spend every free moment caring for me. I want to thank you for your love and company. I pray that you continue to receive the blessings of our Lord Jesus Christ."

Father Sellisi smiles and tries to comfort the man who has become a hero to so many at the Vatican, especially him. "Dear Monsignor, it is I who should be thanking you. By the way I have some very good news!"

"Good news? What is the good news?"

"I have been trying to keep up with the work that has piled up since…" Father Sellisi hesitates for a moment not wanting to upset Msgr. De Marinis in any way.

A smile crosses the monsignor's mouth as he says, "Please Giovanni, I know the Parkinson's has made it impossible for me to continue, but that does not mean I am without interest, after all I have done my work for the church for more years than I can count. Please continue."

Father Sellisi puts his hand on the monsignor's shoulder and says, "You always know what to say when I cannot find the words. I have been keeping up with all the requests for the holy rites of exorcism that have been coming into your office, but as of late what has happened can only be called miraculous."

"Miraculous? Tell me what you have found"

"My dear monsignor, the vast numbers of petitions for the holy rites of exorcism that had been coming to your office daily have virtually stopped. All of these matters relating to petitions which were under your review in the past also seemed to have abated dramatically. In many of the cases I have been told, by the local priests involved, that the demons have been cast out; the victims of demonic possessions have returned to their past state and are once again in the light and blessings of the Lord. It is truly a benediction."

Msgr. Amodeo De Marinis is delighted to hear this news. "Giovanni, do you realize what this means? Satan has lost this battle and, for now, he has been vanquished albeit only for a time. As we know, however, you must keep vigilant, do not ever let your guard drop, even for a moment, for if you do that is when Lucifer will take over and corrupt the body and the soul of those who are weak."

"That is what you have taught me monsignor and that is what I have learned and I pray that I never will fail you or the church in my calling."

"Ah Giovanni, that is so good to hear. I have told Cardinal Castelli that I am no longer able to continue in my role as chief exorcist of the Holy Church of Rome. I have asked him to consider you to assume the responsibilities of my office. I have asked him to bless you in this undertaking. Dear Giovanni, may the Lord bless you and protect you."

Father Sellisi is stunned by the news, "But my dear monsignor, this cannot be; the church needs you, those possessed count on your power to free them from evil and I cannot succeed without your holy guidance."

"Father, you are much stronger than you believe. You have the faith that is needed to save the souls of the possessed and I have seen it with my own eyes. I have witnessed your devotion and reverence for the holy work of our Church and with God's help, the blessings of Jesus Christ and the Holy Spirit, you will not fail."

"But father…"

"Dear Giovanni, I grow tired, let us resume our talk when I have rested."

Father Sellisi resigns himself to the fact that he will have to finish their talk later. "Yes, of course. Sleep well monsignor." The priest gets up from the chair besides the bed and leaves the room and quietly closes the door behind him.

Monsignor Amodeo De Marinis was not really tired; he was glad for the time to pray and wished to do it alone. "Dear Lord, thank You always for Your blessings and thank You for a lifetime of doing Your work; the work I love."

An unfamiliar voice speaks, "You are most welcome Amodeo."

Amodeo is a bit unnerved, "Who is there? Father Sellisi is that you? I thought you had gone."

"It is time Amodeo; your work is finished and you have done well. Let us go home."

"Lord, is it really You?"

"Yes, and you have earned your eternal reward; the peace of Heaven and the love of God the Father."

"Will you hold my hand?"

"I already am."

* * *

The White House – Washington, DC – The White House announced today that President-elect John Paulding will nominate billionaire businessman Harry Lieberman as the Secretary of Commerce. Mr. Lieberman is the founder and Chief Executive Officer of the retail giant "Harry's Place" as well as a number of other companies. Harry Lieberman had previously endorsed the candidacy of Dr. Thomas Houston and that is why, for many, this nomination came as a complete surprise.

At the press briefing held a few hours ago, President-Elect Paulding was asked why he nominated someone who previously supported his potential opponent. Paulding replied, "Given that the economy of our country had been left in such a sad state, we should put politics aside and look for the best person, with the best skills and background to get things moving again and Harry is the first person that came to mind."

When Harry Lieberman was asked to comment he said, "President-Elect Paulding and I had a very frank and honest discussion about both our visions for the future of America and I think we were both very surprised on how much we actually agreed on. My first order of business will be to streamline the rules and regulations governing how we do business in the United States and look to have frank and honest discussions with our trading partners in hopes of leveling the playing field. I consider this honor to be the high point of my career and I am most grateful to President-Elect Paulding for having given me the chance to make a difference."

The vote to confirm Harry Lieberman as Secretary of Commerce will take place in a few weeks. He is very popular with both parties and his appointment is expected to meet with little or no opposition.

In the audience at the press briefings was Harry Lieberman's daughter, Amanda Sellers. Ms. Sellers, the beautiful and famous actress was beaming with pride when she told reporters how proud she was of her father.

* * *

Mabella Restaurant – Commack NY – My uncle, Chief Spartaco 'Al' Barese was there to greet everyone at the door. He couldn't help but smile at being there with all of his family and friends. When Beth and I arrive, we are delighted to see Uncle Al so happy. Of course, I couldn't allow that to continue so I said, "How the hell did they ever wind up choosing you for Suffolk County Police Commissioner?" I look around to make sure no one is listening and ask him, "Come on, cough it up, you bribed the County Exec, right?"

"I sure did! By the way when you open your safe on Monday, there might be a few hundred coins missing, but don't worry I'll have the police look into it!"

We laugh and I hug him and say, "Congratulations Uncle Al, I'm so proud of you."

"Thanks Chris, I can't believe that it happened to me, but now that it did, I can't wait to tackle the craziness that I'm sure is part of the job."

Beth and I mingle and we are having a wonderful time laughing with family and talking with some of my uncle's friends and co-workers including the retiring police commissioner. Beth and I look around and see Uncle Al's girlfriend, Eileen Silverman. She is standing over by the bar talking to my cousins Aurora and Henry so we both go over to greet her. "Hi Eileen, I see you're getting to know my cousins."

Eileen smiles and says, "Yes I am; they are wonderful and I am so happy to meet them. My son and daughter are here somewhere and I know they want to say hello to both of you."

Being the wiseass she is, Beth says, "Well I know where they can find Chris in a few minutes…by the buffet table. He'll be the one stuffing his face."

"Ha, ha; very funny", but Beth looks at me and smiles. She puts her arms around me, kisses me and says, "I wouldn't change a thing." The four of us talk for a few minutes when I hear my uncle tap his glass with a spoon and ask everyone to please quiet down as he has a special announcement. He walks over to where Eileen is standing, followed by her son and daughter and he looks at Eileen and smiles. Eileen, who had been widowed five years earlier, met Uncle Al at, of all places, the roast chicken display at a supermarket in downtown Huntington.

It is easy to see the love that they both have for each other as he gets down on his knees. Eileen gasps and is overwhelmed as my uncle pulls out a small jewelry box and opens it. Inside there is an engagement ring with a stone about the diameter of a 1910 Liberty Head Dime in Mint condition.

"Eileen, I have never known a woman who is as beautiful, funny, generous, caring and thoughtful as you. I can't guarantee that things will always be perfect, but I can guarantee that I will always love you." With Eileen's children happily looking at their mom and smiling, Uncle Al then asks, "Eileen Silverman, will you marry me?"

Eileen just stares at Uncle Al and we all can see tears coming from her eyes. She reaches down for his hand and he gets up. She touches his cheek and kisses him and whispers "Yes." Uncle Al takes her hand and places the ring on her finger and they just hug each other as the room erupts in cheers, applause and laughter.

* * *

Price Clinic for Cancer Research – Miami, FL

FOR IMMEDIATE RELEASE

It is with great sadness that the Board of Directors of the Price Clinic for Cancer Research announces the passing of its beloved founder, Dr. Spencer Price. Dr. Price, a recognized worldwide expert on battling the scourge of cancer, had been actively engaged in the fight during his entire 62-year career.

Over the years, Dr. Price has discovered and developed techniques and therapies that are now recognized as revolutionary treatments for various types of cancers. The Price Clinic for Cancer Research has gained recognition from a number of sources including health agencies, clinics and treatment centers both in the United States as well as more than 103 countries around the globe. A staff of more than 106 scientists, doctors, research associates and support personnel have been inspired by his dedication and the leadership role he has played for decades.

Dr. Price passed away Sunday at age 84 from complications arising due to his battle with colon cancer. He had fought the disease for a number of years and asked all who knew to keep his condition private. The directors and staff ask that in lieu of flowers, contributions in tribute to Dr. Spencer Price be sent to Price Clinic for Cancer Research.

* * *

The Dolby Theatre – Los Angeles, CA – Last night, Hollywood elites gathered in mass at Los Angeles' iconic Dolby Theatre for the 2023 Academy Awards. Television audience numbers for the awards have shown a dramatic drop over the years, but that didn't deter those glamorous actresses and handsome actors from dressing in elegant designer gowns and tailor-made tuxedos as they stroll down the red carpet.

The big winner of the night was the suspense thriller "Tina is Gone", featuring Amanda Sellers in the starring role. The movie, having been nominated for 8 academy awards, has been called by some critics as sordid and extreme in its content, but it has been enormously popular with general audiences around the country. "Tina is Gone" has won awards for "Best Picture", "Best Actor in a Dramatic Role", Best Actress in a Dramatic Role" and three other academy awards including "Best Screenplay." The screenplay was co-written by the very talented Amanda Sellers and first-time writer, Christopher Pella.

In accepting the award for Best Actress, Amanda Seller, thanked the academy and had special thanks for two people who inspired the storyline. She told the audiences present at the event and those watching on television and online, "I want to take a moment to mention two people who made this all possible. Beth Della Russo, the woman I had the honor of playing in the movie and Chris Pella, the man at the center of it all. Chris was the inspiration behind this true-life drama and who, without his bravery and that of his uncle, this film would never have been made."

A smiling Amanda Sellers looks down to acknowledge Chris and Beth who are sitting near the front and smiling back at her tribute. "I have to say that throughout the entire scripting and production there seemed to be someone or something guiding our every move, kind of like some angel looking over us just to be sure we got it right. I think we did and I hope you agree. I want to thank the academy for this award and thank you, Chris, for sharing your story with me."

When it came time for the award for "Best Screenplay" to be presented, Ms. Sellers accepted and gave her thanks to all involved. Mr. Pella, who also accepted the award, said, "I want to thank the Academy for this honor and I also want to tell my uncle, Police Commissioner Al Barese, and let him know that I'm not sharing this award with him."

To date "Tina is Gone" has grossed over $320 million domestically and nearly $730 million worldwide.

* * *

Seminary of the Immaculate Conception – Huntington, NY – I picked up my invitation that was sent in the mail. I opened and read it:

You are Cordially Invited to attend the
Special Celebration of the Naming of
"The Paul and Catherine Della Russo Study Center"
At The Seminary of the Immaculate Conception
A Special Mass will be presided over by
Bishop Victor Teller

Reception to follow in the Conference Center
RSVP Father Aiden Langford by September 4th
Formal Attire

I heard from Beth that nearly all the invited guests replied that they would attend the event and I was very happy for both Paul and Catherine. After I read my invitation, I realized that I would need to buy a tuxedo. At that exact moment my phone's ringtone goes off and I see its Beth calling.

"Hi, what's up?"

"Did you get the invitation?

"Yep!"

"Well, are you going to take me or what?"

"Beth, I just opened my mail about 30 seconds ago."

"I don't care, are you going to be my escort or what?"

"Of course, I just wanted to leave you hanging for a while."

"Oh, really."

"Just kidding, calm down Beth, don't make yourself crazy."

"What are you wearing?"

"I saw this fabulous black and gold sequin tuxedo with a florescent pink ruffled shirt and a red, white and blue bowtie that lights up when you sing "God Bless America!"

"Get ready, I'm coming over and we're going shopping for a tux." and Beth hangs up.

We found a great looking tuxedo and I pick up Beth on the evening of the event. When I arrive, I ring the doorbell and Beth opens the door and she looks absolutely stunning. She sees my reaction and she smiles and says, "How do I look?"

All I can say is, "You look absolutely beautiful!"

She gives me a kiss and a hug and says, "You look really handsome, but maybe we should have bought the bowtie that lights up when you sing "God Bless America."

Beth and I try to get to the Immaculate Conception Seminary early, but cars are already lining up well before the Mass begins. The seminary's parking lot is already full and so Beth and I leave my car keys with the valet and we head inside. There, at the entrance, to greet all the invited guests is Fr. Aiden Langford.

He immediately gives Beth and hug and when he sees me, he says, "I know I just saw you at Spartaco's recent celebration, but I am honored to be here, joined by you and the lovely Beth. Christopher, if you don't mind, I would very much like having a brief conversation with you in private this evening whenever you can make yourself available."

"Of course, Father, you seem kind of busy now, but after you've had a chance to greet the guests we can catch up."

"Excellent! I will endeavor to abduct you at the proper moment."

We say our good byes to Fr. Aiden and Beth and I walk away to find our seats for Mass in the pew reserved for family. We look for Beth's parents and we spot them and wave. As we walk towards them, she stops to stare at me and says, "What was that all about?"

I am unsure myself, but I say, "I really don't know, maybe Father Aiden wants to talk to me about Uncle Al's wedding."

Beth is not so sure, but now she is thrilled for her parents and she is smiling from ear to ear. Paul and Catherine hug their daughter and they greet me warmly and thank me for being part of their special day.

I tell them, "From what I hear from Father Langford, he was so excited that ICS was able to do this for you both that he put himself in charge of all this. Congratulations, I couldn't be happier for you both.

Paul Della Russo smiles at Catherine and says, "I think we have another groupie on our hands!"

The family laughs and we take our seat for the Mass. The bishop presides over a truly beautiful ceremony filled with readings from the Bible, along with quotes from the gospels and hymns that capture the essence of what the Della Russo's commitment means to ICS as part of their unwavering faith.

After mass the guests are escorted to the reception area where they are serving cocktails and hors d'oeuvres. I must have had my tongue sticking out because Beth jabs my side and says, "Easy big fella."

I am just about ready to dig in when Father Aiden taps me on the shoulder and asks if this is a good time to speak.

"Well as long as it doesn't take too much time. I was hoping to stuff my face, but I guess there will be enough left for me."

Father Aiden laughs and says, "Let us find a quiet corner as I have something confidential to discuss with you."

I am totally intrigued by this surreptitious get-together and I follow him to an alcove off the reception area.

"Father, you've got my curiosity going and now you have my undivided attention, so what's up?"

"Christopher, I am sure that you have heard of Amodeo's unfortunate, but peaceful passing. He was a dear friend of mine and I know that he felt privileged to also call you friend."

I had found out about the monsignor from a letter I received from his assistant Father Sellisi. "I was very sad when I heard the monsignor had died and I am very proud that he would consider me a friend. His courage and strength in the face of…well you know because you were there."

"Ah yes I was and I want to discuss something with you."

"Sure, what gives?"

"Before Amodeo's passing, we spoke. He told me that he called upon a close friend of his. I believe you met him when we were at the Vatican, Cardinal Castelli."

"Yes, I remember him; he's quite a guy; very smart, very wise and he looks pretty tough."

"Ah yes, smart, wise and tough is quite right. That being said, just before his passing he recommended that Father Sellisi assume the duties of the Vatican's chief exorcist. It is an extremely important role and potentially a very dangerous undertaking. Although Cardinal Castelli reluctantly agreed, he had concerns that Father Sellisi did not have the depth of experience required to assume such a role at this time."

"Well, I guess he would know best."

"Before he died, however, Amodeo also told me that he confessed to the cardinal the essence of the motivation behind out trip to Israel.

"Father, please don't tell me that he told Cardinal Castelli…"

Fr. Aiden stops me before I finish, "Christopher, let me assure you that Msgr. De Marinis would never betray a trust. He did, however, tell the

Cardinal that the trip was necessitated by the Lamb of God blasphemies and that you and I were asked to join him on the journey because of some unique, how shall I put it, aspects of our individual talents. Nebulous, I agree, but the monsignor assured the cardinal, given the presence of such evil, it would be wise to consider a proposal he had concocted."

"Proposal? What kind of proposal?"

"It is comprised of a small, very special grouping, to be overseen by the Vatican under the auspices of Cardinal Castelli and blessed by the Pope. As of now, the council is to be comprised of Father Sellisi and myself."

"Wow! What an honor that must be. Father Sellisi is a true man of God and I am sure you both will do an excellent job! Wow again."

"There is one more element, Christopher and that requires some soul-searching on your part."

"My part, what does this have to do with me?"

"One of the items that Amodeo and I discussed prior to his passing was that you and your special relationships with The Sainted can prove invaluable in the event of some resurgence in the type evil that we had to face during the Lamb of God horrors and the battle at Megiddo."

"Father, you've got to be kidding. I am…"

Father Aiden interrupts, "I will tell you what you are; you are blessed by God, His Son, our Lord and savior Jesus Christ, and the power of the Holy Spirit. You can actually speak with The Sainted, you have heavenly insights given to you by these blessed icons of the Church and both Amodeo and I accept as true that you were given these gifts to help save souls."

I don't know how to respond so try to make light of our discussion. I tell Fr. Aiden, "Father you've got to be kidding. Who do you think we are, "The God Squad?" That's kind of like "The Mod Squad?" well except there's no Julie."

"No Christopher, this is not some fantasy, it is real and it is your destiny."

I am speechless.

"Christopher, let us return to the celebration. You may wish to consult with Spartaco to assess his reaction to my supplication. All I ask is that you give proper consideration this holy charge deserves and let me know of your decision as soon as you can. Will you promise me that you will at least consider this proposal?"

I am silent for a moment, but I tell Fr. Aiden, "Of course, I promise that I'll think about it."

Fr. Aiden smiles, "Christopher, I will be forever grateful for what you have done and I will always remain your friend." Fr. Aiden blesses me with the sign of the cross and says, "May the Lord bless you and keep you." Father Aiden rests his hand on my shoulder and he returns to the cocktail hour.

I take a moment to reflect on what Fr. Langford has told me and I realize that I need some time to think but that will come later. When I return, everyone seems to be enjoying themselves and I see Beth is standing in the midst of the crowd looking for me.

She spots me and says, "Hi, where were you?'

"Oh, Father Aiden corralled me and we talked."

Yeah, about what?"

I don't want to lie to Beth, but I think if I obfuscate a bit, I can fool Beth and technically be forgiven by God. "Well, it was about a project that he would like my help with. It has to do with the Lamb of God horrors that took place and I think he wants me to work with him. Right now, it just seems to be an idea so there is no real focus yet."

"Really, are you thinking about doing it?"

"Yeah, I am, but I don't know if I can make the kind of commitment that this requires. Anyway, I told Father Aiden that I will think about it. But, hey, do you know what I'm thinking about right now?"

Beth holds her fingers to the sides of her head and closes her eyes. She begins to chant a mantra, "OMMMMMMMM…I see marinated mushrooms, Grana Padano; I see sausage and peppers, I see Chicken Marsala, I see eggplant parmigiana. Wait, my vision is getting foggy…sorry Chris, I can see no more."

I stand there in amazement, looking at Beth, slack-jawed I tell her, "You are a clairvoyant! I…I never knew; never had an inkling, but you got it right; perfectly correct. I can't believe the woman I love can read my mind!"

"Oh, I can read more than that and when you're ready, you can tell me what you and Father Aiden really discussed."

I should be dumbfounded, but I'm not. This is Beth and, other than Uncle Al, she knows me better than anyone else. I love her and she loves me and I know we are meant for each other.

Beth and I walk over to the buffet, but for some reason I don't feel that hungry. I am going to propose to Beth next month and I start to think, if I take on the role as outlined by Father Aiden, I'll probably be gone for periods of time. How can I do that to her without making her suspicious or angry? Then I think to myself, maybe I should let Beth know of my special gift and relationship with the Sainted. I have all these questions, but no answers.

Beth nudges me and says, "Come on Chris, you've been waiting all day for the feast, fill your plate and let's find a quiet corner to talk.

"Okay." Beth always knows what's in my mind and in my heart…and the best way to them both is through my stomach.

Personal Notes by the Author

I don't know if any of you who have read all of The Sainted Trilogy are even interested in some of my personal musings, but I have to get this down on paper for my own edification. The Sainted Trilogy, Book One "Evil Awaits", is my first attempt to write a book, any book, fiction or non-fiction and the process proved to be far more difficult than I had imagined. Difficult yes; impossible, no, but for me it was an enlightening experience. I sincerely hope you enjoyed reading all the books in The Sainted Trilogy and I would love to hear from you with your thoughts and comments.

Now that I am prepared to put this down on paper or digitally, here is some of what I confronted in this personal foray into the world of authors. Thanks for allowing my little bit of introspection.

Writers Block

I have reserved this last chapter to put down some of my thoughts that arose once I completed all three books of The Sainted Trilogy. The trilogy extends nearly 1,000 pages, hundreds of acknowledgements and attributions, many hours of research and it took nearly seven years for me to complete. I thought that it would have taken much less time, but I hadn't considered 'writers block.'

For those of you who haven't attempted to write a book, in my case a novel, I don't think you will be able to easily relate to my dilemma. For those who have tried to write a book, fiction or non-fiction, you may have experienced this same phenomenon unique to authors.

Strictly speaking, in mathematical terms, if I worked straight through, eight hours a day, it should have taken me a little more than two hundred to two hundred and fifty days to write and perhaps another one hundred to one hundred fifty days for research. In fairness however, there are holidays, vacations, grandkids, friends, all the joys in one's life as well as the normal distractions, so that number may be unrealistic. When I am inspired to write I try to complete at least four to five pages a day. This may not sound like a lot in terms of output, but when you have to develop the story, attempt to research the background information of, say the saints, it can take more time…as I found out, much more time.

Somedays I would sit at my computer and stare at the screen, totally devoid of ideas that I could use to move the plot forward. This is when I felt overcome by what I know now as writers block. In my case I would try to fill the void by doing research or work on other projects, but my heart and mind were always on The Sainted Trilogy. Over the seven years there were periods of up to six months that all I was able to do is reread the pages I had written and make minor changes or edits that I hoped would improve on the story, making it more readable.

I also believe that writers block can also be attributed to a kind of laziness on my part and that could account for some of the slow progress I experienced at times.

In all fairness to myself, however, I did take time off to write a political satire titled "Absolutely, Positively, Genuine, Real Fake News" which I also adapted as a musical comedy, as well as a 'Breaking News' Blog as part of a detour into the world of fake news. In addition, I've also written a short story and the initial pages of two other novels I am writing. I have also adapted the novels in The Sainted Trilogy as screenplays that I hope will catch the eye of a production company that believes the story to be entertaining.

I know these may sound like lame excuses, but this was part of the process, actually my process, as an author. In this regard I became very familiar with writer's block over years and I expect I'll have to live with it until I stop writing or breathing, whichever comes first.

Beth and Amanda

Aside from being a supernatural suspense thriller, The Sainted Trilogy has other elements, one of which is that it is a love story. The tale evolved into more of a love story than I ever intended it to be. Well, now that you may have read all the books in the trilogy, I am sure that you have your own opinion regarding Chris' dilemma; will it be 'Beth' or will it be 'Amanda' who captures Chris' heart.

I have to tell you that in writing the book this was one of the toughest issues that I needed to resolve as I kind of fell in love with both of these characters. I wrote of these women as accomplished, independent, beautiful, very smart, wise asses both with a great sense of humor and both are in love with Chris. What a lucky guy!

I don't know how you, the reader, feel about this and you might not even care, but for me it was a tough decision. I think Chris made the right choice in the end as I think that Beth is his one and only true love, but there will always be a place in his heart (and mine) for Amanda. What do you think?

Good versus Evil

The eternal struggle...so when someone contemplates the metaphysical considerations behind such a philosophical choice, the net results is that you can't have one without the other. So, when I wrote the various books in The Sainted Trilogy, I felt compelled to illustrate the dichotomy in the most graphic terms.

If the Sainted represent a near perfect measure of human goodness and faith then Satan must represent the consummate evil. My wife, Joan, who after she read Book One of The Sainted Trilogy looked at me and said, "What kind of man did I marry?"

After I finished laughing, I took a bit of time to consider why she reacted in that way. Once I realized the level of evil, violence and murder of the most vicious kind I wanted to convey, I was able to empathize with my wife's reaction. I tried to tell her that you can't soft pedal evil when it comes to Satan. Satan is the essence of all evil and by writing the horrors in extremely graphic terms, I was attempting to illustrate the goodness of The Sainted in stark comparison.

All three books have equally disturbing chapters, but there are two different chapters in Book Two "Revelations", that even I found very distressing. Once you've read the "Revelations" you can decide which among the chapters I am referring to and see if you agree. When I had finished writing them, I seriously considered leaving them out of the final draft, but I decided to keep them in. This is because I always felt it is important never to allow evil to be viewed in anything less than what it is; hideous, vile, corrupt and egregious in the starkest of terms and all emanating from one, single source; Satan.

The reason I even brought this up was because of my next quandary…

Satan

There was a review written for the first edition of "The Sainted". The reviewer, Alicia Smock, wrote, *"One character, though, Medico must be applauded for and that is Satan. He gave Satan the perfect personality: just the right amount of attitude and sass to make him how anyone would imagine him if they were to meet him on Earth and one who likes to play games with his victims. Satan is perhaps one of, if not THE, hardest character to write in any genre and Medico nailed it on his first try."*

I felt that Satan, the fallen angel, Lucifer, the defiant purveyor of evil incarnate, needed to have a personality that his victims would find compelling. These souls are too weak, too greedy, and too hedonistic to bother to look beyond themselves. In their interaction with Satan, they would become totally engaged by this charming, funny, handsome demon that has taken on human form and in the end, they have damned themselves.

To say he is merciless, viciously malevolent, sadistic and vile should only be thought of as his good qualities. Throughout The Sainted Trilogy, however, I have given him a charm and sense of humor that might endear some readers to him, but don't be fooled, he'd ruin you and damn you to the fires of hell in the blink of an eye.

Still, I hope you think he made The Sainted Trilogy more enjoyable to read.

Chris written in the First Person

One of the writing styles I employed has been called into question. That is due to the fact I wrote our hero, Chris Pella, in the first person versus all other characters being written in the third person.

Some readers may consider this disjointed, but I had a purpose. I did this intentionally because I think the reader needs to have empathy for what Chris has been given, the ability to communicate with The Sainted and finding his purpose in life. Throughout the trilogy we are able to get into Chris' head to see how he deals with it or even how we might have dealt with it had we been given the gift.

I want Chris to be viewed as a sort of 'everyman' who tries to do what he thinks is right and sometimes he wins and sometimes he falls woefully short. This is kind of the way it is with the human condition; how would you have reacted if you were put into Chris' place? I think that Chris' character being written in the first person helps bring you closer to him.

ACKNOWLEDGEMENTS

On September 4th 2016 Pope Francis canonized Blessed Mother Teresa as Saint Mother Teresa of Calcutta.

I have been fascinated by this woman for many years after seeing a documentary about the founding, her leadership and the good works of The Missionaries of Charity. The images are still vivid in my mind; Mother Teresa and the Sisters of Charity tending to the sick and dying among the poorest citizens of Calcutta. She walked among these people providing comfort and solace to those who suffer from deadly diseases and afflictions; many near death. St. Mother Teresa would hold emaciated, dying babies; she would hug old men and women who suffer from contagious diseases. She would feed them, bathe them and most importantly, pray with them and for their souls.

What is so revealing is her love of the Lord, Jesus Christ, the holiness in her heart and the need to serve all people, no matter what their faith. This selflessness gave St. Mother Teresa her reason to exist. Was this unheard of? No, it was the path that many of The Sainted have taken and St. Mother Teresa was not the exception, she was the rule.

As always, I need to express my profound gratitude to The Sainted who, throughout the centuries, define what is best in all of us and worthy of the rewards found in Heaven in the arms of God and His Son, Jesus Christ. I also want to thank the sources of information that I have used in addition to the events, information on the saints, their lives and their miracles as well as the people and the news items cited in the book. Some of these truths are evident in recent events, others are conjured up in my imagination and some have roots in the truth, but require a story to make them readable...I hope.

St. Agrippina of Mineo

St. Bessarion

St. Catherine of Alexandria

St. Christopher

St. Dionysius the Areopagite

St. Gabriel the Archangel

St. John the Evangelist

St. Jude Thaddeus

St. Margaret of Antioch

St. Michael the Archangel

St. Maria Goretti

St. Paul the Apostle

St. Peter

St. Raphael the Archangel

St. Raymond Nonnatus

Wikipedia

www.wikipedia.org

http://www.endtimes-bibleprophecy.com

http://catholicsaints.info

http://www.catholic.org

"God Less America" by Todd Starnes, Copyright 2014 Charisma House, All Rights Reserved

http://satanicverses.org

The Bible, Old and New Testaments

http://www.jollynotes.com

http://www.endtimes-bibleprophecy.com/four-living-creatures-prophecy.html

http://biblemagazine.com/magazine/vol-9/issue-1/armag.html

http://www.bibletruthkeys.com/battle_of_armageddon1.html

http://www.biblestudytools.com/dictionary/armageddon/

https://www.biblegateway.com

http://www.generationword.com/audio_series/revelation_audio.html

http://www.biblestudy.org/question/names-for-devil.html

The Geography of Heaven by Ernest L. Martin, Ph.D., 1999 Edited by David Sielaff, 2006

http://www.dailymail.co.uk/news/article-2587215/Sharia-Law-enshrined- British-legal-lawyers-guidelines-drawing-documents-according-Islamic-rules.html#ixzz48YsFzTSf

http://dailycaller.com/2015/10/23/sweden-opened-its-doors-to-muslim-immigration-today-its-the-rape-capital-of-the-west-japan-didnt/

http://www.emedicinehealth.com

http://ilsiciliano.net/page35_st_nicasius.php

http://www.newadvent.org/cathen/11770b.htm

www.breitbart.com (London)

https://www.theepochtimes.com/the-persecution-of-christians-in-africa-and-the-middle-east_2599420.html

https://www.thoughtco.com/king-david-man-after-gods-heart

http://listverse.com/2007/09/09/top-10-most-evil-women/

https://en.wikipedia.org/wiki/The_infernal_names

http://people.com/crime/ms-13-satanic-alleged-killing-teen-houston/

https://www.cnn.com/2016/04/06/us/texas-execution/index.html

http://crimefeed.com/2016/04/5-shocking-real-life-cases-satanic-ritual-killings/

https://www.beautysoancient.com/st-michael-archangel-prayer-english-latin-short-form/

http://www.catholic-saints.net/exorcism/

http://www.ewtn.com/v/experts/showmessage.asp?number=577292

https://www.oddee.com/item_98653.aspx

http://bibleprobe.com/1928exorcism.htm

https://bible.knowing-jesus.com/.../Miracles-Of-Peter

https://the-line-up.com/demonic-possession-cases

https://www.oddee.com/item_98653.aspx

http://bibleprobe.com/1928exorcism.htm

https://www.catholic.org/saints/saint.php?saint_id=127

www.miraclesofthesaints.com/2010/09/prophecies-in-lives-of-saints.html

https://www.wikihow.com/Drink-a-Tequila-Shot

http://www.gazettereview.com/2016/01/most-expensive-tequila-in-world/

https://www.livescience.com/36559-common-blood-type-donation.html

https://www.williamshakespeare.net/speech-from-henry-5.jsp

https://www.breitbart.com/middle-east/2019/05/03/the-vanishing-report-exposes-persecution-of-middle-east-christians-as-close-to-genocide/?utm_source=newsletter&utm_medium=email&utm_term=daily&utm_content=links&utm_campaign=20190503

https://www.romancatholicman.com/confession/

https://www.azquotes.com/author/13382-William_Shakespeare/tag/listening

http://www.newadvent.org

https://www.whatsaiththescripture.com/Prophecy/The.Battle.of.Armageddon.html

https://www.almasdarnews.com/article/chinese-military-gets-new-high-precision-sniper-rifle/

https://www.shenyunperformingarts.org/explore/view/article/e/D6zx3eCDT_w

https://www.oca.org/saints/lives/2017/06/06/101631-venerable-bessarion-the-wonderworker-of-egypt

https://www.visitflorida.com/en-us/cities/south-beach/top-10-ocean-drive-art-deco-hotels-miami-beach.html

http://www.answering-christianity.com/signs_of_armageddon.htm

https://tanzeel-ahad.blogspot.com/2010/06/7-signs-armageddon-according-to-islam.html

https://en.wikipedia.org/wiki/Islamic_eschatology#Major_Signs

http://everything.explained.today/Gog_and_Magog/

saintsresource.com/peter-the-apostle/

https://www.tripsavvy.com/
basilicata-cities-map-and-visitor-guide-1547187

http://saintroccosfeast.org/St_Rocco.html

https://brewminate.com/engineering-of-saint-peters-basilica/

Latroun Abbey, The Trappist Monastery of The Silent Monks

https://www.youtube.com/watch?v=9n3WRiHKTag

https://www.tripadvisor.com/Attractions-g293981-Activities-Galilee_
Region_Northern_District.html#MAPVIEW

Trappists - Wikipedia

en.wikipedia.org/wiki/Trappists

https://www.stbasil.com/news/2019/10/3/god-revealed-in-the-darkness

https://www.nirvanicinsights.com/powerful-prayers-evil-spirits-demons/

It should be noted that the online and electronic media news headlines and articles as referenced in "Megiddo were researched during the period around the year 2018 when I was writing the initial draft. Some of the conditions that I had referenced and written about may have changed for better or worse, but they were accurate at the time I wrote them. It appears, however, that the persecution of Catholic and Christians sects around the world continues unabated.

AUTHOR MICHAEL MEDICO

Michael Medico was born in New York City where he attended Power Memorial Academy. On graduation Mike joined the U.S. Navy and served stateside during the Viet Nam War. After being honorably discharged from the service, he attended Pace University and graduated with a Bachelor's Degree in marketing and advertising.

Michael spent the first ten years of his career at various advertising agencies until he founded a direct marketing advertising agency and served as its CEO for 35 years. He has written numerous articles published in various trade journals and has been a featured participant on business panel discussions and industry workshops. During his career in direct response, Michael has managed many television direct marketing campaigns for a wide range of products and brands that became very successful. Michael has been featured on the cover of Response Magazine and earned a triple platinum album award from Arista Records for his participation in the marketing Arista Records 'Ultimate' Music series.

After the completion of The Sainted Trilogy, Michael spent some months adapting and completing The Sainted Trilogy as a four season/39-episode series for cable or streaming. In addition to 'The Sainted Trilogy', Michael has written the political satire titled 'Absolutely. Positively, Genuine, Real Fake News' that was also adapted as a Broadway Musical; a short story titled, 'The Death of My Father' and he is currently working on two new novels.

Michael and his wife Joan have two sons, Anthony and Richard, daughters-in-law, Shannon and Christina and 6 grandchildren. Mike and Joan spend time between their homes in Northport, NY and Florida.